What readers love about the Decrypter books

"**Takes you on a ride** and refuses to let you off until you reach the very end." *Marie*

"A brilliant read! I recommend this to anyone who enjoys mystery, suspense, thrillers, or action novels. The **detail is astounding**! The historic references, location descriptions, references to technology, cryptography....this author really knows her stuff." *Fran*

"An **action-packed adventure**, technothriller **across several continents** like a Jason Bourne or James Bond movie, but with an actual storyline!" *John*

"**Brilliantly written**. I loved the very descriptive side, which was a good way of visualizing and getting to terms with each new place, as the action takes place in several different countries." *Sean*

"The **description is so rich**, so immensely detailed that it just draws you in completely to its world." *Denise*

"There is **great tension and chemistr**y between the two main characters, Calla and Nash, that has you begging for more." *Pam*

"I found myself intrigued about what could be the **next step in the evolution of cyber systems**. I look forward to

more stories from the author especially involving Calla Cress." *James*

"Calla Cress, still reeling from her recent discoveries, is thrown right back into danger. This is an **exhilarating read** that will have you begging for more." *Richard*

"**Hard to put down** once you start reading it." *Maxine*

"**Great story line** with twists and turns and a **good alternation of action and scene setting** which will keep you on the edge of your seat." *Liam*

"**I can see how this would look on screen** but it may be my wild imagination! The end will shock you!" *Sarah*

ALSO BY ROSE SANDY

THE DECRYPTER: SECRET OF THE LOST MANUSCRIPT

THE DECRYPTER: SECRET OF THE LOST MANUSCRIPT (previously
published as The Deveron Manuscript) is a work of fiction. Names, places,
organizations and incidents are either products of the author's imagination or used
fictitiously. Any resemblances to actual persons, living or dead, events or locations
are entirely coincidental and not intended by the author.

THE DECRYPTER: SECRET OF THE LOST MANUSCRIPT

ROSE SANDY

WWW.ROSESANDY.COM

For those who are curious about the world, its history and the technology that runs it.

THE PRESENT

Calla Cress had never been called a coward, and tonight she would not provoke the first instance. Lungs burning, with a quick snap, she glanced over her shoulder and stepped off the train at St. Pancras International.

He was following her.

She increased her pace and hurried through immigration. Not only could she lose him in the crowds, but she would also make sure the thug stayed off her tail for good.

Calla tore through the station's main concourse, searching for the nearest exit.

Congested with tired night travelers, she hurried through the arrival lounge and burst out onto the boulevard.

St. Pancras, the 'cathedral of railways', towered above her.

Giving it one glance, the wrought-iron framework and arched-glass covering evoked paranoia in her.

She pressed on with labored breaths, her muscles tensing as she shook off the numbness in her hands and the tingling in her feet. Unwilling to yield, Calla felt like an animal in chase, only she was the target.

Weakening legs burned, yet she hurried with resolved steps, crossing Euston Road toward Camden Town Hall, which stood adjacent to a barely visible underground parking.

Tightness formed in her abdomen, shooting discomfort through her body and reduced her concentration. She shook her head to snap free of the trance and dragged heavy feet across the concrete. Her tongue licked the vinegary sting of blood off her bottom lip.

She had to move.

Keys rattling in her hand, Calla found her Maserati on the lower-third parking level, where she'd left it that morning. With a sigh, she slotted the key in the keyhole, sank into the leather seat, and wove the car out into the dark street.

Aware of her fervent pursuer, she stopped at a red light, her palms moist, drumming on the leather of the steering wheel. Calla peered into her rearview mirror. Then her eyes caught his blinding headlights.

"Brute!"

Her foot hit the accelerator.

TheRange Rover charged for her rear bumper.

She swerved around a white Toyota, and the Maserati picked up speed, starting a sixty-mile-per-hour chase through London's tight streets.

Nearly ramming a Hyundai, Calla maneuvered from lane to lane as her pursuant nosed his vehicle toward her tailpipe.

Fifth gear looked good right about now, and she ramped up the engine. The sports car wound through medieval streets, testing its limits in the eastern part of the city. Past several fragments of the defensive, third-century Roman City Wall, the Maserati flew at full throttle.

Hands trembling, she slammed the accelerator.

Her tires smoked. She fed more gas to the engine then peeled off into a one-way street.

Calla rechecked her rearview mirror then swung into Bishopsgate's banking district, toward Monument.

The Range Rover clung to her tail. Eyes ahead, she sped toward London Bridge that spanned the River Thames.

A hiss left her lips. What did he want?

Calla raced across the box girder structure, high above the river reflecting the city lights below.

She twisted the wheel and roared on to South Bank. Without hesitation, she curved into a deserted street behind a line of dated warehouses along the Thames.

Sure she'd broken the speed limit and half a dozen traffic laws, Calla winced.

That was the least of her worries. She wouldn't think about it as the Range Rover surged toward her and cornered her further into a second one-way street crammed with deserted office buildings.

Her eyes locked with a startled young family stepping out of a parked Vauxhall station wagon meters in front of her vehicle. Zipping forward, she smashed a fist on the horn.

Wide-eyed, the family stood motionless as Calla hit the brakes. The decision sent her car spinning several times. A stench of burning rubber stole past her nostrils as her tires squealed a shrill of terror until the vehicle came to a quick halt, meters from the towering Shard skyscraper.

She lifted her head and turned off her engine as the stunned family scurried toward London Bridge Station. Behind her, the Shard stood above the streets of London, like an ominous, glowing glass pyramid whose peak disappeared into the thick London fog. With little movement about, she waited. Where was he?

The drone of a hungry vehicle pumped thunder in her veins as the Range Rover revved its engine. Then the headlights of the steel beast dimmed.

Calla bit her lip.

She leaped out of the car. Confidence sent her marching toward the waiting Rover. Hands on hips, she wanted him gone.

A figure in dark military attire sprang from the Rover and onto the dimly lit street. She watched. His build was hefty, his face concealed behind what looked like a visor ski mask. She wiped beads of sweat from her brow as he advanced and lunged, swinging a punch in a full arc.

Calla sidestepped the blow as it zipped past her nose.

He struck again.

Fingers vibrating, she couldn't move fast enough, and the brusque strike slammed into a shoulder blade. She lost balance. Eyes closed, she crashed backward.

Massaging the knockback, she sprang to her feet and tore at him with an uppercut punch. Her fist caught him in the jaw, and he landed on the rough gravel, opening a one-centimeter gash.

She watched him quiver for several seconds before jumping to his feet. Calla stepped back and forced down a sick feeling. Her shoulder burned from his blow, a strike that had forced an acidic taste in her mouth. She wiped trickling blood from her jawline.

Though the wound stung like fire, she eyed him without blinking. "What the heck do you want?"

Silence.

"I don't have it!" she said.

No response.

She reached for the side of his neck. He caught her hands mid air and gripped them in a lock as his other hand stretched around for the bag she'd strapped around her waist before leaving Paris. Her eyes followed his extended hand.

The Deveron Manuscript was secured within, and she read his intent.

"Give that back!"

He zipped toward the Shard's entrance and scuttled inside

Europe's tallest building. Calla dashed after him. She had no choice.

She wanted it back.

1

The ISTF chairman tugged at his collar. He scanned the conference room as one by one, the participants took their seats.

Calla watched him carefully.

ISTF, and even the government called on her for her expertise in restoration science. Usually looking for the knowledge on what roles languages played in social and cultural situations, she gave him an attentive ear.

Around an oblong table surrounded by several chairs, the meeting mimicked an extended version of the Cabinet Office Briefing Rooms sessions, better known as COBRA.

Diverse as the United Nations, international scholars, government and police officials, plus analysts from five nations huddled around the table.

·   ·   ·

Calla recalled how Allegra, ISTF board member, and friend, had first introduced ISTF to her. Her words still rang in Calla's ears.

"It's funded by five governments—the UK, France, Germany, Russia, and the USA. No agency is more secretive than this group. Only a few know of its existence and call it the International Security Task Force, the ISTF.

These countries came together and formed it before the year 2000, expecting Y2K disruptions that would encourage amateur and professional criminals.

We use the full range of investigative, intelligence, and prosecutorial resources at our disposal.

ISTF intervenes in global criminal investigations, especially near technology and science threats."

When Calla had first joined the agency, her onboarding agent had been clear about ISTF's purposes. "It acts quickly. We have about five hundred permanent staff, ISTF can step in where Interpol, the CIA, and MI6 leave off. We answer to no directive or jurisdiction and are a fierce unit fighting that upholds international law."

Calla had read the briefing notes, noting the governments signed off its funding yet didn't flinch if its investigative schemes were unconventional.

ISTF was above the law and was keen on new science, history, and technologies.

The public remained ignorant of its existence, but knowledge about the group had leaked in online blogs and on illegal websites.

"The government will deny its existence," Allegra had warned Calla.

Allegra had called Calla only the week before to discuss her position at ISTF. "Calla, you know more about anthropology and technology than most. You should attend."

"I don't know."

"ISTF work is top secret and never mandatory. Mason Laskfell thinks highly of you."

"Why?"

"Think about it. At twenty-eight, you are one of the youngest curators at the British Museum in charge of the late Roman and Byzantine collections. And I believe you can do better here."

Apprehension rippled through her. "Even I, the least of skeptics, think the Deveron Manuscript is one huge myth?" she said.

"Go to the meeting at Watergate, then decide."

Calla had agreed. That conversation had only been a few days ago.

"Please settle down. We've got an hour for this brief," the meeting chairman said, bringing Calla back into the room. "Several of you will get a turn to articulate your thoughts on the Deveron Manuscript."

When the lights dimmed, Calla glanced around the room.

Thirty people crammed in the twenty-seater room.

As they compared notes and views, those seated examined the photographs projected on the presentation slides.

Voices murmured in disagreement as a commotion arose over the validity of the top-secret, ancient manuscript.

Calla scanned the briefing notes.

Two-toned and scripted, the seven-page manuscript was written in tainted burgundy and black ink. The calligraphic symbols filled the entire surface area of its tattered square pages.

The chairman turned to the next slide, and Calla guessed most of the on-looking faces coveted a seat within Taskforce Carbonado, the ISTF group that would work with the manuscript.

"After this brief, we'll select ten people for a special operation Taskforce Carbonado," the chairman said.

"We'll build a team from within this gathering to investigate the manuscript's authenticity and lead some of its retrieval efforts."

A blond woman interrupted him. "Why now? We investigate criminal activities and don't deal with cultural heritage."

"The Deveron has resurfaced in Berlin after it disappeared over fifty years ago."

"Still..."

"ISTF's aim is always to prevent crime of any sort, even though our most recent endeavors link to cybercrimes."

"Why now?" she said.

"The Deveron's black-market worth alone makes it a valuable artifact, and therefore, a potential criminal target," the chairman replied

"Excuse me, but surely the German government can tackle this on its own," said a French researcher.

The chairman's eyes dimmed. "Calla Cress, artifact specialist for ISTF, can explain more."

All eyes fell on Calla, and she drew in a deep breath. "The Deveron is a historic, cryptic manuscript. Some think it's an ancient letter, others an instruction manual of some sort."

She took a breath. "The Deveron family, whose ancestry traces back to Cheshire in northern England, first discovered it in 1879, just off Britain's shores."

"Correct," the chairman said. "Research we have commissioned to experts in this room suggests that it details the whereabouts of potential resources that will make crude oil seem like dinner leftovers. Believe me, ISTF needs to get to this first. Our efforts will reap significant economic value for our five governments... and the globe."

"How's that?" interrupted the Parisian. "There's even skepticism here whether it's authentic. The biggest issue is we can't read it."

The chairman pinched his lips together. "There are about

1.3 trillion barrels of oil reserves remaining in the world's major fields, which at present rates of consumption will only last another forty years. Our resources, Miss—?"

"Pascale."

"Ms. Pascale, we believe the document was encrypted to hide certain resources. The light at the end of the Deveron enigma could add several hundred years to that figure. As you know, the rising cost of oil has now forced global governments and oil companies to look at exploiting other resources. But we'll delve into that in a minute."

He searched the room. Was he looking for more cynics? The gathering quieted. None attempted to challenge his perspective, and they waited with silent nods for more revelation.

The Deveron Manuscript, like many others, had plagued her mind. Who could decipher it? Calla squinted as the chairman drummed the podium and waited for the noise to settle. "Nominations for the task force will be made after this gathering. Over to you, Chester."

Chester Hitchens, an animated Museum of London archivist, marched to the presentation stand. A screeching noise fed through the sound system as he adjusted the microphone, lowering it to his short frame. With unsteady fingers, he straightened his thick glasses.

Though he spoke with eloquence, after only a few words, he paused short of a stammer. "The Deveron Manuscript, printed on vellum, first came on our radar in 1962. Back then, anonymous images of the first two pages were sent to the museum for validation. To this day, we do not know who sent them. Although we couldn't establish the nature of the writing, nor its contents, our archivists declared it a manuscript defying all decipherment."

Chester's eyes narrowed, and spots of red darkened his cheeks. He slammed his fist on the desk. "God help us if it isn't a fake."

Calla fought a throbbing in her chest and wiped her brow. Why were they comparing this document to the Voynich manuscript, a medieval merchant's fantasy?

The Yale University-owned document had baffled many linguists and cryptographers for decades, and she was sure they wouldn't reach a conclusion in this forum.

Murmurs erupted as Professor Chiyoko Hosokawa, a Princeton University linguist, and anthropologist, stood. "I agree that the closest script to the Deveron Manuscript's is the Voynich manuscript's own lettering."

"But has anyone seen it? Touched it?" asked a bearded Russian professor.

The chairman approached Chester, laid a hand on his shoulder, and readdressed the gathering. "The task force team will have plenty of opportunities to do so. With the increased threat of fundamentalist groups relying on looted antiquities to fund crime, ISTF must eliminate any peril posed by the re-emergence of this manuscript, including the risk of transferring artifacts across borders. ISTF must possess and analyze it even if the German government disapproves."

Seated close to the door, Calla's throat closed up as the debate continued. She searched her notes.

Her credentials had earned her a seat in this congregation. ISTF was looking for the best from the best.

She passed a hand through her hair as the clock above the projector read 5:50 p.m.

Ten minutes on the clock.

Calla half-listened.

She worked in a museum, for crying out loud, not government intelligence.

She glanced around the room. Where was Allegra? Why would she encourage her to come and not turn up?

The noise level in the room rose.

A second presenter from Munich left the podium, not having offered any new insights on neither the Voynich nor the Deveron Manuscript.

Calla understood none had laid eyes on the Deveron since the sixties, and none of those who had could describe it. Even the projection photos showed only three low-resolution images.

The room overpowered the next presenter—a British Intelligence research analyst.

"Order! I'm not finished yet. We must consider the implications the Voynich script will have on the Deveron decryption," the presenter said.

"We don't know that. They look similar, but there's no concrete proof." The comment came from an Art History professor from the University of Paris Sorbonne, seated in the front row.

The man on Calla's right leaned over and whispered, "I don't know about you, but I could use a break."

Calla's nostrils took in the smell of coffee breath. She moved her head back with a grimace of nausea and nodded in response. She'd heard enough.

Seven minutes passed. If she hurried, she could make it in time to the National Archives. The drive would take her close to an hour down Chelsea Embankment, then toward the A4 motorway.

She bit her lip and tapped her frayed notebook with a glance at the clock on the wall. Calla shuffled her feet, ready to head out. She rose, grabbed her shoulder bag, straightened her khaki trousers, and slid on her trench coat.

Almost on cue, the next presenter concluded their presentation and the meeting chairman stepped behind the mike. "We'll announce shortly who'll work on the Deveron Manuscript in Berlin. Some of you will get a call soon."

Calla barely heard the words.

Philler hated lateness, but he owed Calla a favor.

He'd made it easy for them to become friends when they met five years ago in a training course on SMART technologies.

Last January, she'd translated a manual for Philler, all to impress the brunette who worked at his local library.

She shook her head, remembering the hours she'd poured into the document.

Even at sixty-three, she'd met no one more knowledgeable about computer systems and software besides Jack Kleve, her dependable colleague.

Calla checked the speedometer of her used Audi A3 hatchback. The dark clouds above the London skyline echoed her thoughts. Somber.

After several minutes the automobile came to a traffic light.

She rechecked the light as it turned green. The car ahead of her failed to move.

Without hesitation, she slammed the car horn. "Come on!"

Her voice boomed in the tiny space.

Thirty minutes later, the car pulled up in front of the National Archives Building in the London suburb of Kew.

Calla hurried through the main entrance. On Tuesdays, the offices stayed open until 7:00 p.m. Hands trembling, she checked her watch.

"We're closing in ten minutes."

The voice came from a tired female face behind the reception desk. Calla thanked her and scanned the lobby, pulling out her cell phone from her purse.

"There you are."

The receptionist relaxed her face as Philler trotted toward them. His black-rimmed glasses didn't hide he was aging.

Philler gestured for her to move through the glass barriers. "She's with me. Sign her in as Miss Cress."

"Philler, we're closing. No more visitors," the woman said.

"She's my niece," he lied. "I'll be responsible for her."

The receptionist shook her head. "I'll look the other way."

Calla followed Philler, and they took the elevator to level two. Once there, they moved down the hallway lit on one side by early moonlight peering through the glass façade.

April had promised an early spring this year, and Calla's tension eased at the thought.

Her twenty-ninth birthday would be here before the end of the winter. This year would be different. Calla would find them.

They stopped at a secured door missing a label. Philler produced a chained pass from his pocket and swiped the card reader pushing the door open for Calla. "This is a staff research room prohibited to the public. The computers here have unrestricted access to all known civil servant records. Click on the blue book icon and select 'civil records'. The rest should be straightforward."

He handed her a green Post-it note. "This is the password you'll need. Use it when prompted. I can only give you ten minutes maximum." He straightened his glasses. "That gives me plenty of time to sign out, raising no suspicions. They'll assume I was checking the systems. Okay, I'll leave you to it."

Philler switched on the fluorescent overhead lights and turned to leave. "Ten minutes, tops," he called as he shut the door.

"Thank you."

The door shut behind him.

Hundreds of brown boxes, piled together, stood on gray steel shelves. They formed an endless row of archives on the far side of the room.

Calla felt a chill through her spine. It had to be close to five degrees in the room as she shook it off and moved toward the multi-screen computer on a desk.

She switched on the computer.

Exactly as she'd imagined.

Secure socket layer encryption protected it. Not that Calla couldn't work around it, but there was no time.

She punched in the details from Philler's Post-it.

The computer allowed her entry and lit a screen with four boxes.

Calla chose the civil records icon as Philler had instructed. It was a considerable risk for Philler to let her use the restricted room, but she had only one name signed on her birth and adoption forms.

Marla Cox.

If only she knew if her parents were dead or alive.

She muttered under her breath, "All right. Just be ready for whatever you find."

The computer churned, and she pulled out the only form she'd ever seen on her adoption that came through a court in England.

After several years of research, she'd contacted the General Registrar Office and requested the rights to get all records about her birth and adoption.

A month ago, it had taken every inch of her willpower to apply for a certificate of her original birth entry, and her adoption certificate.

They were incomplete records, lacking information on her biological parents.

She scanned the adoption document. The date came up as twenty-three years ago. All it confirmed was that she'd been adopted at five. Calla fumbled through her bag for what she believed was her original birth certificate.

Place of Birth: County of Essex
Father's forename and surname: Unknown
Mother's forename and surname: Bonnie Tyleman

Many certainties, or better yet, lies, had become clear to her after receiving the documents. What were the myths, and what were the truths?

Could she find any link to her past?

Calla had followed all avenues open to her, sometimes on ancestry websites, sometimes by grilling her evasive adoptive parents who had christened her Calla Iris Cress.

The name Bonnie Tyleman had brought no concrete results.

She'd taken the information to a private investigator two years ago, paying the more significant portion of her savings to locate Bonnie dead or alive.

His investigation identified two Bonnie Tylemans.

The first had changed her name to Marla Cox, several years before Calla's birth.

The investigator found the second registered as a civil servant in a public record.

Armed with that information, Calla continued her search without his services.

The touchscreen monitors took every ounce of technical knowledge she possessed to navigate through the complex software system.

Calla studied the new government encryption program.

Jack had given Calla a quick lesson in working the new capacitive, touchscreen tools such as the ones in front of her.

"You can even use them with gloves," Jack had said.

He'd also given her a quick course in the latest database software.

She slid her finger across the screen, working fast with one eye on the time.

Seven minutes to go.

Scrolling through the windows of texts and flashing images, Calla landed on the catalog database screen.

She stopped.

A bold headline stared back at her:

Civil Servant Commission 1800–present

The cursor blinked, and she entered the name Marla Cox and waited a few seconds.

Twenty entries found.

"Damn, who do I pick?"

She glimpsed to the right of each listing, hoping for a period or date.

None.

"What the heck? I have nothing to lose," she muttered.

She hit the back icon and returned to the previous screen. Calla typed a name that had plagued her mind since the day she'd discovered it.

Bonnie Tyleman.

"Okay," she muttered.

The cursor blinked, searching the database for information. When it stalled, Calla tapped her fingers on the desk.

The machine failed to respond. Philler knocked on the door from the outside.

It was her a two-minute warning.

Palms sweating, her muscles twitched, bringing on a feeling of nausea.

Damn it! She'd waited a long time.

The machine was slow.

She knew enough about genealogy, DNA tests that determined a person's ethnicity, but she wouldn't go to these extremes.

For now, she gave the dawdling computer a chance.

Who had brought her to the foster home?

Why?

Were her parents still alive?

Perhaps they lived right here in London. Maybe in mainland Europe.

Where had she inherited her olive skin, emerald-amber eyes, dark hair, and athletic physique?

No one had ever told her.

Could it be that her parents were Caucasian, or of Asian, perhaps Latin American, French Gypsy, or even Indian descent? For all she knew, she could also be the product of mixed race.

For her twenty-ninth birthday, Calla wanted answers.

Search result...

"Finally," she said exhaling.

Over 200 entries found

"Now what?"

She rose and hit the enter button several times. A drop of sweat fell onto the silver surface of the desk. Without warning, a continuous beep shrilled from the machine's speakers.

"No, not now! Don't lock me out! Come on!"

The screen flashed a warning.

You may not access this information

She slid her fingers across the screen. Her efforts failed as the computer continued with its loud warning.

A hand stretched across her shoulder and hit two function buttons.

Philler's eyebrows knit. "What did you do?" he said, shutting off the machine. "You raised the alarm. We've gotta move. A systems security person could be here any minute. I'm afraid you have to leave now. God knows I'm in enough trouble already."

"Please, Philler, this is my only chance."

Philler sighed. "I can't, Calla. I'm sorry."

The door flung open with a thud. A female data security manager, with a tight grip on the doorknob, blocked their only means of escape. She marched into the room, followed by a male security guard.

"What's going on here? We've registered irregular activity coming from this room," hollered the man.

"Just a routine checkup," Philler said.

The woman's eyes fell on Calla. "And she?"

"Just a trainee."

"Let's go!" the guard shouted.

Calla picked up her belongings and rose, followed by Philler. "I hope I didn't get you into trouble."

The security guard jostled Calla out of the building.

"Hey, it's public property," she called back.

Calla wiped her brow. She'd been so close.

2

C alla glanced up from her laptop as cars zipped past on Victoria Embankment. The morning sun cast its rays on the aluminum café table. It peered in through the square windows that overlooked the river walk along the north bank of the River Thames.

A chill-out track crooned in the background of the tiny yet popular café as morning commuters scurried in and out with their orders.

It had taken her all of seven months to persuade Philler to give her access to the restricted database rooms, and now, her efforts had brought nothing.

"I'll close the window," the waiter said. "Sometimes, the blue skies can be deceptive in April."

The cell phone beside her laptop had been silent all morning. She scrolled through her in-box, landing on a text message sent by Allegra the night before.

Calla,
I've been selected to lead Taskforce Carbonado. I've also chosen
you as part of the team. See you in Berlin tomorrow.
Allegra

Calla set the phone on the table. Jack and Nash were running late.

Dropping her shoulders, she scanned summary notes emailed overnight. Calla didn't know how long she would be on Taskforce Carbonado and needed to get cover at the museum before the end of the day.

The embankment café was already a buzz of activity even at 9:00 a.m., mostly coffee and breakfast takeaways. She liked the busy place. Even with the ear-splitting tumult of clinking glasses and plates, she stayed focused. She tuned out the intrusions and people's voices. Bridging the gaps in her past ranked high on her to-do list.

It was the third time ISTF had called on her expertise in the last eighteen months.

Could she decipher the Deveron Manuscript? Probably. Contrary to some thoughts shared at yesterday's briefing, the Voynich was a fabricated document. However, she would need to see the Deveron text herself to be sure.

She'd sat for several minutes without typing, her screen switching to energy-saving mode.

The reflection in the black screen stared back at her, reminding her of the yesterday's failed efforts.

She could restart her family search by visiting the foster home in Essex, information the investigator had provided.

Somebody there had to know something.

Calla could also look for Mila Rembrandt, a relative she had been told, using an ancestry search company. Her adoptive parents Mama and Papa Cress, had told her many years ago that

Mila came looking for her when she was eight years old. Calla was at boarding school and never learned of the visit until her high school graduation day. She didn't speak to Mama Cress for days.

How could they have kept such information from her? The question still lingered. Why had Mila come looking?

"Would you like another kiwi juice?" a server said.

With a quick glance at the time, she looked up. "Thank you."

The guys were late for the breakfast appointment, and the next ISTF session started in twenty minutes. Calla twiddled her diamond ear stud between her fingers, a pensive habit from her adolescent years, and picked up her glass of kiwi juice. She took a sip before emptying the glass.

A thought dawned on her.

Allegra was a former diplomat and Political Director in the Foreign and Commonwealth Office and had access to knowledge and files relating to past civil servants like Bonnie Tyleman.

If anyone could help, Allegra could.

10:00 A.M.

"You're a million miles from here."

The voice came from behind her. She turned to see Jack approach with an espresso in hand.

"Jack."

Even in a setting as formal as ISTF, today like all days, Jack Kleve was the most carefree person she knew. He wore the usual Converse shoes, Levis jeans, and an Adidas sports jacket, much his uniform, and sported shoulder-length dreadlocks. As he paced her way, he commanded attention.

She wondered why she'd never given him credit for his

sturdy frame, long arms, and broad shoulders. He had toned up in the last weeks. Well, hanging around Nash would do that to any man.

She giggled.

Jack's childlike eyes smiled at Calla as he dropped his bags on the chair next to her and plopped into a seat.

"To what do I owe your tardiness?" she said.

He grinned. "Nash here yet?"

"Not yet. So, were you schmoozing with one of your client list of government agencies? Or, let me see... private corporations, or perhaps a security firm like the gig months ago with Nash at the American Embassy?"

"Hm..." he said with a smirk.

"Don't be bashful, Jack, you've made quite a name for yourself recently. I hardly see you anymore, unless it's ISTF work. I miss us hanging out."

"Me too. But hey, guilty. I was on a call."

She smiled. "When we first meet, you were so keen not to sell on your stuff. What changed your mind?"

"That TED Conference in Edinburgh changed my life."

"And your bank account."

Laughter sparkled in his eyes. "Maybe leaving the Indian Ocean behind had more impact on me thanI thought. I like a good gig."

"Jack, all I'm saying is I miss you dragging me to silly street dance classes."

"I know. We'll do it again soon. When I retire."

"Huh! Never. Jack, you're only thirty-one and one of the most creative entrepreneurs on the TED website and platform might I add. You're just cool and can demand any fee. Possibly any place of employment."

"So, can you."

"Not like you. Now how much did you get for that smart securities job with the European Parliament?"

A nonchalant shrug lifted his shoulders. "Just coz I share everything with you...okay. Seven million."

"Sterling?"

"Sterling. Hey, researching and developing technology takes money."

"And offers you one of the best bachelor pads in London."

"Hey, if it's the only way I can get you and Nash to hang out with takeaway on any ISTF gig, then so be it."

He leaned over and turned her laptop to face him. "Now, what're you up to?" He smirked. "You need to give this a rest. Ancestry.com will not get you any closer to solving the riddle of your past."

Calla giggled. Had she acted wisely, telling him about her family quest? How could Calla resist? Jack was her good friend, and she needed a sanity check sometimes.

Jack gave her a peck on the cheek. "You're an alien, and you know it."

She grinned. "I suppose you'd know. Tell me, Jack, when was the last time you dialed home to your mother ship?"

"There's nothing great to write about Mahé and being a boat boy in the Seychelles."

"Yes, but there's much to say about having a family, however dysfunctional, paying for your own education and earning a gazillion scholarships. Jack, I admire and envy you at the same time."

A smirk flashed on Jack's face, and she edged closer. "Listen, do you think I'm crazy hunting for clues to my background? I mean, wouldn't you want to know where you come from?"

Jack shifted with a nervous grin. "I suppose so, Cal. Your parents were crazy to let you go if they're still alive." He took her hand in his large palms. "I don't want you to get hurt. They may not be all that. A happy family is a dream. No one has one. In your own words, look at my dysfunctional family. Don't let the past dictate who you are or who you'll become. Write your own story. From where I'm looking, you're doing great."

He patted her hand and withdrew it to take a sip of his espresso.

Was Jack right? Calla never pictured what she might find.

He cast a glance at the main entrance. "Ah! Here comes Nash. He's finally joined us."

Nash Shields pushed through the doors. His tousled, sandy-brown hair still wet from his shower earlier that morning reminded Calla he liked to run first thing at dawn. It cleared his mind, he'd once told Calla. He shot them a brief nod. After making his way toward their table, he lowered into the extra seat next to Calla.

He'd been in London on and off in the last three years helping with classified ISTF's intelligence analysis.

Nash's navy-blue blazer hung above his faded jeans. Well-built behind the loose clothes he wore, he liked to stay comfortable. At six-foot-three, his lean build and posture spoke of years of military discipline, though that didn't rob him of the sparkle in his engaging and deep gray eyes.

Once, he told Calla he'd acted as a security adviser to the government. His secret weapon? Fluency in Arabic and a few other languages.

He gave Calla a peck on the cheek. "Hey, beautiful, any new archeological finds I should know about. I find your work fascinating. Did you catch the BBC program last night on the remains of King Richard III?"

His standard American vernacular charmed Calla.

Nash never failed to astound her. Here he was, trendy, intelligent, and just athletic enough to make her self-conscious by looking at him. Quiet confidence dazzled from the intent look of his eyes, and he usually followed it with a sharp sense of humor.

He was extremely attractive. And as she watched him, she hoped he didn't know that fact.

She felt a blush coming on and hated that she was awkward around men she found handsome and, as a general rule, she kept them at arm's length. But recently, with Nash, something had changed, and she could not explain it.

She snapped close the laptop. "You forget, I don't watch TV. By the way, I'm going to Berlin. Allegra Driscoll is leading Taskforce Carbonado. She's asked me to document her work at the Pergamon Museum."

"I know,' Nash said. "The memo came through last night. Jack and I are also on board."

"Are you going to Berlin too?"

"No, we'll be here."

Calla ran a finger on the rim of her empty glass, studying Nash. He took a napkin and wiped away a drip of kiwi juice from the corner of her squirming lips. She removed it from his hand with a grin. "This is a real opportunity for me and challenging work. The Deveron is no ordinary manuscript."

He smiled at Calla, extending her a curious glance. "ISTF has now agreed with Germany for a group of specialists like you to look at it in Berlin," Nash said.

In the last three years, they'd worked together on a few ISTF projects, and many were nerve-wracking assignments.

Two winters ago, they'd worked on an international kidnapping case where a ransom note was left in KIPPA, a unique code language ISTF had developed secretly.

ISTF had stopped the project lacking funding. Frustrated, the kidnapper, also the primary developer of KIPPA, walked off with the language code.

Two days later, he planted a cryptic ransom note in the Daily Telegraph. It mesmerized the media, the public, and caused problems for ISTF.

That had been the kidnapper's intention. Using KIPPA would bring public attention to ISTF.

No one could decipher it, given the kidnapper's reprogramming of the system, using perplexing hieroglyphics.

But Nash and Calla discovered that, though a modern system, it was based on classical cryptography, a Mesopotamian method to be exact. It had been a genuine team effort.

"Allegra is right for this," Jack said.

"You mean *the* Allegra Driscoll. Winner of the Nobel Prize in Literature and the Prime Minister's special representative on cybersecurity? Plus she does a whole bunch of other things. I don't think she was there yesterday," Nash said.

Calla's eyes sparkled with excitement. "That's right. Some of her many titles and no, she wasn't there."

Nash raised an eyebrow. "You seem intrigued."

She was.

Calla's eyes didn't leave Nash's face. They were close friends and colleagues, and the proximity in which they often worked was welcome, but nothing ever developed between them.

Glaring, she wanted to tell him he was remarkable on many levels. With a deep sigh, she admitted to herself that she loved his intellect, physique, and world experience.

Calla gave him a nod. "I'll be working with the best. This is a huge opportunity. It's fascinating watching the woman work."

"Ever been to Berlin?" Nash said.

A sense of anticipation filled Calla. "Once," she said. "I'm sure I can still manage German."

Jack sidled back to their table. They'd not noticed his departure. "Time to go."

While the two had chatted, Jack had left to take a call. "Mason Laskfell is on his way. They'll now disclose detailed assignments relating to the Deveron." Jack turned to Calla. He tilted his head, his eyebrows knitting as if he'd come by peculiar information. "He asked me if I'd seen you, Calla."

Calla had never spoken a word to Mason. Like all organization heads, everyone knew who he was. He never took one-on-one meetings. Except for the few times, she'd seen his name on memorandums he might as well have been a ghost.

ISTF Offices, Basement Level, Technology Museum

Only displays found at the London Imperial War Museum, MI6, and within the CIA rivaled those at the ISTF technology museum. Places Mason Laskfell had explored.

They included machines and equipment used in war and intelligence missions.

Twenty years. Had it been that long since he'd led ISTF?

Yes, it was, and that morning's memo to staff had noted it all.

Told that a closer look at his physique made one think of a striking warrior, he grimaced imagining himself a lieutenant in Napoleon's army rather than the expert cryptographer and capable intelligence analyst he'd become.

Now chief of ISTF's research signals intelligence and linguistic divisions, he thought about the enviable agency position.

How many puzzling codes had he deciphered? Languages, accents, and handwriting?

He'd tried decrypting the Voynich manuscript years ago and failed like others before him.

He would take another stab after yesterday's meeting.

The spotlights above his head illuminated the museum pieces, piercing his eyes. Today he'd chosen a new chocolate suit and a magenta Armani shirt. So what if he cared about his appearance. He judged people by what they wore. In his boutonniere, he also wore a dragonfly charm, sparkling in the overhead lights with sapphires and mini diamonds. He never left the house without it.

Caressing every inch of it, his hand slid over its rough edge, reminding himself of its existence.

Lips compressing into a tight smile, he sighed. How much did they depend on technology?

They'd come a long way even though he hated to admit current times dictated advancement more than he's ever known.

Mason leaned his six-foot frame against the safety glass.

Fatigue gripped him, and he ran a hand through his hair. If it hadn't been littered with streaks of gray, he swore he could pass for forty-five, give or take a year.

He didn't care. Age was rarely a judge of character or wisdom.

Mason felt a minor headache coming on and breathed hard, having heard the rumor the previous week he could read minds, a reason many avoided him. They said this was his primary investigative procedure. Could they be thinking of when he'd once scrutinized a criminal who had beaten the lie detector? When the criminal had been no match for his mind?

"Hmm, I drew a confession from that bastard in all of three seconds, and you can all wonder how I knew that idiot's thoughts," Mason muttered to himself.

He needed more time and checked the schedule on his phone. The Prime Minister's office needed his service for a briefing that afternoon, but his mind drifted elsewhere.

Mason tapped the glass window in front of him, displaying an ancient cryptography system.

How had the Deveron Manuscript appeared again?

Why now?

Was this the manuscript? Was his search over?

He wasn't ready.

The cell phone buzzed, and he twitched.

It was Lillian, his assistant. "Calla Cress is here."

"Send her down to the museum section," he said, his voice echoing off the walls.

Five minutes later, Calla peered through the door into the small gallery. As she inched into the room, sensors lit up above and flooded the stone-tiled floors with artificial light.

Her step wavered, but she strode straight up to him with a fixed gaze, her palms clutching her electronic tablet. "You asked to see me?"

Mason drew away from the glass and watched her, athletic though awkward, she paced into the room with a quick step.

She might just be the bait he needed for Allegra. He would even overlook she'd been untried for the task that he required her to do. Youth and ignorance were what he desired. Calla was close to Allegra he'd been told.

He edged toward her. "You'll be joining Allegra in Berlin."

She squinted. "Is that what you want to see me about?"

Mason ignored her question and slotted the cell phone in his pocket, not once shifting his eyes from her. "Have you been to Berlin?"

She nodded.

Her antics amused him. "It'll expose you first-hand to some crucial intelligence work. Allegra is one of the best. In Germany, her diplomatic approach will be crucial. On Task Force Carbonado, she named you her right-hand person."

Calla kept her eyes on him. "I'm honored naturally."

Mason stroked his chin. He watched her step back, shifting her feet and distancing herself from him. Perhaps she believed the rumors about his alleged telepathic abilities. Good. He could use fear. Intimidation always produced the results he desired.

Mason examined her posture, straight and no nonsense. "Your work in Berlin is confidential, even to those within ISTF."

He stared right into her being.

She tore her eyes away from his, shifting them toward the glass display case. "Why's that?"

"Has Allegra not told you?" he said.

The lights overhead dimmed again as neither had moved in the last several minutes.

Her lips quivered. "She left yesterday for Berlin. I haven't spoken to her, but I'll join her shortly."

Mason moved an inch closer shortening the distance between them. The motion switched the sensor lights back on. "Good. Allegra is a great resource for ISTF."

Calla glanced at the dragonfly on his suit. "Was there something else you wanted to see me about?"

Mason turned his back to her and strolled to the other side of the small room. After a few steps, he gazed at the glass display on the opposite side, showcasing communication systems that went back as far as the First World War. He reached in his jacket pocket and drew out an electronic device. In the dim light, Calla twitched catching sight of the mobile communications unit.

Mason searched for clues in her expression as he handed her the sleek gadget. "Do you know what this is?"

"It looks like a cell phone."

"It's a prototype from our research labs. I've been looking for an opportunity to test this device. My chance has come. You'll test it for me."

Calla delayed a few seconds, then took the phone.

Unlike most smartphones, this was the size of two small, translucent, fused credit cards with dual-sided, touchscreen capabilities.

When stroked, its laser lights light up in blue, displaying an elaborate keypad and different functions.

She slid her finger across its smooth surface, and it recognized her in an instant as the screen produced the words:

Morning, Calla Cress.
Your device will now be configured.

Mason's phone buzzed again.

He ignored it and studied her.

"I want to be informed of anything Allegra has discovered in Berlin. Keep a diary," he said.

"This phone is designed to help you gather information and assess situations. It's different from most smart phones. It has a high-definition screen, layered menus, touch activity, offline caching, and, best of all, it's packed with knowledge on locations." "I see," she said.

"I'm sure you'll discover more as you use it. I hear you're quite techy."

"I get by," Calla said, studying the phone. "I've known about the ISTF research labs designing communication devices. This is an incredible achievement."

He knew the high-tech angle would get her.

Calla ceased her examination and switched the phone off. "Is this necessary? Surely, Allegra will share the Berlin report. What sort of information do you need me to document?"

She wasn't easily fooled. He persisted with care. "Just note your observations. We'll determine later if the information is useful. This could be momentous for your career."

Calla pocketed the phone. "I already have a career. I'll do my best and need to go now. Was that all?"

Mason gave her an abrupt nod. "Have a good trip."

She tipped her head and stole out of the room without turning back. Mason waited a few seconds and then reached for his secure cell phone. He pressed the speed dial. "Slate? Is it working?"

A husky, Italian-accented voice spoke in low tones. "Yes. She needs to have it turned on. Did you activate the function?"

"Damn right, I did."

CHAPTER 3

Day 3

10:03 a.m.
Templehof Airport, Berlin, Germany

Calla knew she would return to Berlin when she visited ten years ago.

Berlin seemed different then, perhaps not as fast-paced and tourist infested.

The vibrant metropolis, built over centuries on the banks of the Spree River, was home to more bridges than Venice.

Strewn with cultural paradoxes and markers of science, the arts, politics, and media, she gazed out her window as the plane started its descent over the overcast city.

The plane landed after the ninety-minute flight from Gatwick. She reached for her overnight carry-on and stepped off the aircraft.

Outside the main arrival terminal, Calla waited her turn in the long queue for one of the yellow Mercedes cabs. The sun peered through the scattered clouds, lightening her anguish. Several minutes later, one rolled toward her, and a Turkish cab driver sprang out, hopping to the curb with a buoyant spring. "*Wohin, Fräulein?* Where to?"

Calla grabbed her carry-on. "To the Pergamon Museum."

He smiled, showing a grin littered with gold teeth, and despite the warm temperature, he wore a woolen winter cap.

"Any suitcases, *Fräulein?*"

His English was accented but understandable. Calla stepped into the car. "No, I travel light."

They drove toward the center of the city. By the time they navigated past Adenauer Platz, in the heart of former West Berlin, Calla was running late.

Traffic crawled, a stark contrast to Central London.

She settled into the leather seat and glanced over her shoulder.

Was it the constant smirks she received from the driver? They seemed to come every five minutes as he beamed gold teeth looking back in the rearview mirror.

Though good-humored enough, he conversed little during the journey. Calla glimpsed back every time the car turned into a new street.

A nagging sensation haunted her.

It had started at Gatwick Airport, then through customs. She peeked once more in the rear window. Nothing was out of the ordinary.

She shrugged and thought about raising her parents' search with Allegra.

At sixty-seven, Allegra had enjoyed contact and interaction with just about everybody. Age didn't deter Allegra.

Calla understood theirs as being a special bond from the moment she met her all those years ago.

Maybe it was the shared love of history. They'd been friends for seven years.

She had never raised her adoption, and Calla wanted to know more about Allegra.

Calla checked her watch.

10:55 a.m.

Her appointment was in five minutes. "How much further, driver?"

"*Nicht weit*. Not far. Not far. Another ten minutes, maybe."

Calla opened her shoulder bag and dipped her hands deep to locate her electronic tablet. She fished it out and turned it on. The itinerary showed that at 11:00 a.m., they were to meet Herr Brandt, the director of the museum, for a private tour of the Pergamon accommodating three galleries. Work began at 11:30 a.m. in a private museum room.

The taxi nosed into a parking space on the busy street, several meters from the main doors.

"We're here. The Pergamon Museum, *Fräulein*."

The triple-winged complex on Berlin's museum island stood perched above the edge of the Spree.

Its neoclassical structure reflected in the water below against the blue sky and scattered clouds. It looked even more palatial than she had imagined.

She stood straight, confident in her assessment. The prominent landmark had sustained severe damage in the war, during the air raids on Berlin. Though the legitimacy of some collections remained controversial within its vast walls, the Pergamon showcased antiquities, Islamic art, and Babylonian architecture she desperately wanted to see.

She wanted to discuss, with Allegra, the Market Gate of Miletus and the Ishtar Gate, including the Processional Way of Babylon, and the Mshatta Façade.

"I think you'll be waiting for a long time," the taxi driver said. "I can't get any closer. The police won't let me. I'll let you out here, *Fräulein*."

Crowds lined the entrance of the building as the late morning sun peeked through the clouds. Calla glanced outside and nodded her thanks. "*Danke Schön*. I can walk from here. Where's the main entrance?"

He pointed ahead. "Up the stairs. I don't think you can go in today. So much trouble is going on."

What does he mean trouble?

Calla reached in her pocket searching for the euros she'd withdrawn at the airport cash machine upon arrival. She handed the taxi driver a fifty euro note. "Keep the change."

The taxi driver drove off, leaving Calla standing in front of the stairs leading to the entrance. She advanced toward the growing queue. Calla hated being late. Perhaps there was another way in.

Police fenced the entry grounds of the museum. Calla stood on her toes, glancing above a group of French students in front of her. Only a few yards ahead, the entrance remained closed.

Calla scrutinized the glass façades. The authorities appeared to have evacuated the museum and had quarantined several evacuees. They waited in an orderly queue on the other side of the main doors.

The cab driver was right. The queue hadn't moved an inch in the five minutes she'd waited.

When the group in front of her made a move, she edged closer to the entryway. Streams of others made their way off the island. Where was the Pergamon pass Allegra had sent her last night by courier?

"*Das Museen ist geschlossen!* The museum is closed. *Le musée est fermé!*" belted a foghorn voice from within the crowd.

The police officer with the megaphone attempted a multi-language announcement down the queue. Calla, when found the laminated pass in a bundle of papers at the bottom of her bag. She stopped the officer when he got to her section of the queue. "*Entschüldigen Sie, bitte.*"

Her German was confident. "*Darf ich bitte rein?*"

She asked if she could go in.

The officer didn't move a muscle. "*Nein, es tut mir leid.*"

"No? Why?" she said.

He continued his parade down the queue, and she began a

chase after him. "Excuse me, sir. My colleague Allegra Driscoll is on the board of the museum. Here's my pass. I'm meeting her here."

The cop didn't flinch. His English was fluent. "Listen, I'm sorry. Nobody is going in today. Now move aside!"

Calla patted her pockets for her cell phone.

The one Mason had given her was in her carry-on. She'd configured it the night before she left London. It was a costly system with a sophisticated GPS program to identify her pre-set numbers and personal details.

With this, she could locate Allegra. Her own smartphone, though more primitive, was in her left jacket pocket.

A local service provider picked upthe cell phone. Her fingers movedquickly, typinga prompt message to Allegra.

> *Held up at the entrance.*
> *Are you inside?*
> *Calla*

The noon rays hit her face, warming her cheeks, making it seem more like a midsummer afternoon.

Calla glanced upward as irritation thundered through her. She video-dialed Allegra.

No pick up.

The voicemail came on. She sent another text message.

Can't get into the museum.
I'm off to the hotel.

Her throat tightened as she placed the phone in her pocket.

"How interesting that we carry cell phones with us. But we choose not to be reached when we're most needed."

Calla zipped her head round following the German-accented, male voice from behind. Prying eyes speared into her. The voice came from a sneering gentleman a few feet away. He must've watched her episode with the police. She ignored his remark.

He caught her gaze and maneuvered closer, extending a firm handshake. "I'm Manfred Bierman. Looks like you're not from Berlin."

Calla shook his hand. "What gave me away?"

"You seem a little lost."

"Could you tell me why the Pergamon is closed today?" she said.

"I take it you've not been keeping up with German news."

She shook her head.

"Please. Allow me to explain."

Bierman wore a dark trench coat with a trilby hat pinched at the sides and could have come straight off a 1940s film set. As they ambled a few feet from the queue, Calla detected hints of tobacco. Cigars maybe.

He led her from the dispersing line toward one of the benches, in the museum grounds.

Calla glanced at the glass entrance. The police, efficient in manner, questioned everyone. One by one the officers took down statements and checked identities.

"The German press has been reporting about ancient

artifacts that went missing from Berlin vaults during the war," Bierman began.

"I see."

"These are due to be returned and inaugurated at the Pergamon today."

"What artifacts?"

"Do you know much about the Pergamon Museum? Or Berlin's cultural history? This is a big inauguration for Berlin."

"Are you looking to be informed, Herr Biermann?"

"I assumed—"

"You assumed wrong," she said twitching her lips. The museum closed in 1939 at the outbreak of war. In 1943 it took just a few hours to destroy it. One of the chief treasures in Berlin's proud cultural heritage, the Pergamon burned as British bombs blasted holes in its structure late in November 1943. Should I carry on?"

Bierman made a move to speak but was cut off.

"The whole wing was later destroyed in February 1945. In the last days of the war, battles on the museum's grounds between the SS and the Russian Red Army forces left its walls blackened and its exhibition rooms destroyed. Shall I continue?"

"I..."

"Several precious items from the museum's collection were removed and hidden in mine shafts. Most were preserved. Many others were looted at the end of the war. Then, the Russians returned much of this so-called trophy art from 1955 to 1960, including the Pergamon Altar."

Bierman let out a short cough. "You are well informed."

"I should be. After all, I look after an entire museum division at the Berlin Museum."

She grimaced.

"You all right?" Bierman said.

Calla nodded, averting his gaze, and placed dark glasses over her eyes. "I know what I need to about the Pergamon."

"Good. Now have you heard of Priam's Treasure?"

Calla was well informed, but somehow he filled her in with great pride as several new police vehicles arrived..

All, except for the last police evacuees, had vacated the open plaza.

Sirens blared across the bridge and Calla and Bierman stopped to watch the commotion.

A moment later, Bierman leaned in. "Priam's Treasure is one of those collections we've been waiting for since it was stolen from us during the war. In 1945 it was taken from a protective bunker underneath the Berlin Zoo, only two kilometers from here."

"Didn't German archeologist Heinrich Schliemann discover the artifacts, mostly gold, copper shields, and weapons, in Anatolia in 1837?"

"Yes, but—"

"If I'm correct, he named them after Priam, King of Troy. Schliemann smuggled the loot to Berlin, convinced he'd found proof of the Iliad's ancient city."

"That's right. It's a treasure of gold and other artifacts from ancient Troy. Schliemann discovered it when he excavated a hill in the Ottoman Empire around 1873."

"Yes," Calla said. "But that's a debatable fact, Herr Bierman."

"The treasure is priceless."

He leaned forward, catching Calla off guard. She edged back as he attempted a whisper in her ear. "There's more," he said.

"More?"

"The other little secret is that five governments know there's another treasure within the cache," Bierman added. "One that was planted, or hidden, should I say? The Deveron Manuscript."

How did he know about the Deveron?

It was classified information. Although she'd come late into the talks about Taskforce Carbonado, nothing had been publicized about the Deveron. She'd not read the full brief but knew many wanted the manuscript.

Calla didn't flinch.

Bierman smirked, grabbing her full attention. "The Deveron Manuscript has vanished repeatedly over the decades. Many are now attempting to determine its true value. It's priceless,"

"How so?"

"It's written in the same script as the Voynich document they say." He bit his lip. "Until yesterday, many believed the Voynich language was a made-up, medieval farce. Thanks to the Deveron, today they're eating their words."

Calla debated whether to entertain his story or move on about her business. She failed to understand what this had to do with evacuating the museum. "How do you know this?" she asked.

"I get around."

She raised an eyebrow. "I guess so."

"Are you still with me?" Bierman said.

Her nod edged him further into his story.

"Last night, a museum worker was inspecting the items to go on display, and he found the manuscript within Priam's Treasure. My guess is whoever stashed it there hoped no one would find it."

"How do you know?"

Bierman reached into his trench coat and pulled out a business card. "I work for RTL, the German media station."

She inspected the card but made no move to take it. Calla suspected he'd paid for the information. The museum worker must've sold him this story. She shuffled her feet on the concrete as a warm breeze caressed her face. "I can see the pride the museum would have in returned artifacts but not enough reason to cause a tourist standstill."

He replaced his card. "There's no verified record of the documents' existence. Yet five western governments are in a bidding war for it. It was last seen in the sixties. From what I hear, photographs were secretly circulated."

Calla probed him further, interested in his version of the rumors. "What's so fascinating about the Deveron Manuscript?"

Bierman pulled out a cigarette from his jacket pocket. With a slight sneer, he tapped it on an overused cigarette case and lit it with an expensive Ligne 2 Diamond lighter. He let out a little laugh. "It's written in a language and symbols no one has ever understood. Cryptographers made comparisons with the Voynich in the sixties before the Deveron disappeared. The manuscript's age isn't determined, and carbon dating tests have left many debates as to its real age."

The fumes he puffed stung Calla's nostrils, confirming her decision never to take up smoking when offered in high school. She fanned them from her face. "Where does the Deveron come from?"

He took another puff, and this time blew the smoke away. "This is something many are questioning."

Calla scanned his face. "What do *you* think the manuscript says?"

Bierman finished his cigarette and tossed it onto the ground. It rolled along the concrete tiles to the rude sneer of a nearby group of Scandinavian women. He shrugged. "Some believe its contents infer to military tactics. Others say it contains insights into world creation. The more adventurous ones think it's a treasure map of some sort." He grinned. "Whether you believe any of these myths, or just value the manuscript for its own historical interest, it still makes it valuable. Look at this."

He fished for a document from his leather briefcase and shoved it in her hands. Calla recognized the memo, a scan of various classified documents identical to those shared two days ago in London. With a rise in afternoon temperature, she shifted her feet, pulling back her hair into a makeshift chignon. A tourist bus from Hamburg parked nearby only for the police to ward it off.

Bierman retrieved the paper and slotted it in his case. "A specialist has arrived today who can translate it."

She'd heard enough, and her thoughts transferred back to Allegra as the light hit her eyes. It all made sense now. Allegra's historical and linguistic expertise with ancient manuscripts would be invaluable in such an endeavor. She'd marked her territory and must've known about this all those months ago when she invited Calla to Berlin. "Thank you for the history lesson, Herr Bierman, but I must go. I'm meeting someone, and I'm late."

"Don't you want to know why the museum has been evacuated?"

Calla had almost forgotten.

"Two hours ago, I heard Priam's Treasure was stolen from the museum vaults."

Calla paused. "That's impossible."

"Oh, yes."

She checked the doors. Allegra had to be inside.

Calla wondered what the holdup *was and* rose. "*Bis später,* Herr Bierman. Bye for now."

Aware she wouldn't get any closer to the entrance, she sent a text message to Allegra.

Can't get into the museum.
Meet me at the hotel.

She proceeded the same way she'd come, down the concrete stairs and over the small bridge.

Eyes blinking, Calla turned to see if Bierman had gone. How had he gotten such classified data in under forty-eight hours?

Calla zipped her head forward toward the street. With no warning, a hurrying pedestrian jolted her.

The blow to her chest threw her off balance in one forceful shove. Calla lost her footing and plummeted to the ground. "Watch where you're going!"

She landed on the concrete with her hands under her chest. Raising her head, she locked eyes with a towering figure hurrying through the crowds of tourists. Calla only caught sight of the back of his head as a conversing tourist whisked by, and with one blink, he vanished.

Her carry-on had landed a few steps from her feet. She reached for it and rose. Her hand slid to her face as moisture streamed from a cut above a bruised chin and left a trickle of blood at her feet.

1:52 P.M.
HOTEL ADLON, BERLIN

Calla held a tissue over her chin. The throbbing pain subsided as she slumped into the waiting cab.

She dumped her carry-on in the adjacent seat. "How far to the Hotel Adlon?"

"Not long. Twenty minutes? Are you okay, miss?"

One eye on her phone showed no messages

She nodded. "Can take the long way to the hotel?" she asked in German.

The female cab driver dipped her head obliging. "*Gerne*," she said.

She started the engine and swerved the Mercedes into lunchtime traffic.

With no messages, Calla reclined on the leather seats as the taxi cruised past the Kaiser-Wilhelm-Gedächtniskirche, the eminent memorial church at Breitscheidplatz.

The damaged tower stretched against the blue sky, a permanent reminder of war destruction.

Savoring the warm breeze that blew through the taxi Calla laid her head back, forgetting the pain from her chin. They continued past Checkpoint Charlie, the former Berlin Wall crossing point between East and West.

The cab driver, looking to make her journey count, insisted they whiz past *Strasse des 17 Juni,* the main boulevard through Tiergarten central park. By the time they'd driven back toward the former eastern part of the city, it was almost 3:00 p.m. local time.

The Mercedes pulled up in front of Hotel Adlon on Unter den Linden boulevard.

The hotel faced that Pariser Platz and hinted at the grandeur of the Prussian capital.

"We're here."

Calla collected her belongings and paid the driver. "*Danke Schön.*"

She stepped out onto the pavement above the grand entrance. The Brandenburg Gate stood to the left. Across the street, the sidewalk was home to several official buildings, including embassies.

Cafés served late lunches, baked goods, and hot drinks. Calla could almost smell the *Butter Kuchen* cakes, *Eierkuchen* pancakes served with lemons and powdered sugar, and sweet, dough dumplings, the *Berliner Ballen.*

Seated café customers basked in the sun, sipping fresh aroma coffee, reminding Calla of her hunger. She set a hand on her stomach and steered through the double doors, clutching her bag as she strode toward the reception desk.

"*Guten Tag,*" smiled the receptionist.

"I have a reservation under Calla Cress."

The woman checked her computer. "Aha, Frau Cress. You're in the Linden Suite."

"Suite?"

"Yes. One suite for Calla Cress reserved by Allegra Driscoll."

"Has Frau Driscoll already checked in?"

The woman hit several keys, clicking her sleek nails over the keyboard. "Let me see. Yes, she arrived yesterday."

Calla thanked the woman for her keys and steered toward the elevators.

The baroque styled Linden Suite spared no luxury for its exclusive guests. The April sun peered through the vast windows of the corner suite with a view onto Unter den Linden.

Garden-fresh white lilies and yellow roses, arranged in a magnificent bouquet on the coffee table, and a chilling champagne bottle awaited her arrival.

The sweet aroma filled her nostrils, giving her pleasant memories of earlier trips to Berlin.

Allegra had handpicked this suite that featured eighteenth-century French antiques and Chinese lacquer work.

The room reflected the appetite of Prussian kings for Chinoiserie.

After the porter gave her a quick tour of the room with its ornate fittings, she inspected the separate marble bathroom and adjacent living space while he waited at the door, ready to leave. "If you need an Internet connection, the fittings here are wired for most international plugs. Will that be all?"

Calla ran a finger on her clotting wound. "Do you have a first-aid kit?"

The porter moved to the bathroom and produced one. He set it on the table in the living room.

"Thank you. I think I have everything now."

She tipped him a handful of euro bills and closed the door behind him. The pain from her accident resurfaced. She grabbed a ripe plum from the fruit basket and bit into its skin before checking her phone.

No new messages.

It had been over three hours. Was Allegra okay? She threw the pit in the wastebasket and picked up the first-aid kit.

One hand on her chin, she located the antiseptic and a small Band-Aid. Calla gulped down an aspirin with the water supplied in the fridge and unpacked her belongings.

Soon, she settled on the upholstered couch facing the window then kicked off her shoes before turning on her electronic tablet.

Tell me, Allegra, what did I miss?

She checked her diary. Allegra had left London a week ago via St. Petersburg, and then onto Berlin.

Calla waited on the sofa staring at the unresponsive phone as she dressed her wound with a thin plaster. Her eyes moved toward the window taking in the details of the suite, a smile stretching on her face. The first-class treatment was Allegra's style. But even after spending much time with Allegra, how much did she know about her government working friend?

No one was like Allegra, even at sixty-seven when it came to elegance. Born into an aristocratic family, she'd been raised every inch the lady. Her charm and ageless good looks were to be envied. Calla liked how Allegra kept her hair in long, black, and gray, woven braids, usually four. Groomed on her head, they flowed like tails behind her. Large, olive green eyes radiated and twinkled when she smiled, distracting one from the sophisticated wrinkles on her face, the only features that gave her age away.

Was Bierman right? If the Deveron existed and was a legitimate artifact, what was it, exactly? What did the British government want with it? Let alone the other four.

If anyone could decipher the historical riddles around this manuscript, it would be Allegra.

Calla stroked her forehead and guzzled down more cold water. It was the most attention she'd ever given the Deveron. Her eyes shut as the aspirin worked its drowsiness through her bloodstream, and she rested her head against the cushions.

Calla shot up at the sound of sharp ringing from the hotel phone. Her tired eyes pulled open as she staggered to the table and grabbed the telephone. "Hello?"

Unintelligible sounds filtered through the line. Then silence.

The line went dead, and Calla held the phone against her ear for several seconds. "Hello?"

Nothing.

She set down the receiver and shot to the window. Lights from the Brandenburg Gate fell onto the carpets. How long had she slept? She checked her watch and realized that her aches had disappeared. Was it really midnight?

Hand on her brow, she moved to the bathroom to check the wound on her chin. As she removed the adhesive, her jaw dropped under her touch. Her chin was spotless. Any sign of an injury had faded. Had she imagined the whole thing?

Allegra!

Perhaps she'd called. Calla returned to the couch and located her cell phone.

No messages. *What now?* Going to the museum at this hour wasn't an option. She found the remote control and turned on the wall-mounted plasma TV. As she scrolled through several channels, she landed on RTL reporting in German. The newscaster stood on the steps of the Pergamon.

"Even though museum officials and police won't confirm, we believe a secret document or manuscript was among the stolen treasure of Priam—"

Images of the earlier closure of the museum flashed across the screen, including a snappy interview with a police investigator. Brightness from the TV screen blazoned into Calla's eyes as she navigated the dark room. In one purposeful reach, she turned on the side lamp.

"Police are not confirming if this was a break-in or if there

has been any damage to the museum. It is still unclear how the culprit escaped with the artifacts."

The rest of the program detailed the history of Priam's Treasure and moved on to other news. Calla rubbed her eyes. Awake now, she called the front desk. "Could you please order a taxi for me?"

"Now?"

"Yes, now."

CHAPTER 4

Nash found his car on Green Street, a few steps from the US Embassy. He checked his watch. He was running late. Gray clouds above showed no leniency. They scattered across the London skyline, creating an overcast blanket that sent a cold current through the darkening city.

Nash tightened his leather jacket. He pulled open the door to his new BMW z4 and checked his cell phone for messages.

None.

Why had Calla left the meeting early the other day? It wasn't like her to go without a word to him.

Perhaps he came across as independent, but the truth was he was tired of being alone. It was time to do something about it.

He had accepted the job not too long ago when the National Security Agency had asked, no, begged him to join them as an intelligence analyst and security adviser. So far, so good, and he even recalled the senior director's words. "Best recruit in the last six months," they'd said.

Damn! He'd left the Marines because he had the itch to travel again. Would he always be a global nomad?

51

Coming to London? It all seemed like so long ago.

So what if he'd trained in the US military, a feat he'd challenged himself with and succeeded. He liked his life simple and uncluttered.

In all conscience, he'd not thought much about his future until he met Calla. She mattered. But what was bothering her? Worry snaked through him, and Calla was at the heart of it.

She was in danger.

Nash cared little for the irregularities that surrounded the Deveron Manuscript.

What had been the hurry the other day? Didn't she see him? He would ask her later.

Now, he needed to make an urgent phone call.

Nash checked the rearview mirror only to glimpse at the tiny scar on his chin undetectable to the naked eye. He smiled to himself. That's how he'd first met Calla, charming, inhibited with piercing eyes, such a curious mélange of emerald and amber.

The car ahead of him honked. He started his engine and reversed, letting the other vehicle out of the parking space, then killed the engine.

Why was it so difficult to tell her? All the military training, the numerous deployments he'd been on in Syria, Iraq, plus the problematic cases he'd worked on in Russia and North Africa, yet this made him want to recoil.

Holding back a sick feeling, he bit his lip knowing he needed to face his father, a man whose approval he craved yet dreaded his rejection.

With one hand on the wheel, he reached for the phone.

The touchscreen lit up as he searched for his attorney's number based in New York.

With the phone engaged, he waited a few minutes and tried again before leaving a message.

"Jonathan. It's Nash. I need to speak with you today."

He clicked it off.

After ten years of service to his country, he'd seen enough.

As a man in service, it had left him feeling helpless. He couldn't lift the family he'd met years ago in Idlib out of the destitution of war or feed the children in South Kordofan beyond handing out food aid bags that would only last a mere week.

Money was no obstacle. So why wasn't he doing what he wanted? He'd done much for others. Why not himself? An army of virtual special agents would do the job.

They would come from various fields in the name of justice, and step in where governments left off.

He didn't need the pat on the back. God knew he'd experienced enough in his line of work, seen criminals walking free, and launching scandalous empires.

He could do something. *Someone has to.*

The cell phone on the passenger seat rang twice. He answered it. "Jonathan? Do you have any news for me? The stakeholders want an agreement soon."

"I'm sorry," said Jonathan on the other line. "Your father refuses to release the funds."

Nash's face heated, picturing the actual words his father had probably used. He clenched a fist and brought it down hard on the dashboard.

Would the old man not give up?

"After all this time. Jonathan, doesn't he understand me?"

"You two haven't always seen eye to eye. This bothers you."

Nash tugged at the collar of his shirt. "Why can't he let go, Jonathan?"

"You're his only child. He only wants the best. George hasn't always accepted your choices, Nash, but he's always been proud of your accomplishments."

Nash already knew the answer to his next question. "Was there something wrong with the proposal?"

"No, Nash, it was impeccable! I've been your family lawyer

for a long time. I think it is purely a conflict of interest. He thinks the money could be put to better use."

Nash was quiet for a long time. He would have to revert to plan B.

"Is there something else, Nash?" Jonathan said. "Something's up. You are the most patient person I know, and it's not like you. You seem quite focused on this. Are you in trouble or someone you know? A girl?"

Nash breathed hard. "I first saw her at the British Museum, but she doesn't recall, then we met properly at Denver Airport, three years ago at check-in."

"I knew there was a girl involved."

Nash let out a quick breath. "I was traveling back from a skiing holiday, and she'd been on an anthropological trip. She was in such a hurry and when she got to the counter; sure she'd missed her flight, she knocked over my skis. I tried to retrieve them, and as they crashed to the floor, they clipped my jaw. She was struck with horror."

"I love a damsel in distress story," Jonathan said.

"That's just it. I was the one struck and in distress. I'd only seen her once before in London when Jack took me to the British Museum. She's the most beautiful thing I've ever seen."

"Wow, Nash. You deserve the best. What happened then."

"I cupped my chin with both hands as gasps, and concerned glares from the queue erupted at the American Airlines counter. I then gave her the okay sign and threw my head back laughing. Nothing was missing or broken. Just a small cut."

"So you were injured by cupid's arrow more than anything else, I see."

"She was funny. Calla chuckled and begged for someone to produce a first-aid kit. She found a Band-Aid in her cosmetics bag and placed it over my almost nonexistent wound. And then said the craziest thing. 'Phew. No damage. By the way, are you taking skis to London?'"

"I like her already."

"The long flight back to London with adjacent seats perhaps changed my life. With my background in political science and intelligence analysis, our conversation and interests were so well matched."

"I bet that's not all you did."

"Hey easy, I wanted to get to know her, so much so that we chatted the entire nine hours and forty minutes. By the time we stepped off the 747 flight at Heathrow, I knew my life had changed, all thanks to crossing paths with the most arresting woman I'd ever met. A girl who seemed to be oblivious to her beautiful appearance."

"So when did you see her next."

"Three months later. Neither of us disclosed our links to ISTF until we found ourselves a few months later working on a joint classified case in Jakarta. She'd been brought into ISTF on specialized projects for her in-depth knowledge of modern and ancient communication methods and for her skill in multiple languages."

Jonathan gasped. "So she works for ISTF too?"

"As a cultural agent. She's actually a head curator at the British Museum."

Nash let out a quick laugh. "Calla can impress any group of bureaucrats."

One thing bothered him, though. Calla could pore over artifacts, codes, symbols and language structures with ease, yet she would deflate after moments of genius into quietness and allow distance between them.

Nash concluded it was sadness or even loneliness. He once asked an innocent question, a compliment. "Where did you get your stunning dark hair?"

Her eyes that usually sparkled with clarity darkened, the amber in them overpowering the emerald glow.

"She impressed you. And by the sounds of it continues to do so," Jonathan said interrupting his thoughts.

"Calla's incredible and doesn't know it. She understands

phonetics, symbols and history like no one I know. And, we work well together."

"Nash, if I didn't know you any better, I'd say you're hooked."

He *was* hooked. He'd known no one like her; straightforward and unpretentious, coupled with a no-nonsense attitude.

"So, is all this business with your father have something to do with her?"

"No. But it makes me think of who I want to be and who I want in my life."

"I see," Jonathan said.

"It's my money, Jonathan."

"I know, but we need your father's signature. Give it three years. When you reach thirty-five, he can't affect your decisions. You can do whatever you like with the inheritance from your grandparents."

The silence, even with a typically upbeat Jonathan, was unbearable.

"I'm with you on this, Nash. We can always try again."

"Thanks, Jonathan. I know you tried."

Nash switched off the phone.

Where had it all gone wrong in his family?

Day 4
BERLIN, 0.58 A.M.

The chill in the night air prompted Calla to zip up her thin jacket. The streets were clear, and the museum terrace was empty except for police officers strolling around its gates.

In the midnight stillness, Calla made her way up the stairs, through the inner court toward the entrance doors. She advanced as far as the glass façade to the police line guarded by officers chatting. They spoke in hushed tones. Two armed cops, in khaki green jackets and white headgear, obstructed the entrance, smoking strong cigarettes.

They watched Calla progressing toward them and lifted their heads.

The older police officer held out a hand to stop her. He swerved toward her, questioning her approach. "*Was machen Sie hier?*"

"I'm here to see someone," Calla replied in German.

"The museum closed hours ago," he said.

Calla approached and faced him. "Can I speak to the inspector in charge? I may have information that may help you?"

The younger looking cop glanced at his partner to see if he would comply.

"What information do you have?" retorted the older man.

"I'm sorry, but I can only share information with your superior."

He grimaced, eyeing her for several seconds as he stroked his frosted mustache. "Who are you?"

Calla churned words round in her mind. "I'm with the British Museum in London. I work with Allegra Driscoll, and I believe she was here this morning."

The police officer paused for a moment, then raised his chin. "Can I see your papers?"

"ID?" clarified the younger cop.

Calla glanced from one cop to another and searched in her pocket, producing her museum identity badge. She reached into her other pocket and fished out the pass Allegra had given her. "Look, here are my credentials. Is Allegra Driscoll here? I need to see her."

The armed men studied her documents with a cautious eye. After what seemed like several impending seconds, the older man pulled out his police radio and turned his back to her. An impatient voice left his lips, and she peered past him, observing a tall man within the museum entrance. He stood with two other officers and museum officials and spoke into a police radio. Calla guessed he was the chief, although she failed to make out his face in the moderate light.

"Yes, she says she knows Frau Driscoll," mumbled the cop.

The man within the building made his way outward and crossed toward them. The cop who'd questioned Calla handed her credentials to the approaching man of authority.

"I'll take it from here," he instructed.

The two police officers let Calla past the police line and drew away from the entrance.

A lump rose in her throat. *Stay calm. You're only looking for Allegra.*

"I'm Raimund Eichel, the inspector in charge. *Was kann ich für Sie tun?* What's your business here?" he said, switching to English.

Calla supposed her German would be less problematic than his English. She wanted to turn back, abandoning the whole plan but with confidence, she extended a hand. *"Calla Cress von London."*

With eager eyes on her, Eichel accepted her handshake. His sturdy grip nearly jolted her arm socket. She managed a weak smile. "I'm looking for my friend, Allegra Driscoll. We were to meet here yesterday. I'm part of her delegation."

Eichel had been studying her credentials as she spoke and shot her a quizzical look. "You know Allegra Driscoll?" he said, more as a statement than a question.

"Yes."

Eichel stepped back and tilted his head toward the doors. "Come this way."

She obliged, grateful to escape the frigid night. For a day that had been sun-drenched, the clear star-speckled sky had invited an unforgiving cold front. Eichel led her through the museum entrance. Even with the dim lights, Calla couldn't have prepared for the grand exhibitions ahead of her walk.

The Ishtar Gate, about a minute into their stroll, commanded an audience with its blue and gold tiles depicting lions and aurochs, the ancestral forms of domestic cattle.

Ordered for construction by King Nebuchadnezzar II of Babylon, Calla could just imagine the respect it once drew in ancient Babylon. They went past the main Processional Way leading to the Gate and swept right through.

Their pace had slowed down, perhaps a gift from Eichel noticing her amazement at the display.

"Your first visit to the Pergamon?"

Calla's focus had been on the exhibitions, and she'd hardly detected the dipping of her jaw. She closed her lips. "Coming here always seems like the first time," she said.

Eichel unlocked a concealed door at the end of the gallery.

Calla hadn't noticed the hidden entrance, invisible to the untrained eye.

Through the door, a group of museum officials and police investigators sat at low tables, examining notes and photographs.

Stuffy and crowded, Calla assumed it was the main surveillance room.

Flat monitors lined the walls displaying every inch of the museum.

She recognized some of the security systems, having advised the British Museum security team on safe, unobtrusive methods of protecting displayed Italic and Etruscan antiquities.

For now, the room served as the temporary headquarters for the investigation.

The officers acknowledged Eichel and carried on about their work.

Calla refused to believe a simple theft had caused the commotion, as Bierman had explained.

Eichel ambled to an adjacent room before proceeding down a dimly lit stairway that led to a lower level.

She tailed him. Had coming here been a good idea? It was too late; the next room changed her mind altogether. Her eyes gaped at an immense vault, the size of a high school gymnasium. Filled to the max, the space boasted ancient Egyptian art, sculptures from old Hellenistic ages, to artwork from Greek and Roman antiquity, mosaics, bronzes, jewelry, and pottery.

One wall stored Islamic works covering the entire region of Spain to India from the eighth to the nineteenth centuries and several other precious, priceless items awaiting display.Calla breathed in the sight and glanced around. When was he going to get to the meat of the tour?

Rubbing her arms, she held them in an embrace for warmth. "Listen, do you know where Allegra Driscoll is?"

Eichel marched ahead and halted by a worktable with a clear label.

Priam

The table was empty.

CHAPTER 5

C alla's eyes drew together. "Herr Eichel, I'm worried. I've not heard a word from Allegra all day. It's not like her not to be in touch. We were to meet here today."

"I wish I knew, Frau Cress," he said and faced her for the first time since entering the room.

Eichel rested his frame against the aluminum table as Calla tapped her fingers on the table. "The hotel informed me she ordered a limousine for the Pergamon first thing yesterday."

Eichel peered past her, back the way they'd come. When he was satisfied they weren't being overheard, he motioned for Calla to sit down and she sank into one of the workstation chairs.

"My police officers aren't privy to the information I'm about to reveal. So, I need your cooperation. How well do you know Frau Driscoll?" he asked.

Calla shrugged. "We're colleagues. I've known her close to seven years." She thought for a few seconds. "She's a good friend."

Eichel took a seat beside her. He studied her face and leaned forward, his voice hovering in soft tones. "She was here. In fact, she was the last person alone with Priam's Treasure." He took a deliberate pause. "And with the Deveron Manuscript."

"So it's true. Both have gone missing."

He stood erect, veered to the corner of the worktable, and picked up a tenth-century sculpture. When he'd studied it, he set it down with a gentle thud. "She came as you say." His hands slid into his pockets as he paced around the table. "It was earlier. Around 6:00 a.m." Another pause. "I gather it was to work with the artifacts before they went on display. We cleared her credentials yesterday."

She said nothing as Eichel monitored Calla's every reaction. "You work for the intelligence arm of your government, don't you?" he said.

Calla opened her lips to speak.

"Don't. I know Allegra was with ISTF," he said, his face breaking into a grin. "Do you know about the Deveron?"

He waited for her response.

She gave none.

"It supposedly contains formulas and scientific clues that have helped perform military miracles and wonders in history. Your friend Allegra was here to verify those claims," he said.

Calla held back a smirk. Each account she heard of the Deveron Manuscript had a new twist to it. She rose with an awkward step and scrutinized Eichel's round glasses. "I've heard the rumors. Educated people can't believe this document can do all you claim. Why have these so-called formulas never been tried before? What's to say a document dating what is it, six hundred years or so is of any value to military intelligence today?"

She slid her hand along the worktable and picked up a small brass plate and examined the exquisite Islamic designs. "Besides, aren't you interested in finding Priam's Treasure instead of a mythical document whose existence hasn't even been confirmed?"

Eichel smirked and moved over to where Calla stood. "Come on, Frau Cress, you're a smart historian. Even I know there's some truth to the rumors."

Is he fishing? Calla placed the item down and faced Eichel. "What are you getting at?"

Eichel stroked his chin. "I think the document is older than most people think."

"How old?"

He shrugged. "Who knows? I'm here to investigate the disappearance of prized treasures. I was at a dead end," he said, smirking at her. "I now have you and your connection to Driscoll. We've secured Priam's Treasure. It's down here. Only one item is missing. We're not sharing this information until we put together the pieces of this puzzle."

Eichel's voice coaxed for a reaction. "Do you see?"

It was, at times, easier than others to follow his English. Now that he seemed to get onto something, his sentences weren't entirely comprehensible.

"The real crime is that both Allegra and the manuscript are missing. They've been...what do you say? Abducted from the museum?"

Calla's pupils dilated, and she fired him a quizzical glare. "Abducted?"

"You mean she's been kidnapped?"

He tilted his head to one side. "No. Vaporized. Vanished into thin air! Look at this."

He led her to the end of the vault, and then through another narrow staircase behind a cement pillar. They entered a slender doorway, hidden within the walls.

The moldy room formed part of the maze under the museum. Past the narrow entrance, brushes, easels, small bottles of solutions, and dyes, including several other artist tools, cluttered the small chamber. Its minimal size suggested it served as a private work area, perhaps used for restorations.

She'd never seen so many artifacts in such a small space.

Her fascination with the room was short-lived as a new sense of trepidation swallowed her. Was Allegra in danger? What could Eichel have meant by vaporized? Eichel hesitated at the far corner of the room. He glanced down and pointed to a hairpin. Even in the dim light, Calla recognized it. Allegra always wore the rhinestone hair clasp, handmade and designed to look like a blooming flower.

"Not a trace of blood, fingerprints, or even a sign of a struggle," said Eichel.

He crouched down. On the floor next to the hairpin lay a strange object, a tubular cylinder. Handcrafted out of thick glass, it was transparent enough to display an empty interior.

"We're not sure where this came from or what it is," he said. "It's a container of some sort, butwe can't open it. It's electronically protected. Have you seen anything like this?"

Calla shook her head.

"A museum worker in Saint Petersburg said it had been sitting with the Priam artifacts for years, even though it was only discovered yesterday."

"Where did it come from?" Calla asked.

"We don't know. However, as I said, one gold item from Priam's Treasure is also missing."

Calla examined the cylinder. "Was it looted from Berlin in 1945 with the rest of the treasure?"

Eichel let out a sigh. "I guess that the cylinder contained the Deveron Manuscript, or the culprit wanted to place it in there."

Calla studied him. The soft eyes behind his spectacles revealed a gentler side to him. He was still looking for clues and dared not tamper with the crime scene.He examined the cylinder with care, sliding it back and forth with a toothpick. "It's locked shut. We've yet to find the access code to this secure system. It looks a little dated, but it's as secure as they come."

"Let me see?"

He raised his head. "You work in intelligence. Isn't this a biometric fingerprint lock? I thought these systems only came into existence this past decade."

Calla knew the security program. The UK government had designed it a few decades ago and patented it to government agencies alone. She tunneled a hand through her loose hair, trying to keep up with the pieces of the story. Was Allegra involved? If so, why?

"There's no way the manuscript could've been taken out of the glass case. Every inch of this cylinder is intact. We have already conducted fingerprint tests, and there's no proof it was there in the first place," he said.

Calla relaxed the muscles in her face. "Why do you think the manuscript was with the treasure? That makes no sense."

Eichel was getting to some point and had revealed more than he wished from the quiver of his bottom lip. He was right about one thing, according to Jack, these security systems were resilient. Eichel was looking for a scapegoat. The manuscript had been lifted from the cylinder with no damage, and, according to him, no alarms had been triggered. There was no sign of forced entry. But why was he telling her all this?

"Are you accusing Allegra of taking the manuscript? That's absurd! Don't you know who she is?" she said.

Eichel cast her a superficial sneer. "You're the only person who understood Allegra's real mission here."

Am I a suspect?

He paced around her. "You know her well. Therefore, we'd like to ask for your cooperation with a few things. What was Allegra working on? What did she discover concerning the Deveron Manuscript? You're a historian. Is it connected to the antiquities of Priam? After all, it was stolen while on Priam's guard."

Calla knew Eichel believed the Deveron stories. He was confident that the two items were equally valuable.

"Your documentation says you're also a linguist. I imagine you're gifted in ancient hieroglyphics and symbols as those on the manuscript. That's why Driscoll needed you here. You must know something," he added.

What were her legal rights? She kneeled beside the hairpin. "I don't know what you think I know. I'm more concerned about Allegra. Are you going to investigate her disappearance? She could be hurt."

"Surely, you have access to her files."

Calla sighed. "Even if I did, I wouldn't be authorized to share anything. Listen, unless you give me more information, I'll just have to contact the British authorities."

He drew back, narrowing his eyes. A beep came from his police radio with a weak signal. He studied it as it flickered before switching it off. "Come. I think you've seen enough."

They advanced back toward the door, and an awkward silence swamped them until they re-entered the security room.

Eichel roamed toward two museum officials and exchanged a few words.

Calla's ear picked up most of the German conversation as the men debated whether to keep her for questioning.

Soon, discussions escalated as police and other administrators determined the next steps.

Faint lights overhead triggered Calla's fatigue. She signaled for Eichel's attention with her hand. "Herr Eichel, before I go, I need to know if your investigation will focus on Allegra's disappearance."

He turned his head and paced to her side. "We've alerted British Intelligence. They'll send someone to help us with the investigation."

"Can I go now?"

"Yes. For now."

He escorted her to the exit of the museum. "Please, take my card. I can't force you but advise you to stay in Berlin a few days, in case we have more questions."

Calla took his card and turned to the door. As she did, he set a steady hand on her elbow, barring her. She glimpsed down at his imposing fingers that gripped her arm. Judging from his stance, he could damage it. "Frau Cress, we'll expect your full cooperation."

"Of course. I take it the investigation here will focus more on the artifacts than finding Allegra."

CHAPTER 6

US Embassy, London

Nash shook David Masher's hand. The lieutenant colonel reminded Nash of a comedian. The man you needed in the Marine Corps. It kept the men in touch with normalcy, a leadership flair that Nash admired. Masher had often used humor to help troops cope with combat and operational stress.

His narrow eyes gleamed at Nash like two pieces of steel. His thick, ginger hair was neat and trimmed in standard keeping with Marine regulations, styled so as not to interfere with the proper wear of uniform headgear.

Nash understood the protocols well. Even then, he didn't miss the strict regiments. The only facial hair visible on Masher was a faint, graying mustache.

The two men steered down the long hallway inside the Marine quarters at the US Embassy. At the end of the narrow hall, Masher pushed open a private office and asked Nash to take a seat. Masher settled into a swivel chair. The position of lieutenant colonel suited his personality.

Nash eyed the silver oak leaf insignia on Masher's uniform,

in keeping with his rank and relaxed, confident that coming here hadn't been a mistake. He could trust Masher.

"Good to see you, Masher."

"It's been a while, Shields. Although I can understand why you left the Marines for a job within the NSA."

Nash knit his eyebrows and fiddled with a sealed brown envelope in his hands. He handed it to Masher. "I need a favor."

Masher took the envelope.

"Could you hang onto this for me? I need you to keep it safe."

"What is it?" Masher said.

Nash's stomach knotted. "I wouldn't give it to you for safekeeping if it wasn't important."

Masher glared at him, his eyes questioning Nash's face, and he gave him a nod. "Okay, Marine. Then, I won't ask. Anything for the man who saved my life twice."

"Much appreciated."

Masher tilted his head. "You okay?"

"Yeah. Just need to attend to something."

Nash rose from his seat and saluted. He hated leaving matters open with anyone, especially a friend like Masher. He'd learned in his profession, often shrouded in secrecy, whom he could trust. And there were few.

Nash headed for the door. "I'll see you soon."

Masher rose behind him, worry lines forming on his forehead. "Nash. Are you in some kind of trouble, son?"

"No, sir, not at all."

1:46 A.M.

Calla clenched a palm. "Goodbye, Herr Eichel."

Her collaboration would be with her own government.

Thirty minutes later, she stepped into the Adlon Hotel

lobby. The night staff didn't notice her arrival except for a knowing nod from the receptionist.Calla rubbed slumber from her eyes as she made her way to her suite. Soft lights fell onto the dark carpeted hallway.

Her body ached from lack of sleep and mounting worry for Allegra, and she'd struggled the whole cab ride with her conversation with Eichel.

Calla paused at her door.

It stood open. An inch wide.

A cold shiver shot down her spine, embracing the dreaded option. *Someone was here.*

She placed a limp hand on the door handle, hesitated, then glimpsed back down the hallway.

No one was about.

Fighting the urge to alert the night staff, an inner probing and natural curiosity made her proceed. She stepped into the quiet room and lingered by the door.

Leaving the door ajar, she stepped forward. Whoever had been, had come and gone.

She listened for any hidden sounds and progressed slowly.

The street-facing windows were open with silk curtains wafting in a quiet breeze. Calla proceeded to the window and closed them. The dining room lights were on the same room where she'd left all her belongings. She inched over to the dark polished desk and inventoried her possessions. Nothing was missing. What were they looking for?

She continued her investigation throughout the rest of the suite, first the bathroom, then the bedroom, the living room, and returned to the entryway dining room. Her chest stuttered, and yet again, she felt as if she was being observed. The feeling pierced her with an invasive prod.Someone had marched into her privacy. What the heck did they want?

Calla ignored the knots in her belly. She'd cured that a long time ago after being bullied in elementary school. She'd outsmarted her aggressor with a blow to her nose, short of breaking it. Since then, Calla had sworn never to live her life in fear. Her persistence and tomboy nature had seen to that. She would fight this bully too.

After a thorough search, Calla decided that the suite was empty. Shutting the front door, she patted the pockets of her jacket for her phone.

Her fingers grazed a bulky object.She fished deep in her left pocket and, a moment later, her hand found and gripped a foreign object.

The temperature behind her neck rose, and she pulled it out with one firm tug. A neat bundle of folded, faded papers was in the grasp of her hand. At first, they resembled old newspaper clippings. She unraveled mashed papers, sheet after sheet. Thin as a stretched woman's stocking, the papyrus unfolded in her hands.

Heart pounding, she peered down at the script, but the low lights made it illegible. Hurrying to the wall, she switched on the overhead lights never once taking her eyes off the papers.

The words were incomprehensible, the lettering unfamiliar and the writing calligraphic. Neat patterns spilled across the aging pages.

In one involuntary measure, her hands rose to her nose and mouth.

The pit of her stomach fell as she gaped, sending the papers floating in drawn-out, gliding movements to the carpeted floor. They landed piled on top of the other.

Calla counted under her breath.*Seven!*

She dipped down next to the historic pile, inches from her feet. "The manuscript!" Her eyes blinked. "It can't be!"

Think Calla, think! Where could it have come from?

She searched her recent memory, but even then nothing made sense.

Did Eichel plant them there? He seemed like the type who needed an excellent investigative victory. But how could he have managed such a devious feat?

She reached in her other pocket.

Wide-eyed, her hand found a gilded, solid gold decanter from Priam's Treasure.

No taller than the size of her index finger, its polished surface was a little scratched and secured in a clean plastic bag.

Calla scrutinized the small decanter and recalled it among the items displayed in London in 1878 before the loot of Troy found a permanent home in Berlin in 1945.

Priam's Treasure had never been exhibited at the Pergamon, or anywhere else on the museum island, only in the neo-Renaissance *palazzo,* now called the Martin Gropius building.

Until this moment, Calla hadn't believed the Deveron document existed.

She picked up each sheet, one by one forming a neat stack in her unsteady hands. The lettering glowered back at her. Along the edge of the sheets, someone had taken the time to lay out what looked like a three-petal flower using secret letters. If only she'd paid closer attention at the London meeting. As she continued her examination, she noticed that, on page three, the writing went round in a design of a star flower with seven petals. The letters, and the hieroglyphics, together formed the magnificent patterns.

One didn't know where to read asthe words ebbed out, flowing in rhythmic streams similar to a runny watercolor painting. They were large, and small, all forming the intended masterpiece. Calla had imagined the manuscript would've been penned from left to right, or from right to left, as with most known scripts. Her linguist and anthropological sides merged to see the manuscript for what it was, a work of art and delicacy.

She examined the writing, accustomed to scrutinizing texts and symbols of all sorts.

Calla didn't recognize one insignia, letter, hieroglyphic or punctuation.

That some believed this was a military document made her frown, for the calligraphy was art at its greatest.

The script resembled that of the medieval Voynich document. She had to be sure. She would pull up the ISTF meeting notes and know soon enough. Calla sprung to her feet not once taking her eyes off the document and the ancient decanter. Her feet stood short of trampling a small folded paper she'd not noticed before. It had fallen out of the manuscript pages and dropped to the floor, inches from her shoe. She stooped down to retrieve it and unfolded it with determination.

What she saw threw her back a few steps. Addressed to her and handwritten with haste, a message in the language of Ayapaneco glared at her.It couldn't have been written too long ago.

Like many other indigenous languages, Ayapaneco was at the risk of extinction. Calla recalled it had been spoken in Mexico for centuries and survived many challenges including the Spanish conquest.

Ayapaneco had triumphed over wars, revolutions, famines, and floods. Only two living souls could speak this language today.

Ironically, they refused to talk to each other.

The Mexican government was trying to ensure Ayapaneco didn't die with the last two fluent speakers.

She remembered studying the language out of interest. Not too long ago, Allegra had suggested Calla work on a month's mission to aid the Mexican government in their efforts to sustain the language. That had been three summers back. She could read the writing but was limited in reproducing it fluently. Whoever sent this to her knew that little detail.

The note read:

Calla,
Get out of Berlin. Take the Deveron Manuscript and the
decanter with you. You're the only one who must translate the
Deveron and unravel its mystery. It must never fall into the
wrong hands. Follow your instincts. Never reveal what you find

to anyone. The manuscript belonged to your parents. It's now your responsibility.

A thundering knock on the front door sent her scuttling to her feet. She stashed the manuscript and goblet under a set of cushions on the couch.

"Who is it?"

"Hotel delivery. A package for you," said a man's voice in German.

She checked her cell phone for the time.

3:23 a.m.

Calla inched to the door and peered through the peephole.

She didn't have a gun and now wished that she'd listened to Nash and gotten one through ISTF. "For your safe

But even if she did, would she fire at anyone?

ty and self-defense. ISTF work is dangerous," he'd said.Behind the door, a hotel porter in uniform stood tapping his feet.

"Leave it at the door," Calla said in German.

"It must be signed for."

"Okay, show me your hands."

The porter raised a white envelope to the peephole, an express, courier package.

"Who's it from?"

He peeked at the package and attempted to read the writing in the top left corner. "I can't say. Looks like it came from London."

She took in a deep breath and dragged the door open.

CHAPTER 7

DAY 5
3:02 P.M.
HEATHROW AIRPORT, LONDON

Calla clutched her carry-on as she stood in line at the immigration counter.

"Next!"

She handed the female officer her passport and waited.

Since opening the door to the porter outside her hotel suite in Berlin, nervous energy had flooded her veins.

He'd seemed credible enough. Yet, she'd concealed the goblet behind her back and opened the door with discretion. Instinctively the porter handed her the package through the door crack. "I'm sorry to deliver it now. Please sign here."

He held out an electronic device for a signature. Calla gazed at the parcel. No information about the sender was evident. She signed for it.

The porter observed her with a curious gaze. "Sorry to come at such an hour. I saw you come into the reception and wanted to get this to you. It was delivered urgently."

"Who delivered it?"

"I don't know."

He left, and she took the envelope back through to the dining room.

Who'd send me a package at this hour?

She shook it.

No odd jingles.

She placed it under her nose.

No odor.

She took a deep breath and tore it open, peeling the thick tape around the edges with caution. After one final tug, she thrust her hand in the bubble-wrapped interior and waited for whatever her hands would discover. The contents slid out without effort, and Calla's eyes fell on the words:

DIPLOMATIC BAG

A document carrier, royal blue in color with the white government seal in the middle and a footnote at the bottom, was concealed inside the envelope.

PROPERTY OF HER MAJESTY'S GOVERNMENT.
ONLY TO BE OPENED BY AUTHORIZED PERSONNEL.

No other message or notes were present. Calla thought for a few seconds. According to international convention packages carrying official papers or other materials were above the law. *These documents couldn't be opened, detained or violated.This is my ticket out of Berlin.*

With no alternative, she placed the decanter and the manuscript within the diplomatic bag. Calla kept the items close at hand on the flight home. There was no turning back.It wasn't until the plane landed that she realized the diplomatic bag was safe from interference but was she?

"Miss?"

Calla disengaged from her thoughts, her shoulders tightening. The immigration officer sat behind a booth. Her gray hair, held in a neat bun, reminded Calla of a ballet teacher she once knew. With good posture and an uncompromising face, the woman's eyes gave nothing away. She studied Calla's passport, flipping from page to page with a cautious finger. Numerous stamps adorned several pages of the European document. They'd been collected in the last several years traveling globally for work, study and anthropological projects.

Calla gripped her carry-on with her right hand as the officer flipped through her passport and stopped at a page. She peered over the counter at the woman's hands.

"Looks like you've done quite a bit of travel?" the woman said.

Calla attempted a relaxed smile as the officer continued investigating the travel document, not once glimpsing up. "What sort of work are you curators doing these days?"

Calla smirked at the officer's ignorance of her profession. "A lot of our work is behind the scenes. We work with artifacts planning, organizing, interpreting and presenting exhibitions for museum collections."

"Interesting. Where are you flying in from today?"

There was no way around this one. "Berlin."

The woman raised her head and studied her face for the first time. She flicked through two more pages and scanned the travel document under a laser light. "I've never been to Berlin. I hear it's a great place." She held out the passport to Calla. "Welcome home."

Calla took a deep breath as the woman stamped her passport and held it out to her. "Next, please!"

Without any checked bags, Calla hastened to the arrival hall toward customs with the exit in her sight. Two uniformed men stood between her and the door to her freedom, and she marched briskly toward the exit without acknowledging them.

"May I check your bags?" insisted one of customs officers. "It's just a random check."

"Why?"

"Sometimes, we sample passengers throughout the day."

Adrenaline fired through Calla's vein as she handed him her carry-on. He handled the brown-leather, hold-all bag and threw it open.

"I've only been out of the country for forty-eight hours. I'm afraid I didn't do much shopping," she said.

The officer dug deep into the various compartments, pulling out item after item, mostly her clothes and toiletries. She glanced at his hands as he fished out the diplomatic carrier. "Hey, Clive. Come over here."

Calla's lips trembled.

"Hey, mate, I've actually never seen one of these." He held out the pouch to his colleague. "I've always wondered what they look like. Now, I know."

He stashed the item within her bag. "It's my first week on the job."

After he replaced all the contents, he zipped up the bag. "Thank you."

Calla stepped out of Terminal 5 into the warm sunshine her heart racing. *What the heck am I doing?* She scurried down the escalator toward the London Underground station, glad she'd left her car and wouldn't need to wrestle with traffic from Heathrow. When she made it down to the Underground, she bustled toward the eastbound, Piccadilly Line platform, heading for Central London. When the train approached Calla proceeded toward the last carriage. The doors slid open, and she veered toward the seats at the back of the compartment, scrambling past disembarking passengers.

Except for a couple with a bubbly toddler seated across from her, the carriage remained empty when the train clanged its doors shut. She plunged into the upholstered seats, and for the first time since leaving Berlin, her shoulders loosened.

Her mind mused over her accomplishment and the risk she'd taken. She'd done as requested and carried the items out of Berlin.Something about the note made her do it, the fact that it mentioned her parents and was in Ayapaneco.It was meant only for her, seeing that just two people knew that she understood Ayapaneco, Allegra, and Izek Vargas.

It had started as a hobby.

The two living souls who could communicate in the language were both in their seventies. Izek was one of them. Calla's fascination with lost words had prompted her to dedicate one summer to learning the grammar basics with Izek. He'd not been easy to sway, but Allegra used her influence yet again to have him instruct Calla. Izek agreed after much persuasion on condition that the government would teach the language to a new generation. Calla decided not to publicize her new skill to anyone, at least not until she felt she could teach it to willing students.

Calla clutched the bag to her chest. *What about the German police?* Perhaps it had been a kind suggestion. She'd find out soon enough.

3:06 P.M.
GUARDIAN NEWSPAPER HEADQUARTERS
NORTH LONDON

"How many will that be?"

Eva Lily Riche admired the pink carnations the florist held in her hands. "Please add white lilies. That's how she liked them," she said in a British twang, though she knew her tone hinted at French pronunciation.

A tear welled in Eva's eye. How ironic the significance of the bouquet. She could never forget her mother.

The florist placed a gentle hand on Eva's manicured fingers. "Are you okay?"

The flowers' perfumed scent brought back pleasant memories of endless summer days in the south of France, the family villa in Eze overlooking the cliffs of the French Rivera where Eva had spent most summer vacations away from the tumultuous life of boarding schools. Those had been the best times with Maman.

School had seemed more like banishment, a place for juvenile girls to be seen and not heard and to be churned into perfection for an unforgiving society.

"Yes, thank you. I'll take a dozen carnations and a dozen, white lilies in one large bouquet."

The florist disappeared through the beaded curtains. Eva had to survive the next twenty-four hours, the anniversary of the day her mother lost all sense of her world. Every year Eva purchased the same bouquet. It was how she remembered her mother, Madeleine Riche, a real socialite in her time, and the woman her father had fallen for. When Madeline slowly lost her memory, her father Samuel Riche confined her to a care unit in Lausanne, Switzerland. Eva couldn't bear to go there. It only made her weep, and ever since, her father had looked at her differently. She'd been his little girl, yet somehow, all that had gradually changed. Why didn't her father love her the same way.

The florist returned with a bouquet. "Will that be all?"

"Yes. Thank you."

The florist hesitated and grasped Eva's cold hands. "Miss, sometimes it's in grief and misfortune that we champion our fears. Rise to yours."

Was she right? Would Eva ever champion the fear of never having her father's affection? Eva managed a smile. "You're kind and wise."

She paid the florist and received the spread, inhaling the aromas as she strolled out into the afternoon sun. The fragrance filled her nostrils as she headed back to the Guardian newspaper office.

Her coffee break was almost over. She paced the few blocks over the moat and into York Way. The office was on the third floor of the Guardian tower. She took the stairs, a firm believer in keeping active and steered to her desk in time to hear the last ring of a missed call.

She slumped into her seat and answered several emails. No stimulating assignments stood out for the week. More galas to attend and celebrity interviews to conduct. She browsed through her diary.

Was the florist's advice sound? *Papa will never be proud of a gossip columnist.* Confidence had been her new friend, ever since she was hired. It hadn't always been this way, certainly not at school. Though born and bred from money and prestige, respect and accomplishment had eluded her. So far fame had sidestepped her too. Proving to her over-accomplished father, Samuel Riche, that she was a worthy daughter remained her focus. He demonstrated higher regard for the boys in the family, especially her elder brothers Léon and Anton.

Léon was a senior executive at Bourgeois Wines, the largest exporter of French wines, while Anton, a Stanford Law School graduate, was a highly sought-after corporate lawyer. Anton also practiced human rights law, pro bono. Samuel and Anton were the only father and son act to be listed on Forbes' list of wealthiest entrepreneurs with a considerable empire comprised of legal firms, luxury brand wines, and global security systems.

"Eva, I need that copy by five," the deputy editor said.

His was the enviable task of taking credit for other's work, including Eva's. "It's done and in your inbox, Simon," she said.

Eva snapped a pencil in half, shot up and walked past several cubicles to fetch some water. When she glanced up above the water cooler, the plasma screen transmitted breaking news on mute. Eva usually ignored the repetitive broadcasts. This time, however, she stopped as an RTL emission from

Berlin presented a special program on the main BBC channel. She edged closer to the screen and turned up the volume.

"Sir, what do you know about the disappearance this morning of the Deveron Manuscript?" demanded the female reporter.

The older man held out a hand to shield himself from the glaring camera lights. A caption flashed at the bottom of the screen:

RAIMUND EICHEL, BERLIN POLICE.

"As we've already stated, we've only confirmed that the missing items from the Pergamon Museum are objects from Priam's Treasure. We're still carrying out a full investigation," said Eichel as his English gave off hints of Americanisms.

"Can you tell us about the circumstances surrounding the theft?" the reporter asked.

"Whoever is responsible knew what they were after. It's still too early to tell."

Eichel glared into the camera lens. "No artifact has gone missing or been damaged on my watch, and this isn't going to be a first."

"What's so significant about this particular manuscript? There's very little information on it. Why would anyone want to take it?"

"I've not mentioned any manuscript!"

"But we've been told that an ancient document is missing. Can you confirm these accounts?"

Eichel's face turned ruby red. "What I believe is immaterial. We work with facts. Thank you!"

Eichel set a hand in front of the camera lens turning the screen black as Eva's eyes remained glued to the screen.

Eva had hardly noticed the three colleagues who'd stopped to follow the emission. "This is it," she said.

Curious gazes fell off her three observers.

She'd already left.

The train submerged under a tunnel, squealing on the tracks and howled throughout the carriage. Calla recalled information she'd kept concealed for years.On her right ankle, just above the bone lay a coin-sized birthmark. It resembled a tattoo, so much so that, at Beacon Abbey Academy, an exclusive boarding school, the head teacher reprimanded her presuming Calla had paid to have a tattoo. That alone constituted grounds for expulsion.

It had taken a trip to the local hospital to verify the legitimacy of the birthmark. The border was calligraphic, with rows of petals designed in sync. In the middle lay a depiction of a three-petal flower and two unreadable symbols. She'd always imagined they looked like Egyptian hieroglyphics but now, having seen the manuscript, she thought otherwise. Calla recognized the two inscriptions. This alone had convinced her to follow the instructions of the note in Berlin.

At the age of five, when Calla left the foster home, a few documents were sent home with her adoptive parents, detailing the nature of the birthmark, given its unusual form. It was easy to think the birthmark had been intentional with its obscure characters carefully etched in tiny letters.

There had to be more to the Deveron Manuscript. The markings on her ankle were too similar to those of the Deveron. Other questions loomed in her mind. How had the manuscript and goblet found their way into her pocket in the first place? Why must it not get into anyone's hands? Who were these wrong hands? Governments, politicians, mercenaries or just anyone who wished to pay the highest price? Calla peered out the window, her reflection enhanced by the dark tunnel.

The train navigated into West Kensington Station, and she disembarked walking the seven minutes from the station to her apartment.After a short hike, she stood at the gated entrance and found her apartment keys.She could think a little clearer in the safety of her environment and would begin systematically by heading to Allegra's house.

Calla stopped short of opening the door. She fumbled with her keys, her mind trying to recall where she kept Allegra's set.

It had been a warm afternoon when she'd met Allegra at the local supermarket. She recalled her amusement. In her own charming way, Allegra tried to explain to the cashier how pomegranates were grown and where they originated. Allegra had bought about five kilos worth, which naturally sparked off a conversation with the cashier. Overhearing the discussion while standing behind her in the queue Calla had filled in the missing elements. "Pomegranates are from modern day Iran and have been cultivated in Caucasia since ancient times."

Allegra glimpsed back, and both burst out laughing. It was invigorating to meet someone with interest in foreign cultures. The two naturally bonded despite their age difference and a friendship began. A few weeks later, when Calla explained she was looking for a new challenge, Allegra told her she knew of an exciting opening. Little did Calla realize it was to work as a curator for the British Museum. That was seven years ago.

Calla slotted the key through the keyhole. She inhaled, then paused before pushing the door open and dropping her travel bag on the floor.

She scanned the room. Her studio apartment was enviable by many standards. With a mezzanine floor, large enough to fit a bed and a closet just above her kitchen and bathroom, the apartment suited her. She kept it neat and minimalist, a habit she'd acquired in anticipation of nomadic life. From the day she'd set foot in the home of her retired missionary parents she'd expected not to stay there for the rest of her life. Life would be one of pursuit of identity and purpose.

Calla tore off her jacket as she studied the quiet environs. Was it just a feeling, or had the Archeology Today magazine she'd been reading slipped off the kitchen table.

She strode to the kitchen counter, picked up the publication and paged through it slowly. Calla had searched for a reference, an item on the Pergamom Museum shortly before leaving for Berlin. Even so. Why was it on the floor?

She reached for a glass in the cupboard and gulped down a cold glass of water before returning to the front door to fetch her carry-on. She removed the diplomatic bag, hurtled upstairs to the mezzanine floor and drifted into a generous landing comprising of a bedroom and the bathroom. Above her double bed, a double-glazed window looked out onto a shared and groomed garden.She unlatched the window and glimpsed into the yard. Arthur had been taking care of her mint. Sluggish as he was at gardening Calla was grateful for her neighbor Arthur, a retired journalist who took pride in giving the garden the attention it deserved.

Calla marched to her bed and knelt down beside it. She located a hidden button underneath her mattress. Painted in the same color as the bed frame, it was undetectable, almost invisible. A small trap door on the floor beneath her bed slid open. It was no bigger than a serving tray. A foot deep and thirty inches wide, it treasured few contents. Those had been her instructions when Jack had helped her fit it.

"I don't want a key. Can't we get my thumbprint for identification?" she'd asked Jack.

"Piece of cake," he'd replied and set about fitting one.

She placed her thumb on the smooth surface, and the metallic flap slid open. Calla reached down the hole and found Allegra's house keys. Allegra had wanted her to have them. "Just in case. Who knows? I may lock myself out."

She jingled the chained keys.

Calla placed the manuscript and the goblet inside the trap door with care and slid her thumb across the edge of the trap door. It shut effortlessly, covering the hole and leaving no evidence of its existence.

Calla shot upward and hurtled back down the stairs. She gathered a few items from her carry-on and placed them in a shoulder bag before bolting the front door and hunting for her Audi on the quietening street.

CHAPTER 8

E va shuffled back to her desk and grabbed the phone. She waited until he picked up. "Alex. Could I come and talk to you?"

"What is it, Eva?"

"I want to follow a story."

Alex Maxfield's office was at the end of the maze of cubicles. He glimpsed up through the glass doors and caught her eye before gesturing for her to cross the ten meters toward his private office. "Get over here."

Eva hung up and cut across the room, passing several cubicles to the glass door that read:

CHIEF EDITOR
ALEXANDER MAXFIELD

Alex had given her exposure when most editors would've just thought she wasn't worth the risk. This fact alone made Eva highly confident around him. She was smart, she'd been told by the papers that rejected her, just not the kind of expertise they needed.

She shut the door leaving the tumult behind her. Alex sat hovering over a document he was reading. "What is it now, Eva?"

The fan in his room revolved, filling the silence between them. Alex was an old-fashioned reporter accustomed to traditional ways. Why use a laptop when the typewriter still worked? Good thing he no longer wrote columns. He only approved and marked copy with his unforgiving red pen. Still, he'd been coerced into investing in newer technologies for the office, including the sleek computers on each desk.

Eva approached him. "I'd like to be assigned to the story in Berlin."

Alex, a middle-aged, heavyset Asian man, with a balding head and just enough hairs to cover his crown kept reading, his eyes focused behind bifocals. Without glancing up, he grunted as he spoke. "What story?"

"The Deveron Manuscript. Priam's Treasure?"

Alex raised an eyebrow. "That's slightly complex for you. Why not stick to the gossip column or fashion? You're a good celebrity reporter with your contacts in that industry."

"No!" The volume of her voice surprised her. "I need this story!"

Alex stopped reading and put the piece of paper down. His thick, dark-rimmed glasses enlarged his eyes like a bug under a magnifying lens. "What's this really about, Eva? You think that you're going to get what you want? Has no one ever said no to you?"

"You don't understand, Alex. I need to do this."

"Not this time, Eva. Now, good day."

Alex smacked his lips and continued reading his document. He marked the text with red ink. Eva guessed the poor journalist would have to rewrite the entire thing. As far as he was concerned, the conversation was over.

"This story needs an experienced journalist, not a prom queen flashing daddy's credit cards. My final answer is *no*. I'm sorry."

The blood in her veins rose to her cheeks, and she placed a firm hand on the back of her neck and steamed through her nostrils. "That's not fair! You've not even heard me out." Her voice quavered. "Don't you know who you're talking to?"

Alex tapped the desk with his pen, awaiting a full-on verbal assault. "Ah! The Riche family card again. You can't pull that one here anymore. I did your father a huge favor by hiring you. Now get out!"

Eva's lips trembled. "You'll regret this."

He stared into her reddening eyes. "Is that a threat, Miss Riche?"

She leaned toward his desk and stooped forward. "No, Mr. Maxfield. I quit and will write this story on my own terms. You'll see!"

She flipped her auburn locks and stomped out of the office, knocking the glass out of the door as it slammed behind her.

4:37 P.M.
ALLEGRA DRISCOLL'S RESIDENCE
WEST LONDON

St. Giles Square was deserted. A quaint little garden square tucked away a few minutes' walk from Hammersmith Bridge. Calla liked walking through the square. She paced briskly along the sidewalk of the iconic common, laid out in the economic boom of the 1820s. Lined with paired, classical-style villas arranged around a central public garden Calla often came here to sit in the shade of its cherry blossom trees. In times of deep contemplation, she sat in the center with the statue of the champion Greek Marathon runner Stylianos Kyriakides edging her on in her thoughts. She often wondered what Sir William Blake Richmond, the sculptor, had purposed in his design.

Calla scampered to Allegra's villa that faced the square and pushed open the front gate. Like the other houses on this piece of land, the residence boasted a stucco front, pediments, and an iconic porch. Allegra lived alone except for Taiven, the butler, and Pearl, the housekeeper. Taiven had served her since Calla had known Allegra, and was often seen walking two chocolate Labradors.

Calla stepped to the front door and buzzed the doorbell. If Taiven weren't around, she would use her key. She waited.

Never having asked much about Allegra's family or relatives the thought whether Allegra had a family, husbands or lovers crossed her mind. Allegra never discussed the topic. Therefore it never made its way into any of their conversations.

As she slotted the key through the door, a light came on in the entryway. The arched entry with ornate, beveled glass pulled open. Taiven, a square-faced, dark-haired butler, held his shoulders erect and cast her a generous smile. He was young, perhaps thirty-five at the most imagined Calla. Striking in appearance, he studied Calla with his ice blue eyes.

He was of Middle-Eastern origin. Where exactly Calla was not sure. Today, like every other day, he wore a black tailored suit, traditional white gloves and a white shirt topped with a light blue tie. She'd never known anyone under the age of fifty to be a butler, or were those her own preconceptions? Well respected by Allegra, Calla wasn't sure when Taiven had started working for her.

"Good evening, Miss Cress."

"Hi Taiven, is Allegra here?"

Was this is a stupid question?

Still, she would be cautious.

He stepped aside to let her in. "I knew you'd come."

She watched him, his nonchalant invitation puzzling her. Calla breezed into the breathtaking entrance as Taiven helped slide off her jacket. Allegra's home was every inch an extravagant household. Calla was never at ease with the ways of the rich and how they were waited on. Her life had always embraced simplicity and modesty.

"How did you know I was coming?" she asked.

"Ms. Driscoll informed me to always let you in. Can I assist you with anything?"

"Maybe," she replied.

She followed him through the landing under a jeweled, eighteenth-century chandelier.

"Taiven, have you heard from Allegra?"

"With regards to?"

He would know soon enough. Right now she needed to learn all she could about Allegra's investigation of the Deveron Manuscript.

"I'm looking for a language dictionary, perhaps in Allegra's office. I need help with some translation work."

Taiven nodded giving away none of his thoughts as he led her through to Allegra's den, past the curved staircase. Allegra loved all things, Victorian. They gave her the feeling of delicacy yet allowed modern feminine expression. The interior of her home was no different, every inch Victorian in appearance and the den was no exception.

Taiven proceeded to a bookcase-lined wall. "This way. You'll find the dictionaries on the third row from the bottom. Here, help yourself."

Calla swerved over past the leather sofa, covered with a red throw, a particular reading spot for Allegra.

"Also, try the shelves by the window," he added.

Calla made her way and knelt down on the carpeted floor. She brushed her fingers along the edges of a few dictionaries and references. Would Taiven stay or leave her to investigate in seclusion?

Taiven progressed to the door. "If you prefer something more high tech you can also use Ms. Driscoll's online files. Her laptop is on the desk there by the window. She created the programs herself."

Calla tilted forward. "Would that be okay?"

"By all means."

She failed to contain her curiosity. "Taiven, have you heard about Allegra?"

He slowly drifted back into the room without a word.

Calla pressed on. "Do you know that the German police and our government are looking for her in what seems to be a case of disappearance? I personally don't believe it. She may have been a victim of Sanax."

Taiven had crossed the length of the room and taken a seat on the edge of Allegra's reading chair.

"So you know about Sanax?"

"Allegra told me about it."

Taiven removed his gloves and placed them in his pocket. "Ms. Driscoll always warned me about this day."

"What day?" she asked.

Taiven ignored her question and stood to leave. "Do let me know if there's anything you need. The computer requires an iris scan in the identification device. Yours have been authorized."

He gravitated back to the entrance and left her speechless in the room. Why hadn't he answered?

4:40 P.M.
ISTF – Intelligence Services, Watergate House

"I have Slate Mendes for you."

Mason shifted in his seat and stared at the interphone. *What's he doing back so quickly?*

He pushed down the interphone button. "Let him in."

A robust man, just short of six-foot-two, coasted into the expansive office. Clothed from shoulder to foot in black he sported a brown leather jacket and stocky army boots as he moved with adroitness. His comportment suggested he was a fighting man. With no step wasted, every motion was carefully drafted. Mason glimpsed up from his work not recognizing him.The man's full head of hair ebbed from his face like frozen waves and fell in brown locks to his shoulders.With a narrow nose, his eyes pierced straight through Mason's gaze.

Mason reached under his desk and lightly rested his hand on the panic button. "Have we met?"

"Ich habe garnichts gefunden in Berlin," said the man in German.

"So you found nothing in Berlin. Who are you?"

The man reached in his jacket pocket.

Mason's hand stirred, ready to activate the button as the man pulled out a sponge looking object and smeared his face clean. Mason leaned forward with a fixed gaze. Accustomed to many life threats the action put him on full alert. He was never caught off guard, a habit from his combat days.

The man, now seated across from the desk, pulled a wig off his head. In calculated movements, he began to rip strips of foil from his face revealing a smooth, clean-shaven bald head. With a long neck jetting out of his long-sleeve muscle shirt, his narrow eyes became more recognizable as Slate drew into form, discarding his lifelike, facial disguise.

Mason's chin dropped. *Military cloaking.*

Unaware that testing of disguise technologies had commenced Mason's lips curled into a smirk. ISTF was experimenting with two core technologies. One made soldiers invisible, disguised in an enemy's infrared and motion sensors. Slate had gotten a hold of the facial adaptation technology or *the mask.*

"They've put in significant efforts here," Mason said. He relaxed his shoulders. "Slate?"

With a focused gaze, Mason lifted an eyebrow. "You're impressive, Slate! You pulled off a disguise that had me fooled."

Slate threw his shoulders back, a wide grin arresting his face.

"I see you had access to my underground labs and got a hold of the *mask*," Mason said.

The ISTF technology labs were working on several prototypes that kept the identity of commandos and agents undisclosed as they carried out undercover missions. *The mask*, as it was fondly known around the labs, used technology that reduced a person's facial signature. It allowed agents to be concealed in a variety of environments, temperatures and lighting conditions. Built into combat uniforms and body suits the mask could be independently used on flesh and equipment. The cloaking didn't stop the ability to breathe, see or hear.

Slate leaned in with one hand on his knee. "The German language training program also came in handy."

Mason raised an eyebrow. Slate was far from fluent in any language. Nevertheless, his mind took on any given challenge. Mason cast him a knowing grin. "I'm really proud of what they're doing down there."

Damn, he was good. Mason recalled the day he'd decided to groom the boy, whose parents had served on his family estate for over twenty-five years. Malnourished, even though he could help himself to anything that fell off Mason's table, Slate had shown much promise and loyalty. He was fearless.

Mason remembered the year well.

1987.

Before that day, no one would have believed that a storm so vast could hit England. It occurred one night in mid-October. A storm its size hadn't been seen in England for close to three hundred years. With winds gusting at up to 100 mph, massive devastation swept the country killing eighteen people. It was later declared a rare event in that part of the world.

Though only ten Slate had demonstrated much capability and courage when he rescued the woman Mason called *mother*.

Mother. Mason could barely bring himself to think of her. She'd been trapped in her smoldering bedroom. The other estate residents had escaped and congregated on the front lawns. Slate whisked to the burning wing and ripped open a small gap through the blazing wood planks for the stronger men to pull her out. Once on safe ground, the tiny boy had been hailed a hero, most of all by a grateful son, Mason.

Victory had been short-lived. That December Mason's mother passed away. The memory of her passing angered him, like a fresh wound left open to flying vultures.

The following summer Mason ensured Slate received a well-rounded education, academic yet militaristic.

Mason withdrew his hand from the button. "What happened in Berlin?"

"I met Cress at the entrance of the Pergamon. I passed off as a local German journalist. She didn't know anything about the disappearance."

"Did you plant the device?"

"Not yet. I have a plan."

Slate pulled out a remote, mobile listening device no bigger than a pen cap. "This'll be planted today."

Mason nodded in accord. "Is Cress still in Berlin?"

"She's back in London. Arrived this afternoon."

"What do we know about Allegra?"

"Completely vanished and with the goods, it looks like."

Mason rose slowly and advanced to the full-length glass window overlooking the Thames. He rubbed his gray, dusted goatee in deep strategic thought. "Did Cress meet Allegra?"

"No."

The sun was setting, reflecting shades of lilac, tangerine, and scarlet on the Thames below. Mason took in the view from his office before turning to face Slate. "I don't think Cress has the manuscript. Allegra wouldn't have risked it. Also, she would have been detected at the airport. I alerted the police the minute I learned of Allegra's disappearance. Have you searched Cress's residence?"

"I searched her hotel suite in Berlin."

"Go to her London place."

Slate grasped the armrest ready to move. "I think it's a waste of time. She wouldn't hide anything there."

"We must be sure. I'll have her emails and correspondence monitored. That's easy enough. However, her outdoor activities are what concern me. Don't let her out of your sight."

Slate rose to leave. "What do we do if Allegra comes back?"

Mason returned to check the slim laptop on his desk. "Given the evidence they have the German police think she was a victim of biological warfare. A particularly interesting one the Russians have been testing called Sanax."

Slate kept his focus on Mason without a twitch. "What's Sanax?"

"Sanax was developed by Biopreparat, a vast network of secret laboratories in Russia. Each has been focusing on a different deadly agent. Our intelligence claims that when Sanax is used in a normal weapon, radiation is sent through the body disintegrating body matter."

Slate stroked his chin. "Is that what you think happened to Allegra? What about the manuscript?"

"Not for a second. Your job is to get me that manuscript."

Mason's interphone beeped, signaling his next appointment, and he clutched tightly at his collar. "If Sanax was used we should start to worry."

"Should we?"

He needed that manuscript. Mason shook the thought away with a wave of his hand. He'd once obtained a photograph of the Deveron Manuscript. That had been back in the sixties. The quality had been so weak he'd not attempted any real translation work. The manuscript then disappeared. With its discovery, just three nights ago by the Russian museum worker, new hope had been ignited. Once the Deveron's secrets were unleashed, he'd finish what he had begun all those years ago.

Even with a seat on the Joint Intelligence Committee Mason had no authority to interfere with the German police investigation. He could intimidate Allegra and Cress, though. "It puzzles me that Allegra refused to use one of my other more qualified subordinates. Cress knows something," Mason said.

He intended to find out what and eyed his attentive wunderkind. "She's our last link to Allegra. Find Allegra, if she's alive and follow Cress. Get that manuscript!"

Slate couldn't move as he steadied himself against the chair for support.

"Get out!"

CHAPTER 9

Calla peered at Taiven from behind a volume of *Lost Languages: The Enigma of the World's Undeciphered Scripts.*Had she shared too much too soon? She replaced the book on the shelf. "Thank you for helping me out, Taiven."

The den, decorated in tones of red and burgundy was perfection. How many times had they sat in here, poring over books and historical documents?

Allegra enjoyed the wooded smell of an authentic fireplace. A Picasso hung over the mantelpiece, an original, no doubt. The only clues to Allegra's past were collected in a series of photographs carefully displayed on an antique chest of drawers. They boasted of distant travels, celebrity encounters, politicians and other influential dignitaries. There were no depictions of past lovers, a husband or even a family member. There was one image though, of Allegra on a hunting trip with a full-lipped young woman. Calla guessed it had been taken more than a decade ago. She didn't recognize the woman. Was it a sister? A friend? A niece? Calla had never asked.

She placed her elbows on the desk, turned on the computer

and performed a file search on the hard drive for anything relating to the Deveron document.

Why did she know so little about this? She was informed about many secret documents but why had she not paid close attention to this one? Who wanted it and why?Why would anyone take Allegra's life for it?

She found a folder titled 'Deveron'. Calla scrolled through the documents within and came across more files. Allegra must've done extensive research. She navigated through five folders, each focused on the symbols of both the Voynich and the Deveron. Not a single file showed any actual translation work. How had Allegra gotten a hold of the Deveron before two days ago? Calla hadn't even seen a copy of the manuscript before the Watergate House meeting. Had it not been sitting in Russia for at least seventy years? Where was it before Berlin?

The questions flooded her mind as she copied the files onto a memory stick she kept on her key chain. She was yet to find a deciphering dictionary or a cryptography system. She shot up and explored the room, searching through the vast library.

Nothing stood out. She placed her hands on her hips and glimpsed at the clock on the far wall. She'd been in Allegra's den an hour, after which she switched off the computer and left the room closing the door behind her. The late sunset had set in. And Taiven was nowhere to be seen.

"Taiven?"

No answer. Was the housekeeper about?

"Pearl?"

Silence.

She hesitated by the curved staircase that led to the upper rooms of the residence and set a hand on the banister, a golden masterpiece. Would it be out of order if she went upstairs? Her foot settled on the first step. She would take her chances. The lights in the upstairs hallway glared dimly on the first floor. Never once having ventured there, Allegra used this part of the house as her central living space.

The room at the end of the hall had to be the master bedroom.

Calla approached the door and peered back before pushing it open. Darkness greeted her as she groped for the light switch and blinked when she found it. Her breath hitched in her throat.

Almost out of place, the room had a modern interior compared to the rest of the house. Two doors led off the main room. As Calla explored, she discovered one was the bathroom and the other a walk-in closet suitable for any countess. The room responded to a remote control panel at the foot of the bed. Allegra had spared no technological expense. Everything needed for a business, diplomatic, or intelligence call was at arm's length, including a video-conferencing unit in one corner of the room.

Calla found the closet door. Where did Allegra store the things closest to her heart?She dragged the door wider and glanced back her body stiffening. The plasma screen at the opposite end of the master bed illuminated. It was all clear, and she accelerated her investigation. Calla discovered an island of drawers in the middle of the generous walk-in closet. She pulled open drawer after drawer before settling on the bottom one, the only one that was locked.

She patted the top of the wooden drawers for a key. Allegra's dresser was on the right. It displayed some of her collection of perfumes, rare and expensive including Fragonard from the French perfume house. A collection of silver, horsehair brushes lay next to a glass jewelry box. Calla unlatched the container and searched through its contents. Nearly abandoning her investigation her eyes fell on a small key, silver and smooth. She seized it and sidled to the locked drawer. The latch snapped open. Calla's eyes glossed over two bundled documents and a small velvet box. She reached for the container and unlocked it. Her eyes fell on a pendant, a gold chain.

She unfastened it.A man's face glared into her eyes. From

the fashion of his beard and hat, Calla guessed it was late nineteenth century. Slightly faded it was worn and had been finished in Sepia.

Should she proceed? Was this prying or merely looking for clues to help her with the translation? Combing through the stack of documents she came across a birth certificate. It seemed moderately old and tattered but well preserved. There would be no secrets here. Allegra was close to seventy though she looked a flattering fifty. As she studied the barely legible words, her focus was set on the date. The cursive script slanted steeply to the right. Sure enough, as accurately as she could see, it read:

THIS CERTIFIES THAT:
ALLEGRA MAY DRISCOLL
BORN TO SUSAN AND CLIVE DRISCOLL

ON MONDAY, 11 MAY 1881,
AT ST MARY'S HOSPITAL,
MOORCASTLE, ANTRIM, NORTHERN IRELAND

It carried on, but Calla's eyes reverted to one minuscule detail.

A number.
That date of birth.
1881.

5:15 P.M.
WEST LONDON

A biting breeze drifted through the cracked window of Nash's BMW. He half listened to mind-numbing tunes on the radio. With the car maneuvering at moderate speed through commuter traffic, a popular station flipped from old to new songs with the occasional report on weather and traffic. It distracted him. He wasn't really listening to anything. His eyes focused on the road ahead.

Despite the many times Calla had shut him out of her life he couldn't bring himself to resentment. He cared for her wellbeing and battled to comprehend her recent detachment from him.

Why hadn't she contacted him? It had been two days. Too long. Calla's lack of communication swayed him from Jonathan's news regarding his father. He didn't care to end up like the old man.

Alone.

Nash had always identified more with his mother, whom he saw less now due to his frequent overseas assignments. She'd left his father when George Shields resigned from the Foreign Service for a job within the Board of Governors of the U.S. Federal Reserve System.When Nash came home, after graduating from Stanford University with a political science undergraduate degree, he overheard the argument. *"I can't always be in the shadow of your career, George."*

Nash feared the worst. And his fears stared him in the face when his mother left. It shattered his life. It was then he'd known a government job couldn't tie him down forever. He could do better working for himself. And even better if this idea of his succeeded. That way those who got close to him would never take second priority in his life.

The newscaster predicted smooth road travel for the evening's rush hour. Nash wheeled on to an empty roundabout that journeyed toward West Kensington and steered into Calla's neighborhood. Primarily a residential area, consisting of Victorian terraced houses, many were recorded on the statutory list of buildings of particular architectural or historic interest. It was one way of preserving London's extensive history. Listed buildings couldn't be demolished, extended or altered without special permission.

He'd tired of waiting for Calla's call. Going to her apartment made better sense.

His BMW swerved into the quiet street and searched for parking, having driven the thirty-minute drive from his apartment near Hampstead Heath.

Nash nosed into a free parking space across the street from the double-duplex homes that lined Calla's street. Glancing over at her house, he decided to try her cell one more time. He fished for his phone in his pocket and stared intently at the apartments, catching a movement out of the corner of his eye that came from across the street. He switched off the light inside his car and surveyed the street. A figure flashed before his eyes and leaped across the mini-fence, a few feet from Calla's front door.

Nash placed the phone back in his pocket, his eye following the obscured character approaching her apartment. He observed as the burly man picked her lock. A professional, no doubt.

The intruder peered round to see if he was being watched before proceeding through her unsecured entrance. Concealed by the shadows in the street the man shut the front door behind him with caution. Nash toyed with the idea of going in after him and jumped out of the car.

He locked the vehicle, checked for oncoming cars, then shot across the road in a military crouch. He hurdled over the gate, then stood with his back against the wall as he peeped through the window.

Darkness.

The street lamps cast a spotlight on the building, eliminating any desire to be inconspicuous. Nash peeped through the window overlooking the street.

Damn. I can't see a thing! Gritting his teeth, he decided to go around the back. A vehement thud sounded, the noise coming from Calla's front room.

Nash stooped under the window as a dark shadow

approached and peered outside for a few seconds. He edged against the wall, and his ears caught the cacophony of sirens and nearly lost his balance as an ambulance whisked by breaking every speed limit in London. Its alarms screeched, puncturing the stillness of the early evening.

The intruder moved away from the window. What did he want? Nash fiddled with his pockets for his military-grade cell phone. He'd had it since his mission in Syria. Ancient by modern standards, nonetheless, it had the right features he needed and refused to part with it.

He forced down a button and out slithered a thin film of plastic. It resembled a two-inch negative strip but functioned as a night-vision android camera. He placed it over his left eye and glanced through the window again. The trespasser had scurried to the mezzanine floor. Not only was he in a frenzied rush, overturning item after item, but he also didn't care about the destruction he left behind. A thief would have gone by now. This man was after something else.

Nash surged to the back of the building. The kitchen window was closed tight. He slit the latch open with his Swiss Army knife and listened for any inside activity before gliding it open an inch. He hesitated as the man muffled in hushed rasps. Nash strained his ear.

"There's nothing here. Are you sure she has it?" said a muffled husky voice.

Nash concluded he was on the phone and continued eavesdropping.

The voice continued above the stillness. "I've already ransacked the place! She may have hidden it somewhere else." The man paused. "All right." Another pause. "Got it. Okay."

Was he taking orders?

Loud thudding footsteps sounded. *Must be coming back downstairs.*

"I'll try another approach," said the man.

Nash ducked below the window.

Jolts and a loud clamor rummaged through the apartment. He hated himself for not intervening earlier. Something about the way the man had crept into the apartment alerted Nash he was a professional. He suspected he had a weapon. The raider stomped into the kitchen. Nash stole a quick look and witnessed the man pull out a spray can. Thankful for his 20/20 vision, Nash made out the bland words that formed as the man drizzled his can.

Where Is It?

Where was what? The invader turned his head toward Nash's hideout. For the first time since he'd arrived Nash managed a quick glimpse of him. A military type with a burn scar on his right cheek, the moonlight beaming off his clean-shaven head.

Was it a heroic souvenir or a job gone wrong? Nash couldn't tell. He failed to place him but took a quick snapshot with his phone. The man cantered to the window and gazed outside. Nash held his breath ready to jolt him if he came close enough.

With a thud, the front door swung open.

5:39 P.M.

Calla!

Nash opened his mouth, but no words leaked from his twitching lips. He had to get Calla out. He quietly tugged at the window only to see the night visitor leap onto the sink.

Nash dropped to the ground. The man threw open the window and escaped past him, bolting to the street.

Calla turned on the lights. He watched her freeze and dash to the kitchen. She gawked at the message on the wall its paint still dripped in thick, downward streams. Nash raised his head, imagining the fear she felt.

She scuttled upstairs for several minutes. His ears caught the sound of the doorbell, followed by loud pounding.

"Calla Cress!" said a male voice.

Calla stomped down the stairs. From his hiding spot, Nash saw her shudder with confusion. The front door flew open. Two armed constables scurried into the apartment with stern glares at her face. "Come quietly, and you won't be handcuffed," the constable said.

"But—"

Her words were inaudible.

CHAPTER 10

7:30 P.M.

Calla's eyes bore directly into the flashlight aimed at her face, blinding her vision. She blinked several times trying to make out the faces. The constables moved the light from her face. Her vision slowly focused on two figures, a man, and a woman.

"Calla Cress?" said the gruff female.

"Yes?"

"Please, come with us?"

"What for?"

"If you come quietly there'll be no need for these." The constable held out a pair of glistening handcuffs. "You don't have to say anything."

"About what?"

The female constable showed no remorse. "It may harm your defense if you do not mention when questioned, something which you'll later rely on in court."

"Why am I being arrested?"

She ignored Calla's question. "Anything you do or say may be given in evidence."

Calla's gaze dropped on the pair of handcuffs glistening in the officer's grasp.

"Please listen—"

The female constable held out a hand. "Save it for the station."

Moments later Calla was whisked like a criminal in the back of a police van.

7:25 P.M.
NEWLANDS AVENUE, HERTFORDSHIRE
ENGLAND

The Elizabethan style manor in Hertfordshire was a serene place to withdraw from the hubbub of the city. Jack had heard Mason often retreated here, about once every fortnight.

Tucked away on a private twenty-acre hill the eighteenth-century manor was one to be desired by many standards. It had been in the Laskfell family for over a century. Guarded by a fierce army of staff, security alarms and closed-circuit television cameras, the home was the envy of any government security system. The eight-suite estate comprised of three enchanting cottages, a walled outdoor swimming pool, and a generous, landscaped garden skirted the grounds with a series of pebbled pathways and herbaceous borders.

Jack's brow furrowed. Why had the ISTF head invited him to his residence? What did he want.

He rubbed a tic above his left eyebrow as his car negotiated up to the windy hill along the private road lined with apple tree blossoms. He'd never imagined how Mason might live. Judging from what he'd seen on the short drive from the main road, Mason was in a league of his own.

Jack proceeded to the secured iron gate, rolled down his

window and peeked out. A cool breeze crept into the vehicle alerting Jack that even with the sunny weather they'd been experiencing in London the nights were still crisp. He glanced upwards spotting a security camera lurking down at him.

Even the most experienced burglar couldn't penetrate the gated fortress. The doorbell was in reach. He stretched a few inches upward and spotted the keypad that required a pass code.

Jack slid back down into his seat and fished in his bag for the scribbled code.Why would Mason want to meet here? He could've discussed whatever he needed to in the office.

He fingered in the secret digits on the keypad. The gate clanged open, throwing the heavy iron back to reveal stately premises.

Mason had called Jack shortly after Calla had left for Berlin. He'd been persuasive in his manner. "Jack, I'd like to talk to you about government business in private. I need your expertise here."

"Should I come to you now?" Jack said.

"No, I'll have Lillian send you the details of the meeting."

"Could you tell me what it's about?"

"You'll find out soon."

Lillian sent him an email shortly after that with an address and the instructions to arrive promptly. She'd also dictated the code over the phone. Jack was no stranger to ISTF's covert missions but rarely had they involved consultations in a private residence. This had edged Jack's curiosity further.

Jack trusted few ever since he'd left the Seychelles. His mother left his father for a younger man in Mahé at the age of five, someone much like Mason. For a long time, refuge had been secured in his inventions and gadgets. Jack depended on himself and anyone around him had to earn his trust. Mason was nowhere close.

Once inside the main gate, the road progressed to the

private cottage. He put the car in first and ambled up the path, noticing the Roman neoclassical theme with which Mason had selected to decorate the gardens and the lawns.

Several Roman statues graced the grounds and reminded Jack of overbearing Roman gods with the moonlight beaming off their burlesque frames. Jack had stepped into a different world. He took in the planar qualities of the gardens as well as the sculptural details of the grandeur displayed outside the main house. It wasn't at all what Jack expected of Mason, a man who indulged in magnificence. Mason didn't come across as one who completed anything in halves.

Jack killed the engine after parking in the spaces provided, several meters from the entrance of the house. He jumped out of the car as the night air, perfumed with scented magnolias, Amazon lilies and tropical plants that resembled flowers native to Seychelles, wafted past his nostrils. They spawned their fragrance to any passerby as he maneuvered toward the main entrance. Though ancient in its appearance, nothing about the custom-made, stable oak door spoke of primitive. Miniature, nearly invisible, security cameras lined the top frame of the entrance, eyeing Jack's every movement. He knew the camera designs well having created similar technologies for the government.

Jack pressed the doorbell and glanced at his watch. Eight o'clock sharp, as he'd been instructed. The door inched open, and a heavyset, butch of a woman stood at the entry.Her weak chin twitched as she shot him a brief smile and eyed him with curiosity. "Mr. Laskfell is expecting you. Please, come in."

"Thank you."

Jack proceeded through the large entryway admiring the manor's interiors, lavish and expensive.

"Shall I take your coat?" asked the housekeeper.

"No thanks, I'm okay."

She ogled him from foot to mane. "All right. Come this way, please. You'll dine with Mr. Laskfell."

Jack hadn't expected a dinner invitation. Still, he followed her through the hall. The inside of the property was a testament to attention and detail, with the bordering and architraves fitted amid thick oak paneling. He examined a set of double doors opening from the salon through to the family room. To his left, the dining room offered every inch of spectacular and a custom-made, oak staircase led from the lounge to the galleried first-floor landing.

Jack tailed behind his hostess. His eyes focused on a giant dragonfly embroidered in a large vintage tapestry. It hung above the dining room door, dangling upside down, ready to devour any who dared enter. "Is this one of Mrs. Laskfell's favorite species?"

The housekeeper pouted. "There's no Mrs. Laskfell," she said.

"I see."

Jack quickly calculated that the dining table, suitable for any state dinner, seated at least thirty people. Set with gold and white china, and dusted with images of dragonflies of all shapes and sizes, Jack could only imagine a dramatic dining engagement had been prepared. Each table setting was garnished with gaudy gold silverware.

The housekeeper pulled out a chair at the far end of the table, adjacent to the head seat. "Take a seat here. Mr. Laskfell will be down shortly."

She left the room by the far exit.

He surveyed the setting. Elegant dining always made him uncomfortable. He preferred an excellent Jambalaya or Indian curry in front of his plasma TV or seated at his computer. Banqueting was for those who had time to muse.

Jack inspected the treasures from artifacts he didn't recognize, to priceless paintings, swords and sixteenth-century armor. The feeling one would get entering the Musée D'Orsay overrun him. He picked up the fork in front of him. Just as he'd thought, solid gold. Dinner had been set for two. Who did

Mason typically entertain here in the mesh of modern and traditional? The room was also decked with state of the art technology items. He gaped at the interphone system, a Crestron, control unit with Luton lighting, each seamlessly hidden among the more traditional furnishings.

Though Elizabethan, the house had a classical Roman feel to it. Jack's trained eyes warned him that nothing here was old-fashioned. The systems rivaled those he'd seen at the ISTF offices. Why did Mason need so much security? Who was he watching? Who' was he watching him?

Jack's text message alert signaled in his pocket.

He fished it out. It was Nash. He pressed his finger down to answer it, and in the corner of his eye, he caught sight of Mason approaching.

"Ah, Jack. Thank you for coming at such short notice. Please join me for a light supper."

Jack shut down the phone and rose slowly.

Mason's entrance was short of extravagant. He wore loose-fitting white robes, resembling those worn in what Jack could only picture was an Arabian Nights tragedy. He also donned more jewelry than Jack thought was allowable for a man of his stature, including a dragonfly brooch and a thin ring on his right hand.

Jack finally understood who possessed the dragonfly obsession.

Empress State Building,
Metropolitan Police, West London

They arrived at the station within fifteen minutes. It might as well have been an eternity. Calla sat across from the heavyset female cop wearing an open-necked uniform. She had on an attached belt, rank badges on the epaulets of her shirts. She had removed her Private Constable bowler hat. The police van shuddered to a halt directly in front of a skyscraper she'd driven past several times, the Empress State Building. Constructed initially as a hotel it was mostly occupied by the Metropolitan Police of West London.

After a trek up two flights of stairs, she found herself across the desk of a chief inspector, an austere, middle-aged man. The day had been mild and, with the sun's disappearance, the temperature had dropped significantly to single digits. Inside the station, it was several degrees warmer. The chief inspector gave Calla the impression he was sterner than the officers who'd driven her here in a rapid commotion.

"Can I remove my jacket?" Calla said.

His nod was brief as he continued reading a stapled document, marking it up. Possibly a police report. Calla studied the name marker on the inspector's desk:

CHIEF INSPECTOR RIDGES

Her mind wrestled with what she'd discovered at Allegra's house, and what the police would find in her possession. As dire as her current predicament, she retraced her discovery of Allegra's birth certificate.

The date 1881 came to mind. Calla had taken out her smartphone and photographed the certificate before replacing it and leaving everything intact. Her sprint down the stairs was a near collision with Taiven, who was on his way up.

"Miss Cress. Did you find everything you needed?"

Calla held her step, nearly tripping on the stairs. Her stare was one of evasion. "Yeee...ss, thank you."

Taiven stepped out of the way and let her proceed. He said nothing regarding her activities on Allegra's residence floor.

She hustled back to her apartment. When she entered, she

found her coats and day pashminas on the floor, a few inches from her feet. Her eyes then moved through the studio apartment, landing on her living room area.

Cushions had been stabbed on the couch. The phone hung off its cradle. Several books had made their way from well-ordered shelves onto the floor, creating piles of hurdles between her and the stairs. She stepped over the vandalized heap and continued to the kitchen. Having wrecked the items there, the culprit had left an unsightly scribbling on her wall. Even in the subdued light, the paint, in shades of orange, red, and violet still crept down in hideous streaks to the foot of the kitchen wall. Her mind shifted to the manuscript!

She mounted up the stairs, taking two strides with each step, pulled the bundled papers from the diplomatic bag and inspected them. She would leave the objects there until she'd made sense of the chaos. That was when the doors had thudded.

The inspector finished his reading and imprinted the documents with a formal seal. The sudden noise brought Calla back to her present predicament.

"Calla Cress?"

"Yes?"

The inspector straightened a few papers on his desk. "Have you been informed of your rights?"

Calla nodded.

"You're entitled to free legal advice. Do you know why you're here?"

"Not exactly. Your officers weren't entirely the articulating types."

His eyes focused on her with intent, giving away no emotion. "Please sign this custody agreement."

Calla stared at the paper, refusing to comply.

"Would you like to contact someone?"

She shook her head.

He folded his arms, leaning back ever so slightly and studied her from a more focused angle. "Do you confirm or deny the knowledge of a woman by the name of Allegra Driscoll?"

Straight to the point, I see. "Why am I here?" Calla said.

No reply left his lips.

Calla placed her hands on the table. "I believe you need to tell me what this is all about."

He unfolded his arms. "Do you know Allegra Driscoll?"

"You don't need to repeat yourself, inspector." She thought for a second. "What if I do?"

"Don't try me, Cress."

Calla clutched her arms to her chest. "We're colleagues in many respects."

He eased up. "When was the last time you saw her?"

"Here in London, a couple of weeks ago."

"You didn't see her in Berlin?"

He's prying now. She tilted her head to one side. "How did you know I was in Berlin?"

"We make it our business to know everything of a criminal nature."

Calla didn't believe a word of his statement for a second. "You still haven't told me why I'm here."

"We're following up on a lead. Earlier today the German police informed us that you had left Berlin when they asked you not to."

Calla shrugged. "I don't believe that was a crime. Was it?"

"Ms. Driscoll possesses information regarding a theft from a Berlin museum. You were her last contact."

Calla rested her back against the chair. "What exactly am I supposed to know?"

The inspector ignored her question. "What was your business with Allegra in Berlin?"

Should she repeat the same story she'd laid out in Berlin?

The German police would have given them some sort of report. Besides, without a formal charge or accusation, they couldn't hold her here. Calla opened her mouth to interject and stopped mid-sentence as the door flung open with a thud.

She turned her head as Taiven burst in, his lips pinched into a scowl.

CHAPTER 11

Taiven's eyes darted toward Calla. Entirely dressed in a navy trench coat over a very sharp suit, he strode with an authoritative air toward the chief inspector's desk. "Miss Cress isn't required to answer anything at all. You'll release her at once."

The inspector rose to speak, his nostrils flaring. Any attempts at a protest were overridden by Taiven's grip on his shoulders, forcing him back in his chair. "Higher authorities are handling the disappearance of Allegra Driscoll, and I believe the matter is way above your pay grade."

Taiven drew a badge from his coat pocket, and Calla attempted a glimpse at it. From the reaction of the inspector, she guessed it carried authentic weight. "This is out of your jurisdiction," Taiven said as the inspector fell silent, his cheeks flushed.

Calla observed as the two men sized each other's command, each swearing inaudible threats with everything in their being. All these years she'd known Taiven to be a butler. Should she thank him or fear his influence? Taiven finally broke the stares and turned to Calla. He drew his eyebrows together. "After you, Miss Cress."

Calla rose instinctively and paced to the door followed by Taiven. No words were exchanged between departing the inspector's office and the short walk up to the car park.

"Is this our ride?" she said.

Taiven stopped by a silver Maserati Gran Turismo. "Yes."

Probably the latest creation from the manufacturer. She grazed her finger along the metallic polish. "I didn't know you owned a Maserati."

Taiven popped open the driver's door. "It's not mine."

"Oh."

"It's yours."

A beauty no less, decked with modern accessories and excellent artistry, a contemptuous smile played on her lips. "Not on my salary, thank you."

"Please get in the car," Taiven said.

She slid into the passenger seat, and they headed back to her apartment. The swift journey was marked with intense quietness as Calla purposed to let him speak first.

He didn't.

"You've just unleashed a skeleton in your closet," she began.

Taiven responded with a quiet smile as they eased into her street in West London. Taiven switched off the dynamic engine, and Calla paused several seconds before opening the door on her side. He reached for her arm. "It's time you and I had a chat. But before that happens, please go and get the manuscript."

Calla shrunk back into the leather and pulled the door shut.She'd not breathed a word to anyone. The note had forbidden it and yet here was a dual-identity government official whom she'd always known to be a butler, bailing her out of mayhem.

Taiven laid a hand over hers. "Calla, you can trust me. I was the one who sent you the diplomatic bag to get the manuscript out of Berlin."

Denial was the most natural option, but she needed help. Calla resigned her will. "Okay."

He rested his head on the back of the seat. "By the way, you no longer live here. Before Allegra left she asked me to let you have access to her estate and research."

"Why?"

He checked the time on the car clock. "It's not safe here for you anymore. Your belongings have been transported to her estate. Please hurry."

Once in her apartment, Calla ran up the flight of stairs. All her essential personal belongings had been removed. Signs of the evening's earlier events remained even when much had been removed in such a short space of time.

At the top of the mezzanine stairs, she reached for a button and released the trap door under the bed.

She'd almost forgotten about the birth certificate. She fished down the dark panel and found the blue diplomatic bag and opened the carrier. The Deveron Manuscript and the gold artifact were still there. She added the data drive, some notes she'd gathered over the years regarding her adoption, and zipped up the bag. She now had everything.

Downstairs Calla found her carry-on and her passport and paused at the front door, inhaling the night air. "God, I hope I know what I'm doing."

"Evening, Mason."

Mason took the head seat next to Jack.Within minutes the housekeeper served a vintage wine, a seafood platter of oysters, crab, lobster, mussels and giant shrimps on a bed of ice and lemon.

Though he'd been raised by the ocean most of his life, Jack wasn't a fan of seafood, especially cold seafood. When the meal had been set he ate politely, washing down each bite with iced water and an occasional sip of Meursault white wine. By the second course of sautéed *foie gras*, garnished with a crispy, cinnamon-flavored, duck pancake, Mason began to engage in small talk about, travel, art, and history.

"You like dragonflies?" Jack said.

Mason finished chewing. "In Japan, dragonflies symbolize strength, courage, and happiness."

"Are those things you aspire to have?"

Mason wiped his mouth with a serviette. "Who doesn't?"

Once the meal was over the housekeeper cleaned the table.Jack studied Mason as he took his time wiping his lips with a napkin. Mason rose from the table, taking his glass of wine with him. "Let's have drinks in the den. Mrs. Hawke, thank you for a lovely meal."

She nodded and cleared the dirty plates.

Jack called out to her, "I won't have any more drinks, Mrs. Hawke. I'm driving."

"In that case bring me a brandy, Mrs. Hawke. Mr. Kleve and I'll have some cigars," Mason said.

"I don't smoke."

"A man conscious of his health. This way please."

They proceeded through the landing to the salon opposite the dining room. Its decor and set-up mirrored the former room. When the housekeeper had finally left them, Mason handed Jack a cigar.

Jack shook his head.

"You sure?"

"Yes."

Mason lit his cigar. "I need you to create a program. A discrete surveillance program. It's a matter of national security."

Jack had always been a little skeptical of the man's behavior since he took over ISTF two years ago. He squinted an eye. "Who's the target? Surely we have enough systems in existence that could do the task."

"I need something a little more custom-made. Nothing that can be traced to us, or ISTF. A science project if you like."

What did he mean 'us'? Jack shifted into the seat across from the fireplace. "How so?"

Mason stood gazing into the fire. He flicked cigar ashes in the smoldering furnace, the placid flames reflecting in his face. "I need intelligence on three enterprises. Three people to be exact: Rupert Kumar, Margot Arlington the Republican governor, and Samuel Riche."

Jack knew these names. They were already under surveillance at ISTF but on a low priority level.

"Aren't we following these people already?"

Mason now turned away from the fire. "I need something more, deeper surveillance into their private affairs. This matter requires the utmost confidentiality. Jack Kleve, you're the most intelligent asset we have at ISTF. I know your file well. You're a seasoned graduate of a top university with a sharp technological and entrepreneurial mind. I've seen some of the developments you've presented at the TED shows. I know you're on loan to us, choosing to work temporarily on Operation Carbonado. We need people like you." He flicked his cigar again. "Drop everything you're doing and make this your number one priority."

Jack's voice choked with caution. "I understand."

"You're to speak to no one about this."

"What may I ask are we hoping to find? Is this anyway related to Operation Carbonado? These people pose no threat to us."

Mason drew back from the fire and took a seat next to Jack. His eyes pierced into his soul as Mason provided no encouragement. "Trust me, this is crucial."

Jack's phone buzzed on silent and moved his eyes from Mason's glare. "Okay. I think I have an idea what you may want. The system I have in mind requires personal contact with the targets. Can that method of contact be arranged?"

Mason's mood eased. "You mean someone will need to be in

personal contact with each of them. I can arrange that provided it's easy to plant."

Jack shot to his feet. "I should have the devices up and ready for trial in a day or two."

Jack's phone beeped again. Another text message from Nash.

He ignored it. "I'm sorry, but I need to leave now. Was there anything else you wanted?"

Mason escorted him to the front entrance, turning one last time toward Jack. "This could work in your favor. I know you applied for the international technology award and for NASA's exclusive technology program."

Not even Jack's mother knew that. Jack despised the rigorous background checks and security measures that he'd endured to be part of Operation Carbonado. After all, ISTF had scouted him and not the other way around. The closer Jack stood next to Mason, the more discomfort he felt. He couldn't accurately pinpoint where it came from, but he needed to tread with caution and cover his back.

Mason held out a hand. "This project could help you achieve that."

Jack responded to the offered gesture and shook Mason's firm hand. "I'll keep you informed of my progress."

Once outside the residence, Jack progressed to his car, cursing under his breath. He'd failed to plant the very bug that Mason wanted. On Mason.

It was in the front seat of his car.

CHAPTER 12

"Let me get you something to eat. I take it you've not had a bite all day."

Taiven threw open the door to the estate.He was right. Calla hadn't eaten since the flight home. She'd not even had a moment to speak to Nash or Jack.

She stole a quick glance at her cell phone.

1 2 MISSED CALLS

Taiven settled Calla in the kitchen. His hands worked with ease pulling cabinets open and whipping up a whole wheat club sandwich, garnished with a generous portion of Roman lettuce and baby cherry tomatoes bathed with Caesar dressing.

Taiven moved toward the refrigerator and produced what looked like a platter of Camembert mousse and smoked pule cheese. "You've had an ordeal. Perhaps an explanation can help you with some of the puzzles. Eat now. You can't do this on an empty stomach."

He left her to eat in silence. Though hunger had been suppressed by the day's events, she was grateful for the nourishment. Several minutes later Calla leaned against the steel of the kitchen stool. It was the first moment she'd settled since returning from Berlin. She rose and grabbed a travel size bottle of bicarbonated water from the fridge and found Taiven in the den flipping through a book by the shelves.

"Has Pearl settled for the night?" she asked.

"I'm not sure."

"Taiven, are you an MI5 agent?"

He closed the book he was reading and strolled to the window, flicking a switch to close all the shades. "This is your home now, Calla. Ms. Driscoll wanted it this way."

Didn't he hear me? Aware that he wouldn't answer directly Calla skimmed her mind for the most important questions she wanted to be answered.The manuscript? Allegra's disappearance? Or Taiven's alleged employment by Intelligence Services?

He asked her to sit in the chair at the desk and took a seat across from her. "Please hand me the manuscript."

Calla pulled the papers from the diplomatic bag. Did Taiven know about the note? Initially, she'd assumed it had come from Allegra. Calla pursued the matter. "Why did you send me the diplomatic bag?"

"It was the only way to get the manuscript out of Berlin. We can't risk it landing anywhere?"

Calla grimaced. "We?"

"Yes, *we.*"

"But isn't that suspicious? I'm already a suspect in Allegra's disappearance. Why else would the police want me?"

"You're safe for now. But not for long."

Calla glared at the manuscript cradled in Taiven's hands. A broad smile grew on his lips as if the document meant more to him than anything he owned. "It's very detailed. Not what I expected."

"Really?"

"Oh, yes."

She threw her hands in the air landing them on her thighs. She stood up. "I should just hand over the manuscript to ISTF. You seem to be one of their agents anyway, or even the government. Why shouldn't I?"

Taiven studied her face that must've revealed traces of fatigue. "I'm afraid ISTF isn't as trustworthy as we would like it to be. There are many non-compliant folks."

"Why was the manuscript left with me and who sent it? You? Allegra?"

Taiven's eyes narrowed. "Perhaps this can help."

He came over to her side of the desk. "Allow me."

From the top left drawer, he pulled out a notebook. Calla had seen this earlier in her search around the den but had ignored it assuming it was a private diary of some sort. He flipped through a few pages before handing it to her. "Here are some notes Allegra gathered. The last time anyone knew of the manuscript's whereabouts your parents were its guardians."

"Guardians?"

Taiven continued. "Allegra tracked them down many years ago when she investigated the disappearance of the manuscript. She later found them, though I'm not sure how or where."

Calla's eyes lit up. No one had ever spoken of her real parents. "Allegra knew my parents? Why has she never told me?"

"I don't know."

Taiven shuffled back to his seat. "When Allegra found them they wanted to know where you were. She'd traced you down through the foster home, and then through your adoptive parents. She watched you for several years before recommending you for assignments with ISTF. However, when she was about to let your parents know about you they vanished without a trace."

Calla's eyes followed his every movement, watching his lips to make sure nothing fell on tired ears.

Taiven's eyes softened. "Allegra established that this manuscript isn't what it seems."

"How do you mean?"

"Its purpose is more profound. Many have lost their lives, or even vanished, while trying to find its true nature."

"I didn't know people had lost their lives? Who are these people?"

"Contrary to popular knowledge this document has passed through several hands. It's a lot older than you think."

"How do you know that?"

"For one, your great-grandparents kept it safe during the Second World War, and after that, your parents did as well before they vanished while on a secret service mission to Russia."

"Are you saying they worked for MI6?"

"They had a special understanding of cryptic languages, even those alien to most people. They contributed to the unsolved cases division."

"Why?"

"Our government likes to follow intelligence and happenings beyond normal realms. It's not only the Americans."

Calla grabbed hold of every sentence he dropped about her parents. Her eyes welled, sparkling in the reflection of the recessed lighting above her. She shifted in her seat and, wiping an intrusive tear away, she edged forward. "Taiven, are they alive?"

"I'm not sure."

"Do you know where I can find them? I'd hoped to speak to Allegra about them in Berlin."

Taiven shifted to the other side of the room in thought and his voice clogged with emotion. "All Ms. Driscoll knew about them was that they served at MI6. I'm so sorry, Miss Cress."

"Oh," she said.

"Members of your family have been protectors of this manuscript for centuries. The treasure isn't in the manuscript itself but what it guards."

Taiven's hands slid across the old papers spread across the table. He pulled out a magnifying glass from the desk. "Let's take a closer look."

Calla turned her attention back to the manuscript. "What language is this, Taiven?"

"I'm not entirely sure but let me see if this might help. Allegra collected cryptography systems. I'm not sure if it's a language or merely a cryptogram. Maybe we can find out."

What was it the note had said? She reached for it in the back pocket of her jeans and scanned it again word for word. "Taiven, this doesn't help much. Did you see this?"

Taiven took the note from her hand. "Ms. Driscoll's instructions were to place it in the diplomatic bag. She must've written it herself."

"Does it mean anything to you?"

Taiven studied the note again before shrugging. "I don't understand the language. All I can say is that guardians are all within the same family lineage."

"I don't follow."

"Look here." He showed her a cryptographic system he'd pulled from one of Allegra's shelves. "Some of these might help."

Calla examined it. She headed over to the full library and surveyed a handful of cryptography systems. They were cataloged in chronological order, possibly by Allegra herself. Many were ancient, some newer.

"Taiven, I've never studied these methods. I don't know where to begin. I'm not familiar with these ancient cryptographs."

"Therein lies your task."

Calla hoisted herself on the edge of a large couch, next to the shelves. How did he know all of this?

She still didn't know who *he* really was. Butler, agent or—? Instinct told her she could trust him. "Is Allegra alive?"

"I don't know. But I'm certain she meant for you to have this manuscript. She believed in you from the moment she met you."

Calla chuckled. "We met in a grocery store."

"Call it chance, call it destiny. It is what it is."

Calla smiled though her amusement was short-lived. "What about the police? Won't they be back?"

"The police aren't your main problem."

How could he guarantee that? She had the feeling he was right.

He reached for an envelope from his pocket. "Allegra left this for you."

She grasped the short note and paced the room reading it carefully. "Says here that if Allegra doesn't leave Berlin with me that I should consider her gone. This is her will. I don't understand. She's left everything to me."

"That would explain the Maserati. It was ordered for you a month ago," said Taiven. "Welcome home."

Calla refused to digest this new piece of information. Nothing made sense. Perhaps it would by morning.

"It's really late. I'm tired and have a long day ahead tomorrow. I need to get a head start," she said.

Taiven nodded. "There's something else."

Calla couldn't imagine what other hidden revelation he'd failed to pull out for the night. He left the room for a few minutes and returned with a document. "Ms. Driscoll also had this prepared for you."

Calla took the document from Taiven.

"It's a diplomatic passport. You now have diplomatic status when you travel. It'll help with the police situation. Just sign here, and I'll have all of this notarized before the morning is out."

Too tired to argue she nodded. "Thank you, Taiven."

"You should find everything you need in there."

He turned to the oak door and gave her one last glance. "You're safe here, Calla. Good night."

Without looking up, Calla responded. "Good night, Taiven."

The door remained ajar, swinging lightly.

"Taiven?"

The chief inspector of police cursed under his breath. They'd left in such upheaval. He hated being overpowered by these government types. The station was quiet now. Most officers had gone except for two or three on the night shift. He fumed at his prisoner's hasty departure and rose aiming to get a good glimpse of the station floor.

The cubicles were empty.

He continued to the door, separating the main floor and his private office. He gave the space one more look and closed it behind him, locking himself in the solace of the warm area.

He picked up the secure phone and dialed a number from memory.

"Yes," a grumbling voice said.

"Mr. Laskfell. I arrested her."

"And?"

"I was interrupted."

"She mustn't begin any translation work on that manuscript."

"What should I do when I get her?"

Mason's silence stretched on the line. "Where's she now?" he said.

"A government agent, probably from MI5, picked her up."

"Follow them."

"Can I use my discretion?"

"Yes!"

The phone disconnected and the line shrilled. He replaced the receiver and collected a few things, turning the lights off before unlocking the door of the office. A giant man by many standards, he left the room walking with swift movements through the open seating workplace, scattered with messy desks, cluttered to the brim with files.

How anyone does this job day in day out, he didn't know. At the end of the room, the inspector turned into the dark corridor that led to the lifts. Clasping his coat and briefcase, he pressed for the ground floor. The double doors dragged open, and he stepped inside the isolated chamber.

As the doors began to pull shut a man stood mid-stride staring at him from the corridor. The man glared at the inspector and shuffled toward the elevators, not once easing his gaze off the police inspector. The brisk walk turned into a sprint stopping short of the closing doors as the steel frames nearly slammed his nose. It was just enough time to catch the inspector's smirk.

The man stood in the hallway questioning what he'd seen.There was no mistaking it. He'd witnessed an extraordinary resemblance to himself.A body double *and* a remarkable reflection of his own frame, only the likeness refused to surrender to his command.

His identity had been stolen.

Literally.

The quiet elevator sailed downward as Slate whistled. He clasped his hands to his chest as the elevator advanced to the ground floor.

DAY 6
6:46 A.M.
West London

Calla woke in a cold sweat. She couldn't piece together her environment as she focused her eyes on the dark room. Had she slept in her clothes? When she'd come into the room the night before she'd collapsed on the bed, poring over Allegra's notes and must've drifted off to sleep. The bedside clock blinked red, the only sign of movement in an otherwise still room. She could just make out the numbers.

6:46 a.m.

She scrambled off the master bed, upholstered in baby blue and white, matching the rest of the furnishings. Grateful for the few hours' sleep, even with so much still processing in her mind, her stomach rumbled with hunger. She traipsed to the adjacent bathroom before sliding under the shower and dragging on underclothes, a spare pair of jeans, and a light green sweater. She headed downstairs for breakfast.

When she drifted into the kitchen, Calla found Pearl rigorously working at a lamb dish. Pearl seasoned the meat and glimpsed up from her work when she saw Calla approach. "Good morning, Calla. I remembered you like a honey roast lamb. I'll have this ready for dinner. What would you like for breakfast?"

Calla attempted a smile as she settled onto a kitchen stool. "I'll just have a green tea for now."

"All right. I'll get one for you."

"Thank you."

Pearl, a bright Brazilian woman, moved around the kitchen with duteous ease as she brewed a pot of steaming tea. Calla spoke above the clamor of the boiling kettle. "Is Taiven up yet, Pearl?"

Shock flashed upon Pearl's face as she stopped what she was doing. Her ebullient Brazilian accent rose to a high pitch signaling nervousness. "Taiven hasn't worked for the Driscoll family for decades. In fact, he left years ago in pursuit of employment elsewhere. We haven't heard from him since, at least not since I started work here. *Santo Deus!* He'd be an old man by now."

CHAPTER 13

Calla cruised out of West London steering the Maserati into the busy city streets.

What was Taiven? And, now, his disappearance... Was Pearl right? Had Taiven been some sort of phantom or was he shrewd enough to go in and out unnoticed?

*Is he a piece of my imagination like my bruised chin in Berlin?*Yes, he seemed young for a butler. Nevertheless, Calla still felt she could trust him. He'd given her renewed appetite in her quest. Her parents could be alive, and he'd supplied her with more information than any archive or document she'd come across.

She steered into St. Pancras International and parked in the provided parking garage on Goods Way. She paced the short, three-minute trek to the British Library, the largest public building constructed in the UK in the twentieth century. Designed by architect Professor Sir Colin St. John Wilson, it mimicked a cruise liner ship.

She moved swiftly. Her instincts had been right. If the computer hadn't timed out at the National Archives, she would have discovered more about her parent's work with the Secret Intelligence Service. The manuscript they guarded and possibly deciphered was now her only clue and rested securely in her shoulder bag.

She had to start with the facts. ISTF believed that part of the Deveron document had been deciphered even though the details were sketchy.

Her cell phone rang, and she answered it. "Hello?"

"Calla?"

"Nash?"

"Where are you? You okay?"

Calla closed her eyes, sighing deeply. She trusted Nash with her life and needed help. Could she tell him? She'd not been ready to disclose any of her recent discoveries to anyone, still trying to make sense of it all. "I'm at the British Library. At St. Pancras."

Nash's voice bathed her ear, a hint of concern touching it. "When did you get back?"

Calla scurried through the main entrance. "Yesterday afternoon."

"The commotion here is all about Allegra's disappearance. Operation Carbonado is on hold."

Calla relaxed whenever she spoke to Nash. He had a way of making her feel unpretentious and capable. She shoved a hand into her pocket and paced the floor nestling the phone to her ear. "Really."

"Please tell me you're okay," he said.

"I could use a friend."

"I'll be right over."

His involvement was a risk for him, yet she needed Nash's heightened sense of judgment evident in perilous situations. He was resourceful, a trained field man, an intelligence analyst, and a brilliant linguist. Most importantly, he alone understood her complexities, yet never questioned them.

"Are you sure?" she asked.

"I'll be there in an hour."

Forty-five minutes later, Nash strode through the main entrance of the British Library as Calla sat in the lobby flipping through some notes. She raised her head when she saw him.

He approached with a sure stride and enveloped her in a secure embrace. "I've been trying to reach you."

She sank into his chest and exhaled, his enticing scent washing over her. She shut her eyes as he stroked the dark locks of her long ponytail.He could be trusted, and they could cover more ground together. When she tilted her head upward and gazed into his persuasive eyes, his shoulders curled forward. Nash pulled back from the embrace and cupped her cheekbones. "Why didn't you call me?"

"I don't know. I'm sorry."

"I was worried about you."

The library was filling up with intrigued scholars, students, and the odd tourists. Still caught in Nash's arms, she pulled away. "We need to find somewhere quiet to talk."

"Let's go to one of the reading rooms. There must be a quiet corner in there somewhere."

Nash led the way with Calla tailing behind.

Though a regular at the library Calla glared upward, admiring the glass tower of gold-tooled, leather-bound books known as the King's Library. They passed tables of engaged conversationalists who went about their business on the floor of the main reading room, surrounded by an astounding 67,000 books.

"I'd like to go to the Manuscripts Reading Room,"Calla said.

"First tell me what this is all about."

He navigated through to the central seating area under the panoramic domed roof with Calla keeping pace. Rows of desks and benches lined the main floor with dimly lit lampshades. They secured an isolated spot in the corner, close to several bookcases.Nash pulled out a seat for her and settled into the opposite chair. "Okay, so what are we doing here?"

Calla leaned forward and whispered. "I have something from Berlin that I need help with."

He raised an eyebrow. "Why the secrecy?"

She hesitated and then surrendered. "It's to do with the Deveron Manuscript."

10:12 A.M.

Nash propped closer. "The manuscript's gone. Don't you know that?"

Calla slouched down like a fugitive deer in hiding.She looked like she was searching her soul for a decision on whether to tell him everything and her revelation would require his every commitment. He peered into her eyes ready for whatever she had to say.

"I need your help with something. Can you keep a secret?" she said.

"Try me."

"We can't involve our governments or any authorities."

Nash puckered his lips and edged in, glaring into her eyes. "I'll always be here if you need me and will keep any secret you want me to keep as long as you promise to trust me."

Calla grinned and contracted her eyebrows. She then produced the manuscript, all seven pages neatly held together with a metallic paper clip. "The vaults here contain some cryptographic systems that may help me translate this."

Nash's forehead wrinkled."How did you get the manuscript?"

She shushed him, grasping his right hand and peered around to see if anyone had overheard. "We don't have much time. We need to do this before they come after us. I'll explain, but we need to get going."

So this was the mess she was in. With his protective nature alerted he decided to cooperate. "Now that you have this. Oh yes, somebody's bound to be after us." He inhaled deeply. "Who's coming and what are we looking for?"

"I've been trying to figure that out for the last forty-eight hours. I don't know. Can we move now?"

"Yes, ma'am."

She made little sense, yet Nash obliged, hoping an explanation would surface sooner rather than later. He shadowed her lead back the way they'd come. Could he reveal that he'd seen a prowler at her house?It was probably best to wait until he knew the full context of her story.

Their ISTF credentials allowed them access to the Manuscripts Reading Room, situated a short walk from the main reading rooms. They entered what Nash believed was the quintessence of the entire facility. He knew Calla came here from time to time. Only seven months ago she'd worked on deciphering first-century Greek texts from the city of Oxyrhynchus, the so-called City of the Sharp-Nosed Fish, written on fragments of papyrus found in Egypt. Naturally, she'd succeeded, a talent of hers he'd always found enlightening.

The main room was discreet, quiet and a handful of inaudible readers and staff, some gloved and relentlessly cautious, pored over rare books, manuscripts, and other documents. Calla whisked her head around and set a hand on his shoulder. "We want the cryptology section."

She approached a short, dark-skinned woman with wide chestnut eyes, a strong chin. Her midnight-black hair was worn in a tight bun as she sat operating the information desk. "Can I help you?" she said, her lips stretching into a polite smile.

"Hi. I'm Calla Cress, a curator at the British Museum doing some research on ancient, cryptographic systems." She glanced over at Nash, and then back at the woman. "I need to look at some cryptography systems you have here. Can you help me locate the right section?"

"Please sign in here. I'll need to see your passes."

They drew out their badges, and she nodded. "What you're seeking isn't on these main floors. We've had some recent renovation work, and various manuscripts have been moved to a temporary, cryptology section. Can I ask which cryptology system you're looking for in particular?"

Calla eyed Nash briefly as he faithfully tried to hide his curiosity about the same thing.

"Ancient cryptology," she answered.

"I see." The woman pulled out two electronic visitors' cards. "You'll need to go down to the underground tower block in the library storage space. There are four floors. You're looking for the last floor down."

"How do we get there?" asked Nash.

"Take the stairs behind you. It may be easier but make sure you avoid the water tank system on the same floor. There's some major work on it at the moment. Present these to the security guard when you arrive, and they should be able to help you."

The woman drew a rough sketch of the location on a small piece of paper. "You'll have one hour from the time you scan these cards."

They thanked her and headed for the stairs. Nash had watched the exchange quietly. As soon as they were out of earshot his interest plagued him. "What cryptology systems do you have in mind?"

"Let's go down and see."

"I'm with you all the way on this Calla but what are you doing with the Deveron Manuscript?"

They reached the stairs, and Calla stepped two steps ahead

of him. "The manuscript belonged to my family, and I want to know why."

"What? You sure?"

"I found out that my family was in possession of the Deveron Manuscript decades ago. I think it has something to do with my adoption."

"How'll the Deveron help you learn more about your family's past?"

"I've reason to believe it is connected to their disappearance. If I find out what they knew about it then maybe I can find them." She paused. "Dead or alive."

Nash acknowledged her conviction. "How do you know your parents were connected to all of this?"

Calla fell silent, struggling for the right words, something that didn't happen often. "Nash, are you a person of instinct or blind faith like me?"

"Go on—"

"Allegra told me she knew them," Calla said.

He accepted the statement but believed it to be a white lie. Nonetheless, he had to go along with whatever she surrendered. It was the most he'd ever heard her talk about her personal life. Calla marched ahead leading their descent onto the lower floors. "I've been reading some of her files. Operation Carbonado believes the manuscript is a cryptograph, leading to the secret locations of meteorite activity that NASA confirms fell on Earth centuries ago. The meteorite brought unknown, valuable elements to Earth. That's why our governments want the manuscript so badly. The elements, similar to carbonado diamonds, supposedly contain chemical compositions not found or known on Earth. They possess implausible energies. Enough to make our nuclear plants combined seem like a child's science project."

"So ISTF may be right after all. And what do you believe?"

She played with her bopping ponytail. "I actually believe it. The explanation seems scientific enough."

"Enough to ignite greed from five superpowers."

She took another eager step. "I also think our governments' intent for the diamonds isn't entirely honorable."

He glanced down at her. "I agree with you on that one. But what makes you so certain?"

"Let's just say that I think my parents found the diamonds, or at least one."

That revelation he wasn't expecting.Calla glanced back at him and raised an eyebrow as Nash's eyes quizzed her face. "Are you telling me your parents found what we're all busting our energies to find?"

"I don't have all the answers, Nash. But if I can hang onto this document long enough to find them then that's what I'll do. Allegra has also done some incredible research on the Deveron. The hieroglyphics, like the Voynich, don't exist in any known human language. And in her notes, she references something here that may help us."

"Is the writing authentic?"

Calla resumed her haste down the last few steps. When they reached the bottom of the staircase, she rested a hand on the sidebar. "I don't know what I think. All I know is that my parents were responsible for the Deveron Manuscript. If cracking its code draws me closer to finding them then that's the risk I'm willing to take."

It was a massive milestone for her as the subject of her parents had always been a sensitive matter. He knew he had to tread lightly. "Did you find out who they are?"

She lowered her head. "No."

They gravitated through to the fourth, lower ground hallway, following the temporary signs to the cryptology department as the woman had directed. Within seconds they found the door she'd indicated. At the entrance, Calla handed the cards they'd been given to the nonchalant security guard. He scanned them and repeated some clearly memorized reading room procedures. He then placed the cards in Calla's hands.

"You can't take any large items into the reading room and can make a maximum of twenty copies with the copiers provided."

Calla glanced at Nash. "Thank you."

The man sank into his seat. "Do you have any questions?"

Nash responded. "No."

"In that case, you have one hour from now. Please put on these gloves."

Two minutes later, wearing cotton gloves, they inched through the dark, woody room. The humidity was kept to a minimum, and the dry temperature helped preserve the more mature texts.The interiors produced smooth timber odors as books stood piled as high as the ceiling, mostly as an afterthought rather than by design.

Calla picked up a chocolate-cover volume entitled *Polygraphiae* by Johannes Trithemius, a 1518 rare volume and the first printed book on cryptology. She avoided handling the book with sharp movements and, instead, held it from underneath. Using two hands, Calla supported it by placing a provided mat beneath it for easier lifting and moving.

She turned to Nash. "Should we split up? We'll find it faster."

Nash scrutinized the cramped room. "Gladly, but what are we looking for exactly?"

"A very small book."

"What kind of book?"

"A small handwritten book."

"That doesn't help me, beautiful."

Her cheeks flushed yet she kept her focus. "Allegra's notes say that my parents translated part of the Deveron Manuscript. They transcribed the cryptographic system they discovered in a small book. At the same time, she believes that they discarded the Deveron Manuscript in Priam's Treasure while on a mission to Saint Petersburg. It's as if they wanted nothing to do with it."

Nash crossed his arms. "You know more than was revealed at the meeting last Friday. I watched you across the room as you counted the minutes while the archivist spoke."

Calla offered him a mischievous smile, a trace of haste ringing in her voice as she spoke. "Back to my parents. They wanted the book to be as far away from the Deveron as possible. But also secure enough to be found. I think they hid it in the rare books section in this library."

"Okay. So it's a journal of some sort?"

"I wish I knew. I've never seen it. I only went by Allegra's notes."

"Why did Allegra keep all of this from you? She must've known you were looking for your real parents all these years."

Calla shrugged. "I don't really know, Nash. She was probably cautious."

They split directions, scrolling row after row for anything that resembled a journal. They searched different shelves.

Manuscripts tired and worn and rare books lined several rows with some volumes abandoned along the bookcases. Calla continued past cryptographic systems that were used during the war as well as ones more ancient.

Nash squinted his eyes. This wasn't a frequented room.

Calla drew toward a Polybius checkerboard, a device invented by the ancient Greek historian and scholar of the same name. Known as a knock code, it was used to signal messages between prison cells. She then crossed over to an Atbash, a simple substitution cipher for the Hebrew alphabet. The row ended there.

They stopped mid-stride as footsteps moved at the door.

"Your time is up. I'm sorry, you have to leave now."

The security guard peered at them as his frame filled the door's entrance. A vacant look arrested Calla's face, and she turned to Nash.

"Nash, I'm not leaving without that book."

Nash leaned into her. "We'll find it. We just need to think. Where would someone hide it?" He surveyed the room. "Let's recheck the rare books."

In one forward movement, Calla began a nervous pace up and down the aisle. "You're right. If this book wasn't meant to be found, then it would be tucked away among rare books. If a book isn't checked out for thirty years, or possibly a generation, it's written off. Eventually, it's boxed off to some warehouse or destroyed."

"Maybe that's what your parents intended," Nash said.

"But why not just destroy it. Why place it here?"

He raked a hand through his hair. "That way there's no blood on their hands, so to speak. Or they just needed it to be found by...just you."

Calla smiled, grateful for Nash's support. She imagined she'd made no sense since meeting him at the library. Yet, here he was encouraging her ambitious pursuits. The rare books area comprised of one short section tucked away in the back, lined along two shelves. They each took one shelf and scoured for anything resembling a journal, notebook or even a scroll.

Calla rested her hand on the top row of the shelf. It shook and without warning, one leg collapsed. The heavy steel tipped, plummeting hundreds of volumes in her direction.

Nash threw a hand on the top of the shelf, balancing the edges with his weight.He tilted the collapsing shelf and swiftly placed a fallen book where the leg had broken. Pulling his hand away, his thumb slipped off the spine of a book the size of a cell phone, bound in plum velvet. He drew it off the fixed shelf where it had been camouflaged by shadows cast by the shelf's edges.

He secured the shelf firmly against the wall. Calla breathed a sigh of relief and set her gaze on the book barely larger than the palm of Nash's hand. She eased it out of his hands. Its velvet cover felt smooth under her touch, and not a speck of dust rested on its engraved exterior.

"Nash, it has the same symbol as the one on the manuscript."

An exact replica of the hieroglyphic she'd seen on the first page of the Deveron Manuscript rested in the bottom corner of its cover. For several moments they inspected the furtive symbol, which was beginning to feel more proverbial now. Without warning the door swung open.

This time, another security member shot her head through and cast them a long glare. "Your time is up!"

Nash's grin broke into a cocky smirk. "We'll be right out. Thanks for your fantastic help."

She stood still, and for all of five seconds, they thought she'd escort them out. Instead, she hesitated a few more seconds before striding back to the door. "Start moving, please," she said and marched out of the room.

Calla placed the small journal in the back pocket of her jeans. "We're taking this," she whispered.

Nash lowered his voice. "Calla...what? Why?"

She laid a hand on his shoulder. "If you observed carefully it doesn't have any barcodes or chips. This book isn't part of the main collection. Trust me, I work with artifacts all day."

She drew it from her pocket and flipped through its pages. "It even has the key we need. I'll bet the library doesn't have it listed as inventory."

Nash's jaw dropped slightly, unable to disguise his astonishment. In all the months he'd known Calla, he'd never seen her so determined. He watched her with amusement. "After you, Miss Cress."

They shot the security woman wide grins as they coasted

out of the room. When they crossed over to the main entrance, Calla gripped Nash's arm in warning. "Here goes."

He shook his head in amusement. "Still with you, beautiful."

They inched toward the revolving gate. A uniformed staff member watched as library visitors made their exits and entrances. Heavily secured with cameras the exit stood only a few feet from where they waited for their turn through the turnstiles. Calla fumbled for their passes. She handed Nash his and took note of two security systems in front of the exit. Standard for commercial retail and library environments they'd not paid attention to the protective system on the way in. Nash glided through the security barriers tapping his pass on the indicated reader without interruption. Calla placed her pass on the reader and traipsed through the bars. *Okay, here goes nothing.*

"Step back, please!"

She flipped her head around only to face a security member.With shoulders curling forward, anguish settled in her gut. Nash made his way back toward her.

The guard eyed her for several seconds. "Miss Cress. Says here that your pass is due for renewal. Make sure you get it renewed if you want to keep using the facilities."

With a curt bow, he rounded on her and turned to the person next in line.

They found Calla's Maserati in the garage and Nash surveyed the dim parking area before giving the all clear. Calla sank into the driver's seat and then flipped the book open.

Two streets over an obscure figure lurked from behind the wall. It made its way toward the library entrance.With his face concealed by shadows cast by a black baseball cap, he moved with quick steps, determined to see it for himself. He disappeared into the British Library. There was no need to take the stairs or the elevators. He merely sauntered through doors and walls until he reached his destination. He stood outside the Manuscripts Reading Room and then pushed his head through the door, defying nature and physics. He floated into the room, scouring each shelf and looking over the shoulders of quiet readers. None acknowledged his presence. He clicked off the device that had tele-transported his body, from several miles away. The technology was sound and would give him several minutes. The neuro-biologists had prepared him well.

He found the fourth floor below ground and pranced upon the cryptology shelves. The area had been deserted and, with no one loitering about, he took a seat on a table facing the shelves. Closing his eyes, he stretched his arms above his head. He wore all black, but there was no obscurity in him.

He opened his eyes in time to see a swift, shadowed man shove a knife to his neck. The aggressor didn't speak but kept the glistening blade at his Adam's apple.In one rapid movement, he hoisted the attacker's hand from his throat and launched him to the floor. The attacker turned and gawked at him, pulled out a firearm and aimed its barrel at the looming figure's chest.

Still seated at the table, the figure clamped his hand on the gun in one sharp maneuver. The firearm disintegrated into ash and settled like powdered flakes at his feet. The weapon had been no match.

Slate recovered from the loss of his weapon. With only his knife to defend himself, he stood back bewildered by defeat. No one had ever crushed him in combat. Would this be a first?

He stared blankly. "Who are you?"

The figure rose, close to seven feet in height. Slate turned to flee as the man moved one step toward him, cutting him off at the door with a swift neck strike. The impact slammed Slate against the door frame and, gathering his wits, he scrambled toward the exit.

Slate plummeted to the ground, rose abruptly and fled out of the room. He glanced back once, and then no more.

The towering man retreated, reverted to his modest six-foot-three and turned to the shelves muttering. "Good girl. You got here before he did."

He came out from under the shadow of his dark baseball cap. His face was now visible.

CHAPTER 14

Calla wound down the window and leaned forward. She inserted the key into the ignition and swung the car out of the parking lot and took a deep breath. The sun beat down through the windshield onto her face as she maneuvered traffic through Central London.

Thirty minutes later the Maserati pulled into a parking space in front of the estate in West London. On entering, Nash dropped his shoulder bag in the Persian chair in the entryway. "Are you sure we can use Allegra's place?" he asked.

"This is where I'm staying for now."

They moved into the den where Calla drew the blinds and took a seat at the desk.

Pearl appeared from the kitchen. "Your phone has been ringing all morning, Miss Cress." She set it down on the executive desk.

Calla glanced at Nash. "Mason," she said. "I won't answer it."

Nash took a seat across from her. "What does he want?"

"I don't know. He gave me that phone before I went to Berlin and treated me like some sort of technology, illiterate person."

She switched on her electronic tablet. "I forgot to take it with me. He wanted a log of all Allegra's activities."

"Really?"

She cast Pearl a grateful smile. "Thanks, Pearl. Just ignore it," Calla said."We'll be working in here for a little while. Please don't worry about our lunch. We can help ourselves in the kitchen."

"All right. In that case, I'll make sure you have something to help yourselves to."

Pearl left quietly. Nash hunched over the table examining Calla's movements. "What do you plan to do?"

She pulled the journal and the manuscript from her bag. "Get to work on this."

She spread out the Deveron Manuscript across the desk as Nash considered its intricate design and make. "It's mind-blowing, isn't it? Someone took their art seriously."

"I agree."

"This is where I need your investigative eyes and genius mind." She passed a hand through her ponytail and pointed to the diagrams she'd noticed earlier. "Look at these three shapes. They form a three-sided illustration."

"Why's each figure marked with different symbols?" Nash asked.

Calla shrugged. "Let's check the journal."

She lifted the journal's velvet cover and slid a finger through its pages, tracing the lines of writing that grew smaller and more cramped at the bottom. "Someone created a cipher for the symbols in the Deveron, an asymmetric cryptograph. You know, in which there are two related keys to unlock a message."

"You mean just like with computers over the Internet? At the NSA, we've used asymmetric cryptography. We create a pair of keys to encrypt and decrypt a message so that it arrives securely," Nash said.

"Exactly, we have to think in those terms." She continued

flipping through the book's delicate pages. "The journal must've clues to unlock the Deveron."

Calla stopped at a detailed handwritten page and rubbed her forehead. "Someone created a set of encryption keys when the manuscript was conceived, one which they kept private and another they sent to a second party."

Nash raised his eyes to her. "That second person is the one who wrote the Deveron Manuscript and encrypted the manuscript using the key sent to them by the first person."

She nodded slowly.

"How'd you figure that out?" he said.

"It's actually an effective way of encrypting. It's been used for centuries."

Nash tilted his chin upward. "That means the second party sent the Deveron document back to the first person so they could use their secret key to read the manuscript."

"Exactly. So what we have here on the third page of the journal is the original, secret key created by the first person," Calla added.

Nash leaned back and placed his hands behind his head. "The person who created the keys must've wanted his own way of interpreting the information he was sent, even if this meant nobody else did."

"Right. They used a secret code, one that wasn't mathematical."

Nash rested his elbows on the large desk. "I think it will take us some time to interpret. You take the first three pages, and I'll take the next four."

After two hours of silent decrypting, Calla peered at Nash and moaned in exhaustion. They'd each grabbed pencil and paper and begun the lengthy process of analyzing each Deveron symbol on their respective pages in relation to the key provided by the journal.

"I think I have something now," Calla said.

They assembled the papers they'd transcribed. Nash scanned his written lines. "There are three puzzles we need to unravel. Here is what I found."

He shared his scribbled notes:

> *In three dominances you rule,*
> *move and have your being.*
>
> *1.*
>
> *Tongue unites your realms*
> *Should it dissolve, a state of confusion erupts.*
> *Here, I first crafted you and lay you down.*
> *Now men seek you for all you say.*
> *Without it, you lack sanity.*
> *No dominance.*
> *I lay to sleep where I first awoke.*

Calla glanced at the notes and then at him. If the riddle hadn't caused more perplexity, Nash's face took on the task as his eyes narrowed.

Nash laid a hand on the manuscript scouring its delicate pages. "What does it mean? Why do they use the word 'dominance'?"

Calla tugged at her ear before a wide smirk settled on her lips. "It's telling us that language is power. 'Dominance' or 'ruling' is coveted by men and women. My pages look a little different, but I think I have the other two 'dominances'."

Nash took the journal in his hands and studied the manuscript. "But what is the purpose of the letter?"

Calla's eyes lit up as she rose. "This is a guide to three destinations. Your destination or the first dominance is talking about language. It's pointing to where language was first crafted,

Babel." She circled the room. "What happened at Babel that defines language today?"

Nash shrugged. "I'm not a religious scholar but wasn't Babel the place history records as the birth of languages. Everyone spoke one language before the great flood in biblical times."

"Exactly. Some think the events at Babel were the cradle of civilization," she said.

Nash scratched his head. "We can't look for a place whose existence and actual location is debatable?"

"Hm, I think it's merely telling us that at Babel history turned. We as a human race began speaking different languages yet more and more we're migrating to mastering one language to survive."

Nash smirked. "English, I take it. British or American?"

"Very funny." Calla snickered. "Think of it," she said. "If you want to have any global influence, English would be useful."

"But English isn't the prominent language when it comes to population."

"I know, but it is by the number of countries where it is spoken."

"That's true."

"We need to find the original *cradle* or birthplace of that language."

Calla squinted, peering down at his bright eyes. "Nash, we're onto something. If this is a map, I think I know where we need to go. I'll get the car ready."

2:00 P.M.
FEDERAL CRIMINAL POLICE OFFICE
STAFF APARTMENTS, ORANIENBURGER STRASSE, BERLIN

Eichel stroked a photo taken of Calla Cress at Tegel Airport. *She can't be a day older than twenty-seven.* He studied the passport scan provided by Berlin Tegel Police. She was twenty-seven, almost twenty-eight.

His stomach rumbled, an atrocious reverberation reminding him that dinner should be ready any minute. Not another day of coffee and pastries. He needed a proper meal before this night shift.

Eichel couldn't remember the last time he'd slept. The past forty-eight hours had included several sessions of questioning, mostly museum visitors, and staff. This had been coupled with endless periods spent poring over any police reports on the Deveron document, foreign and local.

A dead end.

He stretched his fisted arms above his head, drawing out a long yawn. He needed sleep badly. Tired lines and dark circles around his eyes made him look older than his fifty-three years. He brought his hands down and tapped his fingers on the table as his nostrils detected a burned smell. When the smoke alarm went off, he shot up from the dinner table.

Anjte had done it again.

"Are we having burned offerings?" he mumbled.

He crossed the hallway from the eat-in living room to the kitchen. His boots pounded the wooden floors of his modest home—staff residence really—as he stomped to the kitchen. As chief investigator, he'd been given an apartment on the same street as his offices. Not exactly what he would call home. Home would be Dresden. At least his first home.

He barged into the smoke infested room as Anjte, his dark-haired wife, bent over the oven. The sound alarm pierced through the apartment, deafening his ears. Eichel found a kitchen stool and hopped onto it to turn off the smoke alarm.

She shot him a contemptuous smile as she rescued the remains of her dinner. The stench of a burned casserole consumed the kitchen as he descended from the stool. He traversed to the windows, flung them open and let in a waft of fresh air. "Why can't we have a decent meal in this house? I need to eat before I return to work."

His mutterings were ignored, the result of twenty-one years in a questionable marriage. Anjte continued about her business. Eichel scowled and headed back to the dining room. "I'll get some takeaway *döner kebab* at the Turkish place downstairs."

Back at the dining table he gathered his notes and paused to glimpse at Calla's photo again. She'd seemed honest enough when he spoke to her. Was she telling the truth? He couldn't let this opportunity slip away. He had to redeem his failure. It had been a lengthy investigation three years ago, and he winced at the thought of a repeat. How he regretted the events of that night.

The weather office had predicted strong gale winds, quite unusual for October. On that drizzly, autumn night frantic banging on his door woke him. He thought of his decision of taking a staff apartment, doors away from the police station. With sleep clogging his vision he fiddled to the door and opened the latch only to see his faithful deputy.

Peter stood at the door staring dumbfounded at Eichel, like a child who'd suddenly found answers to a treasure hunt. "We've found the underground hideout. It's a few miles from here, in Kreuzberg."

"I'll get dressed and meet you in the car."

Though he'd sounded awake earlier, he'd masked his distresses by consuming six beer cans and downed a bottle of Red Label, another night of immersing his unhappy marriage in liquor. In no condition for police work,groggy-eyed and barely able to walk straight, he made it down to the car within ten minutes.

Why hadn't he told Peter the truth? Fifteen minutes later they steered into Kreuzberg and what used to be the impoverished district of Berlin. The dregs of its past still resonated in the quarter's streets, characterized by high levels of unemployment and some of the lowest income earners.

Eichel said very little until they stopped outside the detained apartment block. "Who are we after?"

"A thirteen-year-old."

"That young?"

When Eichel and Peter stormed into the room, three other officers interrogated the boys who'd been instructed to sit on the floor.

It was a massive case. Everyone had said so, and Eichel was at the helm. He'd spent months investigating smugglers who brought young boys into Germany from less fortunate milieus, transforming them into criminals. Eichel had always maintained that it was a sickening case of organized crime. That night they'd failèd yet again. Not one ringleader was among the detained adolescents.

Eichel swore under his breath. He stumbled toward one of the boys who'd been notorious for supplying drugs on the U8 metro-line. Eichel's anger consumed him. He grabbed the youth, thrust him to the ground and threatened to beat him senseless. The on-looking team of police officers accustomed to seeing Eichel collected, shuddered with remorse.

Peter and one other cop held him back. A redeeming action, but not for long. Suspended and subjected to months of anger management Eichel bore the weight of humiliation.

The case lingered as police couldn't arrest the adolescents until they turned fourteen and corruption continued under his nose. Peter took over the case and found the drug lords. The boys were arrested almost eighteen months later, leading to several convictions. The Berlin chief of police, knowing Eichel was to thank for the case's successful conclusion, shortened his suspension from a three years to sixteen months on one condition. Eichel was ordered to attend an alcohol addiction program.

That had been twenty months ago.

Now that he oversaw the Deveron case spoke volumes. He'd proved himself, and most importantly, no one matched his investigative expertise. Eichel shut off his computer, returning to the evening's case. He mentally organized his tasks. He knew his office needed him. Otherwise, why place him in charge of one of the most significant cases at the station?

He would prove himself again. Eichel slid on his black leather coat that hung over one of the dining table chairs. He reached for his cigarettes from the table and stashed them in his pocket. Looking over the notes he had gathered the day before he shook his head in frustration. He understood how chemical vaporization due to radiation worked. He'd seen this when he spent time with his father, a young cop working with the Russians as part of the *Stasi*, the former East German, Ministry for State Security, in East Berlin. His father had been too junior to access confidential files. Even then, those bold enough whispered about Sanax, a chemical being developed in Russia. Had Sanax been used on Allegra Driscoll?

What was Cress running from? Or, toward?

––––––––

1:15 P.M.

Nash furrowed his eyebrows. "Where exactly are we going?"

Calla's face beamed. "To Oxford."

"Why?"

"In 1762 the *Short Introduction to English Grammar* by Robert Lowth was published. Robert Lowth was a Church of England Bishop, an Oxford Professor of Poetry and," she paused, "the author of one of the most influential textbooks of English grammar."

"But why is that the *cradle* of the English language?"

"Because grammar is the framework of any language, the starting block."

"But this Robert would have died centuries ago."

"True but he's been named as the first in a long line of English usage commentators known for judging and describing the English language."

Nash tilted his head. "Okay?"

"We're not after him, we're after something related to him."

Nash rubbed his creased forehead. "Perhaps the city in which he was born?"

Calla shook her head. "Not the city but the place of work. The person currently doing his job may be able to tell us more."

"So we walk right into Oxford University and tell Mr. Robert's replacement to give us whatever this map is pointing to?"

"The manuscript clearly says we're after something the human race has panted for like water for centuries."

The mid-afternoon sun struggled to seep through the blinds. Calla marched to the windows and dragged the shades upward. "If we leave now we won't be able to see anyone by the time we get there. I suggest we leave in the morning."

Pearl crossed the hallway and stuck her head through the door crack. "Will you be dining here tonight, Mr. Shields?"

Calla crossed to where she stood and let her in. "Pearl, please put Nash in one of the guest rooms. We have an early start tomorrow."

As they exited the den Nash bent down and whispered in Calla's ear. "How does she know my name?"

"Hm, ...she must like you."

Several moments later, the den lay still, abandoned except for a silent witness on the desk. A smartphone. The light from its monitoring device blinked red. It kept recording, having registered every word, syllable, and breath.

Eichel pushed open the front door and stood by it. "I'll be back in the morning before six," he called to Anjte. He made his way back to the Pergamon Museum. If nothing stuck out in his mind, he'd follow his only lead. Calla Cress.

The artifacts belonged to the Pergamon. However, he was no fool. There was little evidence that the Deveron Manuscript was actually robbed from the museum during the raid in 1945. *Who am I to judge? I only have to make sure it gets back.*

If anything, Priam's Treasure had been brought back to Germany to strengthen ties between the Russian and the German governments. Both sides now agreed that Priam's Treasure belonged to Germany. His assignment was to ensure the inauguration went smoothly. So far that hadn't happened. Bringing the stolen items back would redeem his position.

He marched to the police room. This time, fewer police officers pored over evidence in hopes of piecing the Deveron puzzles together. Herr Brandt, the museum director, stepped in. "Herr Eichel, I was hoping to find you here. When can we reopen the museum? This closure is bad for business."

Eichel shifted his weight from one foot to the other and nodded a greeting. "As soon as there's no more threat."

"Can we open tomorrow?"

"I'm sorry, Herr Brandt. No. I'm only trying to protect the interest of the museum and national treasures."

"Preposterous! What's the hold up now?"

Eichel shrank from his scrutinizing eye. "You can resume operation once we've concluded our investigation."

Brandt cast him a cold glance before stomping out the narrow entrance. Eichel rummaged for his cell phone and dialed a familiar number. "Peter, please give me a lab report on the Deveron crime scene by morning?"

"Jawohl," answered Peter. "By the way, as requested, we didn't stop Cress at Tegel Airport when she left yesterday. There was nothing out of the ordinary."

Eichel took hold of notes an officer held out to him. "I'm looking at a copy of her exit report. Did she meet with anyone after leaving the museum?"

"Not to our knowledge."

"What can the hotel staff tell us?"

"She received a delivery. A diplomatic package, so we couldn't intervene."

"Is that so?"

"I did find it strange for a curator to receive diplomatic correspondence," Peter said.

Eichel stroked his chin. "It doesn't make sense. The artifacts are gone, and we have no more clues. The Cress woman's meeting with Allegra Driscoll is our only lead."

Peter's voice rang with concern. "I think we should follow the Sanax angle. I dug up research and know that the billionaire businessman, Rupert Kumar, has had links to the development of the chemical. Do you suppose it could have been used on Driscoll?"

Eichel groaned. "Okay, you follow that and keep this from the media. I'm going to London. I have a contact there that may be able to help us."

CHAPTER 15

DAY 7
6:02 A.M.
M40 HIGHWAY

The Maserati zipped out of London on the M40 highway. Early sunrise peered behind rolling hills, escorting them on the curvy journey, giving Calla and Nash magnificent conditions for a drive.

Nash enjoyed the thrill of the sports car's sound as it flew northward out of London. He pressed down the 'sport' button, a throttle-quickening feature that livened up the car's performance, opening up the exhaust cylinders. The Italian creation cleared its mechanical throat until its V8 engine, capable of revving up to the more than 7000rpm, roared like a ravenous Tyrannosaurus Rex.

The speed placed a grin on Calla's face. "They say it's a boy's car, but I'm sure I could corner it as well as you."

Calla had opted to sit in the passenger seat with her electronic tablet, scrolling through research.

Nash negotiated a tight bend. "I'll take you on anytime."

She placed a gentle hand on his knee. "We need to find the

Chair Professor of Poetry once we get to the University, a certain Dr. Norman Guilford."

"Will he talk to us?"

"I hope so. He's been in office three of his five allocated years."

Calla scanned a Guardian newspaper article she'd pulled up on Norman Guilford. "There's nothing unusual in this man's career. He's fairly elderly as is the privilege of most professors. They work as long as they like."

She glided her fingers over the touchscreen. "His duties, among others, include lecturing on poetry, giving public speeches each term and generally encouraging the art of verse at the university."

Nash quickly glanced her way before returning his eyes to the road. "I'm still not sure if this is getting us any closer to deciphering the manuscript, Calla."

"Be positive."

The northwest route out of London took them through commuter villages, displaying a prime example of the wealth trickling out of London. They sliced through the Chiltern Hills, an area of natural magnificence with its discreet hamlets, stately homes, shimmering chalk streams and intensely wooded valleys.

The hills were bounded on the south by the River Thames and to the north by a long line of scarp slopes. After crossing ninety kilometers flying on mostly triple lanes, they reached Oxford. Nash swung the car up an alley and parked on a quiet street near the town's central railway station.

"Let's walk from here," Nash said. "It's only a short distance to the university campus."

Calla pulled her cell phone from her pocket. "We need to find the Faculty of English."

He cast her a sincere smile. "The most illustrious school of English in the world, I take it."

"That's right."

After a ten minute walk, they found the facility, an arresting building on the corner of Manor and St. Cross Roads. Calla hesitated, standing a few meters in front of the contemporary building, a structure made up of three interlinking cubes of different sizes. The effect was a stock of large cubic blocks built in buff brick as if carefully selected to complement the stone of the neighboring Holywell Manor and St. Cross Church.

She inspected the long strips of plate-glass windows, boxed in metal frames that broke up the brickwork. Calla stopped to breathe in the fresh air. "Think of all the great works and minds that have come out of these very premises."

Nash puckered his brow.

She bit her lower lip in anticipation,as a drop of rain landed on her cheek. She wiped it away. Above them, the clouds gathered, yet the sun held out. They steered through the faculty, which housed a central common area, lecture theaters, and other study rooms. The internal construction was formed by different sized brickwork, astutely woven together at various levels, which gave the area a reasonably uncluttered feel.

They continued up a staircase, leading from St. Cross Road to the English and Law Libraries on the top floor, settling on the upper level of the building for several minutes. They took in the glass ceiling and galleried central space of the Bodleian Law Library.

"We need to ask someone for information," Nash said. "It's close to 9:00 a.m. I'm not sure when classes get going but let's ask someone here if Guilford is anywhere close by."

On the far side of the library, they spotted a group of students. Calla approached them, walking up to a ginger-haired, chatty girl who conversed with her serious-looking friend.

"Hi, we're looking for Professor Guilford's office," Calla said.

The girl tossed her hair from her face. "Most faculty members don't have an office in the St. Cross building. You're looking for the English Faculty Library. I think his office has recently been moved there." She pointed to the door ahead and gave them exact directions. "I think he's also lecturing right now."

"Thank you," Calla said.

They followed her directions to the lower medium-sized cube. Once inside they spotted the office the student had indicated, which stood behind a half-open door. A young woman sat at a desk concentrating at a computer.

Calla poked her head through the door. "Hello. We're looking for Dr. Guilford. Would it be possible to speak with him?"

The student assistant reflected as she toyed with a pencil in her hand. "Professor Guilford will be done in a few minutes. You can wait in here if you'd like."

Calla and Nash took a seat in the cramped waiting space. Sun rays drilled in through the dusty windows, casting light inside the structured stone room. The student continued reading some work on an iMac that hid her from view.

Nash shot up, probably because he felt that he needed to do something. He forged ahead to the wall behind a cluttered desk on one side of the room and carefully eyed various displayed accolades. Several framed newspaper clippings hung, each taken from noted literary journals and publications. A mounted article dating back a few centuries drew particular interest.

Nash placed a hand on the framed certificate. "I take it Robert Lowth was a keen critic of William Shakespeare?"

He seemed to be addressing himself, but it drew a curious look from the student. "Yes, interesting isn't it?" she pointed out.

Calla joined Nash and set a hand on his broad shoulders. "Lowth was known as the first critic of William Shakespeare's plays."

"Indeed, he was," thundered a compelling voice behind them. They flipped round to see the owner of the commanding tone.

Short and elderly, a robust man, exercising a distinctive stage voice, leaned against the door frame contemplating their curiosity. The graceful gentleman extended a hand. "I'm Professor Guilford. Are you waiting to speak with me?"

Calla drew in a deep breath. "Yes, professor."

Guilford ambled into the room. "How can I help you?"

Calla watched the professor, amused by his poise and delighted that his reception was a somewhat cordial one. "I'm Calla Cress, a curator from the British Museum in London. This is Nash Shields, my colleague. We were wondering if you could tell us about Robert Lowth."

"For research purposes," Nash added.

"I see. Please come into my office, and I'll see what I can do."

The pair escorted him through a door off the waiting area and marched into his private office. Piled to the brim with books Calla and Nash searched for a seat in the small area. Volumes piled up across the entire shelf spaces. Some hardbacks had even found a home on the floor. Though cluttered the room breathed of sophistication in its own distinguished way, speaking of solace, study and exuding the pride of an eminent scholar. More honors adorned the walls, this time more personal to Guilford.

Professor Guilford eased into a seat at a large desk. "Please, sit down."

Calla and Nash squeezed onto the tired sofa opposite him. "Thank you, Dr. Guilford. We're conducting some research on the topic of the formalization of English grammar and the English language at large. Could you possibly tell us more about Lowth's work here?" Calla said.

"What is it about Lowth that intrigues you?"

Calla glimpsed at Nash. How much could they reveal? She placed her palms on her lap. "Was Lowth what one may call the father of the English language?"

Guildford twiddled his thumbs "I'm always intrigued by anyone wishing to learn." His face broke into a wide smile.

"Well, it all depends on what perspective you're looking at. Oh how rude of me, can I offer you a drink?"

"I'm fine," blurted Calla. She glanced at Nash.

"No thanks," he said as his eyes scanned the room with heightened interest.

Calla questioned Nash's gaze. *What are you looking at?*

Almost non-detectable to the human eye, small calligraphic scribbling repeated in patterns along the edges of the wallpaper, circled the entire office.

Nash turned to Guilford. "Tell me, professor, I'm quite interested in the inscription patterns on the wallpaper. Do you recognize the script?"

"Ah," said the professor his eyes gleaming. "Many have inquired about those. Rumor has it that Professor Lowth wrote those symbols himself. In recognition of his contribution to the English language and the university we've left those there."

"Do you know what they mean?" Calla said.

"Not exactly. We've always thought of it as art."

Nash strayed his gaze from the scribbles and back to the professor. "Intriguing."

Norman edged against the back of his seat and intertwined his hands. His eyes questioned Calla and then Nash. "Is there anything else you would like to know?"

Calla met Guilford's gaze. "Could you tell us more about Lowth and his work with the university?"

The question was politely addressed to disguise the awkward nature of their most recent discovery. Nash directed Calla a sharp glare.

He was onto something.

———

11:53 A.M.

165

Guilford continued. "Lowth was a Bishop of the Church of England, a scholar and a professor of English here at Oxford. He's the author of one of the most influential textbooks of English Grammar…"

Calla and Nash half listened.Her mind mentally registered the symbols on the wall, almost second nature by now. As she tuned out Guilford's narrative, she grouped them according to type, her concentration categorizing each symbol as it circulated the wall.

Some were new, but most were similar to those in the Deveron.

"…In 1762 Lowth published *A Short Introduction to English Grammar,* a piece of work that he's proudly remembered for. He was prompted by the absence of simple and pedagogical, grammar textbooks at that time in history. He sought to remedy the situation."

Guilford paused to breathe. "His grammar book and other works are the source of many of the prescriptive common foundations and beliefs studied in schools."

Calla stopped listening altogether, absorbed by the entrancing lettering. *Had no one ever thought to look here?*

She interjected, securing more time. "What distinguished Lowth?"

"His works established him as the first in a long line of usage commentators who critiqued the English language."

Nash had also spent several minutes scrutinizing the material on the wall. His attention returned to the one-sided conversation. "Where can we learn more about this Lowth?"

"I'm sure you can find something in our library or pick up a copy of his famous work in any good bookstore."

"Thank you, professor," Nash said.

"Is there anything else you wish to know?"

"You've given us much to work with," Calla said.

"I'm pleased you came, but you could've found this information in any reference book."

Nash searched his face.

"True, but better to hear it from the horse's mouth, so to speak," Calla said as her mind caught Nash's drift.

"Ah, a sense of humor. I like it. If you'll then excuse me, I have a lecture to prepare for."

They marched out of the office. The hallway had crowded with students and professors hastening back and forth from lectures. They wandered outside into the sunshine, and Nash searched for a secluded spot away from the main entrance.

"Did you recognize any of the symbols?" asked Nash as he plopped onto a bench on the grounds.

"Yes," Calla said. "We need to go back in."

"You think Lowth put them there?"

"Him? I don't know, maybe someone else." Calla mused. "It's almost lunchtime. Surely the professor will take a break. We need to head back."

"I'm loving your plan, but then what?" Nash said.

"Something took place in that office when Lowth occupied it as professor of poetry. We need to find out what it is."

Nash checked his watch. "All right."

They took turns watching the entrance. After thirty minutes Calla paced back into the facility and emerged minutes later with a triumphant grin. "Let's go, soldier."

———————

They returned to the professor's office and hesitated by the locked door.

"What do we do now?" Calla said.

A handful of engaged students lurked at notice boards and chatted on cell phones. Nash set a hand on the handle and studied the lock. "It's a spring bolt. Do you have a credit card you don't use?"

"I wish." She dug her hand into her bag. "Use this."

He took the credit card from her and wedged it between the

door and the frame. Holding it within the crack against the door border he wiggled and forced down the card toward the latch. Sensing resistance, he bent the card away from the doorknob. It slid, freeing the lock.

"A bit old school but it works. Let's do this fast," he said.

Calla stole past him in a fast movement that loosened her hair, falling wildly behind her back. Dark as a raven's coat against her skin the mane flowed rhythmically as she moved. Nash watched biting down a smile.Only now did he realize its length and dark radiance. He'd never seen it unbound, reminding him of the new resolve she'd mastered in the last twenty-four hours.He smirked and followed. Once inside the office, the two prowled to the walls. Placing their hands against the detailed wallpaper, their fingers traced the symbols looking for patterns. Calla fished for the journal from her bag and studied a page with several encryptions as Nash strode back to the front office. "I'll stay here and watch the door. What does the inscription say?"

Calla had to pace the room a couple of times to complete the task. She set her fingers along the symbols and read them slowly. "It's a bit repetitive but what I have so far is, *'Beware the test, beware the prize'*."

A noise from the hall caught Nash's attention, and he slipped back into the hallway pulling the door behind him. "Keep going. I'll stand guard outside."

Calla's fingers rested on the wall, brushing the material with caution. Without thought or force, her hand slid right through the concrete.

A nervous chill slid down her back. *How?*

What was happening to her? She breathed hard and concentrated. The symbols glowed, almost electronically. Had an invisible switch reshaped the physics of the wall? She would ask questions later.

An easy break-in. She inhaled. *Hm, I wonder?*

Instinct told her to proceed. She eased ahead and disappeared through the wall in what could only have been possible in a psychotic dream. Coming out on the other side she glimpsed around. Her eyes couldn't distinguish what she saw ahead of her. Caught between ecospheres, she faced a blinding light ahead and blinked every few seconds as she followed its lead.

The path grew narrower while the gap she stood in reeked of dampness and mold. Stretching her hands in front of her for guidance she fingered her moist environs, unable to grasp object or form in front of her. The pathway before her was dimly lit and she began a slow pace toward the now flickering light.

The more she progressed the further the light bounced away.Hesitating, her eyes glistened in the light's dim glow as she tried to identify an advancing, lurking silhouette.

She charged back the way she'd come. After a few stampeding steps, she came to a halt. Was it curiosity? *I want to see you!*Not knowing where strength was sourced she whisked her head around and found herself face to face with what she thought was a man, but his comportment suggested otherwise. Inches from him she stumbled backward.He drew what looked like a weapon and swung it in her direction.A gun she could deal with. *Maybe?*

This was no gun.

She failed to identify the weapon and braced herself for combat she'd never experienced.Calla retreated and found her back flat against the wall she'd penetrated. Her assailant slashed the air with his weapon that, without effort, extended into a steel dagger glowing with computer code. With hands crawling up the wall Calla scratched for an entrance through which she could reenter Guilford's office. Unlike her journey here none became apparent.Her only option was to duck from his steel or fight back.

With what?

How? She raised her arms and slammed the assaulter with her fists. Not one of her agitated blows touched him as he cornered her up against the concrete.She slid to the ground, her pained arms shielding her face. She closed her eyes and as if by mishap, plummeted, back first, into the professor's office. Her aggressor pursued.

"Nash!"

The assailant edged closer.

"Nash!"

Adrenaline fired through her.

The office door burst open. Nash surged toward her cowering frame with tunneled vision and chopped a horizontal fist at the assailant's neck.The seething man took evasive action, blundering backward as the strike deflected off his massive frame.

Nash recoiled shielding Calla from the onslaught. Fury flared from the masked assailant. Nash clasped his injured hand and examined it.

Calla drew back and a sense of vulnerability swamped her. They couldn't pry off the digital mutant. Her eyes scanned the room for any item they could use in defense as the assailant whipped toward them. Short of impact, he disbanded like condensation before their eyes.

"What was that thing?" Calla said and staggered to Nash's side.

She suppressed her urge to curse.

Nash's eyes narrowed as they met Calla's with a stare.

A light flared north of Calla's position, followed by fluttering near the drapes, signaling that the assailant had resurfaced. He perched by the door like a falcon. Calla blinked her eyes several times as the man re-emerged by the window, and then by the desk. Each time he appeared, he morphed an inch taller, and a breadth wider as his deafening cackle filled the room.

He was looking for something. Calla thought hard. Was it a man, a shadow, a spirit, a form, a computer? He flickered like a loose wireless connection. This thing was digitally manipulated, a computed cyber vision, with a blow to match ten agents.

It moved like a man, but nothing in his godlike strength gave Calla the confidence that they were evenly matched.

Nash reached for her hand and drew her to his side as the figure crouched, ready for another assault. Nash's fist tightened at his side. Could he fight this thing? Without warning, the attacker reached for the journal and ripped it out of Calla's hand.

She held her breath and, in an instant, he dissolved through the wall.

With heightened senses and a moist brow, Nash's eyes fixed on the direction he'd taken. "What the heck was that?"

1:41 P.M.
SCHOOL OF ENGLISH
OXFORD UNIVERSITY

Silence gripped the room.Calla shriveled as if breaking free from a spell and found she could move.

With a focused squint, Nash concentrated on something outside the window. "It's him." He scooted to the glass pane. "Let's get that journal."

Calla obeyed and followed him. They left the office racing back through the empty floors of the faculty.Nash shot out of the building with Calla flurrying behind. They dashed toward the southern grounds of the college with Nash sprinting and Calla keeping pace behind him. Footing determined steps they collided with several wide-eyed students and staff.

She caught up with Nash for a second. "I see him."

They chased in the direction he took and hounded after him toward the extensive gardens around Worcester College Lake. The escaping figure increased pace, not once glancing back at his pursuers.

He vanished.

Calla came to an abrupt halt. "Nash!"

He drew to a reluctant stop as she caught up with him. She hunched over clasping her knees and regained her breath. "I think he's gone," she said.

They glanced back at the campus from the grounds of Worcester College, one of the primary institutions of the University. The imposing eighteenth-century building stood behind them, haunting them with its neoclassical style as they stood watching for their assailant.

Calla glimpsed to one side of the construction, noticing a row of medieval cottages, perhaps some of the oldest structures in the town. She glared ahead. "What do we do?"

Bathed in the stillness of the meadows overlooking the water the peculiar tranquility was cut by a few wandering ducks and the quiet whistling of the weeping willows.

Nash squinted an eye, eager to do something as he paid attention to movement by the lake. "Sh—"

The digital-like silhouette re-emerged. In a flash the man arched himself behind Calla and seized her arms from behind, her gaze still face-to-face with Nash. She shrunk from his seething breath, over her left shoulder. His head was veiled with chain-mail and a burnished helmet, similar to those worn by medieval knights.

Calla zipped around and studied the long cape that covered him from the shoulder down. It was like being trapped in a virtual reality nightmare. Only it was very real. The digital vision could physically hurt them.

He grunted through his closed helmet, snorting at Nash, even from behind his ornate façade. Was he real?

She tried to wriggle sideways, imagining the severe damage this knight-like being could cause both of them. Nash moved without haste threading his way purposefully toward them until he trapped Calla between him and the assaulter. Before he could launch a defensive maneuver, Calla reached over her side, caught the man's wrists and hurled him forward. The momentum threw both her and the attacker to the ground and toppled Nash backward.

Nash stood still. Calla gasped for breath and shuddered violently. She groped the man's arm and wrestled him with the passion of a terrified tigress. She pinned his arms securely behind his back and drove her whole weight over him. He liberated his hands with sudden force and with grunted breath caught her wrists and forced her arm backward. She heaved her upper body evading his grasp and chopped a vertical palm at the base of his head.

He screeched in pain and attempted to wrench his arm free to no avail.Calla had found a weak spot at the base of his neck where his shoulder bone began. She kept her grip on him. "Okay, whatever you are, hand it over. My journal. Who are you anyway?"

Having never fought anyone let alone an opponent twice her weight, Calla's adrenaline soared to new levels with her new might. "Give up?"

Nash's jaw dropped as he cast an incredulous stare at her. "Looks like you've got the situation under control—"

Her aggressor struggled under her force, writhing on the ground underneath her weight.She angled his arm with a force never before unleashed. Not knowing what to do with him she glanced up at Nash, who stared dumbfounded at the powerful hold she had over her opponent.

The man stopped struggling as she loosened his arm a little at a time.

"Okay!" he said.

Calla relaxed complete grasp over him and vaulted to her feet. Following suit, the man shot up and stretched upward backpedaling a few feet away from them.For the first time, Calla and Nash considered his real stature. Close to the height of a closet, the manlike figure towered over them, possibly at seven feet.

His tone was low and breathy. "I've waited a long time for you."

"Me? Who are you?" Calla said.

"Call me Watcher."

Nash pushed forward and drew his semi-automatic pistol, aiming with precision at the man's head. "Don't you move an inch—"

The man leered at his firearm.

Calla held Nash back. "It's okay. He's not going to hurt us."

Nash resisted and kept his gun steady. "That's not what it looked like a minute ago."

Watcher pulled off his helmet. His eyes glowed like a slow furnace. Something told Calla he was anything but ordinary. His complexion shone in the sun's rays, giving his whole form a tinted ruddiness.

She squinted as the sun burned through the clouds and reflected off Watcher's body. Everything about him suggested authority. "What are you? Where did you come from?"

Watcher studied both of them. As he spoke his glow disappeared, and his radiance dimmed. Looking to the sky, in one elegant movement, he reached back with both hands and pulled out a rounded, dark wood container. He placed it in Calla's hand. "Take this."

He then withdrew the journal from under his clothes, flickering like a bad connection as he spoke. "I believe this is yours. I had to be sure."

Calla took the items and held them with a steady hand. "What's this?"

"I sat there in that room and studied those inscriptions on the wall. Day and night I wondered if you'd ever come."

With a protective hand on her shoulder, Nash raised his chin and took a skeptical step forward. Fear twisted her gut as Calla glared at Watcher's intimidating height. "What do you mean?"

"You're the first to correctly read the symbols in over two thousand years."

Calla lifted the lid of the opulent box, its weight nearly dragging her hands down. Nestled inside was a dark rock. Porous and charcoal in color, it was comprised of millions of cramped crystals clustered together. She lifted the rock out of the box and held it against the afternoon sun. Rays of violet, amber, and scarlet reflected off its serrated edge.

Nash relaxed his shoulders. "What is it?"

Watcher turned his back to them and strode toward the building. He zipped around. "You've begun on a course that's not easy. If you choose to seek all that it offers you'll find what you're looking for."

"And what's that?" she asked.

"You've only got a few days to gather the other two rocks. If not, their energies will be utterly useless. They need to be reunited."

Watcher resumed his steps toward the lake. "Be careful. Many will try to stop you, especially him, the mind hacker. He mustn't take possession of anything you find."

"Who?"

Watcher leaped up into the air and vanished with the briskness of lightning.

Calla and Nash gaped skyward, half-expecting Watcher to return.

Nash pursed his lips. "You sure you wanna go on with this?"

With every ounce of courage she possessed, Calla

straightened her shoulders. She knew Nash would accompany her each step of the way if she asked. She gripped the rock tightly and studied his confident eyes. "I'm not sure what just happened, but I have to find out, Nash."

For a moment he appeared too stunned to move. Returning her gaze, he exhaled as he secured his gun. "I'll come with you. After what we just saw who knows what may come next."

Her heart sighed in gratitude. "Thanks, Nash."

Something behind Nash grabbed his attention. He angled his head slightly, focusing on an object several hundred meters away. With a hint of admiration, she studied his austere body. He didn't move a muscle of his deftly sculpted arms and what had to be a set of healthy, washboard abdominal muscles that slenderized to a firm thirty-four-inch waist. Tossing away her distraction she followed his fixed stare. With his jaw tightening Nash remained in an attitude of frozen calmness.

And then stillness.

Stagnant air settled around them.

More stillness.

A bullet zipped past Nash and launched itself straight at Calla's heart. Nash broke her fall, cradling her weight in his arms.The container loosened out of her hands, releasing the black diamond onto the cool grass.

She stopped breathing.

CHAPTER 16

The cymbals clashed. The trumpets made their discernible entrance and engulfed the small room. The string section floated in the background like vapor seizing time and space. As the horns burst into dominant allegro, they imprisoned Slate's heart, escalating to a terrifying crescendo. The pace of Gustav Holst's *Planets* continued in a tumultuous jumble, floating through the top floor apartment where Slate reclined on a sofa, his feet resting on the coffee table.

His eyes were closed and his hands nestled behind his head. He took in every note and bar of the tantalizing symphony. *What was on Holst's mind when he composed this piece?*

The blinking vibration of his cell phone interrupted his thoughts. He reached for the remote control and silenced the music that had infatuated his mind. He glared at the phone. It lit up blue whenever there was movement from Cress's handheld device, a prime indicator as to whether she was using the application he had bugged on her smartphone. He slid open the top cover to check for activity.

She couldn't have survived that bullet.He closed his eyes and turned the music back on, reflecting on his last encounter with Cress. *What was that thing that had followed her to the library?*

Whatever expertise it employed had been extraordinary. He wasn't moved by the unexplainable. To him, everything could be justified logically and rationally. He believed in technology and science. This person had plenty of it. What was it Mason had said? "Cress should be quite easy to eliminate."

One down, one to go.

Why had Mason not let him just kill her in Berlin? Easy and fast. That was simple enough.

She was a simple curator with a linguistic gift. A gift that he knew Mason coveted more than life itself. What was so special about her gift? Slate really didn't care. It didn't really matter now, did it?

The phone buzzed again. He checked it once more. There was movement on his tracking device. He silenced the music and scrambled to his feet. *Damn it!*

From the voices on the recorder, he could hear a man talking plotting something. Must be the soldier type she had been with earlier. Another man's voice sounded. Had they taken her phone? His receptor had been slightly damaged at the library.

Slate listened intently, but all he could gather was Cress was in trouble. *Hurt? She should be dead! Impossible.*

He shrugged it off. The bullet had gone straight into her heart. No one could have survived his accurate shot. Slate never missed or wasted a bullet. He would check again in an hour. Right now he had better things to attend to.Slate owed his life to Mason, the only father figure or family for that matter that he'd ever known. Somehow, he couldn't help but conclude Mason was a self-seeking, egocentric man who used and abused whomever he pleased.

Over the years Slate had made quite an affluent living serving Mason's dishonest assignments. It all sat in box 6207 in an offshore bank account in the Cayman Islands, mounting up interest.

He'd done enough and wouldn't be Mason's errand boy any longer. How many years had it been? Too many to count. Most of his life it seemed. He had sacrificed his own life for Mason and turned into the one thing his mother would wince at, a common-place criminal. The sacrifice had come at a price too, but wasn't entirely wasted. He had seen the master in action and had learned a few things along the way.

He reached for a steel ring wrapped around his right middle finger. Nothing about it spoke of elegance or beauty. But to Slate, it was of more value than anything he owned.

He pulled it off his finger and placed it on the table near him. Locating his electronic tablet he reached for the Swiss Army knife lying on the table. With the corkscrew tip, he stabbed at a black point on the ring. The top shell slid off revealing a series of electronic chips.

He forced out one chip, no bigger than a baby's fingernail, and found the custom-made memory device he'd ordered from a foreign supplier. He slid the chip inside and placed the memory stick within the electronic tablet. It lit up and the application he sought loaded. He scrolled through a list of classified names, a list of all the clients Mason secretly concocted with. These weren't in the interest of the ISTF. He should know since he'd helped do most of the clandestine work himself. But it was his bargaining chip, should he ever need it.

That afternoon when Slate had left Mason's office he had seen three new names on Mason's screen. Unfamiliar with any of them he flinched. Slate was always privy to everything concerning Mason. Still, Mason had never mentioned these three names to him. A day would come when Mason would no longer need him. He wouldn't be caught off guard.

Slate memorized the names. Samuel Riche, a name he'd seen in the newspapers, Margot Arlington and Rupert Kumar.

What did Mason want with them? The blue light on the phone flashed in rapid blinks. He shut the program and replaced the chip in his ring. His attention turned to the phone. "What's wrong with this damn thing?" His marksmanship had never let him down.

There was no way Cress could've survived that bullet.

5:03 P.M.
SHOREDITCH, EAST LONDON

Calla gripped her arms, digging her broken nails into her bare skin. Where had the cold come from? The fatigue? She rubbed her arms, yearning for warmth. Her bare feet soaked in a pool of blood.

An ice-cold sensation began a slow agonizing decent through her veins, close to sub-zero temperatures.

She tried to stand, but her legs resisted. Her immobile knees, now weakened, locked together, stiffening with a chill as the wind swept over her drenched skin. Snowflakes caressed her cheeks, perhaps the only upside in the gloom. Her thoughts spun round and round, trying to arrest any recognizable memory.

The cold eased, and heat seeped into her aching muscles.

She slowly opened her eyes, making out undetectable images and movement in the near distance as more voices sounded. *What happened? Where am I?*

Her hazy vision became clearer until she could make out decipherable forms. Meanwhile, the voices around her grew louder and more distinct. She lifted her head and glared upward. Jack and Nash sat across the room in debate over an item resting on a cluttered table.

"I can't believe you guys found this!" Jack said.

"Well, actually, it was given to Calla," Nash said.

"Do you know how many people are looking for this?"

"I'm not really sure. Could you examine it? I don't think it's like any carbonado diamond we have on file."

Calla turned her head toward the discussion. A movement stirred behind him. "Calla. Thank God you've come to."

Her chest still heaved with ferocious pain. But as she moved her limbs the stiffness and discomfort eased. Calla could scarcely recall what had led to such a substantial headache.She placed a hand on her chest. Slowly the pieces started to form in her mind. They'd been in a field or was it a valley? No, it was Oxford. She remembered a tall warrior-like man. *The thing! Watcher!*

He had fought her until she'd overpowered him. How had she managed to do that? And then. Blank.

She couldn't recall anymore.

Nash paced to her side and knelt on the floor by the couch. His eyebrow arched and his lips tightened, revealing a single dimple on the right side of his cheek.

"You just escaped a nasty bullet," Nash said.

"Bullet?"

Relief flooded his eyes. "Yes, a bullet."

Calla fought to make her heavy limps move. She lumbered upward and relaxed her shoulders. "How?"

Nash settled in a seat beside her. "The bullet knocked you senseless, but—"

He stopped, waiting for a response.

"And?"

"As if by instinct, you held the rock to your heart," he said glancing at the carbonado.

Calla's eyes begged for more information. "Yes?"

He hesitated once more and set a gentle hand over hers. "You then...disappeared for a good several seconds. The next thing I knew I caught you before you hit the ground with the stone still held to your heart."

Calla took in every word of his story, trying to connect them with the pieces that were still hazy in her memory.

Nash managed an encouraging smile. "I think it saved you. You were gone, outta sight with enough time for the bullet to steal right past you? You then you disappeared. I panicked, coz I couldn't find you."

Could it be true?

Jack joined them, standing a few feet away.

Calla glanced around the room. "Where are we?"

Nash rose slowly. "I called Jack. We need his help."

Jack held a peculiar stone, balancing it between his hands.

"After I saw what the stone had done by shielding you from that bullet and changing the chemistry of your body, I knew we weren't dealing with an ordinary carbonado. Jack can help us find out what this thing is," Nash said.

Nash was right. Jack could probably conduct geology experiments to see where the stone had come from. But, most importantly, what would science tell them? Was the rock a danger?

Jack threw Calla a grin as he slid off a mini torch from his head. He wore a white lab coat and latex gloves. "Welcome to my humble abode. This is my private lab. I come here to work on things I don't wish others to know about."

Calla scanned the room. "Impressive, Jack. It takes a bullet to my heart to get an invitation here."

Jack smirked. "I've done initial tests on the stone."

"What have you found?" Calla asked.

"Carbonados, or black diamonds, have always been a mystery, even to the scientific mind."

"What do you mean?"

"Some researchers have a theory about their origin."

Nash interposed. "It's literally...out of this world."

Calla's shoulders slouched. "I'm listening."

"Researchers are still trying to figure out where they came from. Normal diamonds, such as the ones jewelers work with, come from deep within the earth."

Calla's eyes lit up. "Yes, and they came to the surface through two volcano eruptions that happened about one billion years ago," she said.

"That's right. What we have here is different," Jack said. "Carbonados are older than three and a half billion years. They must've come to Earth in a non-conventional way."

"What way?"

"Well, let's see. Also," he added. "Most diamonds can be found all over the world. Carbonados are only found in Brazil and Africa, except this one."

Nash took the stone in his hand. "One theory is that black diamonds came to Earth during an asteroid event that struck when the two continents were still one."

Calla wrestled the theory. "Isn't that what ISTF documents say, as well as NASA reports?"

"Correct. The only difference is they don't have studies on this stone," Nash added.

Jack's eyes lit. "Not only is it bulletproof but, so far from what I've seen, the compositions aren't present on our planet. It's quite remarkable."

"Is there more?" she said.

Nash interjected. "Carbonados have hydrogen in them, suggesting the diamonds formed in a unique environment, like a star."

Calla tilted her head. "So this stone isn't from Earth?"

"Nope. When I examined it under infrared radiation, I found a spectrum similar to a type of diamond that exists in space," Jack said.

"So what are you saying exactly?"

Jack strode the length of the tiny, windowless lab. "From the initial research I've done, there're three explanations we can use. One, this stone is formed from the original solar nebulae or interstellar dust cloud. Two, it's produced by the high temperatures and pressures of the Earth's mantle or three, it's the result of an interplanetary impact."

"Are you serious?" Calla said,

"Yes, and the funny thing is scientists don't agree on any of the three theories," Jack said.

Calla peered from Nash to Jack determining if she should believe them. "There must be an explanation."

She'd regained her senses now and was fully alert. These were her best friends. They wanted only what was best for her and they were dead serious.

Jack shook his head. "Not really. Even if the source of carbonados is still not proven I think it's amazing that portions of a cooled star could survive, travel across billions of miles to Earth and be preserved for us to find."

"Hm—"

"They're literally *falling stars,*" Jack added.

Calla threw Jack a wearied smile. "Okay, what else have you discovered?"

"There are significant nuclear materials contained in this rock. But what amazes me is that the materials inherent in the stone are non-toxic and are off the charts," Jack continued.

"What materials are those?" Nash asked.

"I don't know yet. This baby has enough juice to power fifty space crafts. My program couldn't read all of it. I think we could be looking at a substance from the outer galaxies, such as a mineral or a gem."

Nash thought for a moment. "But isn't that what Operation Carbonado is all about? The only reason these five governments would get behind this is because of the potential for nuclear energies."

Jack moved back to a computer screen on the desk in the far corner. "Operation Carbonado is full of holes. First of all the reports say that a star exploded and delivered these gems to Earth by an asteroid. But how come none like this have been found? What are the reports based on?"

Nash gripped the back of his neck. "That's not entirely true. NASA has a different take on it. According to classified NASA reports a geologist from Iowa International University analyzed chemical compositions of some volcanic stones found in Brazil and the Central African Republic, similar I guess to this one."

Their eyes fell on the carbonado.

"Like Jack said, the geologist bounced infrared light off polished slivers of the stone, and the resulting scales didn't match signatures for earthly hydrogen and nitrogen," Nash added.

"Why's that?" asked Calla.

Nash took a deep breath. "Because they mimic those found in intergalactic space."

5:21 P.M.

"Whether it's from space or not, as far as I'm concerned, each is entitled to their opinion. I just want to know what my parents were involved with," Calla said, twiddling her right ear stud. "The operation reports also say that a similar stone was found in the sixties, but there is no clear evidence of it. No pictures, no lab reports. Where can we find more about the asteroid theory?"

"Probably from the person who compiled the Operation Carbonado report. I mean the original findings," Nash said.

Jack checked his screen and typed a few words. "That's classified and needs higher clearance than I have, all the way up to Mason."

She hovered for a moment, not having regained her equilibrium. "Where's the Deveron? I want to know more about what Watcher meant when he said he'd waited for me for a long time. Why me?"

Nash handed her the manuscript and the journal. "Calla, you're lucky to be alive. Are you sure you're up to this?"

Calla took both items in her hands. "I'm fine." She tried to ease his anxious look with a weak smirk. "I think there's a connection between what I learned in Berlin and what this stone and manuscript are leading us to. We need to hang on to these and shouldn't let anything we learn out of this circle."

She glanced at both of them. "I need you to swear. This is dangerous for all of us. Can I count on you to see this through to the end?"

Jack glanced at Nash's face and gave her a wink. "The commander and chief has spoken. We're with you on this," he said.

Calla labored over to Jack's work desk and spread out both the journal and manuscript. "Okay, so why did Watcher give me this stone? He said we only have a few days from now to get the other two and muttered something about their strengths expiring if not reunited. What other carbonados?"

She glared at the porous mass of fine-grained rock, now burrowed in her hands. In the light, she rotated it, and it gave off a prism of colored beams that fell on her face.

Jack eased the stone from her hands. "I want to do more research on this. I'll head back to the office labs and see what I can find. But first, I'm intrigued by what you guys experienced in Oxford." Jack studied them both. "Tell me exactly what you saw. What happened?"

Calla was first to speak. "You mean the stone, the wall? Or the Watcher guy?"

"All of it," Jack said. "All the weirdness."

Calla drew in a quick breath. "Well, at first, I was able to press my hands through a wall in the professor's office. I thought it was a wall."

"Rewind," Jack said. "Did you say, thought?"

"Yes, but I was actually there, so was Nash," she said with a quick glance at his face.

Jack encouraged her story with an eager eye. "Then what happened?"

"I was in, as if carried in this other space, and then, he appeared."

"He?"

"Yeah, Watcher. I fought him, and I don't know how, and so did Nash. Then he gave me that box with the stone."

"I'm interested in *him*. What did he look like?"

"Well, that is just it. He kept changing and he hit bloody hard. Then there was armor thing he wore that..."

Jack watched them both. "Have you heard of Portax, a military software that creates an illusion and the physical damage of a robotized machine?"

They both shook their heads.

"It's software was created in ISTF labs about ten years ago after the tech was swiped from a criminal, I believe, but no one perfected it."

"Oh, it was perfect, all right. This guy could hit and combat," Nash interrupted.

"It was a prototype that never worked, only in theory. What you describe sounds real."

"How?" Calla said.

"It's a teleportation software woven with synthetic robotics. It may have also been first stolen from the NSA."

Nash raised an eyebrow. "Really... I don't think—

"If the NSA didn't first develop it," Jack continued, "then someone else did and took it from prototype to finished product. MI6 also knew about it."

"Jack," Calla said. "It was real. I—

"Teleportation software involves matter and energy

crossingfrom one area to another without going through the physical space between them."

Calla crossed her arms. "How?"

"Many ways," Jack replied. "Watcher might also be a Portax illusion of teleportation, merged with some seriously advanced robotics. I think you saw a person charging through the air at the speed of light creating an image and presence of teleportation. It's clever stuff. Wish I had developed it myself."

"You saying it is teleportation, but *not*," Calla said.

"Yes!"

Jack shrugged, "Teleportation could actually become a regular occurrence. Seems it's here sooner than I thought. All it needs is a software to scan your body down to the subatomic level. It then wipes out matter at one point and then shots all the scanned data to a second point. This is where a microchip or even a second piece of software restructures your body from nothing in a fraction of a second. It also borrows from laser 3D scanning technology. Physicists have been working on this for years."

"But what about my touching the wall?"

He raised an eyebrow. "Perhaps you were the subject? Maybe even temporarily hallucinating due to shock."

"Really?"

"I entered the fields of science, geology and quantum physics to prove the weird can happen through human advancement," Jack said. "The energies produced by the Portax software could have caused temporary hallucination."

"Do you really think so, Jack?" Nash said.

"It's a theory, but yes, I think so. Teleporting a person, atom by atom, is difficult, but developments in chemistry and molecular biology have been letting us do it so much more quickly. There is no law to say it can't be done." Jack said. "Guys, common sense doesn't steer or dictate the rules of quantum physics. All you need is to destroy an original to create a faithful replica of the object in question."

Calla digested his words and made a mental note to examine them later.

"Okay, I'm off," Jack said. "Stay as long as you guys want."

"Thanks. Be careful," Nash said.

"Righto!" Jack said as he paced to the door, slipped on a jacket and a leather flat-cap. "I'll see you guys later," he said, shutting the door behind him.

Nash turned to Calla as she sank into the seat at Jack's work desk. He watched her in silence scrutinize the manuscript, and then the journal, unaware of his stare. He had on several occasions thought about a romantic relationship with her. He leaned slightly toward her as she raised her head.

"I was impressed with you in Oxford." His smile, though with shut lips, spread slowly. "Where did you learn that defensive shoulder crank? That's some skillful martial arts move."

Calla backed away from him until she felt the cushion of the chair against her back. "I don't know where that came from."

"You held your own, especially with your grip of death on Watcher. You could handle yourself."

Calla turned her attention back to the screen.

"Calla?"

She turned to face him. "Yes?"

He set a hand on her chin.

She winced. Calla had consistently warded off any romantic approach he'd attempted, and as a result, he'd withdrawn his advances allowing her the distance she insisted on having.

Nash edged nearer and pushed back a wisp of hair that had fallen across her eyes. "Calla. I—"

His hand, gently insistent, moved slowly over her forehead and down her temples, before cradling her head in his hands. His face must've betrayed a hint of infatuation."I thought I'd lost you."

She shrank from the intensity of his affection. "You didn't."

The touch of her intoxicating fingers felt strangely welcome, even though she'd avoided showing her feelings for as long as he'd known her. When he leaned in to kiss her all he got was a flushed cheek. She was unwilling to trust the emotions welling inside, and instinctively reached out to remove his hands.

"Thanks for being there for me yesterday," she said.

Nash had overstepped an invisible, yet clear boundary. He swiveled, turned away and an awkward silence engulfed the room only broken by the sound of an incoming mail on Jack's computer.

Calla turned her attention back to the manuscript as Nash slowly lifted his head. "Why's this so important to you?"

Calla glanced away. "Nash, I've been searching for my parents and my identity for a long time."

Nash decided not to pursue the matter any further. Over the months, he'd observed Calla chase every lead that involved a hunt for her parents' identities, to no avail.

Calla debated whether to reveal what Taiven had told her. She'd still not registered who or what Taiven was. Nothing seemed logical anymore except the yearning in her to continue the journey she'd begun. She reached for Nash's upper arm. "I can't tell you how I know but my parents worked on this manuscript and one of them, or both, were employed by British Secret Intelligence."

Nash's brows knit. "I thought you were an orphan, Cal. Isn't that what your whole search has involved? Looking for information on how you came to be adopted?"

"Yes, but I've reason to believe that my real parents may have given me up for a reason *or* a mission. Then something happened to them."

"Do you think they're still alive?"

"I don't know, Nash, but this is my only lead. They worked with this manuscript years ago. If I locate what the Deveron is hiding, perhaps I'll find out more about them."

He tilted his head. "I understand."

"I've been on a lonely journey for a long time. There's so much agony in not knowing who you're or where you're from."

"I don't like what this pursuit is doing to you." He thought for a second. "But I believe you'll find the answers."

She soaked in the concern that burned in his eyes. Even in the intimate moment, she couldn't tell him what her heart knew. Her chin trembled. "Nash, I'm so grateful for our friendship. Please, let's not ruin what we have."

Nash managed a roguish smile and kissed her on the forehead. "I don't want to lose you. All right, let's see what else we can find."

Calla picked up the manuscript and the journal. "We need to find a bigger space."

They cleared space on the carpet and spread out the ancient papers. Calla focused on the delicate papyrus. "Each of these round shapes, on the outskirts of this circle represents a goal of some sort. We've found one, the rock that Jack has."

Nash sank to the ground beside her. "I read about the Deveron in a classified NSA file published about twenty or so years ago."

"What file was that?"

Nash went over to Jack's computer. "Let me see if I can find it."

Calla rose and followed him. He closed the open application and logged onto a restricted government website.

"How do you have access to these CIA files?" she asked.

He shot her a wink. "Many ways."

He typed in a series of passwords. After moving through a sequence of windows, a file-archiving site popped up. He scrolled through numerous files until he reached the one that he was looking for. "Says here the Deveron document was definitely at British Secret Intelligence Service offices years ago. In 1968. The CIA obtained the document through an MI6 source who loaned it to them for twenty-four hours." He smirked. "Looks like we Americans wanted to run some tests. Perhaps interpret it."

"Does it show what they found?"

"Not much to help us. A British agent repossessed it before the CIA could investigate or even make a copy."

"Where did the document come from?"

Nash read a little further. "Ah yes, at the ISTF meeting they mentioned the manuscript itself was found by a certain Deveron, a person in the eighteen hundreds. It's not clear how."

"So that's why it's called the Deveron Manuscript."

"CIA believed it was a map. How they came to that conclusion is anyone's guess."

Calla shook her head. "I find it ludicrous for the government to be involved in some sort of treasure hunt."

"Aren't they all? This report sides with the asteroid belief. According to this, there're supposedly three carbonados in total. The manuscript leads to their locations."

"That would explain the three circles and the trinity powers on page one of the Deveron."

"One carbonado diamond was found in 1966."

Calla leaned toward the screen. "Where? Who found it?"

"It doesn't say. My guess is if the Deveron belonged to your parents then they probably found it."

"Why was research on the document never completed when it came back to Britain?"

Nash searched further down the screen. "It doesn't say." He turned from the screen. "I've done some digging and think it was stolen. This is how it ended up in the Pushkin Museum in St. Petersburg."

Calla mused over the revelations as her hand landed on her cheek. "Allegra would have known that."

"We have one stone following our translation. This is what I found." He showed her the notes he'd scribbled the day before.

Greater power has no more than this.
Courage is the source of my strength.
Here I fought like a lioness, I ate like a bull.
I danced to your praises, and they ripped me apart.
Yet overall, I remained.
Though I died, I remained courageous and victorious, I was never defeated.

Calla re-read his notes quietly for several minutes and ran a hand through her hair. "This next clue in the manuscript is talking about physical power, strength and maybe even influence. The language used is stronger and more aggressive."

"A power?" Nash asked.

Calla pointed to the circles on the manuscript. "Yes! Look at the main line again."

Nash obliged.

In three dominances you rule, move and ensure your being.

Calla picked up the first page of the Deveron. "History shows us that there are three things the human race covets most: knowledge, through communication and language; power through strength, and wealth through resources. The first circle of knowledge led us to Watcher and the carbonado in Oxford."

"Hmm...this second circle here is, therefore, talking about literal physical power. Like a powerful nation, an army—"

Calla pursed her lips. "Allegra's notes say that the three carbonados are a great distance from each other, possibly on different continents. They can't co-exist on the same axis, like the north and south poles of a magnet. If the second rock is as powerful as the one we have, whoever hid them didn't want them to be near each other. We're definitely looking for a place."

"But seriously, Cal, this riddle could mean anything. It could be *any* powerful nation or group throughout history or modern times."

"Not just any group." She smiled. "Have you ever been to Greece, Nash?"

He fixed his gaze on her then flipped her head back beaming. "We better let Jack know."

CHAPTER 17

6:01 p.m.
ISTF LABORATORIES
GEOLOGY AND PETROLOGY DIVISION

"Fascinating!" Jack whispered to himself. The overhead fluorescent lights flickered off for lack of movement on the floor. He leaned over some documents. With the laptop screen booted Jack made some calculations. He glimpsed behind him. A lone analyst sat three desks from Jack. The man's ears were covered with large headphones, his head bobbing in rhythm to the loud bass of house music that could faintly be heard reverberating. Two others worked on, rows behind him, concealed behind their screens.

Jack had hidden the rock in his leather messenger bag. In about thirty minutes there'd be no one about, just him and the security staff.

On occasion, he would work late into the night. This could be one of them. A janitor appeared on the main floor, lugging a cleaning cart behind him. He switched on the noisy vacuum cleaner and started his cleaning shift. Jack finished up and made his way to the microscopy lab on the seventh floor. It had been a controversial move, but strong campaigning from the geology staff had enabled the installation of a state of the art lab accessible to all ISTF staff.

Not a real geologist, Jack understood enough about sediment rocks and metallurgical substances to determine the materials he was dealing with. His interest in geology had been a hobby from a young age after finding unusual rocks on the Indian Ocean shores of his country. He would examine Calla's stone using the lab's microscopes.

Jack took a deep breath. Perhaps he was a step closer to being all he desired, not decorated with fame or accolades, but a step ahead of criminal mindsets and behavior. Mindsets he was sure ran in his family.

He recalled how embarrassed he'd been when his father was arrested one night for attempting to slice his mother's lover with a broken vodka bottle. Though convicted, his father had walked free after three years in the state penitentiary, leaving a very bitter aftertaste in Jack's mind.

He later found out that his father had harbored pirates who frequented the Indian Ocean, terrorizing western tourists and lived most of his life on the grimy funds they paid. That's why Jack had been so ready to leave the islands. And thank God, his scholarship had seen to it. Nothing around his upbringing was normal, his parents, his house and even the dreads he wore. He had to achieve something phenomenal in the inventions arena if he were to tame the demons of mediocrity that tailed him.

Tonight could be important. It could be one step in the direction of being the best technology specialist capable of designing superior systems that stop criminals. That's why he had joined ISTF when he was first head-hunted by Mason if only to apprehend delinquents like his father. And now that he'd spent some time with Mason zeal was reignited.

Jack saw much of his father's mannerism in the man.

. . .

One by one the night workers on the floor filtered out and the place quieted. Only the night watchman kept him company. The lights flickered again, prompted by movement sensors. The cleaning janitor switched off his appliance and rolled it along with the cart to the next department.

Without hesitation, Jack shut off his computer, picked up his bag from underneath his desk, and crossed to the end of the room. He pulled open the door that led into a corridor and shut it behind him. Jack rode the elevator to the seventh floor. Once outside the lab, he pulled his security card from his pocket that allowed him special clearance.

Seated at a low table a security man leaned against the lab door draining a mug of warm coffee as he snacked on a pretzel. His head was buried in a popular car magazine, and as he lifted his head, he caught Jack's approach. "Ah, Jack! It's always great to have your company up here. It can get pretty lonely."

Jack approached his desk. "Hey Liam, I need to sign in for a couple of hours."

Liam set his reading down and passed him the signature tablet. "She's all yours."

Jack signed in. "Is there anyone in there?"

Liam shook his head. "Not unless they slipped past me."

"Will you need the full power at your station?" Liam asked.

"Yes. Thank you."

Liam shoved open the lab door and turned on the main lights.

"I can take it from here. You don't need to stay on. If you need to go, I can man the machines myself."

"Cheers. Don't forget to lock up. I'll be leaving in about ten minutes," he said as he marched away, head high and chest out.

The lab was arranged around seven microscopy hubs, each constructed as hexagonal tables. At the back, hand specimens, collected over the course of several years, had been stored for various lab exercises. Jack had on occasion used these elements for experiments.

He chose the station closest to the back of the room and set his bag on the table. Turning to the research-grade microscope fitted with a CCD video camera he switched on the overhead station lamp.

Jack waited a few more moments before turning on the equipment. He pulled out the carbonado. As it came into contact with his skin it glowed cerulean and a faint shade of magenta.

He studied the stone. *What the heck are you?* He switched off the light. The rock continued to gleam with intensity around the room. Jack's eyes followed the reflections on the wall as they blazed shades of colors he'd never seen. He placed the stone under a microscope. Under the viewing lens, the luminosity only intensified. He moved on to another instrument at the table, an alpha particle X-ray spectrometer. Created to measure the abundance of chemical elements in rocks and soils, he placed it in contact with the rock. As he maneuvered, a protective layer started to form around the stone, a force shield. *It's responding to light.*

Jack reached for the hand lens, the lab's impressive magnifying glass over on the workbench along the wall. A close-up view of the minerals, textures, and structures in the stone, could reveal much more. He fetched the gadget and placed the rock within its reading saddle. The lens began to calculate. The digital numbers on the small display at the front spun with such rapid intensity that Jack failed to keep up with the speed. Calculation reached apex point and came to an abrupt halt. Had the machine possessed more capacity it would have continued counting. He peeped through the lens. *Uh huh. Just as I thought.*

He took the stone back to the workstation and set it on the table. Walking to a secured locker, he found a radioactive suit.

Once suited he breathed hard, recognizing the severity of what he was about to do. *Look for traces of uranium.*

He had read about ways to safely detect uranium from remote locations. ISTF had started such experiments in this very lab and, now, he would attempt one. The technique was known within scientific circles as near-infrared spectroscopy. Jack returned to the station and switched on a spectrometer. Using a fiber optic probe with a powerful light source, he scanned the surface of the carbonado to identify the chemical properties of its surface. The test produced positive results. How much at this point he couldn't tell though. The energy levels in this one stone alone could power electricity use for the entire globe for weeks. *What was this thing?*

Jack unsuited the research garment, shut off the machines and put the rock in his bag. He turned off the lights and exited the lab. Outside the lab door, Liam's hands were folded across his chest, having nodded off at his station.

"Great!" muttered Jack under his breath.

The coffee mug on the table had spilled over, leaving a brown coffee stain on the closed car magazine.

Jack's hand nudged him. "Hey! Liam?"

Liam's body stiffened. He roused, fixing his sleepy eyes on Jack's face. Liam scanned him. "What is it? Heck, I didn't realize. I...must've been exhausted."

Jack helped him up. "You should go home."

"Uh, yeah. Sure."

Liam set the spilled coffee cup upright and wiped the table surface with tissues from his pockets. Jack patted Liam on the shoulder as he turned to go. "Okay, good night," he said as he marched off to the elevators.

. . .

Liam now awake, waited several seconds until Jack had turned the corner. He surveyed the corridor. When he was satisfied that it was all clear, he rubbed his facial skin. His epidermis shifted revealing a different face, concealed under his meta-material disguise. He wandered to the broom closet, a few doors from the laboratory. Glimpsing around he dropped his used flummoxing device, a custom-made, thin film that integrated signature reduction capabilities for the face and head region. It landed in the waste disposal and shot down the shaft on the wall.

Slate grimaced, glancing down at the body on the broom closet floor.Liam's lifeless body was still unconscious, gagged more than an hour ago.

Day 8

Eichel pulled out his passport and slid it under the window to the uniformed security guard behind the protective glass. He'd never visited any intelligence services offices before, let alone ISTF. The only reason he knew it existed was thanks to a chance meeting.

He'd met Mason several years ago at the Consumer Electronics Show in Las Vegas. Atraps Technologies Inc., a security systems technology company, had been exhibiting CCTV cameras, including surveillance technologies. Both men had attended Atraps Corporation's keynote speech and witnessed a demonstration by the CEO, a rather young entrepreneur.

Atraps was a small start-up with incredible potential. Though not inventors *per se*, the owners were mastermind visionaries, having taken over the industry in such a short period of time. Their approach to implementing breakthrough security systems had attracted Mason's and Eichel's curiosity. Though small the company had attained incredible success with its neoteric devices.

Government and private owners were interested in acquiring Atraps' technologies. But the two co-founders, Michael and Kyle Atraps, were no fools. As recent engineering graduates from MIT, they sought the highest bidder and owned the rights to each new system they developed. Time was no object. They knew what their discoveries were worth in today's market.

During the demonstration of a new network configuration and administration platform, Eichel and Mason had struck up a conversation. They'd conversed like old friends going out for drinks at the Dynamo Lounge Club. That night Mason had extended an invitation to Eichel. "It would be good to exchange ideas whenever you're in London," Mason had said.

Eichel was taking Mason at his word.

The security gate clanged opened. "Here's your passport, Mr. Eichel. Please go through these main doors for the security scan. You can leave your belongings in a secured locker for retrieval after your visit."

After his security search Eichel stepped into the main lobby and gave his name to the receptionist.

"This way Mr. Eicha."

"Eichel," he corrected.

She twitched her firm lips and escorted him to the elevators. They stepped out onto the fifth floor, into an austere, minimalist lobby. "Mr. Laskfell will be with you shortly."

She left him standing in the middle of the atrium fiercely guarded by security cameras. Was he to sit in the only lounger chair provided in the deserted foyer?

"Herr Eichel. How good to see you again!" boomed a voice from behind.

Mason gave him a firm handshake and put a hand on Eichel's shoulder.

"It's nice to see you again too, Mr. Laskfell."

"Let's go have a chat in the restaurant."

Eichel couldn't understand why Mason didn't want to meet in the privacy of his office, given he'd explained part of the nature of his visit.

"This way. If I remember correctly you told me you enjoy a good English roast. They may be serving one today."

"Thank you."

Mason led him into a busy, staff restaurant on the same floor. It was nothing like any staff canteen Eichel had seen before. It might as well have been a prime restaurant with its bright decor and modish paintings. The tables were strewn with overly elegant tablecloths and full sets of cutlery. The only similarity between this eating space and a regular staff canteen was that one queued up for meals.

At the entrance, Mason requested a private room off the main restaurant from a member of the kitchen staff. The male waiter led them to a closed off glass enclosure. "You can use the Lark room, Mr. Laskfell."

Mason invited Eichel to take a seat. "We'll have the roast and two bottles of sparkling Perrier," said Mason as the man left to attend to their order.

The dining hall overlooked the River Thames and, in the distance, Eichel spotted the iconic Ferris wheel, the London Eye.

"I still have not been up there," said Eichel.

Mason turned to view the observation wheel. "The Millennium Wheel? It's just a frivolity, but we're proud of it."

Mason studied his visitor with a meticulous smile. "What brings you to London, my friend?"

Eichel scrutinized his face. "I wish I'd come under more

social circumstances. I'm investigating the disappearance of national treasures."

Their drinks arrived, and Mason filled sparkling water in the chilled glasses. He offered Eichel one. "You're now based in Berlin? I remember you were in Munich the last time we met."

It had been during his probation that he'd taken a short holiday to Las Vegas arriving in time for the Consumer Electronics Show.

Eichel didn't acknowledge the remark. "Mr. Laskfell, I'm sure you've heard of the details of the Deveron Manuscript. It was taken from the Pergamon Museum along with another artifact. One of your people, Allegra Driscoll, also disappeared from the crime scene."

Mason raised an eyebrow. "Our intelligence arm is looking at this carefully. We've launched our own investigation."

"When we met I didn't realize you were working for ISTF. Must be my luck. I'm honored that you've let me into your circle."

Mason twitched in his seat. "Have I?"

"Just the person I need for my investigation. That's why I wanted to see you. Is there anything you can share with us in Berlin?"

"Like what?"

"Come on, I had a chat with Calla Cress. Something also tells me she works for you."

Mason ignored his comment and inclined his head to one side. "What do you want?"

Eichel searched his face for a reaction before continuing. "Frau Cress came to the museum looking for Frau Driscoll. Her allegiance is to the British government and possibly ISTF."

"Is that so?" Mason asked.

"Have you or MI6 dealt with the Deveron document in the past?"

Mason's head shot forward. The small-time cop was prying. Digging into matters that didn't concern him. "If we have I wouldn't know. It's not a high priority here. We don't investigate historical artifacts unless they pose the utmost threat to national or international security."

Eichel grinned. "But isn't that the myth about the Deveron? An international threat, at least for those that get the secrets it supposedly holds."

"It never crossed my mind," Mason said.

Eichel stared at him for a moment. "What about the Russian chemical being funded by Rupert Kumar, the billionaire?"

Mason twitched under Eichel's stare. "I can put you in touch with our agents."

"Thank you."

Mason stood to leave. "Mr. Eichel, I'm sorry, but I have business to attend to. Do enjoy your meal on the house. Lillian, my assistant, will attend to your comfort."

Eichel jerked to his feet. "You're leaving so soon?"

"I'm a very busy man."

"Of course." A quizzical look struck Eichel's face. "Do you smell smoke?"

Seconds later, a deafening siren squealed through the facility as fire alarms resounded throughout the building. A loud voice took to the in-house public address system.

Attention! Attention!
This is not a drill!

Evacuate the building by the nearest safe exit!
Please leave the building immediately!

Do not use the lifts!
Report to the assembly area!

6:12 P.M.

"Think about it," Calla said. "Who in history has been the most influential when it comes to military power?"

"Oh...I don't know, Julius Caesar, George Washington, Cyrus the Great...Alexander the Great?" Nash said.

"Yes. Exactly. Alexander the Great. The key must be in Greece."

Nash scratched an eyebrow. "Why Greece? There must be a few other military powers to choose from such as... let's see, ones from the antiquity and modern eras. How about those in the Middle Ages? What's your point of reference?"

"Alexander, the young king of Macedonia, became the leader of the Greeks. He was also lord of Asia Minor and the pharaohs of Egypt. He became the great king of Persia at the age of twenty-five," she said.

Nash gave her an encouraging nod. "Okay?"

"Alexander never lost a battle in the twelve years that he led his army across thousands of miles. He founded over seventy cities and created an empire that stretched across three continents covering around two-million square miles."

With eyes that gleamed, she took hold of Nash's hand. "*And*, he was only thirty-three when he died."

Nash retreated and took a seat. "So we're to look for the second carbonado in Alexander's birthplace?"

Calla nodded. "Nash. I know I sound crazy, but it's a hunch. It's all I can think of. Where else can we look? We don't have much time."

"Where in Greece?"

"Pella. The ancient capital of Macedonia."

Nash's lips curved into a smile. Calla was smart and knew what she was talking about. "Okay, but let me call someone I know in Virginia who's an expert on Greek history. He'll fill in any missing gaps for us. We should leave tonight," he said.

She smiled. "I was thinking of using a private jet. Allegra's."

Nash stole out of the room and made his way to the upper floor and then to the bathroom.He bolted the latch. Placing his ear against the door, he heard Calla make a few phone calls. He dialed a number in the US on his cell phone and moved away from the door. He had to dial two times before he got through as he pressed the smartphone against his ear. "Colton?"

"Yeah?"

"She knows about Pella. We leave as soon as flights are sorted."

"Okay, you know what to do."

Nash ended the call and sat on the edge of the bathtub.

He stared at the phone before switching it off. *Yes, I do.*

Staff hurtled to the nearest exits, some in a flurry, others more systematically. Smoke proliferated through the restaurant, descending from the kitchen.Women squawked as they hurled to the nearest exits; the men tried not to show any alarm. Mason was gone, and Eichel decided to move behind the horde of evacuees. Heavy smoke consumed the hallways, leaving an intoxicating dust cloud in its path.

Eichel hastened to the stairs and started a march down the escape passage. The exit led through a dark hall, lit by a single bulb, lined with several secured doors. Eichel followed the crowd, many of whom were coughing.A lone door stood at the bottom of the flight of stairs. As employees maneuvered the narrow staircase, a faint knock from within the steel frame of the concealed door sounded. "Someone is in there!"

Several people scrambled past him impelled by a desperate urge to flee.

None stopped to help.

"Did you hear that?" he shouted above the commotion. "Someone is trapped inside!"

He checked the visitor's badge on his jacket and slid it against the door reader.

It failed to open the lock as the banging inside the room intensified. Two male security guards scurried past him.He seized one by the arm. "Please, you must open the door. Someone is in there."

The first man galvanized into action and thudded on the door as those inside pounded louder.

"Okay, 'stand back," he told Eichel.

Eichel drew back as the first security officer swiped his card against the reader.The steel door clicked open, and the three men threw their combined weight against its resistance, forcing it open.Three tight-shouldered women filed out coughing as their tear-stung eyes tried to gain focus.

"Thank you!" said the first.

The guards marched them out to safety and pointed them in the direction of the evacuating crowds. Eichel intuitively scurried into the room to find stragglers. He took note of a fourth woman, benumbed on the floor.He darted to her and checked her pulse. She was alive but must have fainted in shock. He flung her over his shoulder and trudged with heavy feet toward the door. As he heaved their weights forward, he caught sight of a sign.

Classified File Room

Eichel tried to move his feet, but they wouldn't obey him. He glimpsed back.Tattered and dusted files in brown labeled boxes piled to one side of the room. The far end of the room stored a row of dated computer systems. *Must be the room where they digitize classified files.*

He picked up his pace, heaving the hundred and thirty pounds or so on his back to the main getaway route.When he stepped into the escape passage, a security guard patrolled the halls directing fleers.

Eichel forced himself to follow, then glimpsed back. "Please. Please. Take her out! She's unconscious and needs attention. I'll see if anybody else is hurt."

The security guard hesitated a moment and scrutinized Eichel from head to foot, his eyes falling on his visitor's badge before nodding. "Okay, hurry!"

Eichel shifted the woman onto the guard's shoulders and waited until he was out of sight before returning to the room.

The smoke had decelerated as he glimpsed back in the hallway to make sure he was alone. He padded the piles of boxes and continued to the shelves that stood next to the computer systems. He settled at a machine and pressed down the 'on' button.

The screens failed to respond. *"Mensch! Man!* Must've been automatically shut down as a security measure."

Nothing leaped out at him. He paced back to the boxes and checked each one until his investigative eye glanced at the top box on the second pile and its label.

CHAPTER 18

B*ingo!*
"This must be it!"
He hoisted the heavy box.It collapsed under its weight and spilled its contents over his boots.With his pulse threatening to set to charging he knelt on the floor and salvaged the stacks of bound documents. Soon, his eyes rested on a file.

TOP SECRET:
THE DEVERON MANUSCRIPT

He debated whether to take the whole thing. The decision that followed went against his conscience and every training he possessed. He considered the severity of escaping with it from the building given the mania caused by the fire.Eichel spotted two copiers by the door. Perhaps these hadn't been shut off. Seizing the files, he hastened to the first copier and checked it.Its mechanics roared into operation.

He unbound the Deveron papers and one by one and loaded as many as he could through the feeder. Quiet footsteps thudded the floor by the door, startling him. He pulled himself together and braced himself for an intrusion.

None.

The feeder swallowed more sheets, one paper at a time.

There was no time.

The sirens had stopped. He had to get out. Eichel had managed to copy close to half the twenty-page or so file. He retrieved the originals and bound them, before returning the folder to the discarded stack on the floor. The collapsed boxes wouldn't be questioned given the evacuation.

He placed the copies underneath his shirt and buttoned his jacket. Satisfied with his loot he re-joined the last evacuees out to the assembly area.

Once outside, he breathed in the fresh air, having ignored the amount of toxic smoke his lungs had inhaled during his thievery.He collapsed into a crossed-legged heap on the ground and leaned his head in his hands. A young Asian woman set a hand on his shoulder. "You all right?"

He glared at her. "Yes. What happened in there?"

"The fire started in the restaurant and spread quite quickly. We've been told that no one has been hurt."

Sixty minutes followed before the emergency authorities declared the premises fire and smoke-free. Eichel moved purposefully toward the exit. He kept a steady pace as he removed his spectacles and wiped the smoke off with his handkerchief.

A bitter discomfort settled in his gut. He'd lost his visitor's badge.

Eichel dabbed his brow.

CHAPTER 19

Calla stood on the balcony of her room at the Athina Villa Hotel overlooking the aqua shores of Istron Bay. Her eyes took in the mystical beauty of the beach, brimming with jagged coastlines, miles of archeological interests and the home of the kings of Macedonia.

Her curator eyes were pleased as the view burst with history. Rays of afternoon sun fell on her skin, giving it a warm tingle. She was hopeful.

Dressed in a white tank-top and khaki cargo shorts she tore off her light jacket and wrapped it around her waist.Calla took in the smell of barbecuing seafood from the patio as lunch preparations commenced on the villa grounds. She stepped back inside the room, picked up her bag from the bed and made a move for the door. After locking the room behind her, she made her way to the lobby.

Jack and Nash were already downstairs. Jack dabbed with his electronic equipment, mostly gadgets as Calla dropped her bag on the lobby chair.

"Are we ready?" she asked.

"Yes, except for this little baby that refuses to cooperate," Jack said fiddling with a miniature coil camera.

Nash set down the article he was reading in the American Journal of Archeology and raised his chin. "Yup, all set. I've arranged for us to visit the archeological site. Says here it was once the thriving capital of ancient Macedonia. We've got a private driver."

The concierge approached. "Your cab service will be here in about twenty minutes."

"Okay guys," Calla said. "Let's meet here in ten minutes. I'm going over to the gift shop. I need to find a local paper."

Nash slowly eased himself out of the chair. "Do you want me to come with you?"

"That's okay, I just want a phrase book," she said. "We may need some help out there."

"You sure?"

"I'll just be a moment, Nash."

Calla meant what she'd said. Even as a linguist Greek wasn't Calla's strongest language. She could get by comfortably, but if the truth were revealed, ever since Jack had returned the stone to her, she'd been feeling nauseous and needed a remedy.In the last hour, any movement toward the carbonado sent her heart pounding followed by horror chills.

She stepped into the small gift shop. Magazines and newspapers stood on a stand near the cashiers till. The walls were adorned with memorabilia, exhibiting a cluttered feel. Local attire, posters, picture frames, beachwear and tacky statues lined the narrow shelves, all giving the shop a somewhat peculiar charm. The shop assistant extended her a smile, followed by a local greeting.

Calla approached the counter. "Hi. I'm looking for something for a headache."

The woman reached for a box on a lower shelf behind her

counter. "Yes, I think I have some Ibuprofen or Aspirin that may help."

"Aspirin will do."

Calla waited patiently, her attention drawn toward the newspaper rack. She picked up the *Dnevnik* local newspaper and added it to her shopping. "How much do I owe you?"

"Three euros, twenty."

She handed the woman the exact change, collected her goods and slotted them in her bag. She turned to the exit, hardly noticing a lone woman who'd slipped into the shop. Thick, black kohl lined her eyelids, and she wore a gold and olive sequin headscarf above her peering eyes.

Calla stepped aside, but the Gypsy woman didn't move, nor blink. Her stare tore into Calla. Conscious of the piercing eyes that were focused on her, Calla managed a smile.

The woman shuffled closer and spoke in a tongue Calla had never heard before. Gypsies in Macedonia had their own Balkan Romani language, but the words that fell from the woman's lips didn't make any sense to Calla.

Calla glanced at the cashier who swore at the woman. The Gypsy woman's stare was unwavering as she leaned lightly into her.

Calla moved back. "I'm sorry, but I don't understand what you're saying."

A flicker of surprise appeared on the Gypsy woman who set a hand over her heart as if to express a pardon. She switched to thick, accented English. "Excuse me," she said. "I was so excited to see you, I just had to say I didn't realize you would be a woman. And a fine-looking one at that."

Calla's eyes narrowed as she took a step backward. "Excuse me?"

The woman dropped her hand. "I'm sorry. I didn't mean to embarrass you. I've waited all my life to meet you. Many of us have."

"What do you mean many of us? Who are you?"

The woman reached for Calla's hands. "I'm Aishe. May I look at your hands?" she said as she trailed a thin finger along the lines of Calla's palm. Without warning, she dropped Calla's palms and stared at her ankle. The woman squinted and read the marking on the visible birthmark. To this day it still resembled a tattoo. "Yes, you're the one. Be brave, my little one, the path you tread isn't easy."

"So I've been told."

"But you'll succeed."

Calla took a few steps backward, shying from the woman.

The woman's stare eased, and her eyes bulged as Calla opened her mouth to speak.

"Calla, the driver is here," Nash said.

He appeared at the entrance of the tiny shop, and his eyes moved to the Gypsy women. "We need to get going. There's just enough daylight left for a visit to the site."

"All right, I'll be right there."

She turned to finish her conversation with the woman who escaped through the south exit.

"Wait!"

She set off on a run after the woman who trotted at a speedy pace, past the shops, then through the main lobby before fleeing through the revolving doors.

Calla reached the main doors and turned both ways. Calla glanced both ways once more. The woman stood a few meters away with her back to Calla, hailing a cab. Soon, Calla caught up and set a hand on her shoulder. "Please, wait!"

The woman zipped her head around.

"What is it?" a perplexed Greek woman said.

Calla stuttered her words. "I'm sorry. I thought you were someone else."

Jack and Nash moved to her side.

"Someone you know?" muttered Jack.

Calla fixed her eyes on the woman as she stepped into the cab. "No, not at all."

Mason peered out the window. Samuel Riche's Mercedes journeyed up the driveway to the main house. The mogul's opportunist nature impressed Mason, his greed being the primary ingredient with which Mason sought to conduct business.

Mason watched him carefully and studied the notes Lillian had sent to his phone. Samuel, a sharp-witted businessman, had made his fortune modestly. Born the son of a civil engineer and a mother who ran a local bakery in Lyon, his family had struggled most of his infant and adolescent years. His patriotic father Pierre-Louis Riche had fought in the French Resistance during World War II and always instilled in him the vitality of self-sustenance, the notes continued to say.

As a pupil, he attended the Lycée Georges Pompidou in the suburbs of Lyon before graduating with a Master of Law degree from Université Paris X Nanterre. Riche went on to start his career as an investment bank trainee at Edmond de Rothschild. After several attempts, he co-founded Riche Enterprises, along with his father and brother. Riche Enterprises later merged with Louvel, a luxury goods conglomerate and Samuel remained the principal shareholder. Over the years he'd profited by taking large stakes in French listed companies, in particular, a building and construction group.

Mason looked up from his notes.

Samuel was smart. That's why he needed him. Mason thought back to his telepathic days when he could control a man's thoughts and actions by just looking at them. He was out of practice, but that would all end once he had the carbonados. Few knew what they were capable of, but he was ready. Only one thing stood in his way.

Cress.

Just a detail.

Right now he would attend to Samuel Riche.

Nash pointed to a four-wheel drive, Grand Cherokee parked behind the taxi. "This is our ride."

Calla gazed after the disappearing cab for several seconds before taking a step toward the vehicle. They climbed into the Jeep and drove off through the center of Pella and out toward Áno Koufália. With the windows down, winds wafted through the vehicle. Seated in the back with Nash, Calla leaned her arm against the open window, her mind engrossed in her surroundings.

The ride to the archeological site was swift and the ancient settlement housed the remains of an ancient palace, mosaics, tombs as well as a museum. Here lay the residues of the prosperous capital of ancient Macedonia. Though relatively intact little reminded them of its former glory.

They stepped out of the car and advanced toward the timeworn ruins. The museum was situated at the southeast foot of the hill where the palace of the Macedonian dynasty was once located. Calla glimpsed at the display of pottery, jewelry, and mosaics, her mind questioning if she would locate more symbols as those in Oxford.

Outside the ruins, Jack pulled out a radioisotope identifier, an instrument designed to detect, quantify and identify radioactive sources on the spot. "If we find anything like your first rock here this little guy will let me know."

Nash tread past the damaged pillars followed by Calla. He absorbed every inch of the site with his trained eye as Calla noticed his slight distance. Jack appeared more amused with his gadget than the actual hunt they were on as beads of sweat streamed down his forehead, triggered by the sun.

He approached Calla, fidgeting with yet another device. "I've not used this camera before. It's hooked up to a discrete spot on NovaSAR, a new government satellite. It gives me quicker access to information with any correlation to other materials of similar compositions in nature anywhere in the world."

Nash re-joined them. "By the way, Jack, did you get clearance for the use of that satellite space?"

"Of course not," Jack said.

The scalding sun beat on the back of Calla's neck. This wasn't how this trip was supposed to go. She rested on a nearby stone and pulled a bottle of chilled water from her bag. The fresh stream quenched her thirst as it slid down her parched throat. As she set her bottle down, she noticed a group of Japanese tourists approaching, led by an overenthusiastic tour guide.

The guide's voice spoke in musical tones full of enthusiasm and craft, completely contradicting Calla's state of mind. She pretended not to listen as they steered past her.The guide expounded his knowledge with expertise, his heavily accented voice projecting clearly as he enunciated. "One of the legends about Alexander the Great is that when he was in Gordium, in Turkey in 333 B.C., he was able to untie the Gordian knot. The knot is rumored to have been tied by the legendary King Midas."

"What is this knot?" asked a heat-distressed tourist.

"An ancient prophecy stated that the person who untied the Gordian Knot would rule all of Asia. Alexander the Great is believed to have undone the knot."

He paused with the skill of a learned professor, giving his audience time to digest the information. "It's believed he cut the knot with a sword."

Awestruck, some tourists started snapping pictures of the surroundings, while others, intrigued, tailed the guide hurling many questions at him. It was then that it dawned on Calla.

"Why didn't I think of this before? We're searching in the wrong place."

Nash and Jack shot her quizzical looks.

She shot up. "Alexander the Great did fulfill that prophesy and went on to conquer Asia. His seat of power isn't here. What we seek isn't here. I think I have unloosed our Gordian knot. We're in the wrong place."

Mason had put Samuel on his radar as one of the three most influential people he would target.

Greedy for more influence Mason knew how to give it to Samuel. At the same time, Mason could benefit from Samuel's control and reach. All he needed was the manuscript that would point him to the carbonados.

Mason heard the limousine pull up in front of his grand estate, and the moderately dressed French man emerged, escorted by an army of bodyguards.

Samuel's heavyset bodyguard rang the doorbell.

Mason watched from his phone CCTV camera feed.

"Mr. Riche," greeted Mrs. Hawke. "We're expecting you."

Samuel stepped in, exposing a pair of polished shoes and his square face revealed sincere, smiling eyes. With his sturdy build, possibly acquired playing a business sport like tennis. For a man of his abundant wealth style eluded him even though not a thread or a hair on him was out of place. Infamous for blending uncoordinated tones and hues, his dark hair, though clean and sculpted, was long overdue for a haircut.

Two of his emotionless bodyguards scuttled in after him while the other two remained outside by the car. Clad in dark clothing those inside took cues from him and stayed in the hallway.

Samuel followed Mrs. Hawke to the neoclassical drawing room. She made her way to the bar and busied herself, mixing a

Sambuca con la Mosca. "I believe this is how you like it. Mr. Laskfell will be down in a moment."

Samuel stared at the glass in her hand, before accepting the chilled drink. Mrs. Hawke stole out of the drawing room just as Mason descended the staircase. He nodded to her and reached into his pocket, fingering the microchips Jack had couriered that morning. Nestled deep inside his jacket's lining, a thin film of transparent, nano microchips reposed.

He slipped the bugging device onto his hand. Undetectable to the naked eye it was going to be an easy plant.Once secured, it was permanent and practically irreversible, a distinctive feature Mason had added himself. With the device safely in his palm, he stepped inside the salon. "Samuel, *mon ami*. You grace my humble estate with your presence, please sit down."

Mason shook Samuel's hand.

Done!

Samuel eyed Mason before taking a seat in a vintage armchair. "I like to know the people I deal with, but in your case, I've made an exception, Monsieur Laskfell. Your reputation precedes you," said Samuel, his upper-class English ringing with a sophisticated, French twang.

Mason took a seat opposite him. "I can see we've a lot in common. Thank you for your trouble in coming out here."

"I was curious. Your proposal on paper sounded too good to be true. I had to meet you in person and hear it straight from you."

Mason observed him with a meticulous air as Samuel crossed his legs. "I like your proposal. Can you really expand my global and political influence? I need to take a larger vote in the EU."

"I'm aware of your application for nomination as EU Commissioner for Economic & Monetary Affairs."

"That's where you come in. It's a steep bid."

"This fail-proof deal would guarantee not only a nomination but possible election."

"How will you achieve that?" Samuel said.

"Leave that to me. So far an EU accolade is missing from your resume. I know how to gain the votes you require, including access to diplomatic immunity."

"I assume you're well connected in global political realms."

"Call it a gift, Samuel. That's what I'm good at."

Samuel sipped his cocktail. "I've been very impressed with your brief, so I'm willing to give you a chance."

Mason braced himself against the seat and dusted his suit, removing a hair that had escaped his brush. "I'm flattered."

He opened a box of Gurkha Black Dragon cigars, offering Samuel one.

Samuel raised an eyebrow. "Isn't it a bit premature for celebrations?"

"I think we more or less agree on the proposal."

Samuel accepted a cigar from the hand-carved case and tapped it on the edge of the seat. "What interests me is the fine print."

Mason offered to guillotine his guest's cigar and lit it before handing it back. "Not sure what you mean."

Samuel puffed and blew the smoke away from him, sneering as Mason returned to his seat. "What am I missing here?"

"Let me worry about that, Samuel. This contract will enable you not only to expand your enterprise within the EU, but you can monopolize the US as well. You'll be able to conduct business, or politics for that matter, on your terms. You would be richer and more influential than you've ever imagined."

Samuel glared at him for a moment. "Money I have, what I lack is influence and appreciation. The economic weight the European Union has worldwide shouldn't be undermined." He tapped his cigar in a provided ashtray. "But what do you get out of this?"

"You read the terms of the agreement, I want you to employ one thousand employees of my choice across your businesses, no questions asked," Mason said.

"Is that all?"

Mason extinguished his cigar. "Mind you, they'll be qualified for whatever job they're given."

"It sounds like a family favor. But even I know you have no living family. Or am I wrong?"

Mason ignored his prying. "Have you signed the documents?"

Samuel shifted in his seat. "I have to be sure. Before I sign, I'll only ask one more time. What's the catch?"

"There's none. If you don't sign, I can easily find someone else," Mason said.

Mason knew Samuel was accustomed to negotiating the terms in any business affair, and Mason was the only man who could provide him the opportunity to become a global business influence, capable of implementing structural reforms, including the Single Market, which would serve Riche Enterprises well.

"Nothing is free or comes that easily," Samuel said.

"It's your call, *mon ami.*"

Samuel straightened his shoulders and rose, picking up the contract papers from the coffee table. He took his drink with him to the window overlooking the gardens.

His eyes narrowed. In an instant terror surfaced on his face. A swift bullet shot through the double windows, aimed right at the contract papers Samuel held in his hands.

"Get down!" The voice intuitively left Mason's throat as he took a dive behind his armchair.

Samuel cowered on the floor in time to avoid the sizzling ammunition that struck the edge of a Rembrandt hanging over the fireplace. His bodyguards darted in from the hallway and ascended on Samuel. For a good minute, no one spoke or moved a muscle.

Mason emerged from behind the armchair. "What the—"

Two of his security people, as well as Mrs. Hawke, scrambled in, all three clutching semi-automatic firearms.

"Go see who that was!" he said.

A beefy Ethiopian, part of Samuel's security team, hauled him upward. "Let's go, Mr. Riche! You're safer in your car."

They dragged him out, and within minutes his Mercedes accelerated off the estate, leaving a tire mark on the front lawn.

"Imbeciles!"

The remark left Mason's lips in blurts. With one glance at the window, he spotted his discarded business proposal on the floor.

Unsigned.

CHAPTER 20

DAY 9

5:20 P.M.
Via Di San Gregorio
Rome, Italy

Calla marched ahead of Jack with a focused gaze on the ethereal Colosseum ahead, the long-awaited destination of most pedestrians streaming alongside them.

"What makes you so sure, Calla?" Jack said.

She turned around and faced him as he questioned the quick flight they'd managed to get from Thessaloniki to Rome. Calla spoke words of conviction. "*Imperato Caesar Vespasi anus Augustus amphitheatrum novum ex manubis ac. fieri iussit.*"

"Huh! I'm an engineer, not a linguist. Help here?"

"That's the ghost inscription on the Colosseum, or at least as a few scholars have identified," Calla said.

Jack's quizzical look resurfaced. "Huh?" He shook his head. "By the way, when did Nash say he would join us?"

"He should be here soon. I'm not sure why he didn't travel with us."

"And here he is," said a voice behind them.

Nash appeared alongside them. "You forget that your phone has a great GPS tracking chip."

She eyed Jack. "Thanks to you."

Nash took the manuscript and studied the symbols to which Calla had referred. "I've heard about this. That construction of this Roman stadium may have been paid for with loot that Roman soldiers seized from the Temple in Jerusalem nearly 2000 years ago."

Calla repossessed the manuscript and glossed a finger over the words. "Correct. Allegra's notes say the manuscript could be about 2000 years old. The second dominance is linked to an event two thousand years ago. The clue is here."

Calla secured the manuscript in her shoulder bag. "We misinterpreted the translation and ended up on a detour to Pella."

Even as she spoke she challenged her own statement. Was it really a detour? What about the Gypsy woman?

She proceeded toward the lines that had formed outside the dramatic landmark, eager to progress into the ancient stadium. Rome was serene, a city where contemporary met ancient and neither felt out of place. Calla thought back to a time in her teens when she first came to Rome, starry-eyed at every monument, ruin, and museum she visited. Her love for history had been sparked then and continued to this day. She would always return to Rome, but these wouldn't have been her chosen circumstances.

"We need to find a quicker way in. The Colosseum will be closing soon," Jack said.

Nash glimpsed at Calla. "Didn't the Roman Empire reach its largest size under Trajan?"

Calla grinned, glad she had at least one member on board. "There was this one article in National Geographic. Let me see. I think I have it here."

The queue moved smoothly ahead. Calla took a step

forward and found the magazine clipping in her bag. "National Geographic describes the legacy of the Roman Empire in this article."

She ran her fingers over a passage she'd highlighted. "Rome's influence is enduring. It continues to affect much of modern life like language, literature, government, architecture, medicine, engineering, sports and even the arts. There's so much we owe to Rome. For one thing, many of the words I've just used have their roots in Latin."

"Impressive," Jack said. "But still lost as to why we're here."

"Two thousand years ago world dominance was based in Rome. That's why we need to be here. I found an obscure footnote in the manuscript. It says that the path we need to tread is the same as that of the gladiators, almost two thousand years ago," Calla added.

Jack gawked at the Colosseum's pillars and stones. "Why?"

Calla caught up with him. "Because the Colosseum was opened in 80 A.D. under Vespasian's son and successor, Titus. The reason we're in Rome is that as an emperor, Trajan's reputation survived nineteen centuries, more than any other ruler."

Jack narrowed his eyes. "And?"

"The display of the city's power was played out in the Colosseum," Nash added.

She stared up at the height of the stadium. "When I visited as a teenager, I remembered that the gladiators displayed one of the greatest tests of courage in history in the most powerful nation at the time."

Nash leaned against the stones waiting behind the other tourists. He nodded in agreement. "Power and influence can't be had without courage."

Calla's eyes caught his. He'd withdrawn a little. Did it have to do with her own disengagement? She turned forward and advanced with the moving line. *After all the months we've known each other, why now?*

225

． ． ．

Seven o'clock was the time of the last admittance into the Colosseum. When they made it to the ticket counter at 6:45 p.m., Calla paid for three tickets, and they trailed behind the stream of visitors. They traipsed through one of the eight arched entrances and ambled through the inner corridors.

Calla focused ahead and caught her breath in the stadium's inner court that once entertained up to 55,000 spectators. She had to agree with the guidebook. Despite being damaged over the centuries, the amphitheater was still extraordinary in stature and architecture.

They continued through the large terraced podium. Calla considered how many emperors and wealthy families had taken their places here, looking down their noses at average commoners.

It was nearing 6:55 p.m.

"Ladies and gentlemen, the Colosseum will be shutting its doors, please proceed to the main exit. We hope you've enjoyed your visit today."

The PA message was repeated in four languages. As the trio half listened to the announcement, they observed hordes of thwarted visitors making their way to the exit.

"Okay, guys," Calla said. "We're staying."

With the sun already descending, the lights came on, giving the Colosseum its vibrant glow. They plodded on behind the others. Nash spotted a secluded room in the lower galleries, a few feet from the ticket counter, and alerted the others.

Proceeding with stealthy movements, they halted next to the locked door. He fished out a navigator lock-scope and picked the lock.

In the darkness, Nash drew out a pocket torch from his combat pants and switched it on. Peering into the room he gave the all clear. They stole inside and searched for a spot to crouch. Calla and Nash located a half wall at the far end of the room and hunched behind it while Jack stooped behind an old wooden desk.

"What is this room?" Jack whispered.

"Must be an unfrequented storeroom of some sort. I read on the maintenance sheet that this room is closed from 6:30 p.m. With any luck we'll not be disturbed," Nash said.

Calla tried to get comfortable as she hunkered down on the cold stone beside Nash.

In the dark room, he caught her eyes. In the subdued light of his flashlight, his eyes narrowed. "We should wait an hour," he said.

His face was inches from hers in the minuscule space, and she hoped he wouldn't hear the pounding of her heart. With his nearness, she feared it would leap into a race.

Thirty minutes later, the ancient site fell silent, signifying the visitors' departure. The night staff hustled back and forth. The noise continued for several minutes until a static silence seized the air.

Calla checked the time on her smartphone. It was approaching 7:45 p.m.She searched for the architectural application she'd downloaded, a building plan of the Colosseum, including a classified surveillance schedule."There may be a night guard. We need to tread carefully," she said.

"Hey, you two, how much longer? My neck is killing me!" Jack said as he cowered behind the wooden table.

"Any minute now," Nash responded.

Light from the smartphone illuminated Calla's face as she spoke. "When I was here as a teenager, on a school trip, there was a man, a guide I think. He took us around and showed us an underground room. It looked more like a cage where the gladiators waited before they went onto the grounds."

Nash listened, a tone of sadness ringing in Calla's voice, each time she dug up the past. She swallowed hard. "There was a frame, which I thought was a door. It stood opposite the opening of the grated iron. I remember asking our guide, in broken Italian then, what it was for. He seemed quite taken aback that this frame that resembled a door had been discovered. I don't think he intended it to be seen."

"What did the door look like?" Jack asked.

"Like an arched entryway. He told me that nobody could see it. I thought he was mad. To me, the door was plain as day. Anyway, later I found out that none of the other girls had seen it."

"Did you ever find out what it was?" Nash said.

"Actually, I'd forgotten about it until now."

Calla shifted a little as her foot went to sleep. As she tried to stretch it out, it collided with Nash's thigh. He took her left foot and let it rest awhile on his lap.

Calla sagged against the wall, her voice weakening when she saw the position of her leg. "No. He told our class that it was nothing. Just a wrongly constructed door that led nowhere. He must've seen that the other girls were teasing. I didn't believe him then." She glared into his attentive eyes. "And I don't believe him now. That door may be exactly what we're looking for."

"Let me see your blueprint," Nash said.

She zoomed in on her mini screen.

He pointed to a corner on her image. "According to this, we would need to enter via this complex of rooms by this wall. The blueprint doesn't show the door either. But there may be a better way to see this. Once we get there, I'll use this." He pulled a cable-like metal coil from his slim backpack. It resembled a shower cord, only much thinner in diameter. "If we find an opening in the room this camera will penetrate or even x-ray through the walls."

Calla examined the camera, brushing his fingers slightly. "That's impressive."

Her eyes widened when she saw Jack shoot up. "Jack, get down! Not yet."

"I don't know about you guys, but I think we can go now."

They exchanged a grin. "Okay," Nash said. "I'll lead the way."

They moved toward the door. Nash placed his ear against the door frame.

Jack massaged the back of his neck, hopping with a leg cramp. "Surely if someone were going to hide valuable rocks they wouldn't pick a tourist place that is constantly under surveillance."

Calla laid a hand on Jack's shoulder. "Yes, Jack, but two thousand years ago this was not a historical monument but a place of trade, business, sport, entertainment and a meeting place for some of the most influential people in history. Think of it as Times Square."

She crept closer to the door as Nash inched it open.

"All clear. From now on not a sound," said Nash.

He listened and selected their next position before leading them prowling out of the room. They followed the global positioning system on Calla's phone, and when they'd swept twenty meters, Nash raised his right hand to signal movement.

Lights from the arched domes of the exterior walls provided enough illumination for the main courts and walkways. Nash searched for a concealed route as they crept over cobbled tiles and through dark passageways. Soon he came to a halt at what he believed was the corridor leading to the room Calla had described. "Jack, can you link up to the satellite? We need to know where the security cameras and the alarms are."

Jack fired up his electronic tablet and, within seconds, had located each alarm spot surrounding them. He steered them by navigating Nash past each one until they arrived at the desired spot.

"This is it," Calla said.

The only access to the room was through a dated iron cage.Nash tugged at its grilled front. It was sealed shut. He examined the lock. "There are several motion detectors here."

Voices in Italian sounded behind them. Tiptoeing to the far wall, they thrust their backs against it. The shadows camouflaged their agile frames as two guards strolled past arguing in Italian, sidestepping right past without a glance.

The trio held back until the guards had turned the corner.

Nash set his hand on the cage lock. Using a night-vision lens, he considered the best way to push it open. He pulled out a tiny cylinder from his backpack and opened the screw lid. He then poured the contents into the lock.

"What's that?" Calla said.

"A little trick." He smiled. "It's Aqua Regia solution and melts quite a few metals."

The lock broke open.

"That was quick," Jack extorted.

Nash placed the empty bottle in his backpack and pulled out his miniature torch once more. He searched the room through the grid cage and pulled the iron structure. It screeched open. Their attention went straight to the back wall.

An abrupt clank sounded behind them.

They stiffened in their tracks. Calla and Nash zipped their heads round in time to catch Jack plunge to the floor with his hand on the base of his neck.

His tablet smashed beside his collapsing body.

RICHE ENTERPRISES, LONDON OFFICES

"Papa, I need to speak to you!"

Eva ignored the promptings of the secretary trying to ward her off as she scurried into the boardroom.

"Miss Riche, your father is in a crucial board meeting!"

Eva wasn't fazed. She barged right in the middle of a presentation her father was giving to the board of nine smartly-clad members of his company.

Samuel tightened his lips and glimpsed over at Eva who'd crossed the length of the twelve-seat board table and made her way straight to his side.

The board members sat observing the disturbance. Samuel set down the presentation pointer beside his seat and clicked off the slides.

Eva caught a glimpse of his latest endeavor, an oil rig planned for Africa.Not long ago a reserve of potentially 2.5 billion barrels of crude oil was discovered along Uganda's border. Samuel had decided to bargain with the East African nation's government, hoping to secure an oil production arrangement. The African oil, which lay underneath the forests and lakes lining the border with Congo, appeared to be his next pet project. Samuel scanned the papers on the table and slowly pulled down his reading glasses.

"What is it now, Eva?"

Eva soaked up the attention, pleased that she could still command the attention of her father.

She held her head high. "I want to start my own media company. I need you to help me."

Samuel eased into a seat. "I'm intrigued, Eva." He tilted his head. "What new idea is twirling round in your mind?"

She hunched over him, ignored the others in the room and whispered in his ear. "I need to follow a story."

Samuel sneered. "Even though you're not a man you have more fortitude than my two boys put together. And why can't you do this at the Guardian?"

"I quit."

Samuel set his pen down on the table. "Interesting, and why may I ask?"

"That idiot boss of mine wouldn't let me follow the Deveron

story." She stared at him, hoping he followed her drift. "It was stolen in Berlin. Do you know about the Deveron Manuscript? Governments and individuals are looking for it."

"Is that so?"

"Yes!" She thrust a German newspaper clipping under his nosed. "The German government is on a fierce hunt for it. I want to investigate more."

"Eva—"

She leaned forward. "It will be a story worthy of the Albert Londres Prize!"

Samuel squinted an eye. "I doubt that."

Murmurs whispered across the room.

Samuel rose from his seat and strolled to the window overlooking London's skyline. He turned to face the board. "Putting aside Eva's own ambitions, owning a media conglomerate wouldn't be such a bad idea," he said. "Fellow board members, this way we can further our plans and actually control the public perception of our business interests, including this venture into African oil resources."

He swept back to the table and glared each member in the eye. "How does that sound? Wouldn't adding a media arm to Riche Enterprises be in our interests? Think of it, we could control world perceptions around the new oil rig."

The board each added their opinions.

Some were convinced and one or two were not.

Eva interjected. "If this media company ends up with the only exclusive to what could turn out to be the story of the year then I think it is in your interests to give this some thought *and* a quick decision."

She marched around the room, commanding each member's attention.

Her persuasive manner infuriated cynical onlookers. "I intend to get to the bottom of the Deveron secrets that our governments are hiding."

Samuel took over. "I think we can take a vote here."

He turned to the board secretary. "Ms. Robertson, could you please take minutes on this?"

Raphael Leadstone, a spirited, thirty-something board member interrupted. "I object. What does Eva know about running a media company?"

Eva shot him a daring glance. Raphael had walked out of Harvard Business School with a coveted MBA. He was young and ambitious, in many ways like her. Samuel employed him straight out of business school and had groomed Raphael for a few years now and he'd ascended to a seat on the board quite quickly.

Eva pouted. She knew he saw him as the third son he never had in her.Her lips gathered into a pout as Raphael persevered with his suave tone. "This is another one of those activities we'll throw money at and, when our dear Eva decides she needs a new project, we'll have to clean up the mess after her."

Opposing board members nodded.

Raphael continued. "There was the cosmetics company that folded, leaving a stream of liabilities with which we had to contend. Three years ago, Eva pursued an interest in establishing a girl's college in France, another catastrophe." Raphael turned Eva's way. "I propose we appoint a Chief Executive from the board."

"Why?" Eva said, glaring at Raphael.

"In the interest of Riche Enterprises," he said.

She twiddled with her thumbs. Seven of the nine board members agreed to the proposal.

Samuel marched over to Raphael. "Raphael, I'm appointing you as the new Chief Executive of Riche Media."

Raphael shot Samuel a wide-eyed look. He'd obviously not seen that coming.Heat rose to Eva's cheeks and she gazed at her feet for fear of erupting.

"Okay, the decision has been made. Raphael will steer this media company with Eva as Director," he cast Eva a disdainful stare. "And Chief Editor."

Eva shot up and paced the room before settling in a spare chair by the window. *"Couchon!"*

THE COLOSSEUM
ROME, ITALY

It came swiftly. An oversized outline skulked from behind a pillar in the shadowy hallway. Nash vaulted back, evading an abrupt knockout from the attacker's left hand. He lunged forward, caught the attacker's arm and shoved him backward with a violent heave.

The impact threw their attacker to the ground briefly. Undeterred he sprang to his feet and wrenched forward with a weapon.

Calla examined the dolch brass. A short, gladiator stabbing sword, ideally suited for brutal, close combat. She broke away from his strike only to grasp that whoever he was he'd armed himself with weapons she'd only housed in museum vaults. Had Watcher followed them to Rome?

When their assailant surfaced in the dim light, negotiating calculated steps, she observed his eccentric attire as they stood cornered at the far end of the room. Their eyes followed his heavy paces. His digital form veered toward them, his face covered with a brass visor helmet, matched with a round shield and metal shoulder pieces. His attire was completed with both leather, elbow and wristbands and metal greaves shielding his shins.

Calla was beginning to believe he was a product of teleportation, a research topic in quantum mechanics. But was is possible? Could one hypothetically move between one place and another without crossing the physical space between them.

Nash's eyes scrutinized the heavy armor.

The attacker was a *Gallus. A gladiator!* The gladiator took a protesting lunge forward, bending his massive knees as he reached for Calla. He moved his large hands to her throat, catching wrists instead and clamped them above her head while his free hand thrust his sword at Nash.

Nash was knocked off his feet. He flailed forward for the gladiator's bicep. Throwing his entire weight in the attack, Nash clamped the weakened arm and gnarled it under the gladiator's backbone.

The movement freed Calla, who gasped for breath and staggered a few steps away with a quick shiver of apprehension. She glanced upward. The man's height overpowered her, standing at all of seven feet.

The gladiator dropped his sword, tugged his arms out of Nash's grasp and spun around. He pounced to one side, reaching for his discarded sword and swung its double-edge, charging once more at Nash, who stood positioned in the analysis of the gladiator's techniques.

Nash's eyes narrowed into the assailant's approach without an ounce of fear or hesitation evident in his stance.

The gladiator heaved forward.

Nash sidestepped as the gladiator swept past him and collided with the wall behind him. Calla glanced over at Nash, the shudder in her veins welling into determination. She made a visible effort to pull herself together and with every ounce of courage took a strong step forward, only to witness the heavy man rise, grip Nash by the neck, and knee him with a thud that propelled him senseless.

Nash slammed against the rear wall of the cage and dropped to the floor unconscious. Calla darted toward Nash's limp body and held back a choking cry. The giant warrior threaded toward her with a grin of amusement as she hunched over Nash's wearied body. With an instinct to run she fought fear on all fronts and calculated her options.

Fight him!

She couldn't tear her eyes off the double-edged sword and

the injury it could cause. She sprang up and retreated, her gaze fixed on the silhouette inching in her direction. Calla failed to see his face and as the warrior cornered her at one end of the cage. The action gave her no passage for escape. He stood a mere three feet from her, sliding his fingers up and down the blade.

A ray of light from the arched doorway hit his face and, for the first time, she caught a glimpse of dilating pupils through slanted eye holes.His excessive breathing and muffled grunts filled her ears.

Is this it? The gladiator stepped back and drew a second sword from behind his shield.

Calla shut her eyes. *No!*

When no movement followed, she threw them open and observed him as he held out a second sword to her.

"Come on! Fight back."

His grunted command stunned her, and the weighty sword fell at her feet.He took a step back and with flat feet, braced himself for the attack.

She reached for the ancient weapon and studied the pommel, adorned with gold and silver. Its weight alone astounded her and almost pulled her down.

A new level of adrenaline shot through her charged veins. She raised the weighty metal, drawing it back in her outstretched arms, a newly acquired craft. Calla had never held a sword in her life and had also never fought a man, let alone a seven-foot-one.

He stomped forward with burdened steps and pointed his weapon at her throat. Calla's arms and legs moved with confident skill. She stood perpendicular to her opponent and thrust the sword directly at his chest.The swords met in perfect match.Close to two and a half feet shorter she booted him in the groin, causing him to lose his grip on his shield.

He staggered backward and broke out of the cramped cage.

"Coward!" she shouted. "Ever fight a girl?"

She pursued.

Clashing swords they continued to the bridge levels above the underground rooms in the main auditorium space. Not knowing with what power she battled he was no threat to her as she stretched a high kick to his midriff.

He dropped back to the cobbled turf.She leaped onto his chest with her steel pointed at his neck.Heaving and gasping for air the gladiator tore off his helmet as a sign of surrender.

Calla wanted to see his face, and with what audacity he dared interfere with their research.

As the helmet slid off the first thing she noticed were his piercing eyes, then his white beard and cropped white hair, yet his face showed little sign of aging.

"You made it back?" he said.

He'd used the Roman vernacular.

Latin.

Calla squinted, attempting to understand his drift. She recoiled, tossing the cumbersome sword to the ground. "Who are you?" she said in fluent Latin.

He angled upward. "You're the true proprietor of the carbonado you've come for. You must be the one the rock has waited for all these years. Don't you remember me?"

Calla slowly shook her head.

"Come with me. I have something you need," he said as he pulled himself upright.

Calla glimpsed behind her, her thoughts on Jack and Nash.

The gladiator read her mind. "They'll be fine. We don't kill. It's not our purpose.We train. Come with me."

Calla let him lead the way as she stalked with caution. They proceeded back to the caged room.

"I remember you," she said. "You were that tour guide!"

He spun around having now minimized to her five-foot-eleven height. How on earth had he shrunk? They crossed three hundred yards to get back to the room before reaching the iron gate.Jack lay still, but breathing on the cold stone. The gladiator stepped over him, crossing over to the back wall where Nash also lay still, breathing steadily.

The door stood visibly in the middle of the back wall. It swung back as Calla made her approach. Calla gawked at the contents inside as she stepped into the unique space that resembled a weapon storeroom. Filled to the brim with ancient weaponry of various natures, the gladiator beamed, proud of his trophy room. "These are souvenirs from those who've tried to get what you want."

"What happened to them?" Calla asked.

He smirked. "They walked away. Alive."

Calla's fingers settled on her parting lips at the sight of a gun among the plunder, the most modern of all the weapons. She grasped it in her trembling hands and noticed it was a Secret Intelligence Service P99 Commemorative. She'd seen one before at the ISTF Museum in London.

Following her gaze, the gladiator slowly reached for it. "That, I took from your parents."

"My parents?"

"Yes."

"They were here? When?"

"I really can't tell. It's been years."

"How do you know they were my parents?"

"A young couple arrived here. It must've been at least twenty-five or so years ago. Or maybe more, I can't remember."

He glared at her. "Just like you and your friends they tried to get to this room."

He fished around through the weaponry and produced a wooden box that he presented to her. "This is yours, I believe."

She took the container, identical to the first one they'd obtained previously in Oxford.

"Open it," he said.

Inside she found another carbonado. This one glowed red, gold and blue, the colors of fire.

"Protect this well," warned the gladiator. "There so many

greedy hands looking for that. They're not to be trusted. You've very little time left to unite all three stones."

"But you were saying something about my parents—"

When she moved her eyes from the stone and glanced up, the warrior had vanished.

Jack stirred.

She scuttled back into the caged room. Behind her, with no cautionary warning, the door guarding the weaponry slammed shut.

Soundless.

She studied the space. Only an arched slump in the wall remained in its place. She glanced down at the container in her hands. Had she imagined the whole thing? Jack moved a pained leg as Calla threw herself at his side. "Jack, are you okay?"

He rubbed his neck. Jack regained consciousness and took in a deep breath. Nash roused and rose slowly dusting off his shirt.He reached for his backpack, and his eyes settled on her hands. "What do you have there?" As if suddenly remembering his ordeal he drew in a deep breath. "And what the heck happened to that guy?"

---

1 1 :43 A.M.
TAJANI MARKET PLACE
AGRA, INDIA

Mason sat in a clammy rickshaw, swatting flies away like a common street rogue. The breeze filtering through the open vehicle carried caustic aromas from the marketplace only a few yards from where he sat.

The scents arrested his nostrils. *Could it be turmeric, saffron or Asafoetida?*

Agra, the Hindustani capital bordering the banks of the

Yamuna River, sizzled with an unforgiving scorch, even in April.

Though spring the weather hovered at thirty-three degrees centigrade, a few degree points above his comfort level. He observed busy pedestrians going about their business in the bazaar. Several children played in the dirt with makeshift toys they'd made themselves out of metal scraps stemming from ignored rubbish heaps along the side of the road. It was innocent play, unmarred by the materialistic tendencies he had grown accustomed to in the Western world.

The muggy air forced beads of sweat to collect on his arms, dampening his cotton thin *Kurta*, the traditional clothing for men he'd been given at the airport. Rupert Kumar had insisted he blend in, sending him a driver with a brand-new *Kurta* to pick him up at New Delhi's Indira Gandhi International Airport.

Kumar had insisted they meet here at the bazaar in Tajani. Mason disliked being kept waiting. That was his privilege. Anyone who worked with him or for him knew that.He glimpsed at his watch. They were ten minutes late.

It wasn't getting any cooler.

He grimaced at the idea of Kumar, the best-kept secret in the industrial world. Kumar had more global financial influence than many cared to admit. Perhaps it was because by looking at him his comportment would reveal nothing of the sort. He had discovered three oil reserves on land he owned, all purchased within the last few years. So far no one had questioned it. One was in South Liaodong Bay, another in Kenya and a third along Brazil's south-eastern coast. The three reserves together rivaled those of Saudi Arabia, and Libya put together. That fact alone meant prominent individuals would court him.Mason needed to schmooze him first.

Mason leaned back on the ripped faux leather seats. He tried to disguise his irritation at the tardiness by watching the streams of tourists make their way to the grounds of the Taj

Mahal. He could understand why Kumar had always stayed true to his Indian traditions by settling back in his home city of Agra. The place enchanted him with its spiritual customs, architecture, and people.

The Taj Mahal stood as an idyllic background for their appointment asMason continued waiting in the sweltering rickshaw. Kumar had insisted he would find him and not the other way round. *Fool!*

"That color doesn't suit you, Mason. You seem a little out of place here!"

The high-pitched holler came from across the road on the edges of the market stalls. Kumar beamed a wide-tooth grin, parading in a yellow and white thread embroidered *Kurta* himself. Mason raised an eyebrow. For a man of his stature, Kumar wasn't escorted by hoodlums as with most billionaires.

Kumar looked both ways before crossing the colorful street bursting with rickshaws, cows left to their own devices, and several Hindustani Ambassador Cars huffing out black soot as they drove past.

Mason stepped out onto the pavement. As he paced forward, he scrolled through classified ISTF images on his smartphone. *Yes, that's him.*

When Kumar reached his side, he set an arm around Mason's shoulders. "Please, let's take a walk."

Just past high noon, the marketplace populated with scores of shoppers, tourists, and locals. Several pedestrians made their way up through the lush gardens along the riverfront terrace toward the Taj Mahal, the epitome of Mughal art.

Mason studied the eminent Islamic mausoleum that seemed almost out of place in the urban setting, with its pristine marble façades and cross-axial symmetry. Known as the dwelling of a 'queen in paradise,' its palace gardens, fit for the nobles, lined both sides of the river.

"Rupert, I'm not sure I'm a fan of your choice of venue to do business," Mason said.

Though a skinny man, with quite a musical Urdu accent, nothing about him resonated with witlessness.

Kumar grinned. "That's the problem with you Mason, you're too highbrow. You need to take time to enjoy life."

Mason frowned.

He tried to keep up with Kumar's pace who, though short, promenaded with a swift pace.

"Where are we going?" Mason asked.

A toothless beggar slouched toward them with his scrawny, outstretched arms. Mason waved him away, and the beggar turned to Kumar, soliciting money or anything that he would part with. Kumar spoke a few Urdu words to the panhandler and handed him enough rupees for bread and a meal at the local roadside *Dhaba*. In gratitude, the vagabond blessed him with a musical chant.

Mason disapproved. "Why do you fuel overt crime, Rupert? You know he's going to spend it on worthless drugs or alcohol."

Kumar's scrutinizing eyes searched Mason. "You miss the point. It's the principle. What he does is his affair but wouldn't it be a tragedy to just walk by."

Mason sneered.

Kumar astounded him. He'd always supposed him shrewd and greedy like the rest of them. His plan couldn't fail with this lenient temperament.

They reached the end of the bazaar where two men met them and directed the pair through a dappled alley. Mason peered back trying to retrace his steps.

"Don't worry, you'll find your way back," Kumar said.

Mason puckered his brow and kept pace as they came to a gated, marble court that secured a large red-bricked estate, a modest home by Mason's standards. Within its multi-cusped open veranda, gaunt cows lurked in peace, escorted by a few servants. Unlike the youngsters, he'd seen in the streets the children here were well fed. They romped in the court, jesting with commercial water pistols. When they saw the men approach they greeted them with reverence and carried on about their games.

Mason imagined most of the people around were family members, perhaps household attendants.

Kumar steered Mason through the court and up the ornate arched entrance. "Please remove your shoes, it's a tradition in my home."

Mason was scantily dressed by his measure. *What will he ask me next?*

They strolled into an ethnic-decor salon, with its floor-level, seating arrangement. The room was embellished with sheesham wood. Low furniture and vibrant silk cushions adorned the seats. Mason scanned the room with an approving eye, admiring the multi-colored curtains, the only shield to the invading sun rays.

Kumar hitched himself in a crossed-legged position on one of the floor cushions. "Please, take a seat."

Mason followed suit.

In streams of two, traditionally clothed servants attended to them. One balanced a silver washbasin and towel for them to wash their hands. Several minutes later they served flavorsome vegetarian samosas and *Gulab Jamuns*, local, dulcet dumplings.

"*Gulab Jamuns* are traditionally made with thickened milk, soaked in rose-flavored sugar syrup," Kumar said picking up another sweet."You should try these also. These are delicacies in our country."

Mason recognized the sweets, having sampled some in London. He reached for one and set his teeth into its stickiness.

Kumar turned to the attentive servants. "Please leave us."

They scuttled out of the room. Mason eased into the silk cushion, grateful for the chilled house, which made the high temperatures bearable. Without an air conditioner, the interiors remained cool, thanks to the marble floors.

"Mason, I like your proposal," said Kumar. "I understand that you can provide the intelligence and technology to construct sophisticated rigs for my three plants. You see, I may own the land with the oil, but it's worth nothing unless it's properly extracted."

Mason took in his stare. "I've had my own ISTF consultants evaluate the area, and yes, there's a lot of oil there, especially in Kenya. My people have even drafted the blueprints for your rigs, making sure the latest technologies will be employed for extraction."

"Tell me more."

"My oil drillers have pioneered yet another new technology. Spindle ACCO Drilling Group that manages drilling in several oil fields has completed four successful rotary drilled wells. That'll be more than suitable for your purposes."

Kumar reached for another sweet. He edged forward. "What's your real price, Mr. Laskfell?" He glanced down at a stock of carefully worded documents. "It says here you only wish for me to employ one thousand of your people in exchange for your services."

Those people had to settle within Kumar's empire before the end of the month. *Why does the fool care what I get?* Mason reached for a napkin and wiped his hands. "That's right. They'll be qualified."

"I can't imagine anyone giving away something so valuable for such a ridiculous bargain." He fingered the papers and shoved them in front of Mason. "Here are the signed papers, with one condition." Kumar leaned back on the cushions. "The deal is only valid after my rigs have been built."

Damn fool!

CHAPTER 21

RICHE ENTERPRISES MEDIA OFFICES
CENTRAL LONDON

Eva slid her fingers along the bubble-wrapped desk and chair that had been delivered the previous night. She'd selected only Parnian designed furniture. A small outlet in East London had stocked a few items that they could provide quickly. More was on the way. This was nothing like that cheap stuff she'd had to sit on in her last office. As Chief Editor and Director, she could command this office as she wished.

Eva plopped into the chair and admired the executive Radius desk that didn't disappoint, even for its dear price. The leather chair descended back into a comfortable slouch. *You'll eat your words soon, Alex.*

She stretched for the phone. Eva had requested the business systems department for a secure line.She dialed a Berlin number. Over the years she'd established contacts inside the Berlin police force, however shrewdly. It all started with an old German boyfriend after university. He'd ended up in Berlin as a police officer. Eva wasn't sure why.

They'd stayed in touch.

Time to call in old favors. Berlin was an hour ahead. She tried his cell phone.

No answer.

She left a voicemail, fibbing about a trip she was planning before placing the phone in its cradle. Someone had to know more about the Deveron.

This was the second time she'd contacted the Berlin police seeking information on who was in charge of the Deveron and Pergamon case. She breathed in the newness of her office, barely ready to function as a full-fledged newspaper. She dialed another number in Berlin, the Berliner Zeitung, a local newspaper company.

A woman picked up. *"Ja?"*

"Hello, Frau Fuhrmann. You might remember me. We covered the Berlinale, the film festival not too long ago. This is Eva Riche, the journalist from London."

"Ah, ja," said the confident voice, who spoke with the elegance of refined English, even though her pronunciation wasn't quite there. "Must be quite early in London. Are you working on a story?"

"Yes and I wonder if you can help me?" Eva said. "I'm covering the recent happenings at the Pergamon Museum. I'm following the investigation. Tell me, do you know who's covering the piece for the Berliner Zeitung?"

Heavy breathing, followed by a pause, hovered on the line.

Eva's breathing intensified. "I'm looking for a contact in the police investigation team."

Frau Fuhrmann chuckled. "Ah, Eva! Always on the go. I remember you well. You were the glitzy reporter mixing with the stars at the film festival after parties. I remember the press often mistook you for a film star yourself."

Eva bit her tongue. That was the exact image she wanted to eradicate. She'd been a bit of a party socialite, having naturally settled into it. Her work then was the gossip column for the Guardian.

Frau Fuhrmann snickered. "What would you want with such a high profile case? Even our journalists are struggling to get the exclusive."

Eva stopped herself from swearing. Before she could interject the German reporter proved to be a little helpful. "My colleague Bernard may know. Just give me a second."

The phone went on hold. Eva drummed her fingers on the bubble-wrap as the call-hold music screeched in her ear. Within seconds Frau Fuhrmann was back on the line. "The inspector you want is Raimund Eichel. He's in charge of the investigation. But I understand he's not taking any press interviews. He likes to work in isolation and away from the curious eye of media speculation."

Eva cradled the phone and turned around on her swivel chair, glancing out the window at the morning sunrise view. "Do you have a number I can call?"

"Hold on a second."

More jostling came on the other end of the line before Frau Fuhrmann returned to the call. "I have a favor from Bernard. Here's a number for Eichel's office in Berlin."

Eva took the number down. "Thank you, Frau Fuhrmann. I look forward to seeing you soon. You know, I've my own paper now."

"How nice."

Frau Fuhrmann voiced her goodbyes and hung up. Eva caught a glimpse of Mark, the personal assistant she'd hired at a moment's whim. He'd come early as instructed to start his new job and crouched over his computer, attempting to connect his monitor, aided by the information technology staff. She closed the door, picked up the phone and dialed the number Frau Fuhrmann had given her.

"Hallo," said a man's voice. *"Peter Manuel hier."*

Eva didn't speak a word of German. "Hello. My name is Eva Riche calling from London, do you speak English?"

"A small bit," said the man in a scruffy, German accent.

Eva took a breath. "Am I speaking to Raimund Eichel?"

"Nein. No. This is Peter Manuel, his deputy. How can I help you?"

"Can I talk to Mr. Eichel?"

"He's not here. What is your business?"

"Where can I reach him?"

"What's your business?"

A lie wouldn't hurt. He wouldn't put her through if she admitted she was from the press. *Flattery always works.*

"I'm interested in security systems that can be employed in large companies. I own a segment of Riche Enterprises in London. I've heard that Mr. Eichel is an expert on the subject. I believe he would be able to advise me."

Peter's voice grew louder. "I know the Riche group of companies well. I even applied several years ago at their German branch in Stuttgart. Herr Eichel is in London until tomorrow. But I'll give you his cell phone number."

That was easy.

She jotted the number down. "Where's he staying in London?"

"I believe he's at the Hilton in Kensington."

"Thank you, Peter. You were most helpful."

Eva smiled to himself. Peter hadn't followed protocol.

Eva dialed the cell number.

Eichel was asleep in his Hilton hotel room. His half-groggy eyes focused on the buzzing noise on his bedside table.

He extended his hand and grasped the phone.

"Hello, Mr. Eichel. You might recall we met some years ago in Berlin?"

"Who am I speaking to? How did you get this number?"

"My name is Eva Riche. I need your help with something. I'm currently doing investigative research on the disappearance of the artifacts from the Pergamon Museum, can you help me?"

"Are you a journalist?"

Eva ignored the question at the risk of a hang up. "Could I meet you today? I understand you're in London and in charge of the investigation."

"*Fräuline*, please call my office. They'll give you the official statement. I'm not taking any interviews."

Eichel hung up and struggled out of bed. Rubbing his eyes, he rose fully awake, accustomed to early wake-up calls.

He swore. "Nosy journalists! They've always distracted me from doing my job. Morons! They just get in the way."

8:00 P.M.
WALDORF ASTORIA HOTEL
NEW YORK CITY

Margot cantered to the lounge chair and cranked her neck muscles. She ran her hands through her short black locks. Which part of her mixed race background was dominant, the Polish roots of her mother or her Zimbabwean ancestry on her father's side? Had birth on US soil overridden both? She would never know given the premature death of her immigrant parents.

It had been a hard week. The campaign was in full swing in Wisconsin, Maryland and the District of Columbia. Margot Arlington, Governor of Indiana, could hardly have spared this distraction at a crucial point in her presidential campaign. These were important rallies. The Arlington camp believed that the results in Wisconsin could help boost Margot to victory in the popular vote in the elections, now only eight months away. This would deliver a crushing blow to her opponent.

Margot stood observing the New York skyline from the height of the landmark Waldorf Astoria Hotel. She couldn't afford this break in New York, but it was worth it. She'd come too far. Not too long ago she'd been flipping hamburgers and running from one beauty pageant to another in an attempt to please her insufferable mother. Frustrated with this charade Margot wanted what she called 'a real job.'

At eighteen she enrolled for her bachelors in political science at Indiana State University and later graduated with a Juris Doctor from Notre Dame Law School. Her determination and austere persistence were rewarded with admission to the Bar of the state of Indiana. She astounded her mother all the way to her election as Governor of Indiana, a vital triumph for Margot. Now her eyes were set on an even higher trophy, the presidency of the United States.

Job creation across the country and the economy were to be the focus of her campaign. Margot hoped that her background wouldn't betray her. Her frequent appearances before conservative groups and in the news media had given Margot opportunities to woo crucial support after her unsuccessful campaign for the Republican nomination four years earlier. Many, though, had been doubtful of her convictions.

"Malcolm?" Margot said.

Malcolm, her faithful aid, barely out of graduate school, poked his balding head through the door.

"Mr. Laskfell will be arriving any minute. Do you have the tickets?" she said.

Malcolm nodded and slipped back into the office part of the suite.

He'd been given strict instructions. The Republican Party had been kept on a need to know basis about her dealings with

Mason. She'd instructed Malcolm to keep her communications with Mason confidential and lied, claiming he was a distant relative. "No one in the party is to know of Mason's proposal," she'd told the ambitious aid.

With a hard determination to rise within the ranks of the Republican Party the aid had to succumb to her wishes.

How hard could it be? If Mason helped her get elected, all she needed to do was make sure one thousand of his people were employed in America. She didn't care who these people were.

Malcolm reappeared. "Mrs. Arlington, Mr. Laskfell is downstairs in the lobby. Are you sure you don't want me to come along?"

"No, this is just a social call. You're done for the evening," Margot said.

"Here are the Met Opera tickets you requested. Two tickets for Richard Wagner's *Der Ring Des Nibelungen*. Sounds promising."

Margot smirked. It didn't matter what they were going to see. She'd picked this place for its anonymity. She needed more support and money for the rallies. Mason could provide that incognito.

She wandered into the grand elevators on her floor whose doors were cast in nickel and plated with bronze. On the ground floor, she rambled past the prominent murals in the Park Avenue lobby dating back to 1929 before spotting Mason smoking a cigar in a lazy armchair.

He sported an impressive Bottega Veneta tuxedo and held out a hand to lead her to his Rolls-Royce Phantom limousine.

They exited the building into New York's early evening as the driver pulled the car door open, allowing them to settle in the seats of the car.

Eva had covered more ground than she'd expected for the first day. The clock in her office read 12:40 p.m. She'd spent the good part of the morning researching anything she could find on the Deveron Manuscript. Surely Eichel wouldn't be in his room forever.

Could she take a chance? She knew the hotel well and perhaps she could bribe a few willing money-makers. She dialed Mark's extension. "I'm going out now. Cancel all my meetings for the day, especially the one with Raphael."

Mark nodded trying to keep up with who Raphael was. On her way out, Eva grabbed her coat from the hook by the door and darted out of the building with determined haste.

Kensington Hilton stood in the leafy district of Holland Park. Eva parked her white Bentley in the hotel underground garage and made her way to the elevators that led onto the hotel lobby. As Eva approached the front desk, a silver-haired hotel receptionist leaned his ear over a phone receiver, calming an annoyed customer. With an impatient air, she placed her hands on her hips tapping her stiletto until he concluded his conversation.

He set the receiver down and beamed a smile at her. "Good afternoon."

"Hello," she said with a confident drawl, exaggerating her French accent. "I was supposed to meet my husband here. He's in town from Berlin, on business. Could you tell me what room he is in?"

The man deliberately lowered his head and studied her. "What's your husband's name?" he asked.

"Raimund Eichel."

"Let me see." He typed on his machine. "Ah, here he is. I'm afraid he's not in at the moment. His key is here. Perhaps you can wait for him in one of our waiting areas."

"Couldn't I just wait in the room? You see," she leaned

closer, the fragrance of her perfume whiffing past his nostrils, causing him to twitch his nose as she tossed a flirtatious wink. "I want to surprise him."

A gasp escaped the receptionist's throat. "Technically, we're not allowed—"

Eva didn't want to waste time. She drew out a wad of twenty-pound notes and made sure he saw them as she slipped them under some papers on the desk.

"Listen." She read his name badge. "Gustav? I'm a busy woman. I'm sure this will help any trouble I've put you through."

Gustav slid the money back at her. "Madam, I'm sorry."

"Don't expect any business from me or Riche Enterprises in the future."

She spun on her heels and inched toward the elevators, glancing back once to see if Gustav was watching. Her Stuart Weitzman stilettos clicked with each step on the marble floor. She'd managed to see Eichel's room number on Gustav's screen.

Room 245.

The second floor was her guess.

Eva rode the elevator to the second floor. Soft glowing light fell gently on the empty hallway, except for a uniformed chamber woman.

"Good afternoon," the woman said.

Eva maintained a straight face as the woman resumed inventorying her cart items.

"Could you please open my room? My husband has our key downstairs, and I really have a bad migraine. I need to lie down."

They paced a few meters to Room 245, and the housekeeper slotted her master key through the latch. The door clicked open. Eva took a deep breath. "Thank you."

It was empty, already tidied with the curtains drawn. Eva turned to the nonchalant woman. "You can go now."

The woman twisted her bottom lip. "Do you want me to get you something for your headache?"

"Oh, no thank you. I have some pills in my bag."

The woman lingered for a few seconds before maneuvering toward her cart. Eva pulled the door shut and stepped into the room, spying around for a travel or work bag. Moving with the stealth of a hungry cat her eyes fell on a Rimona briefcase on the far end of the bed. She hurried toward it, knelt on the floor beside the silver case, and checked the lock.

Open.

She checked all compartments. Nothing of use seized her interest, just travel documents, itineraries and crime photographs.

She shot up, her head swimming with anxiety and proceeded toward the somewhat small bathroom near the main door. Turning on the light in the windowless room her reflection on the far mirror made her stop mid-stride. She inhaled a short breath, ignored the reflection and searched for any stashed overnight bags.

Three minutes later, Eva was wrestling with luck, and she knew it. Lastly, she decided to check his closet opposite the bathroom door. Inside the dark space hung a Hugo Boss jacket and a couple of trendy slacks.

"Nice, Mr. Eichel. More style than I imagined for a cop."

As she set her hand on the threads, the room telephone sounded with a classic piercing ring tone. Her heart skipped to her throat. Someone was calling for Eichel. She considered her options for all of three seconds. The front door was only an arm's length away. Eva turned toward it, and before she could reach the doorknob, her eyes fell on a wad of papers jetting out of a long coat in the closet.

"What have we got here?"

She reached for the rolled papers that poked out of the inside pocket. Eva seized them and carefully unraveled the find, scanning the contents with interest. She almost dismissed the documents entirely until her eyes read yellow highlighted words:

TOP SECRET:
The Deveron Manuscript

Classified documents from the British government!

Along the margins, several handwritten notes had been scribbled. Eva couldn't understand the language. *Must be German.*

She scrambled for her work camera from her shoulder bag and photographed page after page. Footsteps plodding in the hall caused alarm to surface to her gut as a shadowed silhouette fell across the floor, formed by the lights in the corridor.

Damn!

A rattle sounded on the doorknob. She sprang back, holding her stomach as nauseating pain shot through her abdomen.

"Driver, raise the divider window," Mason said.

He obliged and drove the limousine out of 49th Street, cruising down Park Avenue. Mason pressed down a button in the armrest between them, which slid open a closed chamber behind the front street, housing a bar filled to the brim, proposing a wealth of liqueur including a bottle of Armand de Brignac champagne.

He lifted two glasses from the glass compartment.

"A hefty price. Celebrating already, Mr. Laskfell?" Her mid-western twang sizzled with nasality when she spoke.

He smiled. "For a splendid lady."

Margot took the offered glass and raised a toast. "Welcome to the USA."

Mason chinked her glass. "I admire a woman who has

255

resolve and ambition. You'll stop at nothing to get that seat in the White House."

She raised her glass slightly. "You don't know me that well."

He sneered. "I'm sorry to bother you at a time when your campaign needs you most but time is running out for your decision with regards to my proposal."

"I, in turn, revere a man who comes straight to the point. With regards to your proposal, there's no decision to make." She took a sip of the champagne, leaving a lipstick mark on the chilled glass. "I've already signed the documents."

Mason smiled. "Well then, this will be a lot easier than I thought."

"How'll this work?" Margot said. "The deal doesn't take effect until I'm in office. Right?"

"Correct. There's nothing to fear. You have a solid lead over all of your competitors."

"Yes, but how'll you make sure I receive the votes I need?"

"Let me worry about that, as long as I deliver on my end of the bargain. A guarantee is even tied to the agreement. It's for your security."

The limousine steered to the curb in front of the Metropolitan Opera. Margot cradled her champagne glass and tapped it with a scarlet nail. "You're a crude man. I would hate to be your enemy."

She unlatched her beaded evening purse and drew out the folded papers.Margot unraveled and extended the documents to him. "Signed and, now, delivered."

Mason reached for them. She held on tight.

He examined her frown. "I assure you, you have nothing to lose."

She released the papers. "Let's hope not."

He stashed the documents in his breast pocket and waited for the driver to open the door. "If there's nothing more to discuss, shall we?"

"On to Wagner now."

They disappeared into the vibrant New York opera house.

Hours later, the couple emerged exploding with laughter like old friends. Margot beamed, her arm secure within Mason's.

"The Ring is one of the most ruthless musical projects ever. I so thoroughly enjoyed that," Margot said.

"Allow me to drop you off at your hotel," Mason offered.

Back at the Waldorf Astoria Margot shook his hand and let herself out of the grand limousine. Mason held her hand and brushed a gentle kiss over it. "It's been good doing business with you. Good luck with the rest of your campaign."

He gave her an approving wink before settling back in the leathered seat. His limousine sidled out toward Manhattan. "To the airport, driver."

He reached for the car phone. "Slate, turn on the signal."

Margot bit her lip as she watched Mason's car steer off. She glanced at her watch. "Time to move, I guess."

Within the hotel lobby, she peered toward the two-ton, nine foot Goldsmith clock.

Twelve past midnight.

She made her way back to her suite. The lights were on when she dragged her aching feet into the lavish interior. The adjacent office bustled with activity.

Malcolm strode in her direction. "You ready for your other guest?"

"As ready as I'll ever be."

She followed him into the adjoining room.

Nash entered the room carrying several documents in his hand. "Governor Arlington, are you all right?"

She nodded.

Nash shot her a severe look, disguising his disapproval of her choice of company. He raked a chair across the floor to her table. "We managed to swap the papers. With Mason on US soil, we've started the process of infiltrating his private computer networks."

"Do you have what you need?" she asked.

He slid into the seat. "Yes. Thanks for your cooperation."

Margot slumped into the seat next to him.

Nash watched her.

"How did the NSA find out?"

"He eased her discomfort with a smile. "Don't feel bad. We've had reason to suspect much of Mason's behavior. I wasn't as successful in busting his movements with Samuel Riche as I would have liked, but I managed to prevent the signing of the deal."

"Malcolm. Got a cigarette?" she said tilting her head to the side.

"You really shouldn't smoke," Malcolm said.

She threw him a chilling look, setting him off scampering to find her Marlboro's.

Margot turned her attention toward Nash. "So now I'm a pawn for the British government and the NSA in return for their silence."

"I'm afraid the presidential race has to be run impartially, ma'am."

Her eyes fell on Mason's original documents as Nash rolled them in his hands.

"What you gonna do with that?" she said.

"It's classified."

"What's your next move?"

He glanced at the time. "Get on a plane back to Europe."

CHAPTER 22

E va's ear caught more muffled jabber in the hallway. She clenched her jaw as treading footsteps neared the door's edge, followed by the sound of a door unlocking. She waited for an intrusion into her investigation.

None.

She waited some more. Eva had snapped enough photos. She carefully returned the papers into Eichel's coat pocket, her eyes catching two names on the documents. Written casually across the top of one of the sheets, several scribbled notes lay under the startling name.

Calla Cress.

How do I know that name? She would find out later. Right now she had to move. Eva quickly scanned the room one final time, and without further lingering she scrambled into the hallway, bustling toward the elevators.Halfway down the corridor, a man headed in the opposite direction. He navigated past her and, for a brief moment, his eyes focused on a note in his hands.

Eva recognized him from the news broadcast she'd seen on the Deveron. Caught up in his reading she shuffled her feet forward and slid on her sunglasses as she brushed past casually. Her face turned to the wall as she stole past him.

Eichel nodded politely and then glared back at her. With her chin down she set off bolting, and within seconds, she'd made it to the elevators. Her trembling hand reached for the call button as a bolt of adrenaline shot through her bloodstream.

She jabbed at the call button. Fidgety hands refused to settle as she glanced back. *What's taking so long?*

Behind her, Eichel started a slow march in her direction. "Hey, don't I know you?" he said.

Eva attacked the control panel in frantic hysteria as Eichel's pace quickened toward her. The doors dragged open, and Eva threw herself into the safety of the busy compartment. "Ground floor, please," she called to the smartly dressed woman closest to the elevator buttons.

As she waited for the doors to shut she caught Eichel's eyes, who had gained considerable ground in her direction. Shudders began to rock her gut.

She caught the eager look in his eyes as the steel slammed shut.

DAY 10
FORE STREET
EAST LONDON

Jack scooped up a spoon of steaming Thai noodle soup. Its piquant taste slithered down, lessening the hunger he had tried to ignore since returning from Rome a few hours ago. The aromatic spices tickled his nostrils and reminded him of dishes his mother used to prepare in the Seychelles. He finished his bowl rapidly and settled back in his work chair by the window of his converted studio apartment.

He lived alone and, in true bachelor fashion, the place could have benefited from a thorough cleaning. It didn't help that a cleaner came in once a fortnight. Jack knew his weakness was sloppiness. He alone could understand his mess.

In the background, Ella Fitzgerald serenaded him with "Moonlight in Vermont," a melodic tune that soothed his soul. Jack's creativeness worked best with his two best friends: music and food.

He stroked his neck, massaging the spot where he had received the blow in Rome. The pain was lessening now. He only had a few hours before needing to re-join Calla and Nash and, in deep thought, he switched on the computer, illuminating his multiple desk monitors.

He keyed in a series of passwords on the console. A video program popped up. He set in motion the fast-forward button for a few seconds until he came to the point in the video that he sought. The footage, recorded earlier of Mason, played on his screen, and Jack took down a series of notes. "Business in India now? I can't imagine it's government related."

He loaded another file and viewed some more footage, most of which wasn't incriminating. His lips curled into a wide grin, proud that he'd obtained an earlier opportunity to plant his bug on Mason. The feat had been achieved by an admirer.

Lillian.

Mason's personal assistant. Mason could easily justify a trip to India, but Jack studied the man Mason kept calling Rupert Kumar. His eyes remained on the screen until he reached a particular frame. Three things in the last few recordings interested him. Mason's unprecedented trip to India to meet with Rupert Kumar was the first. Jack had heard the name, and he took note of the billionaire's details. The second was Mason's trip to New York, to visit front lady and Republican presidential candidate, Margot Arlington.Finally, there was the meeting with Samuel Riche, the French billionaire. Wasn't he that snooty journalist's father? *What's her name, Eva Riche?*

None of the meetings recorded in the footage fell within Mason's jurisdiction or line of work. *What's the connection?*

The front doorbell interrupted his musings, and his eyes turned to the clock on his computer.

He debated whether to go to the door at all and lowered the volume of Ella's serenade, thinking his Jazz had been a notch too loud for the neighbors.

Jack moved toward the front door and glanced through the spy hole. "Who is it?"

Mrs. Hawke straightened her shoulders as she lifted her chin to the peephole. "Jack Kleve? Hello. We met at Mr. Laskfell's residence."

How did she find my place?

He placed his hand on the doorknob. "Mrs. Hawke, do you realize it's 2:00 a.m.? What's so urgent?"

He pulled a torch-like pen from the cabinet near the door and peered with it by rotating the cap lens to one side. Aided by its amplified night-vision feature, he scanned her for any metallic or antagonizing objects, satisfied with the little device he'd created himself.

Mrs. Hawke rose to her toes and projected her voice through the eye hole. "Mr. Kleve, Mr. Laskfell sent me."

She had no weapons.

He set the gadget down. "At this time of night?"

"Mr. Laskfell wants to know if you require any more information for his new project."

"Can't this wait until morning?"

"I was on my way home and thought I would do this last errand for him. He tells me you're a night owl."

True. But so what?

Jack cracked the door an inch. "As you can see, Mrs. Hawke, I'm getting ready to go to bed. What is it that can't wait?"

Even as she spoke her scouting eyes explored the room over

his shoulders. She handed Jack an envelope. "This is from Mr. Laskfell. He said I had to get it to you today."

Jack took the envelope. "Okay, you've delivered the envelope. Is there anything else?"

She spied over his shoulders was shameless, even with Jack's stern look. Jack held back unutterable profanity as he scowled at the preposterous woman sporting her forties hat and coat.

He repositioned the door to close it. "Good night, Mrs. Hawke, you've delivered your message."

She shifted back into the hallway and raised inquisitive eyes before she zipped around and departed.

Jack stared at her for a few seconds and then latched the door. He studied the envelope she'd delivered and narrowed his eyes. She could have sent a message first thing in the morning. He traversed back to his computer and scratched his chin. He'd left the program running on mute.

His body stiffened.

Had Mrs. Hawke seen his footage? Had she caught a glimpse of the bugged material? With the monitor still running he studied the rolling video of Mason and Margot Arlington conversing intensely in the Waldorf Astoria lobby.

CHAPTER 23

C alla Cress. Why was that name familiar? What did Raimund Eichel want with her?

Eva failed to collate the pieces. She recounted her escape from the Hilton.Eva had slipped out of the elevator and raced through the Hilton lobby.Back in her car, she paused to think, catching her breath for several minutes gazing at the mahogany dashboard.She scrambled through her bag for her cell phone, hidden under her day planner. She seized it in haste and slid her fingers over the touchscreen, locating the contacts folder. Not one single person with the name Cress popped up. Yet she knew she'd distinctively heard it before. Cress wasn't a common name; it wouldn't be hard to do a search.

She fired up 'Cyter Link', a professional social networking website to which she belonged.

It too generated no search results.

"Damn it! Why do I know that name?"

A silver Mercedes prowled ahead as it sidled out of a parking space. Its headlights beamed directly in her eyes and blinded her vision for a few seconds. She turned the key in the ignition and coasted her car out of the parking lot. She drove the three miles to her house in Chelsea and nosed the car into the narrow parking space.She strode through the Victorian doors of her villa and set her keys on the entryway table. Her bag landed on the black and white floor tiling, and she raced up the stairs, coming to a quick stop at the library shelves that lined the top of the steps.

Eva slid her fingers along each of the four levels stacked mostly with travel and coffee table books. Her eyes fell on two yearbooks from her former high school, Beacon Abbey Academy, a sought after, independent girls' school that had stood for centuries at the top of Elstree hill overlooking the town and its quaint cottages.

Pulling the most recent yearbook off the shelf, she slipped off her heels and rubbed her sore feet before landing cross-legged on the carpeted floor. She flipped through page after page, reminiscing more than she anticipated.

She tossed the volume to the floor and reached for the other yearbook - the one marking her graduation year. This time, she progressed straight to the graduating class pages. The mug shots were unforgivably appalling, yet her jaw dropped at the picture on the bottom right corner of the graduating class page.

It's her! Calla Iris Cress.

'Most Likely to Succeed', read the high school superlative. How she'd despised the girl. Sure enough, on page three, was Calla Cress delivering the senior class speech, the girl who had been named valedictorian of the graduating class.Eva glared at the leggy, dark-haired creature that had seemed quite awkward when she started at Beacon.

Eva remembered meeting Calla for the first time. Everybody knew that she had moved to Elstree to live with her foster parents, or was it, adoptive parents? That part was not questioned as much as where her real parents were. Her untold story started with a rumor Eva had heard in the school corridors, that Calla had refused to call her parents *mom* or *dad* but insisted on labeling them, Mama and Papa Cress. Calla had always maintained that her real parents would return one day. It had been high fuel for victimization. Everyone felt sorry for the girl who'd been shipped off to Elstree. At least that is what Eva remembered.

Eva questioned how an orphaned girl, whose adoptive parents used to be missionaries, could afford an exclusive private school like Beacon Abbey. She'd never found out.

Calla had by far surpassed her counterparts, academically, in sports and most distinctly in languages and history. The girl could always be found with her nose in books or off representing the school in some sporting event or academic debate.

Even though Calla was popular with teachers and peers alike, she was actually a very reserved girl, who'd rarely put herself forward for anything. This had made her an easy target. Eva giggled remembering some tragic gimmicks she'd pulled in the day.

Yes, now it was all flooding back.

Eva jumped to her feet, found her electronic tablet and ran her finger over the bright screen. She searched the Internet and found the high school's, alumni office number.

"Yes?" said a raspy voice. "Beacon Abbey alumni office."

"Yes, hello. My name is Eva Riche, a former student of Beacon Abbey."

"Good afternoon, Miss Riche. It's Saturday, and I shouldn't be answering the phone. Could you call back during our opening hours on Monday?"

Eva reclined on the bed, staring above at her wooden-carved, custom-made ceiling.

"This'll only take a minute. I'm looking for the correct

contact details for a fellow student. Would you be able to help me?"

The woman hesitated before surrendering. "Who are you looking for?"

"Calla Iris Cress."

"I'm sorry Miss Riche; I would have to gain her permission first. Perhaps if you drop us an email, we can forward your request to her. That is if she is registered with the alumni office."

"Is she registered?"

"I'm afraid I can't give out that information."

Damn!

Eva hung up, rolled off the bed and set her electronic tablet on the side table. She took a sip from her bedside, water glass and attempted another search online. After several endeavors scanning through alumni lists and newsletters, she concluded that Calla was probably not registered.

Well, neither was she.

Eva made one more attempt on the 'Cyter Link' website, including its paid, restricted arm, 'Cyter Link Professional'.

Were there any third-degree contacts that could help?

One name surfaced.

Nash Shields.

How charming!

She rolled back onto her bed and rested her back on the mounds of delicate pillows, a grin forming on her lips. "Hmm... let me see, the last time I saw Nash, he was a marine at the US Embassy in London."

Eva bit her bottom lip recalling the strained rapport that had ended before it had started.

2:07 A.M.
ST. GILES'S VILLA

Calla trudged up to her room, her muscles aching with tension. She hadn't managed to sleep the whole flight back from Rome. She hauled her bags upstairs and discarded them on the bed. Pearl had drawn the shades and turned down the bed. Grateful to have someone like Pearl, who always carried about her duties with grace, Calla eased onto the bed.

She needed a moment or two to rest her muscles and reached to turn on the bedside lamp in the turquoise themed room. Oddly she'd not noticed much of the decor until now. Allegra's taste didn't disappoint. Her mark resonated from every corner. Everything from the hand-carved, king-sized bed, to the Art Deco paintings of musicians strumming instruments, to the custom-made stationery on the writing desk.

Calla removed her cell phone from the bag and charged it by the work desk. Her thoughts reeled back to the gladiator and the words he'd said to her.

He'd seen her parents. It had to have been after her birth. But she wasn't sure. She groaned, overwhelmed by the thought of the monstrous task. It would be impossible without an actual name to use. *How did the gladiator know they were my parents?*

She took these thoughts with her to the bathroom. Even as she threw cool water over her burning cheeks, all she remembered was her five-foot-eleven, slinky frame single-handedly pinning down a seven-foot titan. *How long did he say he'd been there?* She massaged her neck and muttered to herself. "Must be my imagination."

She glanced at the second box she'd secured in Rome. *No one will ever believe me.* Calla took a deep breath. *What's happening to me?* Rummaging through a duffel bag, she'd salvaged from her defaced apartment she found a burgundy filing book. Within its pages, she'd started to gather some notes. She also seized the memory stick with a copy of Allegra's birth certificate, as well as her personal journal.

She grabbed a pen, and jotted down statements the watcher, gladiator and the Gypsy woman had told her. It was her way of documenting the surreal events should she need to recall them later. Calla re-read the notes while toying with the memory device in her hand, trying to piece events and facts together.

Nothing made sense. Too tired to think she shot up and shrugged off her clothes, stripping down to shower. She paused to examine her lanky, yet well-toned frame in the full-length mirror by the dressing table. Her body seemed fitter than she remembered. She couldn't recollect the last time she'd been to the gym even though she'd always aimed to maintain her fitness, having been very athletic most of her life.

She slid a hand over her calves, her abdomen, and her arm muscles. Her body was transforming to the physique of a powerful athlete on a vigorous training program. She pulled on her bathrobe and settled onto the stool by the dressing table. In a wearied daze, she reached for a cotton ball and removed the minimal eyeliner and mascara she wore, carefully sliding her fingers over her eyelids and cheekbones.

Where do you come from, Calla?

Her eyes blinked from the mirror bulbs as she focused on her narrow nose in the reflection.

What the—

She focused on the mirror, her vision piercing through the glass, then the solid wall and right through to the bedroom. She blinked twice, realizing she could essentially decide on which item to focus on and which to magnify. She slid her dressing stool back, screeching the white tiles in the process.

Can I?

She held her breath and peered down at her feet, allowing her vision to penetrate them, the bathroom rug, the chandelier on the ceiling beneath her bathroom until she could focus all the way to the basement of the house. She swallowed hard and shut her eyes, then refocused on the items in front of her. She paced toward the bathroom cabinet above the sink and found an

Aspirin box for her headache. She threw her eyes open realizing she'd sensed her way through the room.

Eyes shut.

Exposure to the carbonados!

Brain damage?

Calla took the pills in one swallow. "I'll call Dr. Olivier in the morning. No use worrying about this now."

She tore her robe open and stepped under the shower stream. She allowed the soothing spray to calm her heightened emotions. Water spurts massaged her stiff muscles, and within minutes she'd left the bathroom and collapsed beneath her bed covers.

Calla shot upright when the alarm on her phone beeped. Awake in an instant, one glance at the time.

6:45 a.m.

Within fifteen minutes she glided down the stairs and strolled into the kitchen, dressed in tan pants and a mauve T-shirt. Her locks, tied in a neat ponytail, swung with her stride.

"Breakfast, Miss Cress?" asked Pearl.

"Just some orange juice, please."

Jack had spread some notes on the table and was in deep conversation with Nash. Calla grabbed a fresh red apple from the fruit basket and settled onto a kitchen stool.

"Someone is onto us," Jack said.

Calla knit her eyebrows. "Who?"

"I'm not sure. I'm more concerned about how. We've been followed each step of the way," Jack said.

"I secured all our equipment and our phones," Nash said, a troubled look crossing his face.

Jack took a bite of his toast and chewed as he spoke. "I know. I also double checked them myself before we set off for Greece."

Calla bit into the apple. "Whoever is tailing us would have surfaced by now? No?"

"But don't you see," Jack said. "They have. How did that sniper find you in Oxford? This is really getting dangerous. We can't afford any tagalongs. We barely made it out from Rome alive. God only knows what convinced the assassin at the Colosseum not to kill us. Who was he?"

Nash glimpsed over at Calla. "At this point, I've resolved to believe anything."

Calla chewed quietly. "Wait a minute."

The pair watched her as she left the room and returned a few minutes later cradling the smartphone Mason had given her in her hands. She switched it off and held it up to Jack. "Could you check this?"

Jack eased it out of her hand. "Hey, I know this phone. I had this one wired especially for Mason. He had me manufacture a few of these for special missions. Where did you get this?"

Jack knew the answer even before Calla could respond. "I can only imagine."

She slumped back onto the stool and glanced first at Jack and then at Nash. "Mason gave it to me. He said I needed an electronic diary in Berlin. I forgot I had it."

Jack set an index finger to his lips cautioning the two not to speak. He removed the back cover of the smartphone and detached the battery. Underneath he disconnected a tracking device that he had planted himself.

Nash took the dismantled device from Jack. "I've seen these bugs before. The durable microchips sustain fire, water, and impact." His eyes shifted to Calla. "Why would Mason bug you? Do you think he knows you have the manuscript or even the stones?"

She shrugged. "I'm not sure."

Calla lifted her head as Pearl served her orange juice and a slice of fresh grapefruit. She accepted the breakfast gratefully and waited until Pearl had left the kitchen before speaking. "Mason seemed more concerned about me making notes on

Allegra's findings in Berlin than anything else when he gave me that phone."

"Why?" asked Nash.

Calla tried to recall her last encounter with Mason. "I don't know. He's a strange pickle. I must admit I hadn't really thought much about it until now. I was preoccupied with other things."

Nash enfolded Calla with one arm. "Hey, you didn't know."

Jack cast them an inquiring look. "I'll get rid of this permanently," he said as he sprang off the stool.

When Jack left the room, Nash tightened his arm around her, his touch making Calla quiver. She drew into his hold, and her eyes moved up to his. It was then that her restraint fell.

He pulled her closer and brushed his lips against hers. She responded without resolve as his hand slid up her back, to her neck, before stroking the back of her head. For several seconds she rested in the sensation, her heart racing.

Her body stiffened, realizing he'd liquefied the iron lock she kept shackled around her heart. She opened her eyes and pulled away. "Sorry, Nash, I can't."

He drew back. "Calla." His eyes glinted with pained emotion. "Just because your parents left, doesn't mean, no one will ever love you. I—"

"Nash. No." The words left her lips, but she didn't mean any of them. "Can't we just keep things the way they are?"

She glanced away from him, knowing she was the only barrier to the affection for which she longed. *You're my best friend. What's wrong with me?*

In all the time she'd known Nash she hadn't felt as vulnerable around him as she had in the last few days. Was it only now that she was awakening to the feelings she had for him? With the quest surrounding her identity and her parents, she wasn't ready to deal with new emotions. Not when it came to Nash. He was a friend she *never* wanted to lose.

Nash released her. "I don't mean to take advantage of the strenuous situation we've both been under in the last couple days." He bore deep into her eyes and held her gaze for several seconds. "I won't do that again."

She opened her mouth to speak but, searching for the right words, he withdrew, edging away to the kitchen counter with his back to her. He dug his hands into his pockets before turning back to face her.

Her tongue weighed down. It was too late. She'd pushed him away. The only person who cared for her more than life itself.

Jack gravitated back into the room. "Okay. That's taken care of. We should be fine now." He stopped in his tracks and calculated the silence between Nash and Calla.

When Nash spoke, he broke the awkwardness as the words filtered out in low tones. "We can't trust anyone, not even anyone at ISTF. Isn't that what the note said to you, Calla? I think Mason wants this manuscript. Otherwise, why would he bug one of his workers? Either that or he has something on Allegra. *And* he wants you to get that evidence."

The discussion on what had just taken place between her and Nash was done and buried. She bit her lip. "How did he know we had the manuscript?"

Nash shrugged. "The bug. Mason is also a key orchestrator of Operation Carbonado, which is what kickstarted the hunt for the Deveron document in the first place. My hunch is he's got a personal agenda too."

Jack edged in. "It's not just government related. I have him bugged as well." He paused and cast Calla a concerned look. "He wants Calla to do *his* dirty work."

"What dirty work?" she asked.

Nash interjected. "To get the carbonados for him.

Otherwise, he'd easily have had you surrender the Deveron Manuscript to him."

"He's mad."

Nash folded his arms over his chest. "I'm still wondering why he sent an assassin after you."

Calla rose to her feet. "What assassin?"

Nash unfolded his arms, crossed to the table and set his palms on the kitchen table. "Calla, the night you were arrested I came to your apartment. I'd not heard from you since you'd left for Berlin."

He paused for her reaction, but she stared on.

"Your house was vandalized by an assassin. He came looking for what I now think is this document. We have to assume that Mason is seriously onto you."

CHAPTER 24

E va searched her memory for the missing pieces. Anguish gripped her. With eager intent, she reached for the last drawer on the low dressing table beside her bed and pulled it open. For several minutes she fumbled through its contents until her fingers slid across a shabby business card from a club in Soho, London's West End district. On the flip side, she'd scribbled Nash's contact details.And as she stared at the number, the memories resurfaced.

Twenty months ago Alex had hurried into her office offering her the opportunity to interview the US First Lady, Beverly Westbrook, on her contemporary fashion style. The interview was to take place shortly before a state dinner arranged for the US President's official visit to the United Kingdom.

Alex was thrilled they'd received clearance for the coveted interview. "We need a good glamour story on the front page,

Riche. Westbrook is a well-respected fashion icon in this country."

Eva arrived at the US Embassy in Grosvenor Square, the home of official American presence in London since John Adams' presidency. Situated in the heart of the exclusive Mayfair district the building was notable for its crystalline cube design, adjacent to a semi-circular pond on one side.

She strutted past the waters toward the security gate with a jittery fashion photographer who fumbled with his equipment as he kept stride with her. Upon arrival at the heavily safeguarded, admissions gate Eva placed her bag on the revolving belt while the security staff scanned her items and prepared visitor badges. Once past the security scanners, they proceeded through a double-door, glass entrance and up a grand spiral staircase.

Then she saw him.

In full uniform, Nash, a detachment commander operationally responsible for the safety of the ambassador and appointed delegates stood at the entrance of the state ballroom discoursing with two lower grade Marines.

Eva's knees floundered a little, quite taken by his lean build and strikingly handsome face as she studied every inch of his six-foot-three build.

Nash escorted her through the security procedure required for her to meet the U.S. First Lady. Eva's coy conduct came off as direct as she walked up to him and whispered something mischievous in his ear. How had she managed to get a private number from a Marine on duty? They went out on a date two days later in Covent Garden. After that, he refused to return her calls until she proposed a trip to Paris, the city of her childhood and real home. "Why don't you just widen your horizons, *Chéri*? You'll see Paris from a whole new perspective."

His positive response took her by surprise. Their second date was on the weekend following the state visit. Eva sought to win his every affection hoping Paris's appeal would coerce him into lowering his guard and provide the ideal backdrop for her flirtatious pursuit.

And then the Marine released his ammunition, wanting to break it off before it had even begun. Nash made that very clear the night they visited *Le Miroir*, a quaint bistro she knew in the northern Paris quarter of Montmartre. A small, casual place, adorned with red and black abstracts and numerous mirrors, its original atmosphere was the backdrop of a very sublime squabble.

"Don't kid yourself, Eva. This isn't going anywhere. Don't you think?"

Not one to accept loss she clutched his collar and draped herself across his lap. The movement knocked their wine glasses over as Eva moved in for a forced kiss.

Recoiling, he heaved her off his thighs and shot to his feet. "You're an interesting one, Eva."

"Is there someone else?"

"Maybe," he said, pity surfacing in his eyes.

She didn't believe him and stammered. "You, too, are a strange one, Marine."

He tightened his jacket ready to make a move for the exit. "Eva, I went on a date with you and came to Paris only because the First Lady asked me to."

"I don't believe you."

"She doesn't trust the way you'll handle her responses from your interview."

Eva didn't take the rejection well. Men never said no to her, especially those that she sought after. Nash didn't fit into the class of men she was accustomed to dating. The latter were all ambitious, pretentious types. Nash was different, the kind of man she wanted to be associated with, mysterious and incredibly attractive.

She struck him across the jaw and cursed with words more foul-mouthed than she'd intended. None of it was gracious. She'd not seen or spoken to him since that weekend.

. . .

Eva stiffened at the sound of her bedroom phone, causing her fingers to drop the business card on the floor. She recognized the number. "What is it, Mark?"

"I'm sorry, Miss Riche, but Raphael Leadstone has been calling for you."

She cut him off. "What does he want?"

"He says—"

It wasn't important enough. "Tell him I'm on a business trip."

"He's called several times already."

"Mark, I can't speak to him now.Tell him I'll call him!"

"All right," Mark said.

"I'll deal with Leadstone later."

Eva hung up and jumped off the bed. She retrieved the card from the floor and reached for her cell phone. Even at the early hour of 7:15 a.m. she recalled Nash was active in the mornings, training first and, with any luck, he'd be out and about.

The phone rang a few times before he picked up.

"Shields."

"Hi, Nash. It's Eva."

"Eva?"

"Come on, Nash you used to call me *Eveeee*."

A minor silence kept Eva in eager anticipation.

"I seriously doubt that?" he said.

"Chéri." She fashioned the most appetizing voice she could muster. "Could I meet you somewhere today?"

Nash didn't respond.

She winced. Eva would need to lure him in slowly. "I've really missed you. I just wanted to apologize for how I behaved in Paris."

"I think you already have. Listen, now's not a good time. I'm traveling this week. How about we catch up when I return?"

She couldn't wait that long. "Nash. How do you know Calla Cress?"

"Excuse me?"

"Calla Cress. Calla and I went to school together, and sadly we lost contact. Do you know how I can contact her? I know you two are first degree contacts on Cyter Link."

Nash flinched as he held the phone. He slipped out of the kitchen onto the rear, outdoor terrace, leaving Calla and Jack in constructive debate over Deveron translation concepts. He closed the door behind him. "What do you want with Calla?"

"I just want to reconnect. We were old friends in school."

"I'm sorry, Eva. I can't help you."

"Nash, please."

He would ward her off. "Okay. I can meet you at a café along the Serpentine in Hyde Park." He checked the time. "In one hour."

7:52 A.M.
CENTRAL LONDON

Nash hopped into a cab on King's Road, a major street stretching through the localities of Chelsea and Fulham in West London. The boulevard was infested with early morning rush hour traffic. He'd assumed it would be the best way to slip out of Allegra's undetected.

"Serpentine Road, Hyde Park, please," he told the cab driver.

His meeting would only be an hour. He had no time for a narcissistic woman whose only ambition was to progress herself above her peers. What did she want with Calla?

279

Eva was trouble. The problematic kind that persisted at the risk of losing all work ethic and appeal.

The taxi halted near Hyde Park Corner Underground station. The trip had gone quicker than he'd anticipated. He put forty pounds in the driver's hand and sprang onto the pavement, soaking in the brisk morning air.

City workers commuted along the bustling sidewalk. He crossed the street and strolled into Hyde Park, past the ostentatious Wellington Museum. His feet moved briskly, and he reached the bar in less than five minutes. When he arrived at the café, a handful of tourists and Londoners were savoring the early morning sun on the outside terrace while others leisurely sipped coffees and sat at breakfast. He scanned the room for a free table to no avail.

"Nash?"

Behind him, he took in the approach of a familiar face. Neil Stone, the café owner. He was a very tall man with a narrow build that always made Nash think of a talented stage magician. Neil's extreme sensitivity to customers made him a remarkable café owner, although he managed to conceal this aspect of his personality with a little smile in the corner of his mouth.

"Neil, looks like business is good."

"Nash, my friend, let me get your table."

"Thanks."

"Will that be one or two?"

"Two."

Several seconds later Neil seated him on the deck overlooking the recreational lake. Nash ordered a black coffee and placed his phone on the table.

"Nash!"

He zipped around. *Never thought I'd see you again.*

Eva beamed a wide smile and floated to his table. She was taller than he remembered. Beaming a broad smile, she wrapped her long arms around his neck.

He turned in time to avoid the rouged rims of her mouth.

Disguising his irritation, he grasped her arms and brought them down to her side. "You've not changed."

She'd dressed for the occasion, sporting an elegant gold and cream, cocktail dress.

"Nice dress. A little early for drinks, though."

"Thank you, *Chéri*. Just something I found at Valentino. How good to see you!"

Nash pulled out a chair for her, expecting to be lied to with every sentence. "Are you well, Eva?"

"I'm doing really well! I've just started my own media company."

"So you're no longer at the Guardian?"

She observed him with coquettish eyes. "They didn't deserve me."

"I'm sure."

She leaned forward and seized his hand. "Why did I ever let you go?"

Nash repossessed his hand. "I was never yours to have." Caution kept him aloof as he changed the subject. "Why do you want to contact Calla Cress?"

A fidgety waiter came to the table to take their orders. Eva retreated slightly. "What're we having, *Chéri?* Let's have some champagne. I feel like celebrating. I've not seen you in a long time."

"No thank you."

"All right. Waiter, I'll have a glass of fresh orange juice."

As the waiter left them to fulfill the order, Nash's jaw tightened.

He wanted this over with.

Fast.

Eva reached for a cigarette.

Nash's eyes narrowed. "You haven't answered my question. What do you want with Calla?"

She lit her cigarette and smiled viciously. "Patience, she's just a friend from school. I've been trying to catch up with her. Just for old time's sake."

With his mind ringing sirens of warning he refused to believe a word she said. "Haven't you been in touch all these years?"

Eva inhaled her cigarette and blew the smoke away. "You've not told me how *you* know her."

Nash disliked it when women smoked. As distasteful as it was, Eva puffed more smoke to the side and put out her cigarette as if on cue. "Listen, I understand you're still upset with me. All I want to do is catch up with Calla. We were good friends in school, and we lost touch. That's all. Why are you so defensive?"

"About what?"

"You don't trust me, Nash."

"Does anyone?"

Eva grimaced at his remark. "She your girlfriend? Didn't think you were the brunette type."

"I know you, Eva. Ambition and destruction are usually tied to each of your quests, and mostly journalistic in nature."

The waiter returned with a glass of the requested juice for Eva. They waited until he'd gone before Eva pulled out her cell phone. "I've come across some top secret information. I'm writing a story on the disappearance of the Deveron Manuscript."

Nash listened, motionless.

Eva paused. She searched his face for a reaction before continuing. "These notes, written by a German investigator, have Calla's name on them."

She calculated his lack of emotion. "I presume he connects her in some way to the investigation. I figured if I could just talk to her, maybe even warn her—"

Nash took the phone from her hand. She'd opened a top-secret image of an MI6 file. He recognized the emblem even with the questionable resolution of the image. He zoomed in to mentally register the information and scrolled to the next few photos.

Eva had gained access to classified information. Whom had she bribed, investigated or seduced to get the details?

Sure enough, Calla's name was in the document. Nash could read most of the handwritten German notes. He stopped at an image displaying a half-photographed page. The words translated read:

Why did Fräuline Cress leave Berlin?

Was Eva's story credible?

The truth was she was onto a lead. One that could potentially endanger Calla.

"Where did you get this?" he asked.

She slowly sipped her juice with an amused grin. "Even I have secrets."

He would follow his instincts. Eva never hunted anything without a motive. He'd learned that in the short time he'd known her. "How do you know this jeopardizes Calla's life? Do you know what the German says?"

"Not yet."

The fact that she'd surrendered the information so readily meant she wasn't aware of its importance. It would only be a matter of time before she would find a German translator. Like it or not the fact remained, the German police were investigating Calla. And just when Calla was incredibly close to finding the answers she needed.

What Eva held in her hands was probably the German police's entire investigation of the case on the Deveron. He returned the cell phone to her.

"Interesting company you keep these days, Eva."

She flinched. "You believe me, don't you? Listen, Calla needs to know this."

"I can't help you, Eva. You should try staying in touch with your friends next time. Although I doubt many would want to."

He rose to leave and reached for his jacket.

"Damn it, Nash!"

She plopped a fast hand over her foul mouth. Nash had expected worse, maybe a whack in the nose like the last time. He'd forgotten how overindulged she was. "Wise up, Eva. I'm sorry but, unlike you, I've principles when it concerns my friends."

Nash motioned to a passing waiter for the bill. "I need to go. I'm sorry I couldn't be much help."

Eva's voice rose, adopting a twinge of restrained desperation. "Okay, Nash. At least tell her that I asked after her? Please give her my number and ask her to call me."

Nash had no intention of raising the matter with Calla. He paid the bill and ambled out of the café with Eva tailing with a stomp in her step.

"I'm taking a cab, can I drop you somewhere?" he said.

She raised her haughty chin as she kept pace and flinched. "Please drop me off in Chelsea, near Sloane Square."

Nash glanced back. She wasn't done with her investigation. He would have to elude her somehow before she drilled him further.They found a taxi at the busy intersection near Hyde Park Corner. Fifteen minutes later the cab parked at a hasty angle along the aisle of stationary cars, just a few yards from Eva's doorstep.

Nash jumped out of the black cab and swung round to pull open the door for her. "Congratulations, by the way, on your new company."

She stepped out of the car, tugging at her crumpled dress. "Thanks."

Nash veered toward the other passenger door. "Stay out of trouble."

As he moved Eva gripped his jacket. Before he could respond, he was caught off guard by her forced, fervent embrace. The sudden confrontation pushed Nash against the car and caused a slight snicker from the on-looking cab driver.

Nash broke the coerced kiss and wiped his mouth, imagining punitive words not suitable in front of any woman. "Eva!"

She chortled, throwing her head back in a rudimentary, girlish giggle. Her infantile tactics had ventured too far for his liking. Nevertheless, he wasn't livid. "I feel sorry for you. Remember you're a mother."

"How do you know that?"

"Intelligence way too classified for your journalistic nose. I hope you're setting a better example for your son."

She stopped her uncouth giggle and, with an air of fury at his unwarranted remark, she stepped away from him. "How do you know about Lucas?"

"Just do yourself a favor and wise up. And in case you're wondering men desire a little mystery in a woman."

Eva recoiled, scowling. In one turn she swaggered off toward her front door.Nash watched her, shaking his head. When she'd gone inside, he slumped back into the taxi, and they wove into traffic. He glanced behind him and for a second was confident he'd seen someone he recognized across the street.He brushed the thought away.

Calla stole into a gourmet grocery shop. She couched and slid to the floor. Only moments before she'd witnessed Nash step out of a taxi.

Calla exhaled quietly before rising from the floor. She exited the shop, turned right and pressed on a few meters up the street. When she reached her destination—Dr. Olivier's private clinic in Sloane Square — Calla knew she'd stopped long enough to see Eva *and* Nash.

She took in a long, drawn-out breath, then exhaled.

"Dr. Olivier will see you in five minutes, Miss Cress."

"Thanks."

The private waiting room was still. An unobtrusive piano piece, the Sonata 7 in C major, by Mozart filtered through the ceiling speakers. Dr. Olivier had once confessed it was a pacifying effect when Calla asked why he played music in his waiting lounge. "Most patients arrive at a doctor's office uneasy about everything under the sun. Medical research explains that several diseases are brought on by preventable triggers like stress and worry. Music massages the stress."

As logical as it had seemed to Calla when she was ten years old, would it soothe her ailing concerns now, including, the scene she'd just witnessed outside Dr. Olivier's surgery? She never forgot a face. It was rare for Calla not to like anyone and all she could think about were the last words Eva had spoken to her. It had been a pathetic school girl threat, but Calla had meant every word. "Don't muddle with me. It turns ugly."

A grim look fell on Calla's face when she strolled into the patients' waiting lounge. The room had changed with modernization taking the drab out of waiting. The doctor had introduced a contemporary, modular seating system. She slumped into a chair and rested her arms on the movable armrests, leaning with ease against the soft seating pads.

I thought Nash was at the estate with Jack. Calla had escaped, hoping her quick departure wouldn't distract either him or Jack.

A terrible pain shot through her head. Since Pella, a headache would resurface every so often, creating insurmountable pain in the left side of her head.

A text message came in from Jack.

Calla glanced down and answered Jack's inquiry.

Jack,
Be back in an hour.

"Calla."

She lifted her eyes to see Dr. Olivier. He'd not changed at all with his bright, ebony eyes that were like two spheres of night-black marble. His thick gray hair, worn professionally, was styled back with decent amounts of gel. He was a short man with a broad, masculine build.

"It's been a long time. I was so happy to get your message. Are you well?"

Calla rose to greet him. "I hope so, doctor."

Dr. Olivier briskly tilted his head as he took her by the arm and shook her hand. They progressed into his office exchanging small talk about her job at the museum.

"What brings you to see me?"

"Where do I begin?"

"Has something happened?"

Calla plopped on the chair offered. "Dr. Olivier, you have always known how to set my mind at ease even when I was in incredible pain."

"I'm flattered."

She considered the best way to explain her recent struggles. "Doctor, I hope this doesn't sound absurd, but I've so much... should I say...discomfort in my body? I'm a little scared."

He took a seat at his desk opposite her. "What's happening to you? Walk me through the symptoms."

"Firstly, I seem to be able to see through things."

The words came out of her mouth before she'd contemplated their meaning.

Without flinching, Olivier threaded his hands. "Explain that."

287

He thinks I'm mad!

Not fazed, she elaborated. "Last night I was able to see through my bathroom wall and floor."

She cringed as the words escaped her lips. *Shut up, Calla! Can you hear yourself?* She anticipated a perplexed reaction yet Dr. Olivier's kind face focused on her in the most understanding manner. He said nothing.

Calla continued. "The result is usually a massive headache."

"When did this start?"

"About a week ago."

"You mentioned that the changes were taking place in your body. What changes?"

She took a deep breath and clasped her fingers around her arms. "Well, it seems to be an increased physical capability, immediately followed by incredible fatigue."

Dr. Olivier switched on his computer and pulled out a notepad. "Have you been eating and drinking well? Exercising? Sleeping?"

"Yes, I suppose. Doctor Olivier, I know I sound like I've lost my marbles, and proposing that I'm some sort of weird mutant, but I wish I were lying."

His empathetic look reassured her. He typed something on the computer. "Is there anything else you have noticed?"

"Such as?"

Olivier thought for a moment. "Oh, I don't know, such as were you able to do these things at a young age?"

Calla pursed her lips, thinking for several seconds and shifted in her tight seat. "I'm not sure: You've always been my family doctor since Mama, and Papa Cress started bringing me here. If anybody, you would have evidence of it."

He turned the screen toward her. Her medical file stared her in the face. "Look here, Calla, when you were five, Mama and Papa Cress brought you in for a routine checkup. They said you had complained about migraines, quite unusual for a girl

288

your age. They also told me you said you could literally see your neighbors through the walls of your house."

Calla rose and scanned the screen as she read his medical notes. She turned to face him. "Did you believe them, Doctor? Do you believe me?"

Dr. Olivier rolled his chair back and twitched a little. "Well, at first I didn't, but then it happened again a year later when you were six and similarly for your seventh-year checkup. Each time, it would be something different. Seeing through a cup, a desk—"

"I don't remember."

"The day they reported you were able to count exactly how much money the woman in the beauty shop had in her purse, they got worried. They started discouraging you, I think, and you never mentioned it since."

"Do you know if it kept happening?"

He edged back. "I'm not certain. I think you scared them. They didn't want you singled out or even bullied at school. They never mentioned it to me again and, before I knew it, you were off to Beacon Academy."

Calla advanced toward the window. She peered down at the slowing traffic and the London skyline above the rooftops. She took in the vivid bird's eye view of the neighborhood before shifting to face the doctor. "Am I crazy, doctor? Have you ever heard of such ridiculous things?"

His gaze followed her as he rose. He drew toward her and positioned a comforting hand on her tense shoulder. "Actually, yes. Look here."

He led her back to the computer, and they took their seats in front of the screen. He stopped at an article from one of his research files. "When Mama and Papa Cress stopped talking about it I dismissed it as childhood escapism until I found this."

He turned the screen her way. "You weren't alone. After this medical paper was published, I heard of three other accounts, one in 1963 and one even earlier. The details are sketchy as they were taken from a doctor's personal journal in the 1880s."

Calla skimmed the headline with the eagerness of a hungry wolf while following his narrative. The title read:

HUMAN WITH X-RAY EYES

"When was this published?" Calla asked.

"Several years ago, probably a decade now. The patient in question must be older than you."

"I don't follow. This reads like a comic book account. What happened to this boy? Here, let me see...he was from Alaska?"

Dr. Olivier rotated the flat screen back toward him and hit a few buttons on the keyboard. "It's quite an extraordinary tale really. Demyan Matthews was adopted from Kinshasa. His parents imagined he was a boy just like any other as he grew up, yet he was mature for his age. He learned to do things more quickly than other children did, like talking at just seven months. At one he could recite poetry, and by three he'd learned the alphabet and mastered how to operate a car.

"When he was ten Demyan went to the hospital with a broken leg. There were complications during surgery, and he complained that he could see into his leg and that something had gone wrong with the operation."

Calla studied Olivier's face. "What was it?"

"It was discovered that cotton swabs had been left inside him. He then had a second operation to remove the swabs. Several months later, he began to notice that he could see inside people and objects. He told his teacher that he saw what looked like a thick cord, two beans and an orange inside a patient. His mother believed him. Although Demyan didn't know the correct words he was describing her intestines, kidneys and the heart."

Calla slumped back against the leather seat, listening intently.

Dr. Olivier leaned forward. "After this happened, on many occasions doctors ran a battery of tests to find out if the little boy really did have x-ray vision. In one case Demyan drew a picture of what he saw inside a doctor's stomach, apparently marking the exact spot where the doctor had a cyst. He also disagreed with the diagnosis of a cancer patient, saying all she could see was a small swelling and not the large tumor they saw. Further tests on the woman seemed to prove Demyan was correct.

"Incredible."

"Demyan was brought to England by a national newspaper and, allegedly, he spotted all of the fractures and metal pins in a woman who'd recently been in a road accident. The woman was fully clothed and had no visible signs of how or where she'd been injured."

"That's implausible!"

"I know. It even baffles my medical mind. Incidentally, the Committee for the Scientific Investigation of Claims of the Paranormal and the affiliated Commission for Scientific Medicine and Mental Health performed more tests on Demyan. They needed to scientifically assess his claims."

"What did they find?" Calla asked.

"The tests were intended as a first stage. If he could pass this, then his claims would merit further research and testing."

"Did he?"

"I don't know. However, as I said, there were two separate incidents a lot earlier. I can print all of this for you to read more."

Dumbfounded, Calla knew she didn't have much time to react to the news. Any minute now they had to leave and find the next carbonado.

"I thought I was losing my mind, but now, I'm not sure what I think. What does it mean? What should I do, doctor? Am I like this Demyan?"

"Look, Calla, I don't want you to worry. You know I discourage anxiety, but I have detected some abnormality in your brain tissue and blood cells over the years. The cells appear to be rapidly developing in your brain. I would like you to see a specialist, a friend of mine, Dr. Bertrand in Paris."

"Who is he?"

"Besides being a distinguished professor in psychiatry, neurosciences, and psychology, he is also a Medical Institute investigator on the committees I just mentioned."

Dr. Olivier reached for the desk phone to locate a number in the directory. "We were fellow students in medical school, and he has a personal interest in this sort of thing. He's been studying this phenomenon for years. I think he may shed some light on your condition." He gave her a consoling look. "Calla, I'm also here to help."

She sighed.

Do I really want to know more?

CHAPTER 25

"*I*f the Deveron document was in our possession how did we lose it?*" cried the first angry debater of the five-member panel.

"How did it get all the way to Russia? And now it's under German jurisdiction," echoed the woman next to him.

The BBC 1 television station loomed audibly through the single-deluxe hotel room.

"That's exactly my point. That manuscript rightly belongs to Great Britain," blurted the journalist hosting the television broadcast.

"Ridiculous," Eichel said.

Eichel had returned to his room half-wondering why the woman had bolted from him. He was sure he'd seen her somewhere before, with her light bounce and her chestnut, shoulder-length tresses. Could it have been in Berlin? He wasn't sure and glimpsed back at the blaring TV set. It was merely background noise. He concentrated better with some sort of clamor around him. It must be all his years working around crime scenes and loud police stations.

He lowered the racket, trying to shut the world out for a moment. This hunt had turned into a drifting, disorganized case. Now that he'd left his badge on the floor of a high-powered, crime-control organization would he be able to escape ISTF's watch undetected? What he thought would be a quick case, and the chance to oversee one of the grandest cultural inaugurations in Berlin had turned into complete mayhem.

The news broadcast concluded, and the channel proceeded with more speculation about the missing artifacts. How had the press acquired the details of the Deveron case? He swore. This was supposed to be a top-secret affair among five governments. He was running out of clues. Eichel marched to the closet in the cramped space beside the main entrance, found his trench coat and dug deep into the breast pocket.

With great caution, he drew out the photocopies and wandered back to the main room. He spread them on the bed until the stolen information lined the entire surface area of his double bed. He glanced at each page before making his way to the mini bar. Without any thought, he grabbed a small Jack Daniels bottle. He found some ice in the icebox and poured himself a drink. He took a sip, guzzling the soothing liqueur. The chilled concoction rolled down his eager throat, calming his anxiety. He emptied the glass and stared at the stacked ice cubes.

"I can't do this!"

Eichel slammed the glass down on the table, his mind reeling back to his suspension. The excessive drinking had started the whole mess. He scowled at the half-empty whiskey bottle and took it to the bathroom. He emptied the remaining contents in the sink and shoved the bottle in the wastebasket. He glanced in the mirror, focusing on his frosted hair. He'd aged more than he had wanted. This isn't where he was supposed to be at this point in life.

If he was going to secure the permanent chief spot he needed to solve the Priam and Deveron disappearances. The last thing he needed was a relapse into drinking. His title would be stripped if he didn't deliver the desired results. Or worse, possibly lose his job.He frowned, perching over the porcelain sink.

His reflection interrogated him. What had gone wrong? What clue had he not examined? Why had he resolved to stealing evidence from ISTF? He'd be caught. Well, maybe they deserved it.

He had come in good faith. They'd not been willing to cooperate. They, meaning Mason Laskfell, a man he had once admired greatly. Mason represented everything he aspired to be: brilliant, canny and efficient.

Eichel threw some cold water in his face and wiped the dampness with the towel provided. He strolled back to the bedroom. With the TV racket beginning to annoy him, he switched off the clamor and sat on the edge of the bed. Scattered papers stared at him, and heavy eyelids shut out light as he reclined, lowering against the pliable pillows.

A thought drew his attention.

"Why did I not think of this before?" He sprang to an upright position. "What was in those damn notes?"

He found the page in question. There in the file report, he reread it.

AGENTS COPPER J21 and SILVER X3

KV2/9681

Agent Silver X3 and Copper J21 are in possession of the Deveron Manuscript. Its origin hasn't been determined.

According to SILVER X3, the Deveron details the whereabouts of distinct carbonados. Carbonado diamonds are relatively porous masses of fine-grained diamond, mixed with graphite and other rare minerals. They were first found in 1843 in Bahia, Brazil. Some have been found in Central Africa.

The origin of carbonados remains debatable; one clue is the presence of odd minerals such as silicon carbide, pure titanium metal and pure silicon metal and iron-chromium alloy. Recent research suggests that carbonados are not necessarily formed by a meteorite impact, but may possibly be fragments of a meteorite from beyond our galaxy.

MI6 – OPERATION STAR

The agents working with NASA and Vladimir Merkov, a scientist and Russian defector, are to verify if fragments of a cooled star could survive, traveling across billions of miles to Earth. They'll determine whether carbonados possess nuclear compositions unknown to man.

OPERATION MEADOW:

Silver X3 reports having established the whereabouts of one carbonado, whose composition he verified as "unnatural."

NOTES:

X3 and J21 have periodically been paired on other severe cases.

Eichel stretched his arms and reached for a section of the report that contained a photo. The caption read:

· · ·

Copper J21 – Missing in Action.

The long-haired woman in the black and white headshot impressed him with her determined expression. She resembled an inquiring child. Her stare pierced his mind, distracting him from what he thought was an intelligent brain behind her charade. He'd seen several, female secret agent mug shots in his line of work, but none appeared so unwavering. Her round face and somewhat oversized eyes gleamed with passion and empathy.

He searched for a photo of SILVER X3, but none was evident in the spread of papers on the bed. He studied the paper with the woman's information:

COPPER J21

Legal name: Not Registered/NA

Special skills: Knowledge of twenty-four languages and twelve ancient dialects;

Experience: Modern military communications techniques; procedures for processing and distributing intelligence data; methods for handling, distributing and safeguarding military information. Deciphering clues and translation.

Other: Possibly deceased. Missing in action during a routine procedure in Russia. Body not found.

File closed

The report stopped there.

Pity, she must have been an exceptional agent. He crosschecked with SILVER X3's details.

SILVER X3

Legal name: *Unknown*

Special skills: *Knowledge of eighteen languages and six ancient dialects. Field agent.*

Experience/Skills: *Involved in the work of code breakers and collecting vital enemy information.Carrying out and reporting on covert intelligence gathering operations overseas. Gathering secret intelligence the government needs to promote and defend UK national interests.*

Other: *Resigned. Whereabouts are unknown.*

File closed

Too many secrets. He found his phone and dialed his office in Berlin.

A man picked up the call. "*Ja*, Peter *hier*."

"*Gruess dich*, Peter. I need you to scan a British agent's name for me. It goes back about thirty years."

He paused, knowing he was venturing into uncharted territory. "Could you use your contact in British intelligence? You know...the one in ISTF?'

"Are you sure you want to go down this route?" Peter hesitated. "What is the name?

"It's a code name. SILVER X3. Call me when you have something. Thanks, Peter."

An agitated gaze arrested his face as Eichel hung up. Was

he breaking the rules again? *It needs to be done.* He thought for a moment. This may come to haunt him one day.

DAY 11
8:39 A.M.

"I'll be back tonight."

Jack shot Calla a concerned look. "Sure? Why now? You know we're on a tight schedule. Nash has also disappeared."

Calla bit her lip. "I know, Jack."

She battled whether to tell him about her conversation with Dr. Olivier. She decided against it as she gave him a peck on the cheek. "I'll see you later tonight."

Forty minutes later Calla glanced out the window of the Eurostar as it set off from St. Pancras International station. The train zipped past green fields and small villages along its quick route to the French capital. About twenty-five minutes into the journey the intercom on the train blurted out a garbled message about submerging under the Channel.

With her hand cradling her cell phone Calla's fingers slid across the surface, and she tapped in Nash's number. She stopped at the last digit and stared at the phone. One last chance before leaving English soil. With the image of him and Eva still fresh in her mind, she fought back the thought. The signal disappeared and slouched into her seat.

It's my fault.

She'd dissuaded Nash for months. Every part of her screamed with regret and with heavy arms and shoulders pulled low, her drowsy eyes fell shut.

"Mademoiselle?"

Calla stirred.

"Mademoiselle, we've arrived in Paris. Didn't you hear the announcement?" the onboard ticket conductor asked.

"Merci."

Calla sprang out of her seat. How long had she slept? She reached for her belongings and ambled for the exit. She marched up the frantic Gare du Nord platform, toward the door of the nineteenth-century structure, hoping to grab a quick cab. Stepping onto the sidewalk, she took in the impressionable and culturally diverse ambiance of the bustling 18th district of Paris. Calla inhaled. Spring in the French capital had never disappointed her.

She waited patiently in the cab line and eventually settled in a cigarette-smoke infested Volkswagen.

"14 rue de Jean-Richepin."

The taxi driver nodded. The street was in Paris's sixteenth district and the taxi worked its way into traffic.

The ride took fifteen minutes.

"We're here, *mademoiselle.*"

She paid him and paced toward the address Dr. Olivier had given her. She hesitated a moment outside the six-story Art Nouveau building.Calla breathed heavily, fighting the feeling of turning back.

Do I really want to know more?

Willing every muscle to relax she rang the doorbell.

"Oui?" came a blasé female voice.

"Calla Cress de Londres pour Dr. Bertrand," she said, asking to see the doctor.

A buzzer blared, and she pushed open the iron gates. She advanced through a cobblestone courtyard toward the main building. At the end of the inner court, the intercom by a second entrance indicated that Dr. Bertrand was on the sixth floor of the limestone building. It took her all of two minutes to ascend the ornate, sandstone staircases.

When she set foot on the top of the stairs, an elegant receptionist sat in the lobby working behind her sleek monitor. Calla crossed the few meters from the top of the staircase toward the door and continued to the reception desk. A pine wood scent enveloped the room, giving it calm gleam.

She dragged her feet along the lavender carpet and made a stop at the receptionist's desk. "*Bonjour*. Dr. Bertrand is expecting me."

"*Bonjour, Mademoiselle*. What's your name?"

"Calla. Calla Cress."

"*Un instant, s'il vous plait*. Please, take a seat for a moment."

The woman left her station and disappeared through the handcrafted French doors. Calla sank into a snug armchair against the wall. Above her hung an impressionist painting. She turned her head to consider its fine brush stroke and scanned the rest of the room. Feeling more like a hotel lobby than a doctor's waiting room she fought the urge to explore the rest of the artwork in the lobby. The sound of approaching pumps signaled that the receptionist had returned in the company of an energetic French-Caribbean man who donned a white coat over a smart suit.

"Hello, Calla. *Enchanté*," he said, extending a hand. "I'm Dr. Bertrand. It's a pleasure to meet you. Please come this way."

Dr. Bertrand's voice rang with joy and a trace of an Antillean island drawl. Calla rose and received his warm, firm handshake.

"I hope you had a good journey from London."

"Yes, thank you."

Calla tailed behind him. How could an accomplished academic like Dr. Bertrand be so calm when he faced difficult cases almost every day and, according to Dr. Olivier, most remained inexplicable?He led her through the establishment. Unlike most doctors she knew, who impatiently clocked the next patient through while trying to make the day's quota, Dr. Bertrand was more conversational, considerate and witty.

Her shoulders unloosened, and she marched down the hall with him.He turned to her as she walked a couple of paces behind. "I know you're on a tight schedule. Dr. Olivier filled me in and sent me your file," he said.

"Is there anything you can tell me based on the information?" Calla said.

"Not until we have done some tests. I appreciate your coming in on short notice. Sometimes it's better to catch the symptoms of a condition while it persists."

"Thanks, doctor."

He placed a hand on her shoulder. "Today I'll only perform some routine scans and tests. I'll have to administer a general anesthetic though. Is that okay with you?"

"Yes, by all means, doctor."

They stopped outside a closed door. "You can change in here. The nurse will assist you with anything you need. I'll see you in a few minutes."

Calla undressed in the changing room. She slid on a clinic robe and noticed that the veins in her arms and legs were raised more than usual. She'd not eaten or had a drink in the last several hours as Dr. Bertrand had instructed over the phone.

A knock sounded at the door. "Ready, Calla?"

She placed her belongings in the provided locker and clanked it shut. "Yes."

Dr. Bertrand led her to an examination room a few doors down from the changing room. The room boasted the latest medical equipment, most of which she'd never seen in her life, a few reading monitors and a large scanning recliner bed. Calla's hand trembled. *Will they find that I'm not normal? Am I dying?*

"Try to relax," said Bertrand probably sensing her paranoia. "Please lie down here on the examination table. We'll put you under for an hour or so."

As two nurses performed the general anesthetic Calla's body responded, and her eyes drifted out of focus as the drugs took effect, sending her into a deep sleep. The last thing she remembered before drifting was Dr. Bertrand's instructions to his assistants.

———

5:19 P.M.
WALLACE COLLECTION MUSEUM
LONDON

"Are you a lover of the fine arts, Miss Riche?"

Eva flipped around. Mason made his way toward her. Her attention had been captured by a terracotta piece by celebrated, Italian sculptor Antonio Canova in the Porphyry Court of the notable Wallace Collection Museum. There it stood, headless and armless, the ancient goddess of youth, Hebe. Eva wished she embodied the same amount of freedom and courage.

Mason had agreed to meet her at the national museum situated in a historic, London townhouse and home to one of Europe's finest collections of paintings, furniture, arms, armor, and porcelain.

"Mr. Laskfell?" she stammered. "Good afternoon."

"What can I do for you?"

Mason had heard of Miss Riche but never once made her acquaintance. He acknowledged she was Samuel Riche's preposterous daughter and, for a journalist, the media articles she landed in far outnumbered those she'd written. Samuel had called in a favor before meeting with Mason. "Just talk to her. She's hard to stop when her mind is set on something."

Mason agreed with reservation. She was a bargaining chip. This meeting would work in his favor.

Eva beamed a euphoric smile. "Thank you for taking time in your schedule to see me, Mr. Laskfell. I know you're a busy man so I'll keep this short."

Mason edged closer to the sculpture. "You still have not told me if you're a lover of the fine arts?"

303

She glanced at the sculpture. "Today I am."

Mason grimaced. "Then why choose to meet here?"

She frowned. "I know you are."

Mason was no time waster, and he could see she wasn't either. All she needed were a few minutes to get his attention. Might as well do that here where he felt at ease, no phones, no distractions, just exquisite art. Eva took a shaky step toward him, her stilettos scuffing on the polished marble. "I need some information on an old school friend. My father said you work for the government and could help me out with information on any soul in this country, living or dead." She veered closer and whispered. "The name is Calla Cress."

Mason drew his eyebrows together, entertained by her movement around him like a slithery serpent. Why would she be interested in Calla Cress?

"What do you need to know about Calla Cress?" he said.

Eva's eyes lit up as they moved to the next piece on display. "So you know her?"

"Are you guessing? She works for me...some of the time."

He lengthened his stride and fixed her with a contemplating look. "Miss Riche, if she's a friend of yours, why are you not in contact? Why would you need a favor from a government organization?"

They stopped by a Rembrandt self-portrait, a canvas coated with a heavy application of paint by the Dutch painter. Eva bit her lip as she eyed Rembrandt's thick, tone-dead coloring on the monochrome portrait, mainly where the light fell boldest. She twitched before she diverted her eyes from the image.

"Mr. Laskfell, I know you need something desperately from my father, and I can help you get it. That's why I'm cutting to the chase. I need to know Calla's involvement with the Deveron document."

Mason jolted his head back, raising an eyebrow. He glared into her purposeful eyes, analyzing her dark motives before treading further along the gallery, partly studying Fragonard's eighteenth-century depiction of a swinging damsel and musing over her request. She was a meddlesome journalist and not one about to share the details of her exclusive.

"Before I entertain your query what is it you intend to do with the information about Cress? She's one of the best contributors to ISTF in linguistics and affairs related to history," he said.

Eva's smile wore into a frown. "That's my business, but I could make it yours. I could share whatever I find about the Deveron Manuscript."

"What makes that valuable to me?"

"I've heard of the government's interest, particularly ISTF's, in the Deveron."

"And?"

"Whereas they may not be willing to get their hands dirty in the sullied work of investigative reporting, I am."

His thoughts exactly. The two were treading on mutual ground. Mason's eyes narrowed. He noted the squirm on her face. "I can give you something to start with. In return, I'll need to approve any copy before publication, or I pull the plug on you."

She shot him a triumphant look. "Agreed."

"Eva. Can I call you Eva? I'll also help you out, on condition you keep me informed of your progress."

"So you *do* need my information."

"Don't flatter yourself. Let's say I just like to know what I'm getting with this bargain."

She extended her hand to seal the deal. "All right."

Mason glanced down at her elegant hand. "I have one more stipulation. Your father must sign the documents I sent him. Their contents are of no consequence to you. He'll understand my drift. I'll expect them on my desk within twenty-four hours."

"I can't guarantee that, Mr. Laskfell. That's papa's affair."

"Make it yours, Eva. You came for my help. If you want it,

then you'll give me something in return. That's how this little proposition of ours will work."

Mason was driving a stringent agreement, but this was his last offer, or there would be no deal.

She shook on it. "Okay."

Mason fished out his phone and made a couple of calls while strolling through the gallery.

Eva turned her back, pretending not to eavesdrop.

He toyed with his phone. "I'm sending you a file now."

Her eyes lit up as she swerved around. "Oh. Here's my number."

"I already have it."

Eva's shifted back a step. "How do you—?"

"It's my business to know my enemies and—" He eyed her reaction. "My friends."

The files flooded in, one by one keeping her cell phone beeping several times. She opened one file, and eager eyes scanned the information. Though miniature in font size on the screen Calla's employment file stared back at her.

Calla floated and floated, a weightless flight above the ecosphere. The clouds brushed her cheeks, some gently, some with a moist, steamy punch. She navigated above mountains, over fields, through distant cities, across calm lakes, over rough oceans and past wild savannahs, with her omniscient mind controlling her direction and speed toward her desired destination. She soared above planet Earth.

Even in her wandering, she knew there was a purpose, a task she had to fulfill. Her mind told her that she was on a journey to visit three places and her flight scooped her to the northern hemisphere of the Earth, hovering above England.

Nothing about the architecture, the roads and the fields she saw acknowledged the century. It had to be several centuries back. She landed outside an unassuming cottage, perhaps a shack. Night had fallen, and she traversed the walls floating into a candlelit room. Though crammed with men and women talking, and some laughing, jovial children scribbling on the dusty dirt floors, including a delicious stew in a boiling pot, no one acknowledged her presence. As she listened to two men talking by the fire, she saw Watcher. Unable to hear the dialog there by the fire Watcher received a box from a white hooded man in long, flowing robes. The minute Watcher had the box he held it close to his heart and bowed to the hooded man. He then turned to leave and glided right through Calla.

His sudden exit through her core caused her to stumble backward, and she drifted through space. Her next destination took her through the Tuscan hills of Italy. She flew above the resplendent fields and advanced over a zigzagging, cypress tree-lined road that edged toward a picturesque Tuscan villa. Roman women gathered lavender and poppies in the meadows. Their giggles filled the late summer's day. Like her last destination, these women didn't see her. She glided around them freely smelling the robust bouquets they collected.

In the distance, she saw two men walking in the meadows. Their voices were deep in conversation. One strutted adroit in elegant pace, a gladiator it would seem. His white-hooded companion traipsed alongside, his face shielded from the world. The hooded man placed a small black box in the gladiator's large palms. The box resembled the former one.

As she hovered by the men, they didn't see her curious gaze at the container. She could almost reach it. She stretched her hand to touch it. A drop of rain landed on her cold cheek, and dark clouds covered the sky.

The droplets pelted first in faint streams, and then in showers of hail. Calla sought to fly above the raging storm. Even with the thunder and lightning, she flew through the clouds unharmed to a third destination. It was unknown to her. All she saw were rows of huts, mud houses, banana plantations and palm trees. Soaring above the most beautiful beach she'd ever seen, with its sandy white terrain, she descended and landed on the soft sand. With each step she took, the warm sand massaged her feet. This time the hooded man in white clutched a third box, walking a few feet in front of her. Where was he going? She followed him as he left the beach and entered the rain forest land. Heat scorched the island. Without warning a strong wind pulled her with a mighty force. She ascended further and further away from the hooded man and into the heavens. Her vision was blurred.

"Calla," said a French-accented, male voice. "Calla, wake up!"

Calla came to and focused first on Dr. Bertrand's perched face, then the nurse's. She slowly turned her head, facing the window across from the examination bed.

She regained consciousness.

A doctor's torch gleamed into her eyes. "How do you feel, Calla?" Dr. Bertrand asked.

Her voice stammered as she spoke. "Fine, mostly drugged."

All she could think about was the hooded man and what she'd seen.

Dr. Bertrand set a hand behind her head. "You've been under for about an hour, but you should be fine soon."

Calla's eye twitched, and she trembled.

"It's a normal reaction to the anesthetic," the doctor said.

Her feet were heavy as if they no longer belonged to her and she struggled upright. "Am I all right?"

Dr. Bertrand helped her stand. "We won't have the results for another twenty-four hours, but I'll be in touch as soon as I have them."

Calla nodded slowly. "*Merci.*I'll wait to hear from you."

The clock on the wall read 3:45 p.m. Her Eurostar train with direct service to London, would be leaving Gare du Nord train station just before 6:00 p.m. that evening.

One and a half hours later, her body recovered from the drugs. Moments later, Bertrand escorted her to the reception. "Try not to worry. I'll be in touch very soon."

Calla forced a smile and turned to the receptionist. "Could you please call a cab for me?"

Rain pelted on the windshield as the taxi made its way to the station. A tinted Range Rover tailed at a safe pace behind her cab. Several minutes later Calla's taxi pulled in at Gare du Nord station. After it shuddered to a halt, Calla descended and shuffled toward the platforms.

The Range Rover continued past her cab and parked across the street. A figure emerged and made a phone call. "She'll be on the train soon."

CHAPTER 26

5:56 P.M.
Gare Du Nord
Paris, France

Calla trotted up the Eurostar platform and found her seat in the train car. She rubbed her sweaty palms along her thighs, trying to wipe off the dampness that had started almost immediately after the nurse had reversed the anesthetic. The side effects of the medical procedure had left her with mild dizziness, yet she'd managed to navigate her way to the right platform.

Time was running out and whatever was at the end of the manuscript's enigmatic puzzle remained her only connection to discovering the truths about her family. Calla sunk into her seat leaning toward the window. She debated once more whether to contact Nash. But the image of him and Eva loomed in her mind like an unwanted relative coming to visit.

She dialed Jack's number. "Jack, I'm on the train just about ready to depart for London."

Jack's voice was comforting. "You okay? Why'd you go there?"

"Something I had to do."

Jack didn't pursue the matter. "I discovered something more regarding the stones. I'll show you once you get in. You want me to pick you up at the station?"

"Thanks, Jack. I've got my car. See you soon."

She hung up.

The train advanced on the tracks. Calla rose to find the restaurant car. As she balanced to counter the train's speed within the narrow aisle space a man thudded into her right shoulder as he hurried past.

"Hey!" she said.

He kept walking.

Fierce movement drew her eye toward his militaristic frame. He zipped around. She turned instinctively, in time to shield herself from a powerful fist, and nearly collapsed into an empty seat as her knees buckled.

She padded the floor for her shoulder bag and read the intent in his eyes. He wanted the manuscript and reeled with the shudders of the train's speed as he advanced toward her. For a moment Calla struggled to move her body, still in recovery from heavy medication. She took deep breaths until she could raise her head. Before she could move, he gripped her by the neck and shoved her onto the floor.

Her body drew strength from the fall, and she launched her heel into his gut. He collided backward and slammed his nose on the edge of the divider door. She darted away from him, down the narrow passage to the next car, fighting jolts of trepidation as startled passengers looked on.

Her assailant shot up, wiped his bloodied nose and chased after her. She staggered forward, gripping headrests for support, battling the whizzing speed of the train as it threatened to throw her over.The pursuing man stumbled into several passengers as he chased, taking rapid strides in her direction.

At the end of the car, she hurtled herself recklessly into the women's toilet. She slammed the door shut, secured the lock and back-pedaled until she hit the wall she stared at the sinister lock.

She waited her strength waning. Calla needed her full tenacity back and a few minutes would do it. The look in his beady eyes had threatened spitefulness. He would duel for her hide at all costs.

She dialed Jack's number.

No pickup.

She tried Nash.

No answer.

The high-speed train approached the Channel tunnel. The brief announcement was faint in her ear even as she calculated her next move in the putrid compartment. Trapped, a sudden jolt at the door set her heart galloping to her throat. She placed a hand on the lock.

Calla took a deep breath, welcoming the strong desire to see his face. She turned the knob and waited.

No movement.

She crept out of the compartment like a frazzled rat and stepped into the corridor and scanned both ways. She'd half expected another strike.

None came.

She took a deep breath and retraced her steps to her seat, peering from passenger to passenger in a frantic effort to locate him. With no further antagonism, she sank to her seat and stood alert for several seconds, unable to settle before sinking into the upholstery. Fear trailed through her veins as she armed herself with determination. The sudden flickering of the overhead lights set her on alert as her trained eye scanned the compartment once more.

Soon the bolting train trembled to a halt, jolting her forehead into the headrest of the seat in front of her.

The lights went out.

She waited.

He could force his way toward her in no time.

She curled her fist and gathered more resolve as pitch black arrested the car. After what seemed like an eternity the lights stabilized and switched back on. The train continued its journey.

"Ladies and gentlemen, we apologize for any inconvenience, but we've just experienced a short circuit. The problem has been fixed, and we should be in London in good time."

The train pulled into London's St. Pancras International station. She scurried off the speed train and bustled past disembarking passengers. She would get a head start. Calla gripped her bag, sure of the manuscript's safety and scuttled for the exit.

5:40 P.M.

Mason slid the phone into his slacks. "I'm sure you will find these documents useful. I expect your father's signature tomorrow. Good day."

He strolled to the end of the gallery and saluted her goodbye. Eva slumped into a bench along the gallery wall. Visitors and museum tours didn't faze her concentration as she studied document after document, and scoured the report for any material she could use.

She stopped at one file.

NAME: CALLA IRIS CRESS

Employment: Curator, British Museum, Roman and Byzantine antiquities
Address: 27 Axton Way, West Kensington
Telephone: 0208 777 939 / 0799 212 777
Next of Kin: Sharon and Carl Cress

"Damn you, Mason, none of this gives me what I want!"

She left the museum cursing him under her breath. Museums made her uncomfortable. As if the walls and the artifacts took on an unnerving life of their own, silent witnesses to her thoughts. She advanced toward her car, parked minutes away from the museum. Once inside she scanned the files again and made a note of Calla's current cell phone number.

Could she muster the courage?

No.

Eva and Calla had never understood each other. And, often, their interactions hadn't been cordial whatsoever. Maybe she could hunt Calla's next of kin. Or even better she would follow her for a while. She started her engine, slid into first gear, then wove into the congested streets. It would take longer to reach West London. If only she knew the type of car Calla drove or what she looked like now.

The files contained no photographs.

She reread them. Even though Calla's adoptive parents were listed, the 'whom to contact in case of an emergency' field recorded a completely different name, a Dr. Austin Olivier.

Within thirty minutes she stood outside the doctor's listed practice in West London. Eva waited a few minutes before gathering enough tenacity to go to the door.

She rang the doorbell. A woman's voice answered. Eva searched her mind for a fictitious name, a habit she'd picked up in her journalistic career. "Yes, my name is Rochelle Richards. I would like to make an appointment with Dr. Olivier. He was a friend of my father's."

"Come back in the morning. The practice is closed."

"This can't wait."

The heavy oak buzzed open.

<hr />

Calla glanced up the length of the Shard. She scurried in after her attacker. He'd secured her bag with the Deveron Manuscript and the stones, past the security guards who lay unconscious on the lobby floor. *Got in your way, huh?* She checked on the three men and a woman. They were breathing. One man had endured a massive abrasion on his forehead.

She persevered. *I need it back!*

She squinted in frustration and calculated which way he'd gone. Calla darted to the elevator doors positioned a few steps past the reception desk. She called for it and scurried inside when the doors pulled open. On the twenty-eighth floor she stepped out. For a moment she considered taking the next car to the higher levels until flouncing footsteps sounded behind her. She spun around and caught a shadow disappearing behind the glass wall on her left. He fled out onto an open ledge he'd managed to jar open with a discarded wrench that lay inches from her feet.

She charged after him, toward an abandoned building maintenance unit. The window cleaning cradle system had been installed to polish thousands of reflective glass panes. He leaped, his obscure figure vaulting onto the scaffolding pipes that balanced the unit. They hung suspended around the perimeter of the pristine structure. Ascending upward he used it to support his rapid limbs and swung onto an adjacent scaffolding bridge.

Calla followed suit and watched him use the bridge's frigid cables to scramble higher. Like an irate lizard, her assailant scooted up the cable that had been left for cleaning work. She tailed close behind, not daring to look below. Her rickety feet balanced in determination on the cold steelwork of the cleaning carousels. She held on tight with her white-knuckled hands that numbed with each grip, causing the blood to descend down to the lower parts of her arms.

The pair scampered higher, past the floors of the Shangri-La Hotel housed inside the spire of the Shard, on the fortieth floor of the iconic tower. Calla took in the silence in the night air, almost as if each level she climbed turned the city noise down a notch.

A strong breeze wafted past her, almost toppling her over. The man slipped ahead of her, his boots losing grip on the scaffolding. She reached for him, and he veered his foot out of her reach, and she missed him by mere inches. Calla pursued the grunting climber, eager to retrieve her only connection to her family.

The chase persevered to the seventy-second level of the soaring, thousand-foot construction.After the drawn-out climb, the man pulled himself onto the public viewing platform of the highest spire in Europe. It loomed over the vibrant streetscape of Southwark along the south bank of the Thames.

Calla steered to where he stood in the viewing gallery just above the seventy-two habitable floors. She glimpsed around her. They'd reached the building summit.Both stood still, clasping onto the tension cables of the sophisticated equipment as intermittent gusts of wind currents threatened to topple them over. Neither moved, each studying the other for the first assault. The man edged back, holding onto the restraints while clasping her treasures.

A meter below Calla cringed from the apex of the

skyscraper, at the 360-degree view across London. Unable to see any detail, no buses, cars, people, just rows of lights and track lines resembling converging river paths. She took a deep breath. She tore her eyes away from the oversized urban circuit board.

The man shifted backward, balancing his athletic frame with only a foot of walking space left behind him on the suspension cable. An inevitable drop to sudden death. He swung his foot to trip her and missed. Calla gripped the upper wires and launched both feet off the lower cable. He lunged forward, reaching for her shoulder.

She crouched. With a euphoric grin, the man held out her bag over the flimsy railing. It swayed slowly over the edge of the façade. "How much do you want this?"

She moved an inch toward him as he oscillated the manuscript and her stones in the unforgiving, high winds. Would the building maintenance unit withstand conditions at this height? A loose rope hung on the suspended cabling next to the wincing assailant, mistakenly discarded by the window cleaners. He reached for it slowly with his free hand. If she made a rapid move toward him, Calla could secure the bag and the rope as well. She'd been a good rock climber once and relied on any residue skills from her alpine climbing days.

The man took a quick glance behind him as he stood trapped between her dilemma and the three hundred meter drop. Calla inhaled profoundly and shoved forward with an outstretched arm aimed at the bag. Her other hand reached for the rope the assailant held on to.

The thug tugged the rope out of her reach. Calla caught a sinister smirk on his face.

He'd miscalculated his action. She swiped her waist bag from his grasp. His look of revulsion was the last thing she visualized before she lost her footing. The manuscript and the stones were secure. She glanced down and failed to grasp onto the life rope.

CHAPTER 27

Would Peter consider a personal favor? Eichel pored over the last few sheets of papers he'd photocopied. Peter had often mentioned a former school acquaintance inside the British arm of ISTF by the name of Jack Kleve. Jack must have access to British intelligence. Eichel didn't know him personally, and wasn't one to use his team for information, but this was crucial.

Scratching his creased forehead he wished he had managed to copy the entire file. He strode the length of the room in deep contemplation. Why did SILVER X3 not want to take on the case of the Deveron Manuscript with MI6 and his wife? The footnote on the reports suggested SILVER X3 had required much persuasion. Eichel read further into the endnotes.

After the disappearance of COPPER J21, SILVER X3 lost all attentiveness to pursuing the Deveron case. A detachment to the operation was noted in his manner.

. . .

What happened to COPPER J21 to cause SILVER X3's reaction? No evidence stood out in the documents.

The Secret Intelligence Service convinced SILVER X3 to accept the facts surrounding her demise. Two months after her disappearance, he resigned from service.

Possibly to search for her or her killer. It was common for agents to take personal vendettas. The footnote ended there. Eichel found the personal information section and scanned the report.

The Deveron case required the special cryptanalyst and anthropological credentials of COPPER J21. From 1962-1964, she served as a cryptanalyst with the British army. She read Russian diplomatic cipher traffic from Moscow to Kabul, Tashkent and Turkestan.

Similarly, SILVER X3 was involved in all aspects of directing interception and traffic analysis and working on ciphers. After her disappearance and his resignation, the Deveron case was closed in May 1966.

Eichel read another footnote on the bottom of the following page, dated just a few days ago.

The Deveron case has been reopened. It has been discovered that the document resides within Priam's Treasure at Pushkin's museum in Moscow. It is to be returned to Germany and showcased at the Pergamon Museum in Berlin. In SILVER X3's absence, Allegra Driscoll will lead the operation and verify the Deveron's validity and ownership.

The classic ring tone of his cell phone interrupted his reading. "Hallo?"

"Ja, Peter hier."

"Hallo, Peter."

Eichel disliked getting to the point but he was running out of time. "What have you found out from Kleve?" he asked in German.

"He didn't confirm if he knew Calla Cress. Driscoll only asked Cress to do some documentation work with her in Berlin."

"What could he tell us about Mason?"

"Just some information about Mason in relation to the manuscript," Peter said.

Eichel was intrigued. He'd suspected Mason was hiding something that day at the ISTF offices. "Go on."

"Incidentally, Mason has asked Kleve to trace three prominent people: Margot Arlington, Rupert Kumar and Samuel Riche.

"Will these people pay to get the manuscript and the golden goblet of Priam? Why?"

"I'm not sure, especially the Republican candidate Arlington. The British government seems to have her cooperation with anything related to Mason."

"I see? Perhaps Mason is willing to sell the Deveron to the highest bidder. These three are quite prominent names."

"I don't know. Jack didn't say."

Eichel's impatience got the better of him. "What does Arlington know?" His shoulders dropped. "Peter, I know and Jack are close friends and his friendship with you is outside the realm of your profession. You've often told me of the way you bonded at McGill. I appreciate you taking on a personal request for this case when you didn't have to."

Peter was silent for a couple of seconds. "That's okay. I want to help with this case and Jack was cooperative. I'll send you a video he sent me. Take a look at it. You can draw your conclusions from it."

The video uploaded on Eichel's phone. What he saw told him all he needed to know.

He'd guessed right.

As her feet left the ledge time verged into passive motion. She plummeted with her head facing the earth. Calla's mind spun with bewilderment begging for anyone, anything to wake her from what seemed like a dream. Her lips wouldn't move, neither would her lungs as she gasped for air. Her hands moved to her throat. Although she was free-falling the placid sensation within her spirit surprised her. The city's clamor drowned out, replaced by the steady thudding of her heart, beating with a smooth rhythm.

Calla closed her eyes. *Will I feel anything?*

Her lungs resumed function, and she took a deep breath. The drop that had started as a blitz to ground level suddenly lost speed. She decelerated her descent, stalling impact by controlling her momentum and direction at will. Gravity ceased to exist, giving her the upper hand as she governed motion.

She'd heard of free-falling, but her speed was nothing like the kinematic equation physics had honed. Her eyes remained shut yet she named every detail around her. Cars whisked below her feet like a row of bugs creeping along a beaten path. London Bridge's train network straggled underneath like traveling centipedes.

She governed gravity, and in all of a few minutes, she pulled upright in mid-air until her feet were inches from the sidewalk. She took deep short breaths, opened her eyes and glimpsed up the summit of the prodigious Shard.

Is this real?

She tilted her head down as her feet hovered inches from the concrete pavement that waited for the landing of her suspended, yet steady feet.She examined her body. Not a scratch. Not a broken bone.She fingered her skin with trembling hands, merely hung suspended mid-air as if her body density had dipped below that of vapor. Calla took a few steps defying gravity's pull and inertia. Her eyes squished together at her newfound ability and she focused on the concrete pavement underneath her sneakers. With heightened clout, she lowered herself gently onto the wet ground. She'd not even noticed the spits of rain as they moistened her face. With her feet secured she stood erect and exhaled a deep, grateful sigh of relief. *What in the world just happened?*

She paused on the wet concrete and glared up the craggy pinnacle of the tower, reminding herself of her achievement.Raindrops caressed her cheeks. *Dr. Bertrand will never believe this!*

Rushed footsteps on her left set her on alert as she investigated her surroundings in the open space of the public street in the London Bridge quarter. Someone could have witnessed her plight and descent when she'd landed on the far side of the Shard on Joiner Street.

She turned to her left. Darkness had crept over London's eastern end and, as she quelled the urge to run, she glanced around for her Maserati. A few parked cars lined the streets of the customarily bustling district.

Calla set off running in search of her car as caution kept her alert She darted back to the front of the building, concluding that none had witnessed her aerial escapade.

The Range Rover was nowhere in sight. A young couple frolicked on the side of the street. They halted beside the

Maserati as the heavily perfumed woman gawked at Calla's cut chin, wet hair and dripping clothes. The man deliberated, his stare suggesting he didn't wish to interfere.

"Are you okay?" the woman asked. "You're all wet."

Calla ran a dampened hand through her wet locks, tugging away the snarls that had begun to form with the moisture. It was a bothersome characteristic with her hair when it came in contact with water. "I'm all right. I've got my car here."

Calla stepped into her Maserati while the couple took in the sight of the sports ride, now exhibiting a parking ticket. They carried on about their business having given up speculation.

Within the safety of her car, Calla checked her rearview mirror. She replayed the last hour in her mind and pulled down the window to rip the ticket off the windshield wipers. She placed the wet waist bag on the passenger seat and threw it open. The manuscript and journal were safely nestled inside, along with the two carbonados.

She fired up the ignition and careened in the direction of West London, heading for the privacy of her new home at Allegra's. There would be much to ask Dr. Bertrand when he called her later on that night.It had better be sooner rather than later.

———

1 0:3 5 P.M.
CENTRAL LONDON

A hundred meters to the left, of the adjacent corner of St. Thomas Street, a white Bentley parked within the shadows of the city buildings. An unassuming woman watched within the lavish automobile.

She sat in silence.In her hand she held a mini HD camcorder, recording images out of her window. She turned it off. "What was that?"

Was it someone who may have ended their life with a suicide jump? It could also have been pranksters, known to sneak up Europe's tallest building. She'd heard a scream. Even so, in hindsight, there had been no thud or bump, as one would expect of a falling body. Instead, the form had drifted as light as air.

She waited a few seconds and then some more, before peering down the deserted street, when a spectral silhouette emerged. Eva gripped the steering wheel of her Bentley and contemplated her next move.

Earlier that day Eva had been to Dr. Olivier's practice. She cursed under her breath recalling the unpleasant welcome she'd encountered.

"Miss Rochelle Richards, have we met?" Dr. Olivier asked.

"Not exactly."

"How did you get my number? We're not a listed surgery office. I only take patients by recommendation."

"I'm actually looking for a patient of yours, a good friend. Her life may be in danger?"

"Who are you looking for?"

"Calla Cress."

"What sort of danger is she in?"

"I need her number."

"I'm sorry, Miss Richards, I can't do that. In any case, she is in Paris."

That was all the information the doctor had surrendered. Eva darted out of the high-class practice, crafting her next move.

Calla can't be going to Paris for long. Could she have taken the Eurostar? It was common knowledge that this was the quickest return trip to mainland Europe from London, especially for a day's journey. Eva took a chance and called Mason.

"Yes?"

"Calla is off to Paris. Do you know what flight or train she's on?"

"Let me see."

He returned her query a couple of minutes later. "ISTF intelligence has tracked her and estimates she's on the Eurostar arriving from Paris at 9:04 p.m."

Contacting Mason had paid off. "Thanks for the tip."

Eva arrived several minutes before nine at St. Pancras International and spotted Calla leaving the arrival hall. Even though she'd not seen her in years, Eva remembered Calla's athletic build and long mane.

She followed, concealing herself behind an advertising panel. She then tailed outside and witnessed Calla slinking off with a dazzling Maserati. Eva pursued at a safe distance in her vehicle. She increased her speed, keeping up with the silver Granturismo. As they left the station an oversized, four-wheel-drive monster overtook Eva, hungry after Calla's automobile.Eva's car stopped short of colliding with an oncoming black cab. She steadied her steering wheel and accelerated after the Range Rover.

At a traffic light, Eva lost the two vehicles. She hammered the steering wheel and set the car speeding near St. Paul's Cathedral as soon as the light turned green. Nearing the top of London Bridge, she spotted the Maserati making a sharp turn toward the Shard.

Eva pursued and arrived at the front of the building only to spot the cars abandoned. She jumped out of the Bentley and approached the Range Rover with caution. She gazed at the Shard's entrance. *They must have gone inside.*

With no other option, Eva decided to wait in her car. Several moments later she stiffened when the Maserati whizzed past her. It was enough to catch a glimpse of Calla. Half an hour later she stared ahead of her calculating her next move. Her eyes caught an image diving meticulously off the Shard, head first and then feet down. She sprang out of the car and glared up the height of the dynamic high-rise building. *What the—?*

As the object floated, the news-hungry journalist in her grabbed the camcorder from her dashboard and filmed the entity as it conquered a free fall at a steady speed.

Incroyable! Incredible!

She saved the image and jumped back into her vehicle.

CHAPTER 28

C alla staggered through Allegra's front door chilled, wet and famished. What happened to Jack and Nash? It had been close to fifteen hours since she'd left.

The phone in the hallway rang. *Dr. Bertrand.*

She scampered to pick it up, almost tripping over the rug.

"Calla Cress?"

The voice on the other end of the line was foreign, possibly German. "Yes?"

"Hello, Frau Cress. I need to speak to you."

Calla had heard the voice before. Wasn't it that German cop?

"Raimund Eichel. We met in Berlin."

"How did you get this number?" Calla asked.

"I tried all the numbers you gave me, but they didn't work. I then asked your government for Allegra's number."

She placed a hand on the bag and held it close to her chest.

The European police must be on a hunt for it by now. She'd had a couple of nasty surprises with the Metropolitan police.

Calla decided to play it cool. She set her back against the wall and sank down to the warm floor. "What can I do for you, Herr Eichel?"

He sounded matter of fact. "I'm in London. Would you have some time to help me with my investigation? You see, I have a few more questions about Allegra Driscoll."

I don't have time for this. Calla shifted her feet. "Herr Eichel, I've already told you all I know about Allegra. I don't have any additional information."

"Could we just meet? Please."

A discreet beep interrupted the call, signaling a second caller was trying to get through to Calla's receiver. She recognized the international country code for France.

"I'm afraid I can't talk right now. I've another call coming in." She would stall him. "Perhaps we could speak next week. I have to go."

She activated call-waiting and scrolled to the redial button to pick up the second caller. "Hello?"

"Calla. It's Doctor Bertrand. Sorry for the late call but I know you wanted me to call as soon as I had any news. Do you have a moment?"

A choking lump skulked down her throat, glad she was already seated. "Yes, I do have a moment."

"I wish I could tell you the news in person."

Her heart sank into her belly, and she thought for a moment. "Perhaps I can dial you in via video-conference. Do you have video-conferencing facilities?"

"Yes, we do."

He confirmed the details as Calla reached for a pencil from the hall table. "Give me a moment. I'll dial you on the video-conferencing unit."

. . .

Within minutes, wrapped in a snug bathrobe, Calla sat face to face in conference with Dr. Bertrand. She took a deep breath.

"There're two things, Miss Cress. Have you been in contact with any form of radioactive substances in the recent past? Or even earlier, such as in your adolescent years?"

The carbonados!

"Why, doctor?"

"Your body shows signs of radioactive poisoning."

A distraught feeling crawled through her veins. His words had wounded her. "What do you mean?"

"The results showed that you have a significant amount of radionuclide Polonium 210 in your bloodstream."

"What's that?"

Dr. Bertrand frowned, compassion not once escaping his eyes. "A few years ago Polonium was identified only after the death of a Russian government spy."

"What sort of element is it?"

"There's been much misinformation in the news and other media about what amount constitutes a lethal intake of Polonium 210. Nevertheless, Polonium 210 is one of more than twenty-four known Polonium isotopes, all of which are radioactive. It's a rare element in nature and is present in uranium ores."

"How does one come in contact with it?"

"Doctors on both sides of the Atlantic have begun to seriously consider the possibility of nuclear terrorism. Many were unable to detect Polonium earlier because it doesn't emit gamma rays. Gamma rays are encountered with most radioactive isotopes."

Calla's heart broke. "I'm not sure I follow, doctor."

Bertrand continued. "Unlike most known radiation sources Polonium 210 emits only alpha particles, which don't pierce even a sheet of paper or the epidermis of human skin. They're essentially invisible to normal radiation detectors. Have you had any injections, intakes of substances, recent or previous, that you may deem questionable?"

"I don't know, doctor. So, it's administered orally?"

Bertrand's lips pressed together into a slight grimace. "Gamma and alpha rays are classified as ionizing radiation. If you have inhaled or ingested any such substance, Calla, it can cause significant radiation poisoning."

"I do remember the reports in the media about that case. From what I recall most hospitals can't even detect alpha particles," Calla said.

"My research has been extensive and led me to many thought-provoking cases. Your case is rather unusual. You are right, most hospitals only have the equipment to detect gamma rays, but I've invested in newer technologies."

That would it explain the strange looking equipment she'd seen in his offices. Calla questioned him further, digging her bare toes into the carpet. "Does that also explain the escalation of my vision and physical changes?"

"I can't say. I still need to study your results more carefully to see if we can find a quick remedy to reduce the Polonium and what level of danger you could be in."

The doctor wouldn't use the word *danger* lightly. "I see."

"I don't want to alarm you. The results aren't completely conclusive. If you want we can continue to perform more tests," said Bertrand.

The thought of being a lab rat didn't intrigue Calla. "Can I have a couple of days? I just need to digest all this information."

"Of course. There's one other possibility regarding your symptoms."

Calla held her breath. "What's that?"

"You could also have a genetic abnormality or disorder."

1:30 A.M.

The shaky video played on the mini screen. Fluttering noises and muffled sounds resounded through the gadget's minuscule speakers.

"*Zut alors!* Must've had my finger in the way."

Eva spent the good part of the early hours of the night scouring through the film. The light on her work desk reflected off the mini video screen. Not really sure what she was looking at she played the clip several times, rewinding and zooming in for better observation.

Mason will love this.

He wasn't giving away much, but his position at ISTF was no secret to her father. She'd eavesdropped on several conversations between the two. Right now her interest was in the falling shadow.

At first glance, it could have been anyone. "Mason knows something about this."

With his help, she contemplated getting the images in front of professionals. Eva reached for her phone, and when Mason picked up, she shrilled with the excitement of a playful child. "You're gonna love this!"

"Your clock is ticking," Mason said.

"I've something you'll find interesting, but I can't discuss this on the phone."

12:20 P.M.
MAXIM'S RESTAURANT
KENSINGTON, LONDON

Eva observed the traffic from a quiet table in Maxim's private dining area. She peered at the door hoping to catch Mason's attention as soon as he came in. Several minutes later a waiter ambled in her direction followed by Mason.

As he settled into the seat opposite her, her pulses set to pounding conscious of the scornful eyes that were focused on her. Mason glared. "You have ten minutes."

Eva frowned. "Are we back to *Miss Riche*?"

Mason clasped his hands on the set table and sent a cold stare through her. "I'm waiting for your contribution from your end of our deal."

The waiter returned with a glass of chilled water. Mason arched his squared shoulders, his scrutinizing eyes unsettling Eva as she welcomed a flicker of warning in her gut. For the first time since meeting him, she averted his gaze, slouching in her chair and lowering her eyes. "Take a look at this," she said. "What kind of training programs are you conducting within ISTF?"

Mason kept his focus on her squirming face. "What's your drift?"

She shoved the shaky video in front of his strong face. "Something commissioned by ISTF?"

He took a quick look. "What's this?"

Eva leaned forward, her unsteady voice lowering. "What are you intelligence people cooking up?"

Mason scanned the room as busy waiters went about their chores in anticipation of lunch crowds. He refused to entertain her curiosity and shifted his gaze back to her face. "I thought your story was on the Deveron Manuscript?"

Her finger flipped through some video files, scrolling the side dial of the miniature device. She thrust it once more in his direction. "Look again. Explain this?"

Mason skimmed the video, unmoved. He leaned closer and re-scanned the material. Shaky and noisy at best he made out a falling object from a skyscraper. The amateur shot had been filmed from the ground looking up. He recognized what looked like a human being, gracefully dropping from the Shard.

Eva observed Mason's face as she took him through the footage.

His professionalism kept him guarded and indifferent.

She toyed with the gadget's features and stopped the video, zooming into its pixelated glow. "Do you recognize this person?"

Mason held his gaze but gave away no emotion. He grasped the camera for a closer look and then handed it back to Eva. "It amazes me that you have time for this sort of thing. I thought you were a serious journalist."

Anger crossed her face. "But—"

"Listen, my advice is that you resolve to astute investigating by charting factual evidence."

Dignified and demure as a royalshe pursed her full lips. "You and I know that I'm onto something."

"What exactly?"

"This is Calla Cress. Just before I filmed this last night, she was involved in a high-speed chase that nearly wrecked my car along with several others."

"Time is of the essence here." He narrowed his eyes. "Where's this going?"

"I followed them."

"Highly unlikely. But even if what you say has the slightest accuracy, which I seriously doubt, how does that help you?"

"Calla has found something to do with the Deveron Manuscript." She tossed her hands in the air. "Come on! The rumor on the street is that the Deveron is no ordinary document. In fact, many looking for it believe it leads to new sources of nuclear or other energies! I've done my homework, Mason!"

Eva leaned forward waiting for a response.

He didn't twitch.

Something grew coldly resolute on her face. "You guys at

ISTF have found that nuclear source and used whatever you've found to develop some wicked stuff. At least that's the story I'll print unless you tell me otherwise."

Mason inclined his head, heat rising to his cheeks. "Don't play with fire if you're covered in flint. Your video is very incomprehensible, my dear. My advice to you is, stick to the gossip columns."

"Not likely—"

"I forbid you to publish any of this nonsense."

"I don't think the invention of human flight is nonsense," said Eva. She lowered her voice. "To follow your analogy, where there's smoke, there's fire. My take on it is that ISTF has been using Calla to test some of the nuclear materials the Deveron document has produced. I'm no fool, Mr. Laskfell. I know when I have a story."

"And what story is that exactly? That the government is testing human flight equipment. Every journalist knows that. Any prankster today can create android-powered, mechanically assisted flying techniques."

"What's keeping her afloat? Either ISTF is onto a new technology that governments would kill for, or I'm a raving idiot."

"I beg to differ."

Eva's head swung in a slow, side to side motion. She leaned her back against the padded chair and placed the camcorder in her bag. "I too have heard of the mysteries surrounding that manuscript. Maybe our own government has uncovered a secret so deep that they have no intention of revealing it to the public. Isn't that how ISTF plays?" She mused a little. "Is it even safe? Tested?"

He hunched forward. "Your ten minutes are up."

He threw several bills on the seamless tablecloth and pushed himself up from his chair. "Good day, Eva."

She gripped his arm with both her hands and dug her nails into his tailored suit, her manner ruthless and firm. "Just verify my story, and I'll publish it. I need the full backing support of ISTF. Think of the publicity it will give you. Your discovery."

"Miss Riche, whereas your number one quest is to dominate the limelight, keep in mind that craftier people have more imperative things to attend to."

He filched his arm from her manicured grip and tipped his head before threading his way toward the exit.

She brought a hard fist down on the table that sent her glass hurtling to the tiles. *"Imbécile!"*

CHAPTER 29

Calla threw her eyes open and switched off the conferencing unit. She'd left it on all night and had fallen into a deep sleep until the late hours of the morning. She folded her arms around her as if to cower from the news she'd registered from Dr. Bertrand.

Even though he hadn't said it Dr. Bertrand's face had revealed much. Her mind refused to accept the severity of his words. The news of the Russian agent in the London papers had been a dominant topic at the time. As far as she remembered the spy had died shortly after his hospitalization. Calla had purposely avoided revealing to Bertrand the details of her plunge from the Shard. Why should brilliance be classified abnormal? Perhaps science can't explain it all.

If she were to die soon had her life held any purpose?Calla flopped on the bed and stared at the ceiling. Though she tried to fight them, the tears began a steady trickle, wetting her pale face. Defeat imprisoned her mind.

She made an effort to pull herself out of bed and set her feet on the carpet. As Bertrand's words haunted her, an epiphany crept into her mind. There was one thing that she hadn't tried. It wouldn't be easy, but it was worth a try. Without any more thought or regard for life, she resolved to follow it through. She could at least find who the heck her parents were. The last stone would make it clear. If she had all three, the answers would surface.

If only she could live that long.

12:53 P.M.
MAXIM'S RESTAURANT

Taiven slouched behind a divider at a small table by the door. He followed every word, movement and threat in the room, perched over his coffee cup like a hunting bird. He'd witnessed the glass leave Eva's table and shatter on the tiles only moments ago.

A waitress scrambled to salvage the wreckage while Eva shifted to another table. He sipped his coffee and glared at Eva from behind dark glasses. Infuriated, she tapped her nails on the tablecloth contemplating. The sharp-witted troublemaker had made it quite clear to those impolite enough to eavesdrop on the intense argument, that she wasn't one who would back down.

Thirty minutes earlier Taiven had tailed Mason into the exclusive restaurant as the chestnut-haired socialite greeted him. Even with the passing of the years, Taiven remembered her artful tactics. The girl had always been a tormentor. She'd been Calla's adversary from the moment Calla stepped into Beacon Academy. Taiven had always remained fervent in his duty, a mission that he alone knew and, to accomplish it, he'd had to shadow Calla and all that pertained to the brilliant child.

. . .

337

Calla had arrived at Beacon Academy similar to most new students, reserved and curious yet eager to learn. The academy was a rocky place for those who joined mid-year. Friends had been made, and enemies named too. Pretty soon it became clear who dominated the independent school grounds.

Eva was the one most girls dreaded, wanted to be and the tougher ones despised. Those who sided with her had no inch of self-esteem. Calla spared no time for her infantile mannerisms. In fact, because Calla didn't entertain anything Eva did, it irritated the pretentious elitist. The full extent of Eva's aggravation surfaced when Beacon Academy was invited to go on an inter-varsity school debate against Wycombe Girls Academy. Calla was given the coveted leadership spot and Eva, a natural darer, had intimidated the whole faculty beseeching fair playoffs for the role.

The deciding match took place in front of the entire student body and staff. No effort at all had been required from Calla.

Eva, on the other hand, struggled to keep her history straight, name facts and deliver a credible presentation on US politics during the Watergate scandal. Calla's giftedness and sheer genius overwhelmed Eva, who battled visibly to match the natural academic.

From that day Eva had made it her life's ambition to torment not only Calla but anyone who patronized her aspirations. Taiven later found out that much of Eva's behavior had spiraled out of control after her mother had mysteriously been institutionalized.

Taiven's face surfaced above a local newspaper. He surveyed Eva with a cautious glare and summoned a server for the bill. He waited until the waitress approached and placed two fifty-pound notes in her grateful hand. "Thanks for the coffee. Keep the change."

The waitress took the more than generous amount and

stashed the bills in her shirt pocket, glancing around for spying eyes. Satisfied that the predetermined monetary exchange had gone well, she busied herself at the bar refilling Eva's water glass.

Taiven rose to leave. As he slid past the bar, he dropped a transparent tablet, no bigger than a pinch of salt, into the waiting, ice-cold glass. Taiven stole out of the restaurant by the back door. The waitress picked up the glass and served it to Eva.

1:00 P.M.

Calla changed into a warm, magenta cashmere top, a pair of snug jeans and black boots. She proceeded back downstairs with the manuscript. With her hand over the banister, Pearl stood at the foot of the stairs conversing with Jack and Nash who'd just made their way through the front door.

Nash studied Calla as she eased her step over the stairs, his eyes lighting up. "You're back?"

Calla stepped to the bottom of the stairs, endeavoring to change her mood. She threw him a smile. "And glad to be."

"Jack said you were in Paris yesterday. Was it to do with the manuscript?"

She shook her head.

He edged closer. "Do you want to talk about it?"

She took a deep breath. "Not really. Perhaps some other time."

Nash retreated as an expression of wounded tolerance crossed his face. He narrowed his eyes turning to Jack. "You need to see this report Jack has compiled. His research on the stones is astounding."

She inched closer refusing to look Nash in the eyes. "Really? What else did you find?"

Pearl took her leave as Jack held out a document in his hand.

339

"The carbonados respond to light, and I can confirm the minerals they possess aren't present on Earth."

Calla took the report from his hands. "Are these minerals toxic? I hope you were careful, Jack."

"Don't worry. We'd all be affected by now."

Calla shot them both a worried glance. Only now did she realize the contamination risk they might be in as well. If both Jack and Nash were unaffected by the carbonados, then perhaps her interaction with the stones had begun a rapid escalation of a genetic disorder.

Was this why her parents had put her away? It made sense now. If they knew of the genetic disorder then they would have thought it best to keep her away from the Deveron Manuscript they were working on, *and* the stones.

Jack shuffled into the quiet den with Calla and Nash close behind. "This is exciting stuff. We need to find the next stone."

"It would make sense to have all three," Nash said.

Jack set a hand on Calla's shoulder. "This could put all those questions about your parents and these artifacts to rest."

Calla managed a feeble smile. "Let's check the third and last clue." She reached for her notes, and the Deveron tucked away in her waist bag as she marched to the mahogany desk.

She set the items on the table. Her voice shook as she read her notes. "Here's my take on the third dominance."

Jack shot her a quizzical look. "Are you okay, C?"

She swallowed hard. "Yeah."

Nash's jaw tightened. "What happened in Paris?"

She shook her head, a miserable attempt at denial. "Nothing, really. Let's get back to the dominance."

Even as she read the words, she knew they didn't believe her.

The notes read:

3.
You steal my soul, but you cannot possess me.

I replant. I replenish, I survive and have stood the test of history.
You covet my sparkle, you covet my value,
Yet you can take none of me with you with your last breath!
I am everywhere. I am everyone.
I make men rich, I make men poor.
Yet here I lie in my dark grave where I will remain all my days.

Jack reached for the loose sheet of paper. "What the heck does this mean? Whoever wrote this must've been smoking some of my grandfather's crack."

Calla snickered, appreciative of Jack's well-timed humor. "I thought about this on the train to Paris. This passage is talking about wealth and resources. Don't you think? You know, one of the things the human race craves"

"How do you figure that?" Jack asked. "Your imagination impresses me."

"As yours mine, tech and science genius."

She tugged at a dreadlock of his, her cheeks puckering into an acute smile. "My hunch is oil and other natural resources. Earlier today it hit me that, the richest continent regarding resources is Africa. This has always been the case throughout history."

"Where in Africa do we begin?" Nash asked.

She pointed to a set of notes she'd gathered earlier. "Look, here are the details of the known natural resources in Africa from Alexandria to the Cape. Everything from oil and gas in Egypt, Libya and Algeria, to diamonds in the Congo, Angola, and the Central African Republic, uranium in South Africa, Somalia and Niger and copper in Uganda, Zambia and Zimbabwe."

Nash's expression remained grim as he watched her, concern crossing his eyes. "It still doesn't isolate any one place."

"Africa has 'stood the times of history,'" as the Deveron puts it. Her resources don't run out," Calla said.

Nash was distracted by something on her face. He advanced and surveyed her jaw.

She drifted back a little, her head perking upward.

"How did you get that bruise?" he asked.

Calla hadn't even noticed. She checked her face in the mirror above the fireplace, "Oh. It's just a scratch. Must've been from Rome."

She skirted away from his touch, his attention lingering on her evasiveness. Calla refocused on her notes. "Before we go I need to pick up a few things. I checked the flights to Rabat, none suit us."

Jack's eyebrow arched. "Rabat?"

"Yeah. We're to begin in Morocco," she added.

"Dare I ask why?" said Nash amused by the new destination.

"I'll explain it all at the airport."

"If we get a flight," he said.

A mischievous smile frolicked on Calla's lips. "I was thinking something a little more private."

Jack raised an eyebrow. "How so?"

"Allegra's private jet. I spoke with her pilot about an hour ago. Time of departure, 11:00 p.m."

Jack whistled, impressed by the mode of transportation. "Count me in. Like my buddy here I'll wait for the low down on why we're heading to North Africa. Right now drinks on the house sound like my cup of tea."

She headed for the door. "I'm darting out now for the rest of the afternoon. We can meet at Heathrow say, ten-ish."

Nash followed her into the hall. His face tightened as he spoke. "Where're you going? Here," he reached for his coat, "I'll come with you."

She placed a gentle hand over his heart and raised reluctant eyes to his witheverything in her screaming 'yes.' "No." She managed a smile. "Don't worry. I'll be back soon."

"Calla, why won't you let me help you? You've got to let me in."

"I can't, Nash."

"Listen. Whatever we find or don't find, know that I'll always be here for you."

He meant it. She could tell from the way his dimple contracted. Her hand slid to his face, and he covered it with his as she stepped closer. "Nash, I know. Without you, I would be—"

"Just let me help you."

"I promise to tell you what this is all about, but not now." She hesitated. "I have to do this alone."

CHAPTER 30

Mason's face broke into a grin as he sipped a glass of whiskey on the rocks. He liked his plan. He set the cold drink on a coaster by the video-conferencing system and pressed down the start button that powered the unit. "Are you there, Milan?" he asked.

The left screen lit up, displaying a headshot of a silver-haired, heavyset Italian. "Here."

"Let's check for Sydney," Mason said.

The second screen lit up. "Sydney is on the line," said a woman's voice.

One by one the screens lit up until five monitors representing five time zones were online, Milan, Tel Aviv, Sydney, Johannesburg and San Francisco.

Mason greeted the conference participants and loaded a file onto the system as each participant followed the presentation on their individual monitors.

"Good afternoon from London, ladies, and gentlemen. As you can see from the first slide, we're right on track. Each one of these influential figures was chosen carefully." He observed each glaring associate individually before proceeding. "Once the hosts are within their targeted positions they'll proceed with the following orders. Unknown to the organizations we've chosen the hosts, or hackers should I say, will infiltrate the US government computer systems and the world's largest corporations starting with the firms above, Riche Enterprises and The Kumar Oil Corporation. The hacking viruses will find a home in the RC2 Cloud systems of these institutions."

Tel Aviv eyed his plan with awe and distaste all at the same time. "How does it work?" he asked.

Mason leered at him, detesting the presumptuous idiot. "The hackers steal access to these organizations. They'll penetrate the infrastructures by first embedding into a website hosted on each individual server and then covertly install a command and control infrastructure. Quite simple really. Once these organizations are hacked, it will give us access to eighty percent of the world's technology infrastructure."

"Excellent," beamed Sydney.

Pride dripped off Mason's lips as he spoke. "Once the system is in place it's a hundred percent undetectable by the organizations' substructures. They'll never be able to trace our hackers' activity. The companies will undergo failures, outages and transactions they've not approved but will never know how to stop the havoc. I have handpicked each one of the three thousand hosts myself."

"That must have taken a while. Will they just follow orders?" Johannesburg asked.

Mason circled the room. "They'll not even know they are hackers."

<hr />

3:00 P.M.
BLACKMORE, ESSEX

345

Calla pounded her fist on the blue door of the two-story cottage. She knit her eyebrows as she stood on the narrow entrance porch of the secluded farmhouse.

"Hello?"

No answer.

Calla peered through the open window to the right of the door. Inside, the light in the front room hung swinging without a lampshade.

She rang the doorbell once more of what used to be the Girls' Village Home of Blackmore. Thirty miles west out of Central London, Blackmore was fifty minutes' drive away. A village once termed in the Middle Ages as 'Black Marsh' or 'Black Swamp.' The house was one of three stone-built properties on a converted farm, set in the picturesque countryside in the heart of Blackmore.

She gazed down at a printed-paper in her trembling hand. There in her grip, the local tourist information indicated that the home shut its doors in 1991. The Home had opened in 1876 as a large complex for disadvantaged girls. In 1945 it was converted, accommodating boys as well.

Calla's Internet search had also produced the name of the last director who had run the home. Rosetta Black. According to her intelligence sources, Rosetta still lived here. She hammered once more on the sturdy cedar. She stepped back and considered the plaque on the wall.

Girls' Village Home Blackmore

Even after more than two decades of closure it still hung visibly suspended above the entrance. Calla drew away from the veranda and took a few paces back. She blinked as the sun peered through the dense clouds, causing her to squint as she glared up. Most of the shutters were closed except for those on the second story.

She scanned the driveway. A dated white Peugeot 403 stood in the ample parking space.Calla scrutinized the old brochure of the Home that she'd kept in her stash of research from the age of ten, a fragment of her past that made no sense to her. Mama Cress had given her the brochure one summer during half term when she kept questioning them about her real parents.

She turned to the back page and studied the information again.

The girls who are received at Blackmore Village Home range from infancy onward. Most of our girls stay with us until they reach the age of seventeen, provided a suitable home is not found. From 1876 until 1939 thousands of girls called Blackmore Village Home. Many received excellent training in various professions, and there was always a high demand for Dr. Sterling's well-trained girls. Today we hope to place girls in proper schools through sponsorship or homes through adoption.

Calla would have been five years old when she left the foster home. She remembered little of her life here except for the cottage and the little wooden swing that used to stand beside the driveway, where she would spend several hours.

Alone.

The swing was gone, probably removed to make room for the new driveway. She rang the doorbell one last time.

Nothing.

Shrugging, she turned to leave.

"Yes?"

A gray-haired, woman slowly pulled the door open, wearing what appeared to be an oversized kitchen apron. She leaned on a copper-colored walking stick and eyed Calla intensely with her hooded brown eyes. It was clear she didn't receive many visitors.

Calla gave her a heartfelt smile, turning toward the door. "Hello. I...I'm Calla Cress. I wonder if you can help me."

The woman cautiously slid the door open and peered through the inch crack. "What is it you want?"

"Have you lived at this address long? You see, I was brought here as an orphan. I'm looking for any information on what happened to the foster home and the children—"

Calla stopped mid-sentence, feeling an enormous weight on her mind. The woman's stare remained frigid, and she dragged the door to close it. "Sorry, I can't help you."

Calla had come too far. She'd avoided knocking on this door for months. The answers had to be here. Determined not to be warded off Calla set a firm hand in the door crack. "Please help me." A wrench of misery surfaced in her throat. "I'm dying—" she whispered.

The woman's look stiffened. A tear emerged in Calla's left eye and dropped to her elbow as her hand remained steady on the door. "Please help me. I have a genetic disorder, and I need to talk to you."

An invisible weight lifted from Calla's shoulders. She'd finally acknowledged the full extent of her fraught existence. "Won't you help me, please?"

The frown lines on the old woman's face eased. She attempted a weak smile. "I'm sorry. I've lived here since I was a girl but, I don't see how I can help you."

Calla pulled out a wrapped object from her denim pockets, a laminated photograph. "Perhaps this can help? This is the only memory I have of this place. Do you recognize it and why it was filed with my adoption papers?"

The woman's glare dropped to Calla's hands, and without a word, her feeble hand eased the photograph from Calla's grip. Once she'd surveyed the black and white image, she lifted her gaze to study Calla's intent. "Where did you get this?"

"I've had it since I was baby, I think. You see, it's a photograph of a birthmark. I've had it as long as I can remember. My adoptive parents, Mama and Papa Cress said it was the only personal belonging they took from this foster home."

Calla raised the right leg of her denim jeans. "Here. Take a look at this. It looks like a tattoo."

The woman's eyes widened even further as they fell on the impressive birthmark. She drew the door wide open. "Come in."

Calla closed the door behind her as the gentle woman led her inside the humble cottage. She moved at the woman's slow pace as they trailed past the cloakroom that led one into an inviting living space. Calla studied the arched windows and the rustic Inglenook fireplace, which still emitted a distinct burned odor reminding her of the quiet, winter evenings she spent listening to Papa Cress' stories by the fire. They paced past the room, settling in a retro, orange and brown tiled kitchen with its sixties decor.

The mature woman took a seat at a round kitchen table. "For years I wondered what had happened to you, Calla. We didn't call you Calla then."

Calla pulled a seat across from her and slowly dipped into its synthetic frame, not once taking her gaze off the tender, yet wrinkling face. "What did you call me?"

"Baby. Just, Baby Cress. You were the youngest baby we had in the home at that time."

"You know this photo?"

"Would you like some tea?" the woman asked ignoring the question.

Calla nodded out of respect for the woman's hospitality. "Just milk, no sugar, please."

The woman doddered at a shaky pace toward the sink by the window overlooking the driveway. April showers began a steady descent in the courtyard as the sun disappeared behind the graying clouds.

The woman closed the windows, and soon the whistling

349

kettle broke the serene silence. She brewed two cups of Earl Gray and took her place at the table.

Her voice shook with strain as she spoke. "You were the one we were most careful to place in the right home. That's why you stayed with us longer than most."

She wouldn't interrupt even though everything in her wanted to know why.

The woman slurped audibly from her steaming, tea mug. "I remember the night well. We had been told for months that a baby girl was to come to our home. She needed special attention and delicate care."

Calla tasted the weak tea and set her cup on the table, as the beverage warmed her hands more than her throat. "Why?"

"I remember the couple well. They were well groomed from head to toe. The woman was so stylish. For a village girl like myself, I thought she was royalty." She let out a small laugh. "The man was tall and strong. Everything about him pronounced his authority. But what gentle eyes he had. Especially when he looked at you, Calla, all bundled up with your tiny face in that sweet white bonnet. Your hair, my dear, is as dark as it was then."

The woman reached over and raked her feeble hands through Calla's dark mane. "Still silky like a raven's coat."

Calla listened intently as the woman's narrative sparked her imagination, picturing the man and woman in her mind. These must have been her parents. "What were they like?"

"They seemed reluctant to leave you, but they both signed and agreed that it was for the best. They only had one legal condition, that this birthmark never be removed. That is why we took a photo of it and kept it with your file. The contract stipulated that they would pay your adoptive parents for all your expenses into adulthood. And I remember they said a trust fund was left in your name with a beneficiary."

"Was there a name?"

Any name would do. Please, God!

350

"I don't remember."

Calla now understood. That's how Mama and Papa Cress had afforded her education. They'd always claimed it was a fund they'd inherited. *They lied to me.*

The woman took another noisy draft of her tea. The rain had stopped, and sun rays sparkled off her clean kitchen sink.

Calla investigated further. Perchance this time she would get a response. "What's so special about this birthmark? It's very unusual."

The woman cradled the photograph in her bony hands. "Dear child, they didn't explain anything. The adoptive papers were in order. I distinctly remember they were in a tremendous hurry. I was just the office assistant then, told to administer everything with the new office computers. In the eighties, that was a novelty."

"Did they say where they were going and the reason for my adoption? Where can I find those files?"

"I don't know. The home closed when it ran out of funds. I'm not sure what happened to the files. Destroyed maybe."

"They just walked away?"

Calla's host nodded slowly. "I just took you in my arms and watched as the woman was pulled away from you. Oh, did she cry! We heard her weeping all the way to the waiting car that night."

"What happened to them?"

"I don't even know if they were your parents. The papers didn't have any information about your birth. If I remember correctly it listed them as your guardians."

"What were their names?"

"Oh, if only I had the files. I don't remember." She glanced at Calla's eager face. "As soon as they placed you in my arms, they left. You were such an angelic child. And at five your new parents came to take you."

A tear strained out of Calla's right eye however hard she tried to control it. Her throat lost all moisture.

351

The aging woman took Calla's hand in hers. "I'm so sorry, Calla. I wish I could tell you more. That information was legally classified to protect both parties. They were very specific about that. In fact, I think I remember we were to destroy your files once you left the foster home."

"Why?"

"I remember asking myself the same question."

Calla took one hand back and wiped her damp eyes. "In all the time I was here did I ever visit a doctor? Is there anywhere I can find out more about my medical history?"

The woman's eyes narrowed, and she leaned in closer. "That's all I know."

Calla's cheeks burned, rejection and despair immersing her mind. Her voice clogged with emotion. "It's almost as if they paid the Home and my adoptive parents to take me. Why? What was so wrong with me?"

The woman's disheartened eyes turned from Calla's solemn face as her own sorrow echoed Calla's grief. "I hope that's not true."

Knowing it was the only comfort she could offer the gentle woman drew her into her embrace.

Calla rested her head against the comforting heart of the compassionate stranger. *Why did these people just leave me? They must've known I had an abnormality. That's why they gave me away and asked for special treatment for me.*

Calla's unsteady voice broke through the sobs. "I was a burden to them...a weakling and therefore undesirable."

Everything she'd feared.

Her changing state couldn't be attributed to the carbonados. Jack and Nash weren't affected.

The woman wiped Calla's tears with a thin index finger. What had been a twenty-minute cry in the woman's consoling arms felt like it had lasted all afternoon. Calla lifted her throbbing head and bloodshot eyes from the woman's arms. She wiped moist eyes with her sleeve and sat upright as the darkening cloud cover told her it was getting late. "Do you know what time it is?"

"Let me check."

"I need to go." She fixed intent eyes on the woman's face. "Thank you. I have the closure I need."

The woman cupped Calla's face in her hands. "I don't like the resolve in your voice, dear. Calla Cress, you're your own person. Live your life to the fullest. Just because your parents didn't want you doesn't mean that no one does. You may have been an accident to them, but your life isn't accidental."

The woman's words were still ringing in Calla's head as she headed back to her car. *Nothing matters now. The stones, the manuscript.*

Life...

Rosetta watched Calla hurtle to the Maserati as she glimpsed outside the rain-stained, kitchen window. She regretted the amount of information she'd revealed, convinced that she'd caused more harm than good.

Then again she hadn't given Calla the most vital piece of information. However, that was the one thing the couple had asked her never to tell Calla.

5:58 P.M.
A12 HIGHWAY TO LONDON

Would they have kept her, if she hadn't been a freak? The thought hung in the air as Calla hauled her feet into a run toward her Maserati.She flung herself into the front seat, a piercing pain attacking her chest. Her face mirrored the thunderous discharge that continued to assault most of Essex. *I'll never know family, belonging...*

A bolt of lightning lit the sky, followed by a crack of thunder. She was incapable of love because she'd never been loved. That's why she ran...every time.

From Nash...

Another explosion of lightning.

Terrified at giving affection to the one person who cared for her with a commitment so visible, Calla was incapacitated. The pelting streams blinded the driveway ahead as she revved up the Maserati's engine and accelerated toward the A12 highway en route to Central London.

With the road submerging under voluble streams, brought on by the incessant downpour, the sports car sliced through forming puddles, threatening to curve her off the road.

What would anyone care if I ended it all now?

Surely that's better than mutating into God knows what!

Nash's image formed in her mind, threatening to alter her resolution. She brushed it away.

Nash. It would have been...

Drunk with disgust at herself, her world, her parents, whomever, she stepped on the gas.

Darkness threatened to steer her into oblivion as her vision marred, at best with a brew of tears and precipitation. Not a single car loomed in sight. Armed with a bruised heart and a tortured mind Calla made a decision.

I won't take anyone with me. It only takes a second. Maybe two...

The engine chortled, raucous as it navigated through gushes and thunder. Calla focused straight ahead, her eyes blinded by desperate windshield wipers. She spotted an overpass bridge about a mile ahead. The concrete structure would deliver the demolition she required.

Will it hurt? She swerved into fifth gear, rocketing just under the hundred-and-sixty miles per hour mark, her eyes fastened onto the solid structure.

Now or never!

Nash...I'm so sorry...

With no clear cautioning, an arresting light surfaced from under the flyover. Her gate to extinction. As if to ward her off the dazzling headlights flickered with the ferocity of a panicked lioness. *Where did you come from?*

This isn't what she wanted. She wanted to go alone.She slammed the brakes and shut her eyes. The Maserati failed to conform to will and flew forward toward obscurity.

CHAPTER 31

Mason surveyed the faces one last time. He'd been in conference all afternoon with his counterparts.

"So let's recap, Mason," said Sydney, "the hackers won't be aware of their activity?"

"No."

"How's that possible?" Tel Aviv asked.

Mason leaned against the sidewall. "That, ladies and gentleman, is for me to know."

"But how will you be able to get onto those cloud systems?" Milan said.

"The software is powered by energy and high charge electricity from the carbonado diamonds. With such energy, I can produce a mainframe processor capable of creating a distinct password-stealing botnet, or in street terms, a network of infected computers, from any global system." He surveyed the attentive glares. "Think of it as an upgrade to last year's malware scandal, you know, the one with the software that damaged millions of computer systems. That scandal has been linked to more than $100 million in bank fraud. This will be far superior."

"Fantastic, Mason. How did you—?" Milan began.

"Never mind the details. The hackers carry this technology disease as they work in my target organizations and unknowingly stumble on internal websites with security vulnerabilities. ISTF has identified many such weaknesses in these three establishments. We just need one website for each organization. We then hack the site's software or simply steal an administrative password from a desktop computer to get on the site."

"So the three have all signed?" asked the representative from San Francisco.

Mason strolled around the video-conferencing room. "Almost. Samuel Riche still needs a little persuasion. But that is under control as we speak."

"When will he sign?" Tel Aviv asked.

Mason's hands fisted. He needed Tel Aviv and his influence in the Middle East. He glared at Tel Aviv, an individual who'd always envied Mason's ability to rally an army of believers behind the Deveron Manuscript. He narrowed his eyes. "It will only be a matter of time before I flood Kumar's oil reserves, drive Arlington insane with her lust for the seat in the White House, and ensure that Samuel Riche faces the biggest dilemma of his life."

The room erupted with murmurs of excitement.

"We need entry into Samuel Riche's empire. We need to make sure that all three thousand hosts find their bearings in time," Cape Town said.

Mason took a seat and faced his onlookers. "In the end, the three will have to decide whether they like it or not. There'll be no good option for them."

This time Milan grimaced. "How's that?"

Mason clasped his hands. "Their greed will engulf them. In fact, because their end of the deal is so sweet they're blind to the fine print, even if it stares them in the face."

"When will we have the carbonados, Mason?" Tel Aviv said.

Irritation boiled in Mason's veins.

He clicked on the next slide. It hadn't always been so with this group. They'd never questioned him until recently, starting with Tel Aviv. "In a day or two. Once they're in our possession, the hosts must be mobilized."

Mason contemplated, realizing his need of each participant for the hacks to succeed. "The manuscript and the stones are as good as ours," he said.

"This needs to happen quickly, Mason," Sydney said. "Remember we only have one chance. The opportunity will never come again. There is only a short window to combine the diamonds. Can you confirm that Slate will succeed?"

"I agree," San Francisco said.

His sentiment was echoed by Cape Town.

"And what about Driscoll and Cress?" Milan asked.

"Slate has taken care of them. Cress has suffered a fatal fall I doubt she'll recover from." He pursed his lips and smiled. "I instructed Slate to bring the diamonds and the manuscript immediately. He'll be checking in any minute. Well, if there are no more queries we'll reconvene in a few days once we have the items. That's it, everyone."

Mason switched off the unit.

Where's that Slate?

He lit another cigar. It was coming together as planned. He tipped the ashes into an ashtray and shook his head slowly toying with his dragonfly pin. This time it would be different. He was working with a new generation, one that was digitally minded.Mason examined the technology lab he'd built in the basement of his Hertfordshire home. Leaning back against the leather of his chair he rested his silver-haired head in locked hands.

Mother.

He recalled the night he'd heard the news. She hadn't found the Deveron. *How she obsessed with the wretched thing!*

Once she'd learned of its existence, it powered her usually reserved and unassuming behavior. Her search for it, mostly in China, turned a cultured woman into an inconsistent, anxious creature who, toward the end of her life, lost confidence in her abilities as a gifted government investigator. Ultimately she became withdrawn and took her life, the Deveron Manuscript having consumed her entire adult life.

She couldn't live without it and it still puzzled Mason that anyone could have possessed such unfathomable lust for any object. That's how Mason had first-hand learned of greed, a powerful force that could seize one to the point of losing grips with reality.Greed would consume Kumar, Riche, and Arlington in much the same way.

He rose and pulled a nearby drawer open. He located a faded picture of a woman. She wore a scarlet gown and smiled back at him as she had on many occasions.

I should never have let the Deveron do that to you.

Why did you have to go after it? If you hadn't, you'd still be here.

He replaced the photograph and slammed down his fist sending his whiskey glass flying.

He cursed.

The Deveron had preoccupied his mind for as long as he could remember. All for the wrong reasons.Still, once he had it and the stones, the inevitable had to be done, if only for the sake of the memory of the his mother. The woman in the photograph that he'd lost.

It had to be destroyed. And, he knew just how.

Only a few hours to go.

He finished his cigar, shut down the equipment, then proceeded upstairs, his thoughts reverting to the man in Tel Aviv.

He alone was leading this. Mason dialed Slate's number. Voicemail picked up. *Where's that moron?*

It had been nearly half a day. Slate always checked in. What was the holdup? He left a message. "When you're done with Cress I have a job for you in Tel Aviv."

2:00 A.M.

THESSALONIKI, GREECE

A cool breeze swept through the top floor apartment of the white stone building. The wind puffed out the candles on the oak table as a woman rose to close the battering windows. Her dark-chocolate, waist-length hair swung in the intrusive breeze.

She checked the small clock on the table. Even at two in the morning, she couldn't sleep. Without thought, she returned to her online reading.

Spring evenings in Thessaloniki were disposed to low temperatures and calm. She pulled a knit shawl over her bare shoulders and took in a deep breath. She set down the papers she'd printed and researched a topic on the Internet. The Wi-Fi connection tended to be unforgiving, mostly fading in and often out. Tonight it behaved reasonably stable.

The shrill from a red pyramid desk phone drew her attention, and she answered it.

"*Yia sou?*"

"She came," said the faint voice.

"Who's this?" she said.

"Mila? It's Rosetta calling from Blackmore in London. Oh Mila, she's beautiful and all grown up."

Mila pursed her lips, grimacing. She'd not spoken to Rosetta Black in over twenty years.

It had started.

"Who came?" Mila asked.

"Calla Cress."

She hadn't heard that name in years. The news sent a chill through her nerves as she lifted the phone, taking it to the window with its hanging cord trailing behind. She pushed the cedar open, filling her lungs with gallons of fresh air. "What did you tell her, Rosetta? You remember that you were paid handsomely never to reveal any more than we authorized you?"

"Yes, I do, and with the money, I was able to keep this building and the surrounding grounds. I also managed to find all the girls better homes. Whatever was left I now use to live modestly."

Mila had always liked Rosetta but didn't need her confessions right now. She glimpsed down into the street with rows of bars and clubs. A horde of tourists rambled out of a bar, their intoxicated voices bellowing some senseless English tunes.

The night chill failed to calm her raging emotions. Mila turned her attention back to the conversation. "What did she want?"

"To know all about her records...and her parents."

"What you did you tell her?"

"Only what we agreed."

Mila sat down on the wooden window ledge, rubbing the back of her neck.

"Hello?"

"Yes, Rosetta, I'm still here."

Rosetta's unsteady voice reverberated with unease. "She didn't look well at all. I believe she'd been wounded in some way. I can't be sure. But, most importantly I was worried about her state of mind."

"What do you mean?" Mila asked.

"She looked like she was on the verge of giving up. So I told

361

her about the birthmark. Only what we agreed. You see, she shoved a picture of it in my face."

"Rosetta—"

"I know what you're going to say, but I cared for this girl until she was five. We always knew she was special. When you've raised as many girls as I have you can tell the ones who are particularly gifted."

Mila set her hand on her forehead, hoping to mop away the anxiety she felt. "You may have put her life in danger. The less she knew about that birthmark and her past the better."

"I didn't tell her anything more about it," cried Rosetta.

Mila's forehead creased, tense lines coating her face. "I believe you."

She had personally helped select the right parents for Calla. They believed a retired missionary couple would be best. Fewer complications. Also, being barren for so long, they were more likely to cherish a small baby girl. Mila remembered the interview well. They appeared to know how to keep to their own affairs and were unpretentious. She'd wired funds each month for all of Calla's expenses as a child.

Calla was to be educated privately, an attempt at steering her accelerating appetite for knowledge. Mila recalled the day she had visited Mama and Papa Cress when Calla turned eight. Calla hadn't been there as Mila glowed in the stories and photographs they showed off.

Calla was happy, academic and somewhat athletic, everything Mila would have expected. The couple had done a phenomenal job in raising her and never once questioned any of the demands they were given regarding Calla's upbringing. They truly loved Calla more than most natural parents.

Rosetta's probing voice brought Mila back to their conversation. "Mila, we need to do something. Calla is really not well."

"I can't reappear in Calla's life after all these years. It could ruin everything." She lifted her tired body off the ledge. "No, Rosetta. I can't."

"Please, Mila. Please."

"I'm sorry. My hands are tied. I can't help Calla."

Taiven stood over Calla's limp body.

He carried her off the wet road and reclined her on the back seat of a parked black van.

A woman waited inside. "Is she hurt?"

"Yes," replied Taiven.

"We better move her car off the road. I doubt anyone saw anything."

Taiven steered the damaged Maserati off onto the hard shoulder and hurried back to the van. He would take care of the wrecked car later.

The woman glanced at Taiven and started the car. "Good thing you drove the van straight at her. I knew she wouldn't ram you. She wanted to avoid a collision."

"It's a risk we had to take. It's not in her nature to take life."

They drove for close to half an hour. Calla remained unconscious, elongated on the dark seats in the back of the van. They arrived at the estate at St. Giles Square, close to an hour and a half later. Taiven settled Calla in her room and positioned a hand over her left arm and rubbed unscented medication over her wounds. A warm luminosity left his hand, filling her body with vitality and heat.

Calla stirred.

He slipped out of the room.

Downstairs the door shut. "Miss Cress? Is that you?" Pearl said.

There was no answer.

Calla drifted in and out of consciousness. She slowly rose off the bed and felt her forehead. Her parched throat begged for water. She swung her legs to the floor and made her way to the bathroom for a drink. She drifted back to the bedroom. Calla noticed her bags had been packed for her flight.

She recalled every detail; the meeting with the woman at the foster home, leaving the house, right up to the advancing car. But nothing after the impact. How had she gotten home, alive and unharmed? Her condition was possibly worsening, with a tinge of amnesia. Perhaps someone, or something, had seen fit to give her a second chance at life, at least what would be left of it.

Would she take the second chance? Calla showered and dragged on some slacks and a light jumper before reaching for her overnight bag. She glanced at the time. 10:00 p.m.

Jack and Nash would be on their way to the airport. She made a move for the door.

CHAPTER 32

DAY 13
11:12 A.M.
Rabat, Morocco

N ash held out a chilled water bottle to Calla. "You look like you could use this."

Thankful for her second chance at life, however it came, she beamed at him with new energy. "Thanks, Nash."

He cast her a sincere smile. "No problem."

The trio headed down to the marketplace, better known locally as the *Souk,* with the heat of the African sun beating on the back of their necks. The metropolitan city of Rabat, at the mouth of the Bou Regreg River, had a clear-cut European presence. Like Casablanca to the south Rabat had much French influence as they proceeded down the tree-lined Mohammed V Avenue to the center of the city and traversed into the renowned marketplace.

Jack ran his hands through a set of hanging, silk veils, teasing an eager, toothless merchant who tried to barter with him. "Sorry, sir. I have no ladies to entertain with this scarf, and this one's taken."

With a silk veil, worn in local style, shielding her head, Calla turned to Nash. They curved into convulsions of hysterics as they watched Jack try to avoid a second merchant who'd shoved a handful of jeweled bracelets toward him.

Nash pulled Jack away from the fervent sellers. "Jack, it will take more than a veil to get the girl."

"You should know."

Shaking with laughter, Nash pulled him to the sidewalk. "All right, we'll talk about that later. I double checked with my intelligence contacts. Aran Masud should be at the café at the end of the market. According to the CIA, he's legit."

They forged ahead through the narrow alleys of the bustling market, admiring the spread of exotic fruits and vegetables. Calla took a swig of her water bottle and breathed in the spicy scents of the marketplace. She slung an arm through Jack's. "The most famous resources ever to hit the African continent were those that belonged to King Solomon."

"King Solomon?" Jack asked. "He wasn't African, nor did he live on the continent."

She giggled. "Finally, Jack. You did pay attention at some of my curator talks."

"You give great talks and, believe me, it's great to hear about history when the view is worth watching."

She nudged him by the arm with a smirk. "Pay attention, computer man. You're right about Solomon. The man didn't live here, but his treasures were here. One legend says that the Queen of Sheba, a queen consort whose reign stretched from Ethiopia to Yemen, came with hard questions for King Solomon. She wanted to test him and lugged with her a hoard of camels, spices, gold and precious stones. All for her new man."

"Stones?" Jack said.

"Yes, stones. You know, like rubies, emeralds, and diamonds. She came, questioned Solomon and liked his responses. For some reason, Solomon gave her all she desired and to quote a famous historian, 'some of his royal bounty'."

Nash stepped ahead of them. "Solomon was the wealthiest man ever to walk the Earth. He's also remembered as the *wisest* but wisdom wasn't his only resource. His gold reserves alone would be worth nearly a trillion US dollars in today's currency." He threw a teasing fist into Jack's shoulder. "Now that's bounty for booty."

"She must've been a knockout," Jack said.

They turned the corner into a section of the *Souk*, congested with merchants trading food, vintage clothes, and local souvenirs at bargain prices.

"Sheba returned to the continent with much bounty to her own country," Calla said.

Jack shot Calla a quizzical look. "But where is this bounty? Surely we're not trailing through Allan Quatermain's footsteps?"

Nash grasped Jack's neck in a tease. "Friend, open your mind to the possibilities of history, far beyond a novel character from the eighteen hundreds."

Calla shook her veiled head and chuckled. She locked arms with each of the heat-distressed men. As the colorful, chiffon veil shielded her from the sweltering sun, she exchanged looks with a twinkle of mischief in her eye. "I think Queen Sheba was the keeper of the third stone. Hopefully, Aran Masud can take us to the exact spot she hid it."

"I think I like this queen," Jack said.

They stopped in front of a café in the French-style quarter along a narrow pedestrian street.

"We're on time," Jack said. "Masud will meet us out here."

They waited outside, gazing over the estuary to Salé from the chilled open-air café, spread over several terraces in the Andalusian Gardens. A local man in his fifties, dressed in a *djellaba*, a flowing, hooded garment with full sleeves, approached them. "Jack Kleve?"

Jack stepped forward. "Yeah."

Jack had called in a favor with ISTF intelligence services and confirmed Masud's credentials together with Nash. It had taken a while to find the right contact, but Masud had been assigned to assist them with anything they required in Rabat.

"So Aran," Jack said. "You come highly recommended. Your name surfaced during a search for a knowledgeable guide on the African continent."

"I'm flattered. I've been involved in British intelligence on and off for fifteen years."

"What can you tell us about Queen Sheba's treasures? Have you ever found any of them?" Jack joked.

Masud shook his head. "I've been on many excursions in search of Sheba's treasure, once in the 1970s and once in 1985. Those who have sought it have also abandoned their searches mid-way."

The trio watched Masud curiously trying to ignore his chewing-tobacco stained teeth. How much he knew was a mystery to all of them.

Nash spoke in fluent Arabic. "Mr. Masud, what's your price for a walk down Sheba's trail? I'm not sure how much you know about us, but we're are conducting an archeological study."

Masud grinned, a wide-tooth smile, now revealing a set of scattered, gold teeth. "For you, the price will be £5000. We leave now. We've a long journey ahead on this dark continent."

"Okay," Nash said.

"Cash first. Mr.—"

Calla knew Nash hated carrying much cash with him, but he most likely had anticipated this sort of thing. He reached into his backpack pulling out an envelope of Sterling notes. "Fifty percent now and fifty percent upon our safe return."

Masud took the money and nodded in agreement. He bowed his head courteously. "This way. We need to collect some gear and discuss the details."

They stepped into the busy café.

Slate watched from across the street as the three Londoners, led by a local guide, made their way into the popular café. Three plainly dressed men stood with him.

"Blend in," Slate's said.

Slate spat out his gum on the dusty ground. He cursed. Cress was still alive. Slate had been positive the girl hadn't survived that Shard fall. He'd left the scene at London Bridge armed with that knowledge. He'd scuttled to the bottom of the building to grab the manuscript from her shattered body only to find her gone along with her car. He was now on the hunt for Cress.

A third time.

"Hey," he yelled at the men. "Stay out of sight. They're on the move."

Slate and his men remained concealed. He drew out a retractable mini telescope with an integrated listening device. The image was hazy, requiring a couple of adjustments. When it finally worked, he peered through the eye hole.

Through the minuscule opening, he caught sight of a local man leading his targets to a table. Within minutes a bearded gentleman joined them. Probably a local historian or professor. Slate tuned the listening device, and clear voices sounded even though he had to mentally tune out the noise of the boisterous café.

───────────

Calla studied the two local men as they exchanged a few words in Arabic. Masud turned to them. "You must understand, I've asked my father who has done more excavations than I have. He'll be able to tell you more. Many have sought Queen Sheba's treasure and not found it."

The older man glanced at each of the visitors and spoke in his mother tongue. "What makes you think you will?"

"We don't seek a treasure, just information," Nash replied in Arabic.

"Then you had better be prepared," the man said.

A bothersome grin spread on Masud's face. "We leave in an hour."

Masud left the table followed by his father. Calla, Jack and Nash huddled as a waiter offered them mint tea, accompanied by almond biscuits delivered on silver trays.

"Do you trust them?" Jack asked.

"We have no choice," Nash said.

Calla lowered her voice. "We'll just have to take a chance and hope we get to that lost treasure, or where it was held. I believe someone in King Solomon's circle was the original keeper or knowledge expert on this third stone?"

"Why Solomon?" asked Jack.

"Solomon started great, so to speak. A man full of wisdom and wealth but he didn't end great, I think he gave the carbonado to the Queen of Sheba as 'bounty.' It must've been stashed among his vast resources," Calla said.

"But it's millenniums later. Why would these resources be lying around somewhere? Are we seriously looking for a gold mine here?" asked Jack.

"The Deveron alludes to a crafty keeper of the third carbonado, one of great resources. Solomon is the only man ever to have owned resources anywhere near that in history. This must have happened at the time when Solomon had seven hundred concubines and three hundred wives. The stone must be here in Africa," she added.

"Well, it better be because, according to this translation, the stones need to be united within eight days of the first one being found," added Jack. "We don't have much time to jump to another continent. I like this man Solomon" He whistled.

"Whoa! I need his skills. A thousand women? He would need three years to spend a single day with each."

"Hence the thousand and one nights," Nash said.

The comment drew laughter then Calla's face darkened with worry. "Jack, Nash. I'll owe you big time when all of this is over."

Jack leaned in. "Calla, don't even think about it."

She breathed out a grateful smile.

Nash scanned the café, his gaze narrowing into a grimace. "I personally wanna keep an eye on this Aran guy."

"According to ISTF files he's legit and has been very instrumental in this part of the world for us," Jack said.

"Exactly," Nash said. "According to ISTF."

They left within the hour, boarding a chartered flight to Pakuba Airstrip in North-Western Uganda. Masud hadn't really told them much about the destination except that they would land in the fields where the animals roam free, and waterfalls descend over lofty cliffs. Whatever that meant.

Calla peered out the window of the Gulfstream G650 jet. Gazing outside gave her the feeling of gliding, welcoming the enthralling descent toward the valley. They hovered over the northern part of Uganda, surveying diverse vegetation, everything from forests to scattered woodlands disappearing into the Savannah grasslands.

She glanced down only to catch her breath as she took in the sight beneath them of the roaring Murchison Falls. The thunderous falls on the Nile River spanned between jagged cliffs, forcing their way through a seven-meter gap and dropped a spectacular forty-meters into the placid river below.

The plane landed at a bare and dusty airstrip. Moments later a local driver met them and guided them to a white safari van. When Masud greeted the driver, he introduced him as

Makumbe. Dark as midnight Makumbe put to mind the thought of a bolt of lightning. His attentive brown eyes were like two disks of wood as they turned to view the curious travelers. Glancing down at them he stood close to the height of an attentive ostrich.

"Makumbe will take us to Paraa Lodge where we can drop off our things and use it as a base. He'll also lead our trek to the trail by the falls, where I'm sure you'll find what you seek. We leave in thirty minutes," Masud said.

Nash shook the driver's hand. "I hear the animals in these parts are unforgiving."

"Only if you interfere with them," Makumbe answered as he displayed a large set of pearly teeth.

He packed them into the safari van and settled into the driver's seat. The four-wheel drive steered off the lodge promptly at 6:00 p.m. local time. Forty-five minutes later they tore around a sharp corner, skidding to a stop at the top of the roaring waterfalls. They stepped out of the van, admiring the view of the boisterous, foaming waters. Masud gathered the group and spoke with an authority unsuited to his minuscule height. "We'll hike from here. Are we ready?"

Masud and Makumbe directed the pack of hikers on the dirt path. How they would traverse the treacherous rocks, and tumultuous waters was anyone's guess. Calla's other concern was the unpredictable beasts of Africa that roamed the area. She'd read that perilous cheetahs ran free and uninhibited, not to mention the water buffaloes that charged opponents, weighing in at 1200 kilograms each.

Meters from the summit of the falls Calla addressed the *déjà vu* impression that played on her mind. She recognized the view but wasn't entirely sure why.

She'd seen the falls before. Her dream from Paris hung vividly in her mind as she replayed the picture of the hooded man. Was this the path he'd taken? Could that dream have been a sign that she was on the right track?

Nash trekked with sure-footed steps ahead of the group,

walking alongside Makumbe. "We're almost there," Makumbe said. "Just a few more meters."

A crimson sunset had formed over the falls and, from their height, they gawked at the vast valley from which they'd come.

"Stop!" Makumbe roared.

A deafening shot exploded in the trees behind them, turning their attention toward screeching, black-headed, Gonolek birds that shot out of the *Ensali* trees and littered the evening sky.

Nash withdrew his pistol. "Get down!" he ordered the company around him.

One by one they dove face down on the cleft path. Five shots fired above them, followed by a tear gas can, landing inches from Jack's feet. He reached for the irritant and cast it several meters from the group.

Calla covered her eyes as the oozing can spread a cloud of mist around them, causing inflammation in their eyes, noses, and mouths.

Nash kept a firm grasp on his 45-caliber semi-automatic pistol.

Calla glanced upward and caught a glimpse of an oncoming ambush through the smog.

Four camouflaged men enclosed them armed with automatic firearms and meshes of fibers, woven in grid-like structures that could only have been fishing nets. As one of the hoodlums took a menacing step forward, he was caught off guard by Nash's aim. With a savage heave, the man drove at him with the butt of an army shotgun.

Calculating a defensive strike Nash surged forward and slammed the man's arms, stalling his vertical attack and sending him staggering backward as the goon dropped his gun. Nash kicked it to the side and struck him in the chest with a tight-gripped knuckle fist that drove him to the floor unconscious.

A second man swung at Calla with a heavy net, lunging violently behind her. She sensed his heated breath on the back of her neck and twisted round. She crashed a fist into his lungs that jarred her hand tight. She froze for several seconds as the blood returned before contending with teargas smoke and eye irritation.

The man's legs buckled under him and he dropped the net gasping for air. Assured looks from Jack and Nash gave her confidence.To restrain him further she gripped his arm and with fisted knuckles, pressured hard above his elbow joint. The pain immobilized him, and he dropped to his knees in surrender. The tread of approaching footsteps signaled the appearance of the chieftain. Calla glimpsed upward and caught a face through the mist. Brown eyes, the color of acorns and a poisonous look on his face that made her think of a deadly eel, it was the thug who'd charged at her on the train, sent her plummeting off the Shard, and knocked her to the pavement in Berlin.

He sported a clean-shaven head. The hoodlum was exquisitely put together, with a musky scent that swooned women and a strong jaw, completely contradicting the peril that stemmed from him. Her eyes narrowed into his stare as Slate emerged through the fogged air, armed with an army pistol and, queerly, a street knife. He quickened his pace and charged his blade at Jack, who heaved backward gripping Slate's wrist into an arm wrestle.

Overpowered by the six-foot-two hulk, Jack rocketed to the ground with a solid kick from Slate's army boot and his head slammed on to a mud-spattered tree stump that opened a fingernail-deep gush on his forehead.Nash's jaw tightened. He lengthened his stride to Jack's aid, eying Slate carefully, who then plunged forward slicing the air with his blade.

Nash stretched an arm for the attacker's knife hand, his wrist scuffing the knife's sharp edge as he shelled a jolt into

Slate's right knee. He stood over Slate's recoiling frame for all of two seconds.

Slate crooked backward, grabbing his kneecap with his free hand. He backed away from Nash until the rough stones of a giant boulder scuffed his back. Slate tightened his grip on his firearm and settled it in the direction of Calla's forehead. He moved forward.

Calla's predicament caused Nash to stop in his tracks as a spurt of anger spiraled in his glare and focused on Slate's accurately aimed handgun. The tip of the cold gun barrel chilled Calla's crown, and a tense shiver thrilled through her senses as Slate lurched closer, his face inching toward hers. In one precipitate effort, he slit a lock of hair that had cascaded to her face and wrapped it around the blade, initiating a riled look from Nash, who stole a step in his direction.

"Not so fast, Marine," Slate said, angling the gun perpendicularly against Calla's flesh without a single glimpse at Nash.

Her eyes fell to the bag around her upper body as she evaded Slate's piercing stare.

"Had enough, Cress? We should stop these body wrestles that I may begin to enjoy."

"Get away from me!" she said.

"Not yet. Maybe you don't want me to. Otherwise, why keep me pursuing you. This may turn out to be more than a manhunt."

Calla lifted her chin. "You've been warned."

Slate let out a shady smirk and turned to Masud. "Get outta here."

Masud bowed his head and hurtled down the dirt path pursued by a frightened Makumbe. With the gun still menacing her crown, Calla shot a glance at her companions. The last thing Calla saw of Masud was the unnerving smile on his perspiring face. As the commotion came to a stilled pause the teargas mist faded. Faces and forms became distinctly visible.

Nash stood defenseless a few meters from Calla, with a tightened fist to his side. Inches from him Jack stooped on the ground, resting a hand on his bruised chest as blood from the head wound seeped to his shirt.

Calla glimpsed round her, an inner surge of intolerance growing to dangerous proportions. The two carbonados had tumbled out of her waist pack.Slate's gaze followed her anxious gape as his knife inched to her throat. "Cress. It would have been lovely." He dug the gun deeper into her skin. "Hand over the manuscript and this time, make sure you place it in my hands."

She gaped at him with eyes that made her fury rise theatrically.

Her reply was calm and confident. "No."

The gun mined a little deeper. "Sure? Now, let's try again. Start with the stones."

"No."

The bubbly flight attendant returned with a can of Coke and handed it to Eichel. "Would you like anything else, sir?"

Eichel took the fizzy drink and gulped it down. It gave him the sugar high he craved. They would be landing at Pakuba airstrip in the next thirty minutes.

The plane cruised over the expanse of the Sub-Saharan African skies. Eichel couldn't stop the sense of anticipation he felt. The stories from his great-grandmother who'd lived to a hundred and eight occupied his mind. She had worked as a nurse in Tanzania at the time of the German occupation, early in the twentieth century. He was only saddened by the fact that he couldn't visit one of the oldest known inhabited areas on Earth and experience her adventures. His trip was to the neighboring land-locked country where he hoped to find Jack Kleve, having left all the necessary meeting arrangements to Peter.

Eichel blinked as fading sun rays blinded his eyes. He stepped onto African soil for the first time, captivated by the green expanse and vivid colors of the country Winston Churchill had once called the Pearl of Africa. He approached a local driver who held a misspelled sign with his name.

EISHELL

"I'm Eichel," he said.

"Welcome to Uganda, Mr. Eichel."

They jumped into a waiting white Toyota and sped toward the heart of the country, en route to Murchison Falls. Eichel stared out the window at the tropical landscape. Merchants selling produce from neighboring farms lined the gateways into the towns as they crossed town after town heading toward the north-western part of the country.

"How much longer, driver?"

"Not long," came the reply.

He thought back to the tip from Jack, through Peter, that had yielded much and pulled out an email printout from his travel bag. It was from Jack addressed to Peter Manuel.

Subject: Africa

Peter,

Mr. Eichel can tag along, but we want no interference. ISTF will deal with Mason directly. We need to apprehend him red-handed. We'll deliver the Deveron document to Mr. Eichel once

*it's secured. Btw, I found something that Mr. Eichel may have
dropped. Tell him to be careful next time.*

Bis bald,
Jack Kleve

Confidence in his private investigation returned. Eichel would
keep his distance as instructed. The ride up the rocky path
toward Murchison Falls rocked the car as it ascended toward
the waterfall that formed part of the Nile River.

The Toyota juddered to a halt.

"The place you're looking for is a few meters past those
trees," said his driver. "I'll wait here."

10:27 P.M.

"Calla Cress, don't test me. Give me the artifacts so we can all
go home," Slate said.

His voice was raspy, Italian probably. Calla shook her head
and turned around to the sound of approaching footsteps. A
shadow emerged from the shrubberies. "I'll deal with this, Slate.
Get back."

Nash caught Calla's eyes, his knuckle whitening around the
trigger of his firearm. Mason emerged from the gassy haze as
Slate sidled behind him.

"Really, Shields. By my last count, you're outnumbered two
to one."

"That's if you passed math. Your numbers don't add up
when it comes to her."

"I'm sure there's no need for your firing skills. Cress will
comply. Won't you?" His gaze stabbed into her soul as he turned

378

to Calla. "Give me the manuscript and, while you're at it, the stones as well."

"How about I don't," muttered Calla.

She studied him furiously. He'd discarded any trace of his alluring persona. He stepped toward her, staring into her outraged eyes. "You know that just by possessing it you're guilty of theft and transfer of stolen goods. I could turn you in."

She bit her lip. "On my last check, I'm the curator and totally credible when it comes to transferring valuable artifacts across borders. I don't see that on your resume."

"Hand it over, or you'll face the same calamity your parents endured."

The words came out of Mason's lips like a steel spear to her side.

Her eyes narrowed. "I don't believe you," she said, her steady tone surprising her and those who watched. "What did you do to the Cress family?"

Nash took a firm step forward to where Calla stood and set a hand on her arm, shielding her from Mason's outburst. "Laskfell, that's a criminal confession."

Mason paid him no attention but kept his gaze on Calla. "This doesn't concern you."

Calla took a step forward.Was he bluffing? What did he know about her parents? She crushed a fist in his tight jaw. "Criminal!"

Mason gilded backward and collided with the ground, recovering from the unexpected wallop. His hand rambled for a folded handkerchief in his hunting attire and sponged oozing blood from his wounded nostrils.

"Don't unleash the past, Cress. It will haunt you until your guts are raw."

"That's for me to decide."

"Your father never had it in him, and neither do you."

Nash came between them, shielding her from his menacing approach. "Enough, Laskfell. You know damn well this manuscript is international property, safer in her hands than yours."

Mason shot them a malicious sneer and surged upward. He raised his rifle at Nash. "Back off, Shields. Let the Americans hang onto another agent. My hand may not be as steady as it used be to so don't make me stumble."

Nash's hand cramped on the trigger. "Her problem is my problem, Laskfell. Keep that in check for your memos."

"Oh, this is boring me to tears. A bit of *déjà vu*. If I recall that's the same thing your father said, Cress."

Mason crooked the gun in Calla's direction. "One last time. Hand it over!"

Calm.

With all eyes anticipating Calla's response Jack rose stealthily.Mason's eyes jerked his way.

Jack shot Nash a thoughtful look. It came in two seconds. Nash's boot slammed into Slates' shin, flailing him to the grimy path. The distraction gave Jack several seconds to secure a tranquilizer gun from the inside of his army vest and level it. He detonated it straight at Mason. The dart erupted from its shell and tore toward the giant man's neck.

Slate lunged forward and trapped the small missile with his bare hands, inches from Mason's throat. Mason stomped forward, casting his three opponents a demonic stare. He aimed his multi-shot sporting rifle. A flash of fire exploded from the barrel.

Rapid motion drew their attention. The bullet ripped through Jack's chest. It sent him convulsing backward as a deadly stench of sulfur contaminated the air, making Calla's intestines churn and force a gag. Her mind spun with guilt-ridden emotions and disgust. Her body stiffened as she watched her best friend plunge in slow motion under the force of the blow.

Nash caught Jack as he collapsed backward, sending them both strafing to the wet ground.

Mason's rifle kept aim at Jack's lifeless form. "Now, Cress. Do you still want to hang onto the Deveron?"

Calla grasped her bag and moved it round to her back. She shriveled as she watched her two friends. Mason's firearm lowered a few inches and this time its fury was marked for Nash's head without any compromise on accuracy.

CHAPTER 33

11:09 A.M.
RICHE MEDIA ENTERPRISES
LONDON

Eva clutched her mini camcorder, scrolling through some video files. Technology had never been her strongest skill. Yet she felt she was onto something. She would take this evidence to Mason. Or, had she already done that? Somehow, she couldn't really remember the details of the last twenty-four hours.

Did I stumble onto something big? The only predicament was she couldn't remember what it was. She sprang out of bed and found her work camera on her nightstand, scrolling through the hundreds of images and found some earlier shots she'd taken. Were these pictures of Eichel's notes?

Eva glanced down at her jumpsuit.

Had she slept in her clothes? This never happened unless she was utterly intoxicated.She returned to the images and noticed Calla's name scribbled across the margins of a document. *What is your connection with the Deveron Manuscript?*

382

The last RTL news reports speculated that the manuscript may not be in Germany anymore. She checked the time on the camera's bottom right corner. She'd lost forty-eight hours. *But doing what?*

That was plenty of time for any ambitious thief to embezzle the artifact. She scrolled through the rest of the pictures and videos of her images taken in the city at night. A shadow plunged from London's landmark skyscraper.She checked the date the photograph was taken. Yesterday.

Why was she taking pictures of buildings? She couldn't recall taking any of these images and videos. *What have I been drinking?*

Her one hunch was to maintain an intense hunt for Calla, and if need be, she would use her only link to her.

Nash.

How angry he'd seemed when she kissed him.Eva grinned to herself and headed for the shower.

10:36 P.M.

Calla spied through obscured eyes as her companions recoiled on the ground. She gaped at Jack's lifeless form. Everything in her wanted to eradicate her opponent but not at the cost of another friend. She slowly lifted the tip of the acid-free foil covering the manuscript out of her bag.

Nash caught her eye as he held Jack's unresponsive body on the ground. His voice quivered with courage. "No, Calla." He communicated with a cool, even temper. "Don't do it. Don't let him take this from you."

She couldn't bear the thought of losing him too. *No!*

Nash, I can't watch you die.

Her core had been tested, and it burned for Nash. Any

minute now the rifle could go off, and its hungry mark remained targeted at Nash's head.

"Get up!" Mason said.

Nash carefully lowered Jack's body to the ground and rose to his feet. Not an ounce of desire for struggle was evident in him as he glowered at Mason. With an inflexible glare, he sidled into Mason's personal space. "Pick on someone your own size, Laskfell. She's not it."

Calla opened her mouth to speak.Instinctively Nash raised a hand to shush her protests, his tone firm as the hide on a buffalo's back. "Don't give up on the Deveron, beautiful. Don't let him have it."

Nash turned his focus back to Mason's towering frame. "Now, boss, where do we begin?"

Mason sneered, amused by his dominance of the moment. "This isn't your battle, Shields. Conversely, I could use someone like you. What's she to you anyway?"

"I know what you're up to, Laskfell."

"What of it?"

Nash pulled his shoulders back, his gun firm in his right hand. "How about I spare you some billions, take a confession, and we call it a day?"

Calla watched Mason, her intent gaze piercing his. Nash galvanized into motion and launched for Mason's rifle, knocking him to the ground in a wrestle. The gun loosened from Mason's grasp. He catapulted upward and gripped Nash by the collar. With Mason stamping out in a fury they staggered in a bear-hug struggle that continued for several seconds.

Nash stretched for Mason's shirt and drove his forehead into Mason's nose.Mason grasped his nostrils as blood leached to his hunting attire. The taste of his own blood caused spittle to build at his mouth as he weakened in Nash's grip. Mason smeared the blood away with his sleeve. From the shadows, Slate found his footing, gripped a drooping branch and pulled himself forward tailed by his hoodlums.

"No!" commanded Mason as his hand waved Slate back, warding him off like a disobedient mutt.

The men retreated.

Calla suppressed an urge to intervene, her hand tugging at her shoulder bag. Vehement emotions spun through her hammering pulse. Nash released Mason and thrust a knee into his groin. With pain shooting through his body Mason bellowed out a muffled grunt, a stern look crossing his bleeding face. He cocked his head forward and slammed the top of his head into Nash's front.

Nash shot down on his back and watched Mason charge for another assault. The struggle prolonged, hurling the two men in a ground wrestle to the edge of the forty meter drop of the bellowing falls. As the irate waters smashed their frames, evenly matched in potency and will, Nash's face registered concern.

Sheens of sweat moistened Calla's face as Nash glanced down below him at the angry showers. Sneering Mason's hand held him loosely by his jacket, inches from the waters' perimeter.

"No!" roared Calla as she considered the only support that secured Nash from falling to his death, Mason's sadistic grip.

"Last chance, Cress or he goes over!" thundered Mason, his voice adrift in the growls of the falls.

Calla held her stomach as if pained by a violent spear, her eyes disclosing terror. Mason took one conquering look at her and in an instant, released his hold over Nash. Bleeding inside with the piercing of a thousand thorns she leaped onto the rocks along the edge of the toothed cliff. Nothing prepared her for the splintering of her heart as she watched Nash disappear beneath the drenches of the gushing torrents. As if stricken by a brutal hand her heart and body surrendered to immobility.

Three seconds earlier, as Nash hung over the crashing rapids, he'd barely managed to expel the words he'd cautiously avoided for months yet had to tell her.

Though she didn't hear them, as their eyes met for the last time, he had uttered the same words she so desperately wanted to understand.

"*Ana baḥhibbik.*"

She needed no translator. He'd loved her to his grave.

CHAPTER 34

Calla hung over the edge of the waterfall her body jerking. She glimpsed down at the thunderous pour. With the ragged cliff suffused in the misty moonlight, she glanced back at her sneering subjugators, angry tears coursing her face. There was no reason now to give him the manuscript, nor the carbonados. Like a fierce lioness whose young had been assaulted she launched herself at Mason, seizing his collar and jammed an elbow in the back of his neck.

He fell forward and thudded to wet path. Her fury then turned to Slate and, with one surge, she slugged him in the gut, propelling him to the ground.His grunted moans rang in her ears as he struggled to his knees coughing. Without assessing the damage, she'd left behind, she retrieved the fallen carbonados, placed them in her bag with the Deveron and glowered at her wide-eyed attackers, who stood analyzing her strength and resolve. Before she could pounce on them Mason sprang up, his physical robustness defying age and nature. Calla felt a blinding blow across her cheek, propelling her backward.She plunged to the moist ground and clenched her bruised face.

Mason strode forward and peered down at her, repulsion filling his eyes.He would kill her for the Deveron for sure. Calla held on tight to her ancient treasures. They were all she had left.

Knowing she would gamble her life for the Deveron Mason tugged harder at the bag and crushed his right foot on her hip for better grip. The motion tilted her to the side as her eyes registered the depth of the falls underneath her.

Mason spat on the soggy ground. "Now or never, Cress."

She glanced up at him and then down at the maddened waters. "Never, lunatic. Never!"

In one decisive moment, she hurled herself into nature's fury.

FIVE MINUTES EARLIER...
MURCHISON FALLS

The Toyota Ipsum parked near a baobab tree along the beaten path lined with full-size lush trees and flowering bushes. Eichel was sure he could trek the rest of the way. He'd come prepared, dressed in zip-off safari trousers, a long sleeve mosquito-repellent shirt, and hiking boots. He rocked backward and hid within the darkness of a tree, gripped with alarm.

Calla, Jack and a third man struggled against several assailants. He witnessed Mason fire a hunting rifle that spewed a bullet at the man he believed was Jack Kleve.

It took every reserve in Eichel to keep down. He'd almost given away his hideout.

Feeling like such a weakling for not getting involved in the struggle he reasoned that age wouldn't allow. He stood frozen behind the thick-trunked *kigelia-africana* tree as Mason and his men terrorized the trio. He's staggered forward.That's when

Mason raised his rifle and sent a bullet through Jack's chest and tossed the third man over the falls. Mason then unleashed his rage on Cress. *What man wrestles a woman?*

That had been his cue to help a lady in peril. As courage crossed fear, he progressed forward only to observe that she could indeed handle her own defense to more significant effect than he ever could until she, too, plummeted over the rapids. His body stiffened as Mason, and several men took their escape.

Three minutes passed. He peered over the trees' rustling leaves. *Three murders!*

It was a whisper at best, inaudible to all but him. Eichel's heart stood arrested in his throat. Unable to breathe he failed to make a decision and remained concealed by a boulder, yards from the cliff's edge. He waited ten more minutes, before staggering to his feet. He crossed over to Jack's lifeless frame and checked his pulse as he lay on the ground motionless, where Mason and his men had left him to die.

Eichel felt no pulse.

He knelt beside him and buried his head in his hands in defeat.

"ARGH!"

A loud cough brought him back to the crime scene. Jack moaned, rubbing his bruised head as he coughed uncontrollably, gasping for air.

Eichel scrambled for a bottle of mineral water in his pack. He cradled Jack's head and quenched his thirst with the cold water.

"Jack? Are you all right? That bullet went straight to your heart."

"What happened?" Jack said.

Eichel couldn't bring himself to tell him. "You were sh... shot. How did you—?"

Jack rattled his throbbing head and padded his chest. He

ripped open his shirt revealing what Eichel recognized as a bulletproof vest.

Jack let out a short breath. "Nash told me to put this on. He was right." He stopped, the mention of his friend triggering a recent memory. Jack sprang to his feet and scrambled to the edge of the cliff. One gaze at the deafening falls told Eichel Jack understood.

"They're gone, Jack. I'm so sorry."

Jack shot him a look of doubt.

"It's true. I saw it with my own eyes."

Jack spun around and seized Nash's backpack. He held it tight.

"We need to get you some help," Eichel said.

"What happened to them?"

Eichel glanced away. "Like I said, they're gone. I'm so sorry, Jack. Mason killed them both. They went over. Down there." He pointed to the drop down the boisterous waters.

Jack drove a fist in the backpack then stood erect. "Raimund, if you're right? We're out of time. Let's go!"

11:36 P.M.

A gush of water spurted over her free-falling body, adding to the speed of her descent to the crocodile and the hippopotamus-infested Nile. For the second time in a week, Calla was sent fluttering to her death. She surrendered her fate to her gifted mind. This time she took better control of her direction and speed and drew all the strength she could muster into her subconscious. She guided her fall to safety.

She had cheated death.

Twice.

Would there be a third time? She plunged arms out in a drowned out splash at the foot of East Africa's deadliest falls.

She landed into a well of rapids meters away from a watching crocodile that gawked with its jaw stretched in anticipation.

Gallons of water gushed in endless streams around her, driving her body further from land. Though she welcomed the freshness of the current as it beat against her body, she tore against its force in a stable attempt to flee from jeopardy. The frigid water, mudded with murk, wrenched rapidly with powerful undercurrents, making it perilous for her unmatched muscles.

Her feet kicked the violent tide, and it was then that she noticed the throbbing in her ankle. Shrieking with pain she tore her way against the speeding torrent, struggling to the bank of the river. Dragging her body to a hop, she slinked into a nearby bush, alone, with a drenched manuscript and two ancient carbonados from the galaxies burrowed in her bag. She trembled with the plummeting temperature and huddled in the shrubs clasping her knees for warmth. Her mind replayed Jack's demise and Nash's fall.

Plaguing thoughts circled around her mind as Calla crept on her hands and knees attempting to peer into the distance, tortured with grief over losing more than just friendship. She was breathing, but she'd lost her life. Surrounded by the wilderness, her ankle throbbed with each step. She couldn't go on. It was the brutal landing. Calla searched for her cell phone in her waist pack. Soaked through and through it had stopped functioning. Her tears stung her drying face.

She clenched her fists, a decision that only reminded her that her body was arrested with agony from crown to foot. She had spotted a small village as the group had made its way up the hill. She searched her mind for a name, orientation. Nothing registered. Perhaps she could make it there if she followed the river, but she couldn't muster enough strength as she sat swathed with bruises. Numbness zapped her strength, and she crumpled beneath the shrubberies, meters from the positioned crocodiles.

CHAPTER 35

DAY 14
5:47 A.M

Calla grasped her ankle and limped down the main stretch of the muddy road toward the center of Masindi, a nearby town she spotted from a distance. Day was breaking. The rural municipality looked frequented. She had no idea how long she'd walked. Her strength was diminishing and she advanced toward the town center, grateful to enter the colorful yet remote locale.

The name Masindi that she'd read at the town's gates echoed with familiarity. Samuel Baker, the British explorer, and anti-slavery campaigner had once visited this place. The sun peeked over the distant hills, increasing its warmth through her limbs.

She found her phone.

Damn!

Damaged, she purposed to find some sort of communication method.

The road led her to the center of the town, and she ambled along the stretch of the main street, lined with merchants setting up stalls for market. They prepped sugarcanes, papayas, dried fish, passion fruits, cassava and other tropical crops.

Her feet ached as she strayed away from the main road and rested on the ledge of an all-purpose shop. She placed her hands on her waist and drew in a deep breath. Her clothes, though nearly dry, remained plastered to her skin.

"You okay, my dear?"

She spun around and faced the round eyes of a large, dark-skinned woman with a sleeping baby straddled to her back. The woman's smiling lips were mud brown, and when she walked, her shoulder-length, braided hair swung above the baby's face. A patterned head-tie adorned her head above gleaming eyes. Her hands were fastened around a straw-woven broom and gently swept red dirt off the shop's veranda.

Calla eased herself from her rough seat with a hop. "Can you please help me? I need to get to a phone."

The woman threw her head back laughing. "I think you need more than that. Come with me," she said in her *Banyoro* tribe accent.

The woman led her into the cluttered shop, chock-full with everything from sugar to batteries, all crammed on neat wooden shelves. "You can use my phone."

The woman brought out a sugar cane and sliced moist papaya on a plate. "Eat. Drink."

Calla was grateful for the fruits' sugars that filled her body with renewed energy. The woman offered her a bitter lime drink that Calla swallowed in a flash, causing her tongue to tickle with the tangy aftertaste.

She glanced at the woman. "How much do I owe you?"

The woman cast a shy smile. "That's okay, my dear. Just eat."

Calla's lips curled into a grateful smile as she embraced the morning sun. She munched on the straw-like strands of the sugarcane.

As the sugar energized her body she watched half-naked

children frolic with laughter at her knotted, loose hair. One little boy showed off his self-made wire-car toy, and the bliss in their eyes only made Calla more determined to rid the world of people like Mason.

She thanked the woman and heaved herself upward. "Do you know where I can get a car?"

"My brother has a car. Where do you need to go?" the woman said.

How could she explain that she wanted to go back to the falls and find Nash and Jack, dead or alive?

"I lost something by Murchison falls, and I need to get back with help."

Thirty minutes later the shopkeeper's brother, a giant man, and two other helpers took a Jeep up to the falls. Calla searched through her waist pack and pulled out four hundred-thousand shillings, the equivalent of about fifty-pound sterling. She paid them.

When they reached the spot, Calla had tried all night to forget, there was no sign of a struggle. With the help of the local men they searched the area but couldn't locate Jack's body or Nash's backpack.

Nothing.

Not even the empty tear gas can.

"I'm pretty sure this was the location," she told the shopkeeper's brother and the leader of the men.

He rounded his men up. "We're leaving!"

Calla gripped his arm. "You can't leave."

"There's nothing here. Let's go."

"No, please, I can't leave my friends here."

"There's no one here dead or alive. Let's go!"

The men started toward the car.

Calla watched them leave. "Please!"

The leader shot round and cast her a broad smile. He drew out an ethnic spear from the back of the Jeep.

Calla held her breath as she eyed the weapon pointed at her, its leaf-shaped tip advancing toward her midriff.

"You have something that could persuade us otherwise. Give us the Deveron Manuscript and the rocks, and we'll let you live."

"Are you serious? You know about the Deveron."

"We may be from around here, but news does travel down to the dark continent. We have a good price waiting for those stones and the manuscript." He snickered. "Don't you realize you stick out like a sore thumb in this place?"

"I don't believe you."

He threw his head back, snorting a thunderous cackle. "It was easy to find you. The Englishman's willing to pay well for that bag. He's been spreading the news around the local area all night. We know you have what he wants. Now, hand it over!"

Nausea settled in her gut and blood drained from her face. Clotted with numb dread she shuffled backward and set off at a sprint. Too weak to contest them and a will to match she sprinted down the rocky path.

Her foot struck a loose root that threw her off balance, twisting her already weak ankle. She yelped out in excruciating pain as the men gained on her.

"Not very smart for a government curator," the leader cried.

Calla's fingers crawled in search of the bag that had fallen off her waist, landing a few feet from her. Her tortured ankle forbade her to move, and she massaged the wound to relieve the pain.

As she cringed on the ground, the gang leader set a heavy-booted foot over her injured foot. Pain shot up her entire body, and she let out a piercing scream.

He grasped the waist pack and grazed her skin with his spear. "Thank you."

She pierced burnished eyes into his core. "The *Banyoro* people don't hunt humans. They hunt beasts."

He eased his foot off her throbbing ankle. "Not this time. Good luck finding your friends."

Calla gawked in disbelief as they parted. "You can't leave me here!"

The bulky spear-man glanced back. "Pay us, and we'll take you back to the village."

"I have no more money."

He belted out laughing, another deafening eruption. "Then we'll leave you to the fate of the Savannah! Happy Safari."

The other men snorted and followed their commander back toward the Jeep.

Moments later the Jeep started, and she watched it accelerate. Soon the only sounds she heard were the whistling titters of forest birds and the anarchic munching of the creatures of the grasslands. She shot upward, landing in unbearable pain.

Seconds later, movement inches from her caught her ear, and a lone shrub stirred inches from her feet. She sat up, eyes widening as large drops of tropical rain began a heavy descent.

She gripped her arms for warmth and scuttled backward catching sight of abandoned caves in the distance. There would be shelter in there.She advanced steadily toward them dragging non-compliant limps.Calla stopped to breathe, her anguished lungs heaved for air.

Move!

Burdened clouds, pregnant with rain and thunder gathered above her, before bursting down in relentless downpours. The tropical rain transformed daylight to darkness as the unforgiving waterfall behind her commanded the edge of the cliff, mirroring the desperation in her spirit.

A few kilometers to the south lay the desolate African wilderness. Further beyond, in the Savannah grasslands, the sound of elephants heading for shelter with the stampede of death in their rushing feet alerted her.

Calla trudged with heavy strides along the riverbank, scampering inland, away from the river, toward higher ground.

Meters ahead, she spotted rock-strewn caverns. They stood a stone throw away from the waterfalls' edge.

Her eyes took in the sight. Could these be the caves? She'd heard about them. She staggered into the legendary caves many feared to approach, home to hundreds of fruit bats and pythons.

Safely inside she set her back against the soiled wall and tried to ignore the moldy stench attacking her nostrils. A low flying bat slashed its way through the tangled vines that obscured the cave's entrance. It caught its long, dog-like muzzle in her hair. Screeching with hunger, it heralded its army, a swarm of plaguing bats lunging toward her as they emerged to hunt for food, emitting a series of sharp clicks with their famished tongues.

A deafening cacophony. Calla drew in a deep breath. Legend held that no one had ever escaped the bat caves unharmed, at least not without losing their sanity. The last person ever to leave the hollow caverns left traumatized with a disease the locals called *Maramagambo*—without words. Exploration of the caves had led to trauma and exhaustion, and the patient in question hadn't spoken for days.

Calla clawed past the assailing army, gasping for air with each shaky stride. She scurried outside. Her wet safari shirt and trekking combat trousers hung sheared by twigs on her body, drenched with sweat, rain and red mud.

Her disheveled hair trickled with heavy droplets, challenging her visibility and balance. As the rain attacked her nose and cheeks, she scuttled to a deserted mud path.

She dared not look behind her. The rural footpath enlarged into a potholed road heading further away from the river. Steep and barely visible the trail threatened to give way to slick mudslides, and Calla stopped to rest with her hands on her knees.

Calla mustered every ounce of strength and rose. She

continued her quick dash down the mucky footpath as fast as her hiking boots would allow. With her heart throbbing in her chest a piercing pain probed her thigh. Perhaps she could run to the nearest town in about four hours.

Maybe six.

It might as well had been a day.

Nash? Jack? Why did she drag them into this mess?

Would there be time? Would anyone believe her? Who could she trust? She slipped and landed with an awkward thud. Her sore ankle twisted inward, sending sickening pain up her leg. As it rapidly swelled, agony threatened with any further movement.

Calla struggled to stand as the extreme downpour showed no sign of stopping.

Calla's eyes glimpsed through the blinding showers and she made out a deserted, vast grassland across the raging river below.

A rapid crack of a loose twig on the trail behind her interrupted the brief pause. Fear gripped her core.

She zipped round to face her pursuer. *A beast!*

Its front right hoof hoed the sludge in rhythmic motions. Calla stood immobile in his path as the male water buffalo prepared to charge. The wild bovine bore into her stunned gaze.

It could crush her with one movement

1:40 P.M.
CENTRAL LONDON

Eva raced through London's streets ignoring all traffic regulations. Her white Bentley cruised toward Riche Enterprises. She pressed down the button for the car phone system. "Mark, I'll be in the office in a few minutes. I emailed you some images a few minutes ago. Look at image twenty-seven."

"Ah.The one with some documents and scribbled notes," Mark said.

"That's right. Get that printed for me and find me a good German translator."

Traffic remained congested in the city, but Eva managed to skulk her car to the Riche Media offices in Holborn's busy district within twenty minutes.

"I've got the documents you requested on your desk," Mark said as Eva strode into her office.

She asked him to come in and close the door. Littered with more images than she had requested her desk was a mess.

Mark advanced into the office with a wide-tooth grin. He slumped uninvited across from her. "I found this name in the documents."

The words TOP SECRET on the first page had been circled as well as SILVER X3.

Eva studied the words Mark had circled. "What's this?"

Mark was extremely resourceful. That's why she'd hired him. How he did it, she didn't care, as long as he got it done. When founding her new media company, she had decided to hire only journalists, even for the administrative posts.

Eva wanted the best of the best. There were many out there toiling to find a job in a marred economy. Mark had been fired from a prestigious corporation that was struggling to save its image after the hacking scandal hit media companies in London. He was an exceptional investigative journalist who was sacked for participating in the bugging of two politicians' private cell phone lines. Mark also had been involved in the details surrounding the bribing of two charged police officers. Somehow he'd escaped conviction. His defense team successfully pointed to the lack of hard evidence. Eva didn't care when she read his resume.

She shot him a long look. "Do you have the translations?"

Mark pointed to two separate documents he'd asked a legal in-house translator to work on.

"What bells are ringing in your head, Mark?"

He fingered through the translated documents. "When I reported for the Holzworth-Bendel News Corporation we used to do some undercover investigations on the Secret Intelligence Service. We would also pay off some ISTF agents for information, the corrupt ones like us, of course."

Eva listened intently.

Mark maintained a straight face, unembarrassed with his revelations. "That name came up very often with regards to the Deveron document. I remember speaking to this one agent whom I coerced for a legal name for the agent. He didn't know it but, after a cash handover, he revealed that he could get me an address. That was all he was willing to do for the sum we had paid."

"Go on," encouraged Eva.

"I wanted to track that agent down. But before I could pursue it I was fired and well, you know the rest."

"Why did you want to follow the agent and the Deveron Manuscript?"

"It wasn't the Deveron that really interested us. Rather some of us wanted to expose the government and ISTF for malpractices such as empowering agents to commit all kinds of atrocities in the field. That was all before the hype began around these new developments with the Deveron."

"What's the address?" Eva said.

Mark scribbled the details on her notes. "I've had this memorized since the initial investigation. I believe he or she resides there. Whoever this man or woman is they know more about the Deveron document than anyone. They must. Look here, even the German cop has taken an interest by making notes on them."

Mark found Eichel's notes and compared them to the translation he'd placed on Eva's desk. "According to these notes, the German police are still baffled. Perhaps we can beat them to it."

Eva beamed. "Good work, Mark. That'll be all."

Mark stood to leave. "I would advise you to take some sort of protection on this one. Do you own a gun? This person is a former agent. They may not like trespassers."

With that, Mark left. Eva found the address online and keyed in the details into her cell phone's global positioning system. Judging from the satellite images, it was an unusual postcode for a manor home.

A small footnote had been blogged below the address.

The castle was abandoned seven years after a fire caused by lightning. It's still privately owned, but there's no evidence of anyone living there.

Eva fetched her things.

9:29 A.M.
TEN MILES FROM MASINDI
NORTHERN UGANDA

The man tossed Calla's bag to Slate. "Here's your loot! Where's my cash?"

Slate grappled the bag and tore it open. He peeked inside eyeing the manuscript, the journal, and the two black diamonds. "Where's the girl?"

"Not my problem. Only the bush can tell."

For a moment Slate contemplated embezzling the items and selling them to the highest purchaser. Should he really give them back to Mason? If only he were smart enough to know what to do with them. Could he hunt out Mason's clients himself?

He placed the items on the camp table and threw two-hundred-thousand Uganda shillings at the men. "Take your money and get out of here."

CHAPTER 36

Eva caught sight of the manor home at the end of the gated driveway. The drive from London had taken her close to two hours along the M14. Her global positioning system had served her well, and the curvy countryside drive hadn't fazed her. It had actually given her time to process the information she'd received from Mark. Why had SILVER X3 abandon the Deveron case?

She slouched against the door as she drove up the path.

Her white Bentley decelerated up the ramp and drifted to a halt at the entrance of a red-brick English home. Eva imagined that it had once been a gentry home. But right now she was keen to meet its current owner. Despite the rumored fire the property was in good order except for a shattered window here and there, probably caused by the occasional unwanted guests.

Must be a recluse.

Eva scanned the local newspaper clipping she had researched on the fire. No one had been hurt. The owner had battled the fire with the local fire brigade saving much of the timeless property.

She sprang out of the car and surveyed the manor grounds. The courtyard to the south with it gables, lofty chimney-stacks, and a residual, staircase turret was quiet. The place had to have once been a fabulous home.

Eva glimpsed to the charred east wall, a souvenir from the fire, imagining what a high-quality renovation would do for the place. She circled the grounds twice before making her way up to the front door.

She pounded on the solid oak. No acknowledgment came from within. She stole to the west side of the property and peeked through the window. The window ledge forbade any clear visibility, its elevation higher than she'd anticipated. Leaning a knee up on the windowsill she peered through the broken glass. A tattered curtain veiled her view. She hurtled down the stonewall. Her high heeled boot wedged in the openings between the stones.

"*Connard!* Idiot! Not my new boots!"

Eva stooped down in an attempt to rescue her footwear, tugging at the thin leather.

On the east side of the building, away from prying eyes, a man stood at his sink glancing out. Discarded dishes, cutlery, and cups piled the kitchen sink to the brim. The floors crawled with unflustered ants, and minuscule guests scavenged whatever crumbs they could salvage on the pest-ridden floor. Despite the unkempt condition the house clearly showed clues of its former state.

The man ripped open a soda can and guzzled its contents. His gaze drifted toward the courtyard.

His eyes bulged, and he swore under his breath. "What the—?"

He turned his eyes to the end of the court to see if the sign he'd posted a week ago was still on the lawn. From where it stood it was as clear as foil.

PRIVATE PROPERTY – NO TRESPASSERS

Squatters and teenagers had wrecked his property for months, thinking the place abandoned. Could he blame them? He hardly resurfaced from the lower floors where he resided. He stationed his half-empty can on the counter. "I'm sick and tired of you youngsters thinking you can use my property like some sort of weekend camp out for alcohol, drugs, and God knows what!"

The man rambled toward the kitchen door and picked up his Blaser R8 Barrel Rifle. He left the house by a back staircase that led out into the courtyard. "Hey!"

Eva flipped around. She yanked her shoe from the stone gaps, injuring her big toe in the process. She glared up at the distinguished silver-haired man. He approached, dressed in worn denims and a plaid shirt under a brown leather jacket.He would be her father's age and the anger in his eyes disguised his face. Yet his gun barrel communicated louder than language as he marked it at her.

UGANDA, 9:31 A.M.

The beast edged closer, his hooves thudding in a charge.Paralyzed into stillness Calla held her breath.She couldn't run.Not with her ankle. She recoiled in a backward crawl as the charging water buffalo made its move toward her. Calla gawked at the animal for several seconds.

She shut her eyes tight.The thudding hooves shuddered to a halt.

She opened one eye. The animal stood motionless with its gaze still upon her. It edged back, retracing its steps without turning around. She studied the giant mammal. He wasn't looking at her but at something behind her. In one move the beast bolted in the opposite direction.

Calla whipped her head around. Her wounds pulsing in a mania of agony, the scorching sun blinded her vision. A silhouetted figure stood arched over her. She coughed and squinted for a better look. Her vision was hazy, but someone stood peering down at her. A woman with three long braids. *Can it be?*

Calla's lips mouthed a whisper. "Allegra?"

Allegra cast her a grim look.

Calla's eyes focused. She tried to stand. "Allegra, is it really you?"

"Don't move, Calla, you're badly hurt."

"How...how...how did you find me?"

Allegra helped her stand on one foot.

Calla's words shot out in a raspy whisper. "You're alive!"

Allegra smiled. "Be still, Calla. It's time you met your family. Let's go!"

CHAPTER 37

Allegra reached out and grazed her hand over Calla's wounded ankle. The pain subsided a little. "We need to move now."

Allegra hoisted Calla's arm onto her shoulder. The pain eased, and Calla hopped alongside and stopped to glare at her. "We can't go. Jack and Nash were—" She paused to inhale. "We can't leave yet. I took this thing too far, Allegra. They were all I had."

Allegra's calm face saddened but she continued walking, supporting Calla along toward a waiting Land Rover Jeep. Allegra helped her into the front passenger seat. "What happened to them?"

Calla carefully placed her injured ankle on the floor. "I've so much to tell you. It all started with the Berlin trip. What happened to you in Berlin?"

Allegra didn't respond.

Calla shifted in her seat for comfort. "Then came the carbonados and now there's this thing Mason's done."

Allegra's eyes lit up. "The carbonados? Did you find them?"

Calla relaxed her head against the headrest, glad to be able to recline comfortably after the run in the wilderness. She glanced over at Allegra's expectant face. "You know about the rocks?"

Allegra nodded.

"We found two," Calla said. "I used several of your notes and the black journal we found at the British Library to translate the Deveron."

"The journal was there?" Allegra asked.

Allegra closed the door on Calla's side and glared through the open window. "Tell me on the way. We're running out of time. If you only have two of the stones time is running out to find the third."

"I don't have the stones," Calla said.

"But you said you found them."

"Yes, but I didn't get to the part where—" Her tone lowered. "Nash and Jack are gone, Allegra. Mason... His thugs took the stones."

Allegra frowned and hurtled round to the driver's seat. She jumped in the car and started the engine. "I'm so sorry, Calla. Well, at least we have the manuscript."

Calla glanced ahead. "No. That's gone too."

"This is worse than I thought."

COTSWOLDS, 4:20 P.M.

"Who are you? You kids should stop playing around my property!" bellowed the man in a monotone drawl.

"I was just—" Eva said.

"You seem a little old for a teenager."

He glimpsed over at her shoe. "Then again judging from

408

your shoes and car you've spent a few years out of college. Or is it a gift from daddy or a boyfriend?"

Eva frowned, her foot aching from the abrupt slip. "I...I'm looking for someone."

"French, I see. You a tourist?"

"No."

"Can't you read the sign? I would imagine anyone who drives a Bentley Continental GTC would have some sort of literacy level. Get out!"

Eva leaped onto the ground with a hand on her pounding foot. His words were aggressive, but Eva detected his nature was anything but hostile.

His rifle marked her face. "What're you doing on my property?" he demanded.

He could aim an accurate shot from the twenty-foot distance. She was sure of it. Eva didn't shift a muscle. "As I said, I'm looking for someone, sir."

"Who?"

"I don't have a name, just a code. Agent SILVER X3."

The man glanced away from the ocular lens of his gun and hesitated. "Do you think I'm an idiot? How dare you come here with such rubbish! I'm tired of you kids treating my property like it was your own holiday retreat."

Eva lost all fear. "Are you agent SILVER X3?"

The man prepped his firearm and advanced forward.

Eva swallowed. He wouldn't hesitate to fire that gun. She took one step closer, her eyes firmly fixed on his. "I'm a journalist investigating the Deveron Manuscript." She gaped at his lime-colored eyes. "Tell me if you're SILVER X3? The agent who worked on this case for the Secret Intelligence Service. Maybe thirty-some years ago?"

The man didn't answer.

Eva took another quivering step. "Can you help me?"

The man raised his rifle and fired a shot in the air. "If you don't leave in five seconds I'll do more damage to your shoes than that wall did."

He leveled his gun at her feet.

She delayed.

"One!"

She took a step back.

"Two!"

And another.

"Three!"

She bolted to her car and fidgeted with the door handle until she jerked it open. Eva dared not look back. She dove into her seat, imagining his eyes were firmly fixed on her, and they would be until she left his property.

The engine throttled, and she let her window down. "Have it your way," she said. "Whatever you're hiding, I'll find out! Here!" She flung a set of papers out the window that landed on the gravel. "In case you change your mind."

The car sped off, screeching as it spun its tires, tossing the grit of the pebbled courtyard.

The man waited until the convertible sports car had disappeared. He advanced toward the discarded pile and retrieved the papers.

He filed through them cussing. "The last damn thing I need!"

11:27 A.M.
NORTHERN UGANDA

Two men waited at the bottom of the Murchison Falls. They'd held onto a net for hours suspended halfway down the

410

waterfall.

"That's him," said the first man.

They hustled to the netted lump and fished it out of the water. Gallons of water drenched their faces, but they managed to lug the mass.

Nash moaned from a bruise on his arm within the mesh and coughed up water. The sturdy African men cut him loose from the mangled fibers and hauled him to a waiting pickup truck.

Shivering, Nash opened one eye, catching a glimpse of his captors. Unaware he was conscious, in one precise heave, they threw him head first in the back of the pickup. One of the men pitched a thin blanket over his wet frame before scuttling to the front of the vehicle.

The truck started a slow drive up the road, slugging the mud as it veered into a dense forest.

Where were they headed? All Nash could see were the wide range of different flowering plants, fungi, gaping chimpanzees, and lanky, ironwood trees. Other species of primates unfamiliar to him lurked within the mahogany trees. Along parts of their journey, severe overgrowth made it difficult to travel without the thugs halting to use cutting tools.

Nash's head hit the hard steel edge of the pickup. He raised his neck. His hands had been tied behind his back and his mouth gagged. He scanned the back windshield of the two-seater pickup not recognizing the thugs. The truck advanced down the hill, swaying from one side of the road to the other in an attempt to evade deep potholes.

A dense fog had settled after the rain covered the widespread area, reduced visibility to a quarter of a mile or less. A light drizzle started a descend over them. Nash shivered and only hoped he wouldn't catch pneumonia in these morning hours in the Savannah grasslands.

What had happened to Calla? Was she out alone in the

wilderness? Had Mason killed her? He was capable of it. An involuntary grunt left his gagged lips. They'd been so close, and it infuriated him that he had failed her.

Several hours later the truck stopped within a humid, forested area. One of the hoodlums came round the back and pitched Nash a bottle of water. A beefy man untied Nash's hands and legs and removed the mouth strip. "Get out!" he said.

Nash gravitated upward and threw the blanket to the ground. He swigged the still, bottled water and observed what looked like an orderly military camp of scattered khaki tents. Four-wheel drive vehicles lined up along the edge of the camp and several men dressed in camouflage gear paraded the area.

"Nice of you to join us."

Nash swung his head round as Mason turned toward the pickup. Two armed men from the *Acholi* tribe paced alongside him, towering Mason like corn stalks. Nash had read about the peoples of Sub-Saharan Africa. They were a *Luo* people, said to have come to northern Uganda from Southern Sudan. They were skilled hunters identified by their use of nets, spears and long, narrow shields of giraffe or ox hide in war.

Nash rose and proceeded toward Mason with distaste nagging his conscience. "What did you do to Calla?"

Mason raised an eyebrow. "She was responsible for her own fate."

Nash could feel himself shaking with anger. "You won't get away with this."

He took one step forward.

The *Acholi* man fisted his hand.

Nash hesitated. "Interesting company you keep. Will I need a spear?"

11:22 A.M.

412

Allegra's Land Rover jerked along the potholed road and swerved into a dense forest, home to numerous species of gawking monkeys and chimpanzees. Several minutes later they emerged onto a flat terrain on the other side of the tropical forest.

Calla's ankle throbbed with immeasurable pain. "I need to see a doctor about this injury."

Allegra glimpsed over and smiled. "Where we are going we don't need doctors. I just hope we've not run out of time." Her eyes glistened with understanding. "Get some rest. You've been through quite an ordeal."

Allegra's voice had always consoled her, and now, as always, it exuded with prudence and acumen. Calla tried to sleep, her eyes settling on the dashboard where they caught sight of a folded newspaper, Riche Media Times. It looked like a regional paper, and she reached for it and spread it open. The front page carried her photograph. A snap taken at Heathrow airport only days ago.

Her jaw dropped as she read the headline.

Theft of Priam's Treasure: Is This Europe's Hunted Woman?

European police are on the hunt for a runaway British Museum curator, Calla Cress. Could her flight be connected to the theft of Priam's Treasure?

Eva Riche of Riche Media

Calla set the paper back on the dashboard. She kept her hand on its folds as she processed the report.

Allegra had fallen silent, fixing her eyes on the jerky road. "That's why we need to hurry."

CHAPTER 38

C alla stared ahead in silence as Allegra sped the four-wheel drive through uninhabited terrain. The sun scorched her arm as it rested on the window's edge. Calla refused to think about the news report and Eva's cunning tactics.

The ride continued in strained silence as Calla's mind tossed around unanswered questions she hoped Allegra could address. How had Allegra found her?

"Allegra, where've you been? I thought you were dead," Calla said.

Allegra tapped her pointed fingernails on the steering wheel as if hunting for the best way to phrase her answer. "There's so much I need to tell you but let's wait until we get to the Cove."

"To *the Cove?*"

The Jeep stopped by a large terrain overlooking a well-maintained, corn and banana plantation. A herd of giraffes lined the otherwise deserted land while a handful of water antelopes scurried raucously in the remote distance.

Calla turned her head when sneering hyenas crossed the terrain with their young. "What is this place?"

Allegra sprang out of the Jeep and onto the ground. She found a smooth stone and aimed it high toward the center of the fifty-foot space.

She returned to the car and waited. Within seconds the vehicle started a descent into the ground as if suspended on a natural elevator.

At first, Calla presumed it was another attack, but Allegra's calm face reassured her. The car descended further into the ground until it came to a sudden halt. For a moment or two, the two women sat in the dark.

Without forewarning, sharp fluorescent lights flooded the view ahead of them with blinding force. Due to the number and variety of vehicles parked ahead of them, Calla supposed the Cove to be a sizable underground garage. Yet nothing here resembled any garage she'd been in.

Bathed in white light the gleaming floors extended for what seemed like miles. Cars neatly lined the edges of the room, leading to what appeared to be a glass door.

Allegra clambered out of the car and advanced toward two uniformed men walking toward them. Their white uniforms dazzled with a hint of silver in the glaring lights.

The first man greeted Allegra with a firm shake and a smile. "Do we have the manuscript?"

Allegra shook her head.

"The carbonados?"

"No."

The men continued past her and gently helped Calla out of the car. The first man strapped Calla's arm around his neck allowing her to hop alongside with him on her good foot. Both men wore short crew cuts, one blond and the other seemed to be from the Far East, possibly Korean.

At the end of the garage, the Asian man pressed a button on the wall. "This injury will need immediate attention."

His gentle conduct calmed Calla, and she instantly relaxed with the two strangers helping her through the glass door.

They took the cut-glass elevator when it dipped down a long visible shaft. The elevator had no numbers, just various shapes of all forms and lights. She recognized a few of the symbols similar to those on the Deveron document. "What is this place?" she asked again.

No one responded.

Allegra threw her a knowing smile and glared up in anticipation of arrival at their destination. "This is the Cove, a sort of headquarters. Actually, we have a few littered across the continent. Each continent."

Calla's attention was captured. "Who is...*we*? Are they all underground?"

The men laughed casually as Allegra set a warm hand on Calla's arm. "Not really. They are where we need them to be."

The glass doors dragged open, and they came out into a large hallway. The floor shone with bright shades, bearing a resemblance to an office, with contemporary fittings of various shades of cream, pearl, and white.

Calla gaped at the spectacular interiors. Even at several feet below ground, they were inundated with natural light. How was that possible? It was one of the most beautiful interiors she'd ever seen. Calla imagined the plants and vegetation displayed around the place benefited from the spectacular light, giving the rooms the only hint of color.

Allegra led the group down the corridor. "The Cove, or Coves if you include the others, are probably history's best-kept secrets. This place has been here for years."

Calla fired Allegra a sharp glance and followed her lead. "Really?"

"Yes."

They came to the end of the passageway. One of the men led them through a bustling workroom reminiscent of an industrious, design and development office. Several more uniformed people bustled behind electronic tablets that were at the cutting-edge of computing technology.

The room rang with modernity, the latest technology, and several office accessories Calla had never seen. The computers and gadgets looked like they were at least fifteen years ahead of their time, putting to shame some of the developments in the R&D labs at ISTF and if she had to guess, the NSA and the Government Communications Headquarters put together.

They ambled past various cubicles with people of every race and tribe chatting in huddles.

Calla admired the ceiling, decorated with dazzling crystals. "Are those real?" she asked Allegra.

"Of course! They power this place. All the energy used to manage this place runs in those natural crystals. Those are similar to photonic crystals. Crystals have puzzled the world for years. We've actually learned to engineer them for industrial purposes. Crystals, rocks and minerals are at the heart of most of our exclusive capabilities."

Calla wasn't sure she understood. She anticipated a logical explanation at some point, although right now the view made for deep contemplation.

At the end of the main workspace stood a glass office. How long had it taken to perfect such an establishment? Years and lots of money. *NASA's workstations don't hold a candle to the technology in this place!*

The blond man pressed a square button, opening the door to another white office space. Seated at the desk was a tall snow-haired man sporting a distinguished goatee. His wide forehead and thin eyebrows gave him with sophistication as he spoke with someone on what Calla could only imagine was an ultramodern wireless phone. It put the ISTF smartphone Mason had given her to shame.

His lean, elegant build and gray eyes exuded intelligence and Calla turned when he saw them walk in and came around the desk. "Allegra. How'd it go?" asked the man. Though he spoke, English Calla was surprised she couldn't place the accent.

"We found her," Allegra said. "Meet Calla Cress."

The man shifted his eyes toward Calla narrowing them slightly. "Welcome. I've waited many years for this occasion."

Calla examined and quizzed him with her stare. "How so?"

The men helped her down onto the chaise lounge across from the white marble desk. She hoisted her bad ankle onto a waiting cushion at the end of the upholstered sofa. "Thank you, but who are you?"

The man knelt on the floor beside Calla and examined her ankle. Despite his hands-on approach in assisting her, he was the man in charge.

"My name is Vortigern Aspel. Please lie back," he instructed.

Allegra gave her a reassuring look. Calla obliged. He examined her swollen ankle and laid a hand on the clotting lesion on her jaw. His hands felt warm and exuded a faint medicinal aroma of angelica oil. The gentle massage eased some of the pain.

"This'll give a boost to your immune and nervous system and will help you maintain mobile joints. If only we had the rocks. This would be such a simple procedure. Quicker recovery. But you'll be fine."

He rose steadily. "Calla, you're the one everyone here has been waiting for. You alone are the person who can lead what is promised to be the world's greatest enterprise."

Calla cast Allegra a questioning look. "What enterprise? All I want is to find information on my family and now to help my friends. What's left of them."

Vortigern acknowledged her surprise. "Have you not noticed that you're not like others? You possess instincts and knowledge that you don't understand, nor know from where it stems?"

418

Calla felt herself shrivel at his comment. "I'm sure there're others who can do the same things."

Vortigern rose and paced around her chair. "I understand. Have you also seen that when you use these abilities and physical strength, they leave you in such a weak state such as now?"

Calla searched her thoughts. *How can he know that?*

Vortigern set her at ease in a fatherly sort of way, reminding her so much of her Papa Cress. She slid along the seat placing her back upright. "I saw a specialist in Paris. He informed me that I probably have a genetic disorder. The other probability is that I was exposed to Polonium 2 1 0, probably contained in the two carbonados we found."

Vortigern glared into her eyes."Hmm—"

"The doctor explained that the Polonium could have aggravated my genetic disorder and that's why I have incredible strength followed by unbearable exhaustion, like now. I read the report myself," Calla said.

Vortigern tilted his head, studying her as Allegra approached the chaise longue, her movement barely perceptible. "Calla, I've known you a long time. I'm sorry I had to leave you when you needed me most, but it was for everyone's good."

Allegra glimpsed over to Vortigern. "Perhaps there's a simpler way to explain this, Vortigern. Shouldn't we start with who Calla really is?" She glanced into Calla's eyes. "And most importantly, why you have memories and dreams that you can't explain."

Vortigern asked the two uniformed men to wait outside. Once they'd departed, he drew a seat for himself and Allegra by the chaise longue.

He took a deep breath. "Calla Cress, your story started just before the first century."

Eva sped back to London, thudding the steering wheel with compulsion at every red light. "He's hiding something."

The highway bustled with London commuters on their way into the metropolis. She turned on the radio for the traffic news. Just the usual Friday evening London traffic news.

Her phone rang. She scrambled to connect it to the in-car audio system.

"Yeah?"

"It's Mark. Mason has canceled his meeting with you for this evening."

"What? Why?"

"His secretary said he had to leave town urgently."

Damn! Mason promised me more information! This time she had bargained for the full classified files. Only a few pieces were missing regarding agent SILVER X3. Mason was the man to fill these gaps.

"Eva?"

She cursed under her breath. "Yes?"

Mark's voice rang with concern. "She said to tell you that the deal is off."

The day's investigation had brought her no closer to the answers. Eva slammed the phone down. *"Imbécile!"*

She had kept her end of the bargain. Just that morning, after much persuasion, she'd gained her father's trust and persuaded him to sign Mason's deal. That had been a significant step. She'd been a pawn. Mason had no more use for her. *"Cochon!"*

Blistering tears blurred her vision as she swerved off to the hard shoulder. She rammed her palm against the steering wheel. Ignoring the pain, she lifted her head. "Time I publish the second part of the story. Better me than the Guardian!"

She ignored the warning bells. The government, ISTF, and even her father would probably not back the story. Eichel's notes trickled with scandal she couldn't ignore. The details she didn't know she would fabricate.

What's the worst that can happen? A lawsuit?

She had a damn good lawyer. Her brother.

"Before we go into that we need to take care of your wounds. Follow me."

Vortigern directed Calla to a section of the establishment that housed several rooms and closed offices. As they walked past each shut door, Calla read the various names displayed on each door.

ANALYTICAL ASTRONOMY...CIVIL ENGINEERING...MILITARY ECONOMICS...PRACTICAL COMPARATIVE GENETICS... PRACTICAL CUSTODIAL THEORY...ANALYTICAL HISTORICAL...NANOTECHNOLOGY...ARTIFICIALLY INTELLIGENT BUSINESS...POPULAR CLINICAL SCIENCE... BIOMEDICAL PARANATOMY...

They stopped at a set of clear-glass, double doors. "We keep some supplies in here for emergencies. I may have something to ease some of that pain," Vortigern said.

They settled into what looked like an infirmary. Two uniformed women helped her onto a medical examining table.

Allegra held Calla's hand while Vortigern strapped her arm

and leg bands. "This is just to keep you steady. Each one of us reacts differently to medication."

Calla closed her eyes when she saw the medical instrument Vortigern held in his hand. "We call this a *Cell fuser*. You'll be fine, Calla. We just need to inject some remedial serum into your muscles to give you strength."

"What will it do?"

"The composition of your body is so complex that I'm not surprised your Paris doctor found what he thought was Polonium. You see, that was the closest thing he could probably compare it to. Your body is made up of so many components modern medicine cannot understand."

"But why? Is that what's harming my body?"

"At present, modern medicine cannot help you. You need something stronger."

"What's in this serum?"

Vortigern smiled as he administered the medication. "Think of it as anabolic steroids without the side effects. About a thousand years ago some of our people, let's call them *operatives,* for now, began creating medicines when they realized that they needed stronger elements to modern drugs, yet harmless enough to be given to an infant."

"Operatives?"

"Everything here in the Cove is an attempt to replicate a perfect world through science and technology. Every element we use comes from the Earth. We just need to be creative and know where to look."

She didn't follow but felt the murky liquid shoot through her veins, soothing her throbbing muscles. She reclined further and felt her limbs reinvigorate.

"Your muscles were built to sustain impact, go against gravity and self-defend. All from the research and technology engineered for generations in rooms like the ones down this corridor. But they're not operating at full capacity."

Calla felt lightheaded. "I could have told you that."

They were beginning to communicate on mutual ground. Vortigern withdrew the injection. "What you need now is to train them."

Calla thought for a moment. How was I able to plunge off seventy-two stories unharmed?"

His smile reassured her that she wasn't eccentric, but would she welcome what he would confess next?

"Calla, several years ago operatives in our research and development labs engineered a special chip, which runs on energy much like that contained within the carbonados. That chip when implanted under skin reengineers the molecules within the epidermis and your central nervous system. When your body senses contact with gravity, the chip that acts much like a drug reverses the *natural* physics of gravity. So in essence, giving you the ability to stay afloat, or in other words, fly."

"ISTF has toyed with these kinds of experiments," she said.

"Our operatives are light years ahead of ISTF in their research and engineering. They've been at it for many centuries."

Calla stroked her forehead, glancing straight at him as she searched for plausible answers. "How do you know so much about me? How did I get this way? The chip for one. Was I forcibly injected with random test results? Was I a lab rat? That's not even legal. Was I born this way?" Calla could feel the anger welling in her. She had to know. Though she understood the words, he was saying there were so many missing pieces of logic to their conversation.

She knew he was telling the truth. The last several hours had tested her analytical intellect to the core. "What do my muscles *really* do?"

Vortigern paced around her bed his hands behind his back. "Anything you want. And regarding the chip your father and mother had it injected into their bodies before you were born so you must have it in your genes."

Calla gasped in shock. "Are you saying the chip-enabled me to control movement at will?"

Vortigern nodded a knowing smile in agreement.

"Am I the only one with these muscles? These abilities?"

"Some of us have them, and some of us don't. It all depends on each one's mission. But until we have restored all power to the *operatives* using the carbonados we remain vulnerable."

Calla was now fully alert. She examined Vortigern's wise eyes as they soothed her emotions. "Why does Mason Laskfell want the Deveron so badly? And, how can he be stopped? He seems to have a telepathic ability that gets everyone around him jumping at his command."

Vortigern placed gauzes on her wounds and bound them. "Mason isn't what you think he is. He's been preparing his strategies all his life. From what I gather he's now well-equipped and allied."

He unstrapped her hands and feet. "You reacted fine to the serum."

Calla threw her legs over the side of the operating table. "Thank God."

Allegra's fearful look dwindled. "Calla, your nature is like that of a warrior, a defender, and protector. It may not seem like it, but Mason has feared you for some time. You're the one person he knows can challenge him. He needs the energy in the carbonados to engineer the worst technological disasters for his own aims. However, there's one power that can defy Mason no matter how big a following he has."

Calla perched herself on the edge of the table. "What's that?"

Vortigern placed another plaster on her arm. "That's the one thing that even I don't know. But once we have the diamonds it will be up to you to find out."

Calla managed a weak nod. If he hadn't figured this entire thing out by now how could she? Calla felt all the pain leave her body.

She shot up with a spring as Allegra set an arm around Calla's shoulders. "How do you feel?"

"All new again."

They paced toward the door, and an afterthought emerged. "What happened to my parents, Vortigern? Did you know them?"

He fell silent for a few moments. "I don't know. We never found out what happened to them after the moment they left you at the foster home."

Allegra held the door open. "When your parents dropped you off at the foster home we lost all trace of them and the Deveron Manuscript."

Allegra hesitated, Calla understood there was more to tell. Vortigern caught up with them and pulled Allegra to one side. For several minutes they exchanged hushed words.

Allegra leaned in toward Vortigern, her even voice commanding. "We need to tell her."

"What do you need to tell me?" Calla asked as Allegra glanced away.

Vortigern was first to respond. "Calla, we sent several operatives back to the cliff to look for what's left of your friends. They found nothing. I don't think your friends made it."

"There must be something! Jack fell in the open space above the falls," Calla cried.

Sympathy swept over Allegra's face. "I'm so sorry, Calla."

Vortigern ours ed his lips. "Regardless of whether we find them or not, you should know that you can't rely on them any longer. You can't be tied to these people and get emotionally entrapped."

Allegra averted Calla's eyes and lowered her face. "It's always been this way."

The sharpness of Allegra's tone unnerved Calla.

"I don't follow," said Calla.

They both didn't believe the words they spoke as if they'd been rehearsed several times.

Calla's mind rang bells of warning. "Why?"

Vortigern laid a hand on Calla's shoulder. "We're your family now. Let's just leave it at that. We need to find the last carbonado before Mason does."

Calla watched Allegra turn away, frustration rising in her cheeks. "I've known Jack and Nash a long time. And you, Vortigern, just for two minutes. Why should I believe you?" Her voice clogged with emotion. "They're my closest friends. How can you judge them and tell me whom I can or can't trust or get involved with?"

Vortigern ran a hand through his impeccably groomed hair. "Operatives can't associate with non-operatives in such an intimate way. It has always led to disaster."

Calla struggled with his authority and glanced away from Vortigern with calculated disdain. How could they cast off Jack and Nash, whose help and resourcefulness she'd relied on to get her as far as she had? She would have failed to find the first two carbonado diamonds without them. Her own flesh and blood had abandoned her, her parents. But, not Jack, not Nash.

Allegra interrupted. "First and foremost let's find the third diamond. We can discuss this later." She turned to Vortigern with a warning glance. "The only way Calla can put her friends' memories to good rest is if she acquires the stone and gains confidence in who she is. It'll be better for all of us."

Vortigern retreated. "You're right."

They paced out of the room and turned down the brightly lit corridor.

"How can we find the next stone? We don't have the manuscript or the journal," Calla said.

Vortigern directed them back through the central offices. "If only we could find the replica and Mila."

"What replica?" Calla asked.

Allegra spoke first. "Your parents hid a replica of some sort. In case they ever lost the Deveron Manuscript. I think they gave it to a woman called Mila Rembrandt. She knows how to solve some of the riddles."

Calla studied them both. How did they know this? She pulled out a wrapped item from the back pocket of her denims. "Does it look something like this?"

She held out a photograph.

"Where did you get this?" Vortigern said.

"It's a photo that never leaves my sides. The only thing I know for sure came from my parents."

She ripped open the lamination cover and drew out a thin folded paper. Unraveling it against the light, it confirmed her thought. A replica of three of the seven pages of the Deveron Manuscript.

"I never knew you had this," Allegra said.

"I've always had it. Mama and Papa Cress gave me the laminated photo on my graduation day. I always knew there was a note inside, but I never dared rip it open even though I knew it might have contained the answers I've sought for so long. I guess I wasn't ready to face whatever it concealed. I'm beginning to realize I've feared the truth all my life yet I've always had it with me."

"The truth never lies, Calla," Allegra said.

She sighed deeply. "Anyway, Mama Cress said it was something to guide me through my adult life. I'm not really sure they knew what it was either. They received it from the foster home."

Vortigern took the photograph in his hands and studied the inscribed notes on the back. "These notes meticulously lay out the details of each pattern in your birthmark. It's your family emblem. They mimic the Deveron lettering. But I wonder why your parents left you with this?" He handed it back to Calla. "Keep this well."

"I always have. So the headmistress at Beacon Academy was right after all," she said. "Who's Mila, by the way? Where can we find her?"

"Someone your parents obviously trusted," Allegra said. "She must know more about them and can help solve any last complexities about the Deveron. She most probably helped them write that journal."

Calla thought for a minute. "I know where we can find the third diamond. The manuscript references King Solomon and resources. We foolishly trusted an ISTF recommended tour guide to get us there. We were looking for King Solomon's mines and mistakenly assumed they would be in Africa. We were looking in the wrong place." Her curator training set in gear."King Solomon's treasures may not have been left in Africa."

Vortigern' eyes lit up. "How so? No place on earth could store the wealth of resources he had. They were left with the African Queen Sheba."

"We're not looking for his wealth. Not according to the Deveron. We want the carbonado." She tilted her head with a smirk growing on her lips. Don't tell me that's why you planted this Cove here?"

Vortigern smiled. "As you can see this place needs someone like you."

"Not so fast." Calla turned to her hosts, her analytical mind churning through logic, riddles, and recent happenings. "I'm sure a place like this would have an airplane, no? We're gonna need it to get to Mila."

CHAPTER 39

2:15 P.M.

Vortigern, Allegra, and Calla proceeded several levels up to a closed hangar on the upper deck of the Cove. The trio stepped into the enormous space, housing three Gulf Stream jets, and four helicopters. Calla glanced upwards. Above her, she saw the sun attempting to peek through the light-colored ceiling. The glass structure opened up for planes to taxi onto the ramp at the end of the large hangar, and then outdoor to the runway at the command of competent operators.

Three doors led off to one side of the hangar. Vortigern set a gentle hand on Calla's arm. "This way, we'll talk in the pilot's offices. You need to understand a few things before you and Allegra set off."

Calla stared blankly, her mind still perplexed by a term Vortigern had used earlier. What did he mean by operatives? A secret society?

They sank into two seats that lined one corner of the pilots' offices.

Vortigern filed through an electronic tablet with the

intended flight plan that lay on the table in front of them. "Calla, you're a brilliant historian and curator so none of what I reveal should surprise you."

She gave him a long, shrewd glance.

Vortigern stroked his goatee as he spoke. "During the first century A.D., when most of Europe, North Africa and parts of Asia were occupied by the Roman Empire. A prominent man from Tire and Sidon, which is modern-day Lebanon, came to Constantinople or what we know today as Istanbul, to visit a local teacher by the name of Merovec Cavalerius. Merovec possessed a charisma that people were drawn to. Many thought he could even deliver them from the oppression of the Romans. Merovec was a very wise man, to the point that some of the locals even thought his wisdom far surpassed that seen anywhere in world history. Anyway, this ruler of Tire had enjoyed more success than any man and wanted to know what he could do to essentially never die."

"Are you serious?" asked Calla.

"Yes. Merovec tested him by asking him what his greatest treasure was. The man thought for several minutes. He imagined that his greatest treasure was the price he had to pay to live a long life, say up to even 900 years, as men in ancient times. I'm sure you have heard of Methuselah—"

Calla shook her head, having never believed in ancient legends, just facts.

Vortigern paused looking for acknowledgment.

Calla gave him a blank expression.

He persisted with his account. "Merovec told the sovereign to get rid of the treasure, whatever it was. If he could get rid of his greatest possession, it would clear the way for immortality, so to speak."

"Did he?"

"No, not initially. The man was probably richer than the equivalent of the top ten people on Forbes list put together."

"What did he do?"

"For several months, nothing. He eventually gave his money away, and most of it was spent furthering Merovec's influence. In time, the Romans, who as you know had an unshakable belief in the fact that Rome was superior to any other country or culture, started observing Merovec. The more people they conquered, the greater Rome's influence. Unfortunately, Merovec was like a thorn in the Empire's side. His influence as a leader of wisdom and considerable might was spreading, so the Romans had him executed. They feared Merovec and had every reason to."

"Why?"

"That doesn't matter as much as what happened after his death. The world around him went mad. His execution divided many of his devout followers. In fact, many took off afraid the Romans would annihilate them. They'd imagined Merovec would be one of the greatest leaders the world had seen—much like Alexander the Great, or even Genghis Khan—a real threat to their unassailable Empire. To his followers, Merovec's death was the end of their hopes and cause."

Calla paid attention. She blinked her eyes wondering what this had to do with her.

"Calla, I know you understand this. It's important you do," said Allegra."

Vortigern continued. "After his death, Merovec was buried near one of the seven hills of the city of Constantinople, a secret location.

"You mean the ancient city of Byzantium."

"Yes."

"I know the myth. Government officials fiercely guarded this burial place. They feared his followers would turn him into a martyr."

Vortigern edged closer. "However, something strange happened. A rebellion took place in Constantinople and a few scattered places around Turkey, so strong that the country and some surrounding areas shook with an earthquake."

431

"You're not serious. Was Merovec some kind of magician?"

Vortigern raised an eyebrow. "Merovec, as his followers believed, was different. Though ordinary to most he possessed exceptional, unknown wisdom, especially when it came to engineering and scientific advancement, to the point that most people perceived his developments as sorcery. We like to call him the father of technology. He survived the execution and engineered that earthquake by dropping carbonados in the Mediterranean Sea that invaded the continental Eurasian plates, just below the earth's crust."

"Some of this rings a bell to me. The myths say that those superstitious enough believed the earth mourned him and retaliated in anger. While preparing my curatorship at the British Museum for the Roman and Byzantine collections I heard this story, but since there's so little known or written on Merovec, I, like many of my colleagues, dismissed it as folklore." She searched Vortigern's face. "What kept Merovec alive? And what happened to his followers, *the operatives,* I imagine?"

"Merovec's attempted execution was done by poison. He'd known about the execution plan at the time of his capture, thanks to undercover operatives within the Roman legionary. And, being an expert at toxicology, he engineered an antidote. He used some of the same ingredients in the medicines administered to you today. Eventually, the base drug he used was developed and has been used with operatives for centuries, creating unsurpassed immunity and, if you like, immortality. In essence, this was what the sovereign had come seeking."

Calla sighed trying to digest all the information.

Allegra watched her struggle with skepticism. "Now with regards to the operatives, those who were pessimistic, confused and disillusioned, feared for their lives. They felt powerless and abandoned everything to do with Merovec. They resolved to disassociate themselves from the cause of their leader. They wandered powerless, away from purpose and unity, led by the first rebel Masonius X."

"Mason Laskfell!"

"Yes," retorted Vortigern. He seemed unfazed by her shock. "Masonius and his band of rebels found themselves among average men. You see, all these operatives weren't ordinary men due to the manipulation, modification, and recombination of their genes. They'd been trained and equipped by Merovec to perform phenomenal feats in every field of work. They had special capabilities like you."

Calla raised an eyebrow. "Were they—?"

He cut her off. "Nobody really knew what to call them. We've been wandering without proper leadership for centuries. We operatives stopped using our special abilities for centuries. The further we drifted away from our identity the more ineffective we became. Until one day we were no different from the average human being in strength, intelligence, and ability."

Allegra interjected. "We're all descended from that rebellion, Calla. But some of the rebels and operatives date back from the time of the Merovec's execution. Some have been able to live that long through science, like Mason."

Calla put her hands behind her head. Was it plausible? "I see."

"There's hope for us," Allegra said. "Not too long after the rebellion one operative by the name of Cressidus realized that the rebellion had cost his fellow comrades everything. You see, three to four days after his execution Merovec was found alive in Tire, under a pretense identity. The Romans heard about it and feared him like the gods. He acquired several more followers and intended to regroup his special operatives for generations to come."

Calla was puzzled. "But what was the purpose of the underground movement? What was Merovec's cause? Is he still alive?" She snickered with cynicism. "Around here somewhere?"

Vortigern spoke up. "When we find the third carbonado we will know. Initially, we all thought the cause was to create one unified government across the earth. This way poverty, disease, and the vast problems around the globe could be dealt with, or even eradicated using his superior understanding of the earth's faculties, science, geology and much more. Some still believe this."

"But why are these black diamonds so important?"

Allegra grasped Calla's hand. "After the rebellion, Merovec penalized the rebel operatives by slowly withdrawing all their formidable strength, power, knowledge, and resources. He used many methods threatening with coercion and genetic reversal.Basically stripping them back to normalcy. "

"Did he?" Calla probed.

"He placed the combined energy into three black diamonds, then transported the diamonds, which were too forceful for the earth's atmosphere into the outer galaxy using the power of a volcanic eruption."

"You mean the volcanic eruption of Vesuvius, in 79 A.D. that buried the Roman towns of Pompeii and Herculaneum?"

"Indeed." Vortigern nodded. "That's why the carbonados are incredibly charged with energy, so much so that they caused two asteroids to collide in space. Eventually, they fell back to Earth. The resulting meteorite activity was what NASA's cosmo-chemists observed and have filed in their classified reports."

Calla shot up. "The NASA reports that ISTF used!"

"Yes. Merovec assigned each of the three carbonados a guardian. They were to secure them in secret locations until the chosen operative would retrieve them and thereby revive their powers. The only clue as to the whereabouts of the stones is the Deveron Manuscript."

Allegra focused her attention on Calla's reaction. "Even before you were born, Calla, you were the designated operative to reunite the carbonados and the operatives. Us."

Vortigern leaned forward. "The carbonados give us a second chance."

"Whoa! Hold on a second." Calla said and marched up and down the white reflective floor. The pain in her ankle subsided. "What are you saying? This is ridiculous! You can't believe this. If *I am* the supposed one then why does Mason believe he can use the stones for his own purposes?" Calla scratched her temple. "Come on, Allegra, you're an educated, rational tactician. Doesn't this sound bogus to you? Besides, why me?"

"I wish it were, Calla. Your family, the Cressidus family, was chosen to bear this mission," Vortigern said.

"I know this is hard to believe, but you see, you're different. Even among the operatives, you're unique. Just because the carbonados were meant for you doesn't mean that Mason can't manipulate their energies," Allegra said.

Calla brought her hands together. "Listen, I believe in science, research, history, and facts. Even if I find your story credible, you've not answered a crucial point here. Where do operatives come from?"

Vortigern grinned. "With the advancement of some of Merovec's engineering capabilities, we weren't born like most humans. Merovec was a master engineer and scientist. He could use any ingredient on Earth and outer space to create anything he desired. We're above the average person in strength, capability, and wisdom, but we can't regain that status, not without the carbonados. Think of it as humans with the minds and capabilities of gods—"

"Angels...hmm...and let me see the NSA and Government Communications Headquarters' technology budgets combined," Calla said.

"Very funny. Mason, like us, desires these stones because the energy in them can be resurrected and charged into nuclear, technological, intelligence or any other power you can think of. If he gets them before we do he will finish the rebellion he started."

Calla slanted her head, not entirely sure if he'd answered her question.

———

2:32 P.M.

"One more thing, Calla. Over the years Mason and his mutineers persecuted your family for the Deveron Manuscript." Allegra raised her chin. "The Cress family has protected the manuscript from generation to generation until it eventually landed in the hands of your parents. You were given the name Cress intentionally. Your adoptive parents are the ones who took on *your* name."

"What happened to my real parents?"

"From the little, I know of them they rejected the responsibility of raising you as the lead operative when Vortigern told them of the responsibilities. They knew what the manuscript could cost you all as a family. I think they gave you up to protect you," Allegra said.

"How do you know this?" Calla said.

"Because they worked for British Intelligence Services. They were incredibly gifted people and were paired on several missions."

"So the manuscript was really theirs?"

"Technically, yes. They decided to destroy the Deveron to rid themselves of its demands. From my own investigation, I know that they took the manuscript to Russia when they sat in on talks between Germany and Russia over the return of Priam's Treasure."

"Is that how the Deveron ended up in Priam's gold?"

"Yes. And that's why I had to get it out of the Pergamon before ISTF did."

Allegra laid a finger on her temple. "They were trying to

436

protect you. Mason would have stopped at nothing to harm you, even as a baby. All he wanted was the Deveron."

Calla tried to empty her mind of a thought, but she had to know. "Did Mason kill my parents?"

Vortigern inhaled deeply. "We don't know. What we know is your father rejected everything we have just told you about the Deveron. He set out to prove us wrong and in the process found one carbonado. But the keeper didn't give it to him."

"Why?"

"He'd rejected the operatives, and that made you the next Cress in line."

"What did my parents do with the Deveron?"

"In a nutshell, they wanted to prove it wrong. Your father documented much of what he found in the black journal you found in the British Library. When NASA and the government discovered more than he wanted he wrote a half report for MI6, deliberately flawed to protect you, that eventually went to ISTF. And to ward off the government further your parents must have hidden the manuscript in the Pushkin Museum in Saint Petersburg, hoping it would never be found."

Calla slumped further into her seat. "In Priam's Treasure, right? Because of the controversy over the treasure's ownership between Germany and Russia. And the fact that the debate would linger for decades seeing that many treasures that left Germany during the war never made it back."

"Again, your curator mind serves us well and makes my job easier." Vortigern beamed with renewed optimism. "When we found out that you had been adopted Allegra was assigned to find you. Your meeting wasn't accidental."

Allegra interjected. "Mason's on an extremely focused mission. We have observed him for years. He only needs a few prominent people with enough drive. So far he's covertly socializing with the Republican candidate Margot Arlington, the business billionaire Samuel Riche, and the oil mogul Rupert Kumar. If these three people are controlled by Mason, who knows what else he can accomplish through their vastly growing influence."

Vortigern raised an eyebrow. "That's true, but I wonder if there's another hidden motive. I wouldn't be surprised if something else is driving him. You need to find out what that is, Calla."

DAY 15
3:02 P.M.
Thessaloniki International Airport, Greece

The scorching sun beat down on the runway as the private jet taxied into Thessaloniki airport. Calla and Allegra made their way into the crowded terminal.

"There's more security at this airport than usual," Calla said. "I don't see how we can make it past undetected."

The lines through immigration moved briskly. Calla lowered the black baseball cap she wore, with her hair let loose to disguise her identity. She spotted a traveler browsing through the International Herald Tribune. Newspapers still speculated about the missing Deveron and Priam's Treasure on the front cover. She peered over at Allegra.

"We'll make it through. I organized the credentials myself," Allegra said.

Allegra was more seasoned at diplomat tasks and, for this, Calla was grateful.

"Next!"

The tension left her face when Calla stepped to the counter. The immigration officer took her passport. Calla cast her head down.

The man lifted his head, raising an eyebrow. "British diplomatic service, I see. Are you staying in Greece long?" he asked.

"Just a day."

He tilted his head and studied her face. He stamped the passport and closed her lane. "Please, follow me."

Calla glimpsed back at Allegra who'd ambled through to a different line.

Calla followed him, and caught a glimpse of Allegra watching from behind the cleared immigration point as the man directed Calla to a waiting room.

"What's the problem?" Calla said as she stood with a hand on the doorknob behind her back.

"I can't let you through."

"Anapoulos."

Calla zipped her head round as Allegra scrambled through the door, jolting her slightly forward.

"Do you know him?" Calla said.

"Sure," said Allegra. "Our best operative in Greece."

Anapoulos spoke in hushed tones. "Vortigern alerted us that you'd be coming. I've been waiting for hours to spot you before you went through to another line. Two others have also been on standby waiting for you."

"Who are you?"

Anapoulos hurried across the room. "A friend. We don't have time. Come with me."

They scuttled through the exit door pacing behind Anapoulos. "If you're back within two hours, I can guarantee your safe passage back to your plane."

They stepped out into daylight while Anapoulos watched by the roller doors. "I'll be here in exactly two hours when you should re-board the jet."

Calla shook his hand. "You guys are something else."

Allegra waited a few yards ahead. Calla ran up to her. "What was that all about?"

"Mason isn't the only one with an infiltration plan."

CHAPTER 40

Calla sat in the taxi watching the Greek landscape. She turned to Allegra. "I felt compelled to come back here. I think I met Mila here."

"What did she look like?"

"When I came with Nash and Jack, looking for the second stone, I believe the Gypsy woman I met was Mila. She recognized my birthmark."

"I have hunted for Mila for several years. I hope your instincts are correct. If anything, she knows more about your parents than we do."

Calla watched the revolving entrance of the hotel where they'd stayed. "Mila knew who I was. I should've known it then. We need to find her. If only three people knew about the birthmark, she was one of them."

"Then I may be able to help. I came to Pella years ago when stationed as a diplomat in Athens. You won't find her here. We may be able to find her in the traveler camp not far from here."

. . .

The taxi steered up a curvy hill. Below them, countless rows of vineyards stretched as far as the Mediterranean Sea. The road ended near a row of dusty homes and the taxi halted by a large wanderer site.

"Someone here must know about her if she really is a Gypsy. Operatives take many identities," Allegra said.

"So I'm beginning to learn. She was dressed like one when I saw her."

Allegra and Calla jumped out of the minivan and scanned the camp that accommodated dozens of families, probably descended from nomadic north Indians who'd traveled to Europe through the Byzantine Empire in the eleventh century. Small lodges lined one side of the camp, while some made their homes within converted freight containers alongside cultivated gardens that cultivated tomatoes, peppers, and assorted Mediterranean fruits.

"Be careful. Let's not scare or disrespect them."

They approached two women transporting firewood toward the center of the slums. Allegra moved to one and spoke with ease in Romano. She greeted the two women and strode toward another elderly woman who sat mending a tattered coat. They exchanged a few words before Allegra turned to Calla. "They haven't seen Mila since January. Her life was in danger, and she needed to move on. At least that's what she told them."

Calla had expected to be disappointed but not when they were so close.

"This can't be happening, Allegra."

"We'll find her."

"It's not that. Going on is all I can do. I lost two important people in my life. Jack and Nash's lives have to account for something."

"It's not your fault. Direct your anger at Mason, not your failures."

Calla raised her chin "Then let's go get the carbonado. We'll just have to rely on our instincts and not Mila."

Allegra sighed. "We never could."

DAY 16
6:10 P.M.
SKIES OVER AMMAN, JORDAN

"The captain says we'll arrive shortly at Amman International Airport," said the flight attendant before progressing to her quarters.

"Even I didn't picture Jordan as the location for Solomon's mines," Allegra said.

"It didn't occur to me either until I came across this," Calla said and shoved a tattered clipping of a National Geographic article into Allegra's hand.

Allegra scanned it carefully.

"King Solomon built his temple in Jerusalem," Calla said. "But he needed something to build it with. That's when the thought dawned on me. According to ancient texts, the nation hunted hundreds of tons of copper for the project, including large amounts of gold and silver. And that's why we are here. Jordan's Khirbat en-Nahas site has intrigued archeologists since the 1930s."

Allegra pursed her lips. "For its abundant metals. Solomon would've required great quantities of metal to complete such a task."

Calla's eyes remained meditative. "Coming here is our best bet. Especially now that we have less than forty-eight hours. Copper mines in southern Jordan were active several centuries before what was previously thought. The area we're going to produced copper at the same time Solomon built the temple."

Allegra returned the magazine clipping. "All those years we worried about you. But you can handle yourself. I admit it. The truth is you don't need the operatives. They need you."

Calla placed the paper in the back pocket of her shorts. "Allegra, I started out wanting to find my parents so bad. I still do. Now I only want to find the last carbonado to stop Mason because of what he did to Jack and Nash. I don't know which cause is more justified."

"Perhaps both."

"When my search started it was all about me. Just girlish, selfish ambitions. Now that I've lost him...them—"

"Go on."

"I didn't actually realize that in Jack and Nash I had more than any family can give me."

Calla's left eye fought a rebellious tear. "I miss them so much, Allegra."

Allegra slanted her head, empathy glistening in her eyes. "I know, and I'm so sorry. I held them in high regard. I can't imagine what this is doing to you."

The jet touched down at Amman International Airport, jolting them forward as it came to a halt.

Calla collected her things. "I'm only doing this for them."

<hr />

8:10 P.M.
KHIRBAT EN-NAHAS
SOUTHERN JORDAN

Allegra padded her forehead with a silk handkerchief. "*Khirbat en-Nahas* means 'ruins of copper' in Arabic."

"Even though what we seek is a diamond," Calla said.

They drove thirty-two kilometers south of the Jordan capital in a hired car. Shortly after they found the diggers' entrance of the 450-square mile ancient mining and metallurgy district.

Most of the mine surface area was covered with black

metallurgical slag, and the international team of archeologists had excavated the ancient copper production center at Khirbat en-Nahas all the way down to virgin soil. Several site guards prowled the upper levels of the archeological dig site armed with nothing more than walkie-talkies.

Calla fished out her phone displaying a satellite image of the location. "The depth of the waste alone is more than twenty feet."

The sun had sunk behind the desert valley hills, yet the evening sky still glowed, its exposure illuminating the excavation site.

The site's size alone begged for industrial-scale production and incorporated close to a hundred ancient buildings. Situated in the midst of mining trails the excavations abounded on more than twenty-four acres of black slag. Hailed by historians as the largest copper mining and smelting site of the ancient world it lay in a desert valley between the Dead Sea and the Gulf of Aqaba.

"We should be good to head down the shaft in about ten minutes," Allegra said as she scanned incoming intelligence from ISTF on her satellite phone.

Moonlight broke over Calla's face and she whispered. "It's time."

They watched the lone guard move away from the entrance before they skimmed down several feet on a timber ladder, into a rectangular cavity below ground level, measuring almost twenty feet wide.

"This must be the main dig area," Allegra said.

They eased down until their feet hit the ground and the dusty grit grated under their boots. They paced several meters along the rock structure of the mine wall until they found a rundown opening at the far end of the old space.

"Someone's been here recently," Calla said. "And not an archeologist. Archeological sites are usually divided into squares and use flat mason trowels, not gardening tools." She ran her fingers over a breeding dent in the cave wall. "They also excavate horizontally and don't dig holes."

Calla peered down the path ahead of her that led further underground.

"Someone has tried to dig further than the original excavation," she said.

"Let's find out who," Allegra said.

They shifted through the opening, evading collapsing rubble and pebbles as they scuffled down toward the virgin soil. The archeological teams had left wooden panels making it easier to scout the area without damage to the soil findings.

As the women spiraled further inward, Calla turned on her hardhat headlight. It emitted just enough light for a few steps at a time. Walled in by several feet of mine walls Calla glimpsed behind her. "You okay?"

She waited until Allegra caught up. "There's something I need to know, Allegra."

Allegra rubbed her arm across her face. "What's that?"

"I found something in your house when Taiven first took me there."

"What'd you find?"

"Your birth certificate."

———

Allegra stood motionless studying Calla. Shrugging she rested on a soiled pillar.

Calla ambled back slowly. "Your birthday was registered as 1881. How old are you? I mean, I'm still trying to get to grips with this operatives stuff."

"Sit down and take a breather. Now's as good a time as any to tell you," Allegra said.

Calla sank to a boulder beside her. Whatever Allegra was about to reveal produced more hurt on her face than Calla thought possible of her friend.

Allegra's expression turned grim. "Operative time isn't measured in time as you, and I know it because of the science of aging. They perfected it. And sometimes it can be too long to walk alone. It's in our DNA," Allegra said.

Calla absorbed Allegra's words. "How long is long?"

"It varies. The Deveron Manuscript was created, as Vortigern explained, to lead operatives back to our former grandeur shortly after Cressidus decided to make a bold decision, to find Merovec and reunite all operatives."

"How?"

"Cressidus and his family line were destined to guard it until the manuscript found its way to you. That's what makes it truly valuable. Its uniting factor."

"Could he do it?"

"The Deveron was lost in the 1700s. It was later found by a little boy on a battlefield of Antrim, in Northern Ireland. He was a mere infant and guarded it more as a boyish find than anything else for several years, never really knowing what he had. That was when I was sent to retrieve it shortly afterward. The boy's name was Aston Deveron."

"So you're not one of those operatives that were left to '*roam the earth?*'"

"No. As a baby, I was adopted into an Irish family. Vortigern arranged it. My job was to befriend the boy, retrieve the manuscript and then restore it to the right operative family."

Calla swallowed hard taking in the smell of the dry air, scented with ash and rotten dirt. "You mean my family."

"My adoptive father wasn't really sure what to make of my sudden appearance at his doorstep one morning. He'd been unable to give his wife a child and found a solicitor who helped him obtain a legal birth certificate for me. They were afraid I could be taken from them because no one really knew where I came from. So the birth certificate you found was their security."

"So they adopted you and forged the certificate?"

"Yes, they paid to have it authenticated."

Calla digested the information. "How long do operatives live?"

"Well," answered Allegra, "usually as long as science allows."

Calla sat confounded, but then again nothing in the last week had made any logical sense to her.

"Anyway," continued Allegra. "The boy was about seven when I was adopted. He and I grew up in the same town."

Allegra rose to her feet as if what came next was the most distressful thing she'd ever experienced. "When he was twenty-five, and I was seventeen, we fell in love."

Calla now understood.

Allegra cast her eyes down in guilt. "What happened?"

"Nobody ever tells you what falling in love is like. That you abandon yourself and lose all focus. Well, I lost focus, Calla. I managed to locate your family and get the manuscript to them. That's how your great-great-grandparents inherited it. Right up until it fell into the hands of your father, Stan Cress."

"Was I born naturally to my parents?"

"Operatives are like everyone else, with a little scientific twist. You must know that Merovec is still very much in control of the operatives. No one ever questioned it. You were born naturally."

"I see?"

"Calla, you're unique. Very special because of your task. Trust that, and everything will be okay."

Calla rose slowly, and her boots paced the damp soil. The headlight on her head dimmed. She glanced over at Allegra's face, contorted with anguish and guilt. "Tell me what happened after you delivered the manuscript to the Cress family?"

Allegra drew in a snuffle. "My mission was done. In essence, I had to return back to my station."

"Did you?"

Allegra unconsciously furrowed her brow. "No."

447

"You didn't?"

"I rebelled in my own way and refused to return. I wanted to stay with Aston."

Calla's judgment softened somewhat. "Is that why Vortigern warned me about Jack and Nash? No attachments."

She nodded her head softly, not daring to look at Calla. "The worst was..." continued Allegra.

Calla lifted her head. Was there more? Admittedly, she'd suffered enough.

"I was expelled by the operatives, Calla. Mason's operatives found out about my mission and Aston. I was responsible, Merovec said. They accused me, Calla. Before that Mason didn't know of the Deveron's whereabouts. I got careless in my relationship with Aston." She shot a pained look at Calla's encouraging face. "Mason has conspired to find the Deveron for years. He has now found in this generation a way to finish his plans. That's why I had to take the Deveron when in Berlin. One of the things you'll find is the operatives' advanced use of scientific technology, what we call Military Economics. This department engineered a *transporter-relocator*, a small gadget that when injected into my body was able to literally change my molecular makeup and give me advanced camouflage capabilities. That's how I left the museum and Berlin undetected. You' learn all about that soon. The secrets of the operatives."

Calla digested the confession for several seconds. "You left me alone in Berlin so I could discover all this the hard way, by myself."

Allegra nodded quietly. "I've always believed in you. You're intelligent and logical. I don't think just simply telling you would've convinced you. You had to live it."

Calla searched her face. "How did the operatives allow you back?"

She hesitated for several seconds. "Aston and I got married.

When he died at a good old age of 106, I was left alone. I had nowhere else to go."

Calla kept her expression neutral and set a hand on Allegra's shoulder. "You didn't do anything wrong. Love has to be free and if not, we have to fight for it to be. I know that now. I won't let anyone take that from me. What's been freely given is freely earned."

All tense emotions smoothed from Allegra's face as she managed a weak smile. "You mean—"

Calla didn't have to articulate what she meant. Allegra knew.

"Thank you, Calla.

"Now, let's get that carbonado."

They descended further into the trench. As they ducked under a low crevice murmurs in the shadier corners of the mineshaft caught their ears.

"I know those voices," Calla mouthed.

They concealed themselves within the darkness of the curved partition.

Calla peered round a boulder that stood in their path. "It's Mason!" she whispered. She grasped Allegra's green jacket, shifting her closer for a more accurate glimpse. They watched the activity ahead in silence.

Mason and several of his men, sporting drilling gear, clutched shovels and rock drills.

About twenty of them grunted as they chiseled at one corner of the mine surface.

"They can't find it like that. The carbonado finds its way to the rightful owner," Allegra whispered .

They studied the excavators, some local, some foreign, digging with chip hammers, paving breakers and other heavy equipment in an insane attempt to break through any rock or shaft wall.

Calla made a guess. They'd either bribed the archeologists or forced their way into the mine. The lack of care with which some of the diggers handled the drills and break-hammers suggested that they were mere amateurs.

Calla leaned back gently and whispered in Allegra's ear. "We need to stop them. They'll destroy this historic site."

Movement from a dark corner drew her eye. She propped forward and saw his face.

Nash!

Nash's hands were tied around his waist with cords of natural hemp rope.

Mason shoved the manuscript's pages in his face.

"You're wasting your time," they heard Nash say. "Only she could translate this document with accuracy. I don't believe that level of precision falls within yours or my skill set."

"Rubbish! Operation Carbonado recruited you as the American arm because you too are versed in these ancient manuscripts and cryptology."

A tall man held a gun to the back of Nash's head.

Nash glared at Mason. "You don't intimidate me."

Calla watched and thought on intervention.

Nash hunched forward and booted the thug behind him in the groin. The man collided with the uneven wall and doubled over in pain. Nash raised his wrists to his mouth.

What was he doing? As Calla watched in paralysis, with his hands-free, relief settled in her gut knowing he'd clenched a sharp instrument between his teeth. His hands loosened and, in one swift movement, he seized the gun that had dropped from the thug's hand.

Several attackers surrounded him.

He paused.

It came from directly above. The mine walls shook like thunder, loosened by careless drilling. Missiles of debris shot from the shaft ceiling sending rubble smashing into those who stood underneath.

Nash took refuge in a small cavern off to one side of the central mine passage.Allegra and Calla shifted backward and broke away toward the exit. Flickering headlights dazzled in the darkness as the trapped men tried to break free from under the showering boulders. Mason's body flattened under the weight of shelling rubble.

"Nash!" Calla cried.

He turned his head. Calla coursed toward him, dodging debris and a shower of collapsing rock fragments. Nash saw her and angled in her direction over boulders and rubble as the cave hurried behind him.

"Cal!" He reached for her dusty hand, gripped it, and they raced toward Allegra.

"This way!" Allegra cried, her voice muffled by rumbling.

Through the dust storm, Nash and Calla caught sight of the exit ladder, suspended over the twenty-foot wall. They hurtled toward it, their boots thudding the dirt and clambered up the flimsy wood toward the surface. They surfaced, gasping for air.

First Allegra. Then Nash. Calla got a grip on the rock and lifted her head a few inches above ground level. She reached for Nash's hand as he hung over the edge of the ancient wall, stretching for her hand.

"Nash, my foot's caught."

She glimpsed down and pulled at her boot.

It wouldn't budge.

CHAPTER 41

8:30 P.M.

C alla arched down to check her boot.

"Calla!" The voice came from within the mine. "This way!"

Nash and Allegra glanced back down. "Who's that?" Nash said.

Her foot slid, sending her back down several feet. She receded to the mine floor and glared up at a leering face. "Taiven?" She wiped an arm across her eyes. "What're you doing here?"

"Keeping this from Mason." He raised his arm out clasping a black container. "I believe you could use this."

"You've had the carbonado all along?"

"Yes," he said.

"Why didn't you give it to me?"

A veiled woman stepped in from the shadows. "You weren't ready."

Calla struggled to see the owner of the voice through the dust that had fogged her vision. "Mila?"

Mila stepped into the light. Piercing eyes, full lips, and a strong jaw, just like in Pella. She'd discarded her kohl eyeliner for a more natural look and wore no frills, laces or bangles. As she came into full view, Calla took in her white body uniform, much like those that Calla had seen in the Cove, worn under an Arabian veil. Allegra and Nash dropped down and observed behind Calla.

"This whole time, Taiven," blurted Allegra as she admired the ornate container in his hand.

"I wanted to tell you so many times, but it wasn't my place. My mission was and is Calla Cress."

He placed the wooden box in Calla's hand. "You need to go now and reunite the black diamonds. You only have until dawn London time."

"Mason has the other stone," Nash said.

Taiven's jaw hardened. "The carbonados run on a time clock that was set by a chemical reaction when they exploded into space. Merovec calculated that eight days was probably the greatest amount of time it would take to allow effective use ofthe combined energies of the diamonds."

Calla started to speak. Her hand jerked violently to her lips as the box crashed to the floor. The carbonado rolled onto the gravel glistening its various shades of amber, crimson and ebony.

Their attention was drawn to a thin yet accurate steel cable trailing, attached to a steel net.

Mason's head surfaced from the darkness covered in dust. "Give that here!"

He tossed a net over the black diamond and hauled the rock toward him.

Nash stretched for the carbonado as it hung suspended. Mason swung a clenched fist at him. Nash dodged out of reach, and the blow flew past him, missing his nose by millimeters. He reached with his free hand and seized Calla's bag from Mason's shoulder. He tossed the items to Calla.

Mason padded for his shotgun.

Nash booted it swiftly out of his fumbling hand. "Go, Calla! You don't have much time!"

Mason took hold of Nash's neck and flung him to the ground. He wrapped a wire cord around Nash's neck and tugged tight at the rope until Nash's air supply deteriorated under Mason's grip.Nash convulsed and gasped for oxygen, thrashing and kicking his legs until his struggling body limped like a fragmented puppet.

Taiven darted forward. "I wouldn't do that if I were you, Mason."

"You again! After all these years you show your face?"

Taiven eyes blazed like fire. "Release him!"

"Out of my way!" Mason retorted.

The cave wall shot furious debris that loosened the ground around Mason's feet.

It came from beneath. A wide gap cracked open. Mason lost his footing and broke through a widening rift in the ground as it split, pulling Nash down with him.

"No!" Calla said.

The onlookers shoved to the edge of the torn ground.Shudders of pelting debris kept them from any rescue activity.

Taiven set a hand on Calla's shoulder. "You need to bring together the carbonados now, or we are all spent."

DAY 17

0:20 A.M.
THE COVE, LONDON BRANCH

"Have they found the carbonados?"

Vortigern marched into the room brimming with bustling operatives.

454

"We've just heard from Allegra," a commander said. "They're here in London."

Vortigern remembered the day he'd been entrusted with delivering the stones to the caretakers. He'd been given strict instructions not to fail. The search for the right keepers had been at his sole discretion all those years ago.

He peered down at the three-holed pallet contained within a wooden case, from which he'd once removed the stones. He forced shut the container and admired its exterior. Carved out of mahogany its borders were encrusted with pure gold. It rested on his desk, no bigger than a tissue box.

"They have to make it in time. Those carbonado diamonds have never been in one place since I separated them."

2:56 A.M.
THE SHARD
LONDON SKYLINE

Calla spied through the glass façade of the glimmering Shard skyscraper. Mason conferenced with members of ISTF and a few she didn't recognize. It didn't surprise her that several hours ago her companions had thought him gone, crushed.

Mason had mastered covertness, and warfare like most men learn the art of breathing. She didn't know what craft he used, but he was effective.

Ingenious.

She leered at him as he strolled from chair to chair, clutching a remote control no bigger than a mobile phone. Calla recognized it. He always carried it with him. She'd seen him handle it the day they'd first met at the ISTF Technology Museum. It had to have been instrumental in assisting him, and possibly Nash, out of the rubble.

. . .

455

Upon leaving Jordan, she'd contacted Vortigern about that phone, hoping its global, positioning tracking ID would surface on the operatives' databases and help them get to Nash.

Vortigern performed a covert search on ISTF's satellite tracking site and discovered that not only was the tracking device sending a signal from London but even more peculiar, from the Shard. Vortigern's intelligence revealed that Mason had called for assistance while in Jordan.

Additional data prowling revealed that Mason had recently purchased a few office floors in the skyscraper. Possibly the reason her Range Rover pursuer had been so eager to dart in there a few days ago. Though uncertain about Nash's wellbeing she guessed that Mason intended to take Nash with him wherever he would go. Possibly to use him as barter for the manuscript and the carbonados.

She took her eyes off the remote control. Invisible to the naked eye she fluttered like a hawk on the tilted front of the fiftieth floor. The conference participants listened as Mason spoke and others joined via video-conference. The man Calla presumed was Kumar was full of praise, and his musical voice broke the discussion.

Calla listened.

"Having personally verified the delivery of your blueprints, Mason, I'm impressed," Kumar said..

Mason responded. "We're ready to proceed."

"We're pleased with what we see, Mason," Milan said.

Mason frowned at the screen broadcasting from the largest metropolitan area in Israel.

"So, you still don't have the diamonds?" Tel Aviv mocked.

Mason's eyes were distracted by a screen at the foot of the table. His negotiating card.

"I've got the next best thing. This is worth more to Cress than the carbonados."

Using heightened vision, Calla scrutinized the floors for the exact spot Mason's screen had tuned in. Nash sat on the floor with his head in his hands, held in a secured room on the fifty-second floor. Calla soared round to the other side of the building and coasted to his window. She shut her eyes searching for Nash's exact window. The reunited carbonado diamonds had advanced her ability to see through and manipulate opaque objects.

Nash rose and leaned his arms against the door of a solitary room. His wrists were fastened with what Calla imagined were steel cords that allowed him movement of only a few meters. His head bowed in contemplation, facing the inside wall.

Calla pressed her hands against the heavy glass. It would take a mighty blow. She threw double fists through the twin-skin façade. The glass shattered its many layers until a large puncture appeared, two feet in diameter.

Nash raised his head and glanced toward the window. The fresh air breathed through his sandy hair and as intense moonlight reflected off his bruised face.

He veered toward the perforated window, barely making it.

Calla's upper body permeated through the diffused glass.

Nash's face settled inches from hers, his eyes widening, assessing if he'd seen right. "Hey, beautiful, wouldn't the front door have been the easier option?"

"Since when do I do *easy*?" calla said.

"That you don't." He smiled. "I'm really glad to see you."

His smile could still dissolve her insides. "Nash," she whispered.

He edged closer. "I see it was worth getting those diamonds to you."

He glanced at her smooth, pearl-toned bodysuit, matched with a white headband belted around her forehead. "Is this who you really are?"

A mischievous thought played in her mind. "You're not disappointed are you?"

Nash leaned forward to touch her as if to make sure she wasn't a vision. His hand settled on her face. "Not in the least."

Amused, she eased through the glass and effortlessly loosed his restraints. He watched her move with sureness. Her hair fluttered freely with the night breeze that streamed into the room. She inched forward and, for the first time ever, received his waiting embrace without reservation. She kissed him deeply as if the moment would erase the rejection she'd tossed his way for months.

"I hate to interrupt a tender moment," a voice said.

Calla frowned at the interruption as Slate strode through the door aiming a firearm.

"Mason said you'd come. Let's go," Slate commanded. He waved the weapon in the direction of the door.

She bit her bit. "I think I've had enough of Mason's instructions. How about you, Nash."

She swung a roundhouse kick into Slate's side. The firearm loosened from his grasp and dropped to the granite-tiled floor firing a deafening shot. Slate reached out to retrieve it.

Nash got to it first.

Anticipating Slate's response, Calla seized his hand and crushed it within her grip. Stunned into paralysis Slate squealed in pain. She struck at his throat with her other hand, sending him gasping for air, unable to speak.

"Had enough?" Calla said.

Her stare weakened him until he broke down into huffs.

"You don't need to be an errand boy for Mason," she said. "You know ISTF won't protect you from prosecution and Mason will certainly not stick out his neck for you." She released him from her grasp. "You'd stop him yourself if you could."

He gawked at her, giving away no emotion.

"Mason won't help you when he ends up sliding a feeding pan across bars. But I'm sure government people like Allegra

Driscoll will make sure you get the best legal support or even a deal." She watched for a reaction. "It's up to you."

Slate reeled back until his body edged up against the wall. The pain caused him to heave and grab at his chest. "I don't need you to show me that Mason is a first-class crossbreed.I've seen this coming for some time." Slate drew his eyebrows together. "To him, I'll always be a hit man, paid to venture where he won't dare. Doesn't say much about me, does it?"

"Actually," said Nash. "It makes you smarter than him."

They watched Slate whimper. He seemed to be talking to himself and, for a moment he ignored their presence.

He bolted upright. Slate ceased to babble and eyed the two bystanders before wiping his bloodied nose with his sleeve.

Voices filtered into the hallway. The meeting had adjourned. Calla watched Slate's fury intensify. "Wanna start now?"

He stared at her for a few seconds. "A deal you say?" He shot Nash a look. "This way."

They headed for the door and raced down the dark corridor toward the conference rooms. The lights flickered as they neared Mason's closed meeting.

"He'll be in there a few more minutes. Follow me," Slate said.

"We might need to strategize this a little," Nash warned.

Mason's hoarse voice sounded at the end of the hall. "You made an appearance, Cress."

They swept their heads around.

He stood behind them.

"Looks like your meeting adjourned early. Good, we can get this over with," Calla said.

Mason fiddled with an electronic tablet and focused his eyes on Calla.

Like lightning Slate curved his way past them and launched himself at Mason. Mason's body shifted briskly to one side asSlate sailed right past him, hurtling to the ground.

459

Calla tilted her head toward Nash. "Should we?"

"After you, beautiful," Nash said.

Mason held on tightly to the wireless remote-command tablet and moved backward.

Calla paced forward, studying his intention."Something bothering you, Mason?"

He made his way into the conference room where half the meeting members had left.The group shot to their feet. Mason motioned them out as he made his way to the video control panel.The men shuffled past Calla.

Calla tracked cautiously, watching as Mason operated the control panel.

"I'm afraid you didn't make it in time, Cress." He threw his shoulders back, poised and controlled. "Three thousand of my operatives are in their positions. You forget I had two diamonds for more than twenty-four hours. Enough time to set up my protocol analyzer, a little device that will capture and analyze signals and data traffic throughout the systems of Riche Enterprises, Kumar Oil Corporation, and the US Republican Party."

"Counting your eggs a little too early, Mason?"

"Why Merovec would pick a woman is beyond me. Anyway, his loss. By now my hackers have seized more data than I need. I'm more than halfway there."

Calla edged closer.

Mason cradled his tablet. A sapphire-blue light told her it was in remote control mode. He sneered. "I will transfer the systems to promisc mode, that is, to a mode that will cause the system controllers of these organizations to pass all the traffic they receive to my central processing unit and not their own."

"Looks like you thought of everything," she said.

He arched an eyebrow. "Perhaps you'd better determine

whose side you're on, Cress. Soon that choice will be made for you as the hack will include everything, bank transactions, contract information, client lists, confidential R&D plans, new technological developments, firm secrets and well, you know how it goes, much more. No organization will be out of reach."

He cast a glance up at her. "Impressed yet?"

She didn't budge. "I'm on my side. No one's."

Mason continued. "This way the defenses of each of these systems will be immobilized." He eyed the tablet. "These little gadgets are magnificent. Just one stroke on the screen. That's all it takes." He let out a sneer. "Give Merovec my regards. The coward has let global technology spiral out of control and into the hands of amateurs. It's time I did something about it. You, on the other hand, Cress, are a weak girl. Who are you any way against my mobilized army of hackers?" He studied her. "Why would he pick a weakling like you?"

Calla took another step forward.

Mason clicked his tongue. "Fighting me won't stop my operatives sniffing at everything going on in these organizations, including administering data transfers. This is just dinner. Dessert will be NASA, the NSA and Britain's Government Communications Headquarters."

Calla halted a couple of feet from him. "What makes you think I intend to fight you?"

Mason tilted his head. "Isn't that what we operatives have done since Merovec started his movement? Fight to the end! Yes, I figured that's why you held on to the carbonados. I see that your physical skill has improved somewhat."

Calla's eyes drilled into his eyes. "You forget, Mason. When this conflict began two thousand years ago, it was never a physical one. What you don't realize is that I've found the little lab in your house, thanks to Jack. And yes, I spoke to him only a few hours ago."

Mason lost the grin on his face.

Calla feigned a smile. "Jack placed the three carbonados in your own command center. I then energized and remodeled your software program." She grinned. "I, in turn, hacked *your* little program."

His eyes glared with fury and disdain.

She sneered. "Reverse engineering is an incredibly useful skill. I analyzed your program for its vulnerabilities."

Mason's face grew ashen. "There are no vulnerabilities in my design."

"Really? If there's anything I've learned on this journey with the Deveron it's that knowledge, a.k.a perception is the greater power of the three dominances." Calla wasn't finished. "You see, in this day and age it's not just physical power that wins the battle."

Mason winced.

With his guard down she snatched the tablet from his grip with a confident air. "This is the age of technology. Allow me." She slid her hand over the screen and activated his software program for him.

Mason's eyes narrowed,

"Here we go. By activating this button, I've just whitelisted your hackers and enlisted your three thousand operatives to work the reverse on your program. Each offense you intended to create in these corporate computer systems has consumed up your own systems. You see, Nash got to Arlington, and Jack got to Kumar and Riche."

She slanted her head. "Oops...not too smart for a girl. I'm sorry, I think we're done."

Mason slumped into a nearby chair. All he could see was the last look he'd seen on his mother's face. The Deveron had defeated her and now him.

"It's over, Masonius X. That's your name isn't it?" Calla said.

He raised his head with a flash of anger. "Not so quick, Cress. Like a dragonfly at a bug party, I always serve the last course." He raised his hand from his suit jacket and fired a bullet from a concealed handgun. Calla's eyes widened as the bullet zipped toward her head.

CHAPTER 42

ALLEGRA DRISCOLL'S RESIDENCE,
WEST LONDON

"**D**oes it still hurt?" Nash said.

Calla rubbed her temple.

"Not really. It's just a small reminder. I think I'll miss running from Mason. He really couldn't have seen it coming."

"Calla, I'm glad you took some advice from a former Marine," Nash said.

Calla smiled at Allegra, recalling her cautioning before they left the mineshaft in Jordan. "*Mason, as intelligent as he is, can be predictable. What he's done once he'll try again.*"

That was when Calla had requested the Cove in London to suit her up with as much, threadlike bulletproof material as possible. After Nash's advice to Jack, she figured she'd take precaution. Knowing Mason had once aimed a gun at her temple he would most probably try it again.

She'd also requested the Cove to give her the best bulletproof appliance they had to protect the skull. "It can't be obvious," Calla had insisted. The result had been a rather classy, matching white headband.

Nash held her hand in his. "Mason must've thought you were dead when that bullet knocked you out for several seconds."

"I know, but I had one last surprise for him. He was wrong about dragonflies too. Though dragonflies are predators, they're also vulnerable to predation. That last blow to his head kept him unconscious for several hours. He was still out when the police, ISTF, and MI6 arrived."

Nash stroked her hair. "He's gone now, locked up on remand at Belmarsh and waiting for trial. It's a high-security prison, especially for cases involving national security."

"So where were we?" Calla said.

Allegra settled in her reading chair by the fireplace of her den. "Discussing the return of stolen goods."

Nash moved to the window and folded his arms as he watched the women converse. Calla peered out the window, spotting children riding on their scooters in the spring sun. She turned her head back to Allegra. "I better return the carbonados to their rightful owner."

"Aren't you the rightful owner?" Nash asked.

"Unfortunately, no."

Jack strolled into the room guzzling a can of Coke, followed by a smiling Eichel. "Who do they belong to?" Jack said.

"I'm afraid I can't tell you. Some things must be kept top secret, even from you, my friend. By the way, I want to thank you both for what you and Herr Eichel did. If you hadn't gotten back to Mason's technology room after Africa, I don't think we could have reversed his program in time."

Jack grinned. "Always a step ahead here, history girl."

"You certainly are, Jack," she said.

· · ·

Allegra shot to her feet and ambled over to Eichel who waited by the door observing the group. "Herr Eichel, I owe you an apology about Berlin, but I had to get the Deveron out. I grabbed the first thing I could find." She handed him Priam's golden artifact. "The manuscript had been sealed in there so long, I couldn't wedge it out."

Eichel cradled the goblet in his hands and placed it in a small, custom-made briefcase. "But how did you escape with these items? We traced every exit, checked every CCTV camera and frisked every evacuee from the Pergamon."

"Don't you worry about that. We've instigated a binding diplomatic agreement now. I don't need to disclose that information. What matters is you get what you came for."

Calla moved over to Eichel and handed him the Deveron, carefully placing it in an acid-free, plastic sleeve. "Berlin will be happy to get this back for a while, just until the exhibition is over."

"Thank you," Eichel said. "I'm sorry I can't stay for your celebrations, but I have to get back to Berlin with these artifacts. My flight leaves in an hour."

Eichel shook Calla's hand. "We've closed your case, Miss Cress and we'll be issuing a public apology."

Taiven appeared at the den door. "I have a car waiting for you, Mr. Eichel."

Eichel saluted the group and strode to the door with the artifacts before making his exit.

"Don't you need the Deveron Manuscript anymore?" Nash said.

Allegra smiled. "All we ever really needed were the carbonados reunited." She winked at him. "Eichel just received a replica that Vortigern and I created."

Nash shook his head, at the secrecy in the room and moved back toward Calla. "I'm sorry we couldn't find out more about your parents."

She sighed. "I guess Mila never really knew what happened

to them after they told her to watch over me. She's my mother's sister, that's all I know."

Nash slid an arm around her waist. "Where do we go from here?"

Calla gazed into his gray eyes. "Well, for starters, why don't we go on one proper date? No fights, no guns, no travel, no manuscripts, just a simple, quiet date."

Jack sneered. "How about the new sky restaurant in the Shard? I hear they serve a mean lobster."

Calla smiled. "Fancy a sky meal?"

Nash took her fingers. "Try me."

Calla wandered upstairs and closed her bedroom door. She strode to her work desk and switched on the video-conference system. Vortigern appeared on the screen, beaming.

She took a seat and unmuted her speaking button. "Did you receive the diamonds?"

He patted a silver box on his marble table and opened it. "They've found their true resting place at last. As long as we operate within the provided guidelines, we can continue to stand above any threat to the operatives."

Calla glanced at the glowing stones next to Vortigern. "You saying that we'll never face a threat again?"

"Unfortunately there are no guarantees. You see these carbonados have now given operatives a second chance, a chance to redeem ourselves from the faults of the past. And to continue to follow Merovec's lead."

"Will I ever meet Merovec?"

"You may, you may not. It's up to him."

Calla's gaze dropped to her desk.

467

Vortigern closed the box and observed her. "Calla, have you thought about what I said?"

"Which part?"

"Please don't go through what Allegra went through. It's not worth the pain. She told you herself. We need you now more than ever. This means Nash can never be important in your life."

She frowned and fell silent. *I've always made my own decisions. Right? Free will is a gift no one can possess or take. Right?*

She observed him. Vortigern's troubled look didn't ease her anguish. "I've wanted to avoid telling you this but did you ever wonder why Mason never killed Nash at Murchison Falls?"

"Nash survived a fall, that's all."

"No, my dear. We replayed a satellite video. Mason had his operatives rescue him. I don't know how to tell you this. The truth is Nash's first mission at the NSA was to investigate operatives in the US. It was a highly classified case entrusted to him. The government wanted to know if we were threats to global or US national security. He wrote a report about us that is circulating within the CIA, MI6, and Interpol. Not too long ago we learned through our Cove in Washington that Nash struck a deal with Mason. To this day we don't know what that deal entails but we know Nash backed off his fierce goal to have Mason prosecuted."

"That's ridiculous. Mason is awaiting trial. Couldn't we ask just Nash? He's never lied to me," Calla said.

"For whatever reason Nash isn't bringing forth certain evidence against Mason, even as Mason sits in prison awaiting trial for coercion, international theft, transfer of goods, assault, technology terrorism, mismanagement of funds and possibly murder."

"I don't believe you." Calla's voice had risen more than she'd anticipated. She flopped back in her chair. "Be careful what you say, Vortigern. Nash's cards rack higher than yours. I for one trust him."

Vortigern sighed. "In Nash's defense I believe he has a choice to make, we just don't know if it will be the right one. Even now Nash has the power to lock Mason away for good and reverse what Mason has started. But his conviction is stalling all due to what Nash and Mason have agreed and that NSA report."

"What's in the report? Let me guess, you don't know. Pure speculation."

"Calla, be warned."

"Or what?"

Calla didn't like the look on his face. What did Vortigern know of loyalty, something not even her own family could deliver? Nash had been willing to die for her, and that was enough.

"I'll think about it," she said.

"Don't take too long." Vortigern leaned forward in his chair. "Listen, Calla, to take on the responsibility that a lead operative like you needs you cannot socialize with Nash. You need to trust your own kind—"

Calla fell silent. *My own kind deserted me! Nash has never abandoned me.*

Calla rubbed her temples, hardly noticing the silent footsteps that strolled into the room. Allegra set her hands on Calla's tense shoulders.

Calla didn't stir.

"It's true," said Allegra. "When I found you at the falls I already knew that Nash would be okay. That's why we never went to save him. He means well, but we don't know which way he'll go now after his dealings with Mason. Think of it. Why has he never raised the topic of the NSA report he wrote. We can't take that chance."

"But weren't we able to reprogram Mason's hackers by whitelisting but, most importantly, by using Mason's own telepathic program. He has advanced this platform into a tested technology that can pick up fragments of people's thoughts by decoding brain activity. You and I know we used the same technology to eavesdrop on the hackers' private thoughts and could anticipate their activities before they acted. Can't we supersede this program somehow and investigate Nash in the same way we protected those three thousand?"

She hadn't thought this through. Nash was under operative fire. She had to do something to protect him. Any argument, for now, would do. "We could analyze his intentions. Isn't that what you operatives are good at? Crossing science with humanity until you can't tell the difference. I trust Nash. He would never do anything to harm me."

Vortigern's tone was gentle and encouraging, "I'm afraid that has ethical issues tied to it. Most of Mason's hackers had already resolved to participate in criminal activity and some actually engaged in it. Nash hasn't. He has to be free to act like any other person or operative."

Case in point, Vortigern! Calla pulled away from Allegra. "So what happens now? Do I just go back to my normal life and continue as if nothing is going on?"

Vortigern reasoned with her. "You can't influence Nash's choices. Break it off before it's irreversible."

"Nash would never be corrupted by the likes of Mason. His nature is allergic to the kind."

"No," Vortigern said.

Allegra's tone begged for understanding. "If you have a relationship with Nash chances are that Nash's memory of you will suffer. Merovec will see to it." She breathed hard. "They did it to me."

"Allegra, you don't mean that—"

"Merovec may interfere with him, and even Jack. He's a master engineer on all levels and his expertise tests reason, logic, emotion, technology, and scientific theory. That's how things have always been. That goes for anyone you connect with on an emotional level. You would co-exist, but you could never have a life together. We're here to help you figure out how to live with your unique capabilities."

Calla protested. "My parents and many operatives have had such connections even to non-operatives—"

Vortigern glanced at Allegra. "That's all changed now that the carbonados are back together. From now on operatives are banned from emotional entanglements of any kind. Such bonds have kept many from executing their obligations."

How could they speak without any thought of what she wanted? Operative or not she was no machine. She was wired like any other person. She glanced at both of them for a second and realized the decisions that had stood in her parent's way.

She nodded her head slowly. "Understood."

"In time you'll learn to embrace who you really are, and we'll be here helping you every step of the way," Vortigern said.

Calla switched off the machine. She started out the window into the square. Allegra's voice interrupted her thoughts. "I tried, and I lost Aston."

Calla scrutinized her eyes and responded in soft tones. "You tried. You pursued what you thought was right without anyone standing in your way. It's called free will."

Calla's voice rang with determination, having encountered a similar resolution once.

"Then I'll not stand in your way, Calla. But I can't let you go without caution. You could risk losing everything, your unique identity, and gifting. The worst part is when you go back to your world, Nash and even Jack may not know who you are. Before you decide, think it over."

She knew what to do.

CHAPTER 43

Calla marched downstairs with Allegra in silence.

A silver-haired man stood at the bottom of the wide marble steps. "Calla Iris?"

She halted and glared at him for several seconds. Calla's eyes widened, as Eva progressed behind the man.

For an instant, Eva's expression changed.

Calla held back disapproval as she set her foot on the bottom stair, her eyes fixed on the two visitors gazing critically at Eva. "What're you doing here?"

Eva took a step back. Her face abandoned pretense and, despite her boldness. Calla watched her unable to breathe. "Wait. Let me explain," Eva said.

Calla's glance shifted from Eva and studied the distinct profile of the poised man with intense eyes framing a handsome, square face.

Allegra stole to the bottom of the stairs. "Stan Cress. I never thought I'd see the day."

Stan reached for Allegra's hand and kissed it before steering his gaze back to his grown child.

Calla kept her eyes on Stan's direct. "What's going on, Allegra?"

Before Allegra could respond, Eva pushed forward. "Calla, I took back the news report I printed."

"Why? Is that an attempt at avoiding prosecution for conspiring with Mason or an effort at evading my indignation?"

"I'm really sorry, Calla. When I met Stan, at first glance, all I wanted was the story published. But something about him reminded me of the relationship with my own father. One that's basically non-existent."

"You've always been a good liar."

"It's true, Calla. For a moment I saw something in your father's eyes." Her voice choked with emotion. "I saw grief mixed with love for a daughter he'd lost long ago. Calla, I would give anything to get that look just once from my father. I've never had it, and I wanted you to have what neither one of us ever had growing up, the affection of a father. It was the right thing to do."

"The games ended in the playground, Eva. We're not sixteen anymore."

"No, darling. I remembered all your birthdays," said Stan as he stepped forward, his luminous eyes exuding mystery.

Was he really her father? *God, is he real?*

"Could you please leave us? I need a moment with this. With him."

"Of course," Allegra said, and she and Eva headed toward the den.

Stan drew in a deep breath. "Eva came looking for me for all the wrong reasons but has helped me find you again. I'm sorry I let you down, Calla."

Calla pressed her lips into a fine line. For the first time, she took in the full stature of the father who'd left her discarded at a foster home entrance.

Abandoned.

Nash joined them by the staircase, his gaze registering shock at the sight of Stan. "Well. I'll be damned! SILVER X3? The golden agent of MI6."

Stan shook Nash's hand. "Nash Shields. You've done me a great service. I'm indebted to you for taking care of her as promised. I know you didn't have to."

Calla's eyes transferred to Nash whose face delivered no reaction. He grasped her hand. Intense eye contact told her he was going to tell her the truth. "I'm sorry, Calla. I couldn't tell you."

"Tell me what?"

His eyes glinted with credibility. Even then he struggled to get out the right words. "About a month after I joined the NSA, I was assigned to Operation Carillion, our code for the US's investigations into ISTF's practices. This brought me in direct contact with Mason's file, especially how he was voted into leading ISTF. Anyway, this investigation also raised the issues surrounding the Deveron Manuscript, especially Mason's willingness to pay ISTF agents and hit men to hunt for it. I, therefore, began to explore the little we knew about the manuscript until I ran into a colleague, Colton, who was heading the CIA and knew Stan. Your father often worked with him on joint cases in the past."

Stan set a hand on Nash's shoulder and gave him a reassuring nod, his face pinched with unyielding determination. "She needs to hear it from me. Baby, I knew the heavy responsibility the manuscript would place on you. I didn't want that for you. I pleaded with the secret service to hide my family. Your mother was still pregnant with you. MI6 refused to get involved in concerns they didn't understand, not really taking the manuscript business seriously. I had to take matters into my own hands. So I turned to Colton when I heard you'd joined ISTF."

Her eyes were pools of appeal. "How did you know I was at ISTF?"

"I'm sorry, darling. I made it my life's ambition to know and always kept an eye on you."

"Everything but make my acquaintance. Why didn't you let me find you?" she said.

"I should have, and I know I can never make up for lost years. Maybe we can start... now?"

Was it too late? Too hard? Too unexpected? Did she feel anything for the stranger calling himself father?

"What did Colton do?" she said. "I mean, what did you and he agree about me?"

"He asked Nash to keep you safe when the two of you started working on cases at ISTF?" Stan answered.

She glanced Nash's way. "Nash?"

Nash caressed her hand. "It's true, beautiful.I didn't know you then. It was a favor for an old friend. Just like any other covert assignment."

Was this their first secret? Would there be more to follow? She recalled Allegra and Vortigern's words but brushed them away without second thought.

Nash gently squeezed Calla's hand. "Colton told me if you ever got too close to getting the carbonados that I had full clearance to take Mason out. I don't think you needed my help with that."

"Nash, you overlooked your own safety for hers. You're one of the most respectable men I've ever had the privilege of knowing," Stan said patting him on the shoulder.

Nash smiled. "We just met. I only had your file to go by. But I'll take that as a compliment." He mimicked a slight salute.

Calla sank to the bottom step, and Stan took a seat on the stair beside her. He shifted nearer, afraid to reach out and touch her. His deep voice had captured her attention. He communicated something in his tone, very close to heartbreak. "I'm sorry I left you, baby. It was never right. Your mother and I just wanted to protect you. When I read the papers Eva left at my doorstep, I knew you were in trouble. That's why I contacted her. I had left it too late. I had to come find you. Even if it meant coming back into your life, uprooting your existence a second time."

Stan's eyes waited. "Eva was the one who found the files I'd worked on for years. She snooped for them in my house. Together we alerted ISTF about Mason's criminal activity, and they put us in touch with Jack. That's how I found you."

Jack sidled into the hallway overhearing part of the conversation. "Stan had an exhaustive file on Mason. It'll help put him away for good."

"Calla, you were the one who knew how to overpower him all along when you suggested he could be defeated not in physical strength but in intellect and by the corruption of his own hacks using a technology bug. That's the mark of a true leader," Stan added.

All fell silent as she glimpsed at the gawking faces. "Stan, Father, could I speak to you alone, please?"

Calla looped an arm through his—a father she'd never known—a relationship she was beginning to understand and question, all at the same time. They walked out into the garden as an azure sky fleeced with passing clouds.

The sun hit his emerald eyes, she'd never once imagined what it had meant for him to sacrifice his family for their safety.

He too had suffered. She stroked his arm in approval. And for one who'd harbored a million questions and rehearsed the moment repeatedly, she summarized her next sentence into one thought. "Father, where's my mother?"

EPILOGUE

SEVEN MONTHS LATER...
ISTF HEADQUARTERS

She'd heard about the kitchen fire months earlier. Several rooms hadn't been in use since that day. Calla strolled through the ISTF offices, clutching a set of papers as she headed to the file room. It would be reopened for the first time today.

She swiped her card at the entrance and found the Deveron Manuscript file along the discarded shelves. Pulling out the file she opened it and saw the ISTF stamp in a drawer next to her.

She stamped the file.

CASE CLOSED

Calla set the file back on the shelf and inhaled a deep breath. Switching off the lights she secured the door and headed to the ISTF Archeological labs. A colleague waited by the door.

"Ms. Cress. Welcome," the cheerful woman with chestnut-colored eyes said.

The assistant directed her to a bright cubicle near the floor length windows that overlooked a quiet, inside courtyard on the third floor at Watergate House. Two men stood nearby sharing a joke. Jack turned when he saw the women approach.

"Hi. I'm Jack Kleve. I'm delighted we could have a professional come down and help us identify the archeological finds in Pakistan. We like to call it the Karachi Brief. I understand your Arabic is up to speed and your historical knowledge comes highly recommended."

Calla smiled and shook his hand. "Hey, Jack."

Jack turned to the colleague seated at the desk next to him. He had his back toward them. "This is Nash Shields. A senior security adviser from the US, also part of the NSA. You'll be working with him on the brief. Our government asked him to help us. It's a great sign of our two countries working well together."

Nash rose from his chair without comment and extended his hand. "First day at ISTF? Hope you'll like it here."

Calla smiled and held the small, wireless, electronic tablet hidden away in her shoulder bag.

I'm sure I will.

The Decrypter and the Mind Hacker
(A Calla Cress Technothriller)

The second book in the explosive bestselling technothriller series

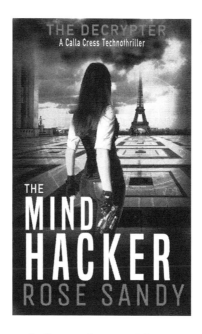

Calla Cress took down the world's most dangerous man. She made one mistake. She let him live.

A billionaire behind bars, once the secret service's most brilliant code breaker, is luring the world's smartest minds into his prison cell. They leave in a coma and seconds later a lethal hack snakes through one government system after another.

Meanwhile, Calla Cress, museum curator turned undercover cyber-security agent, faces the biggest dilemma of her life. She's harboring a dangerous secret buried in the deepest vaults of technology history.

In a few hours, she'll have to make a decision that will change her life forever. After an explosion rocks her hideout in Colorado, Calla wakes up halfway across the world at the whim of a powerful, unidentified organization demanding she produces the whereabouts of a missing MI6 agent who can disarm the billionaire's hacks. Powerful people are prepared to kill to obtain the cryptic secret the agent kept.

There're a few obstacles: Calla has never met the agent who has been missing for 30 years. Can Calla find the only person who ever challenged the enigmatic billionaire?

With only a handful of clues left in a mysterious sixteenth-century anagram encrypted with a sequence of codes, Calla, NSA security advisor, Nash Shields and tech entrepreneur Jack Kleve are thrust in a dangerous race across the globe. With each haunting revelation, they soon realize the key to disarming the hacks comes at an astonishing price.

The Decrypter and the Mind Hacker is a fast-paced, suspense thriller, charging through government secrets, world history and computer fraud that will have you wondering whether technology has progressed beyond human intelligence, changing civilization, and perhaps human nature.

Reader Praise for 'The Decrypter and the Mind Hacker'

"A female James Bond with a Matrix twist." Amazon reader.

"Takes you on a ride and refuses to let you off until you reach the very end."

A brilliant read! I recommend this to anyone who enjoys mystery, suspense, thrillers or action novels. The detail is astounding! The historic references, location descriptions, references to technology, cryptography....this author really knows her stuff."

Get your copy here:
'The Decrypter and the Mind Hacker

https://rosesandy.com/the-decrypter-and-the-mind-hacker/

JOIN THE ADVENTURE

SHORT REVIEW

**Thank you for joining Calla,
Nash and Jack on this adventure!**
As an author I highly appreciate the feedback I get from my
readers. It helps others to make an informed decision before
buying.

It only takes a few minutes. If you enjoyed **The Decrypter:
Secret of the Lost Manuscript** please consider leaving a
short review where you bought the book by going here.
www.rosesandy.com

BE THE FIRST TO KNOW

Be the first to learn about new releases and other news from
Rose Sandy, by joining **Real Time with Rose Sandy**, a
podcast and fun e-update. See you there by going here :
rosesandy.com/signup

While you are at it, swing by the official Rose Sandy Facebook page (www.facebook.com/rosesandyauthor) to join a community of adventurers, history and technology enthusiasts.

Finally, if you enjoy pictures of travels, book inspirations, historical mysteries, science and technology thrills, check out my feed @rosesandyauthor on the Instagram app.

IN THE DECRYPTER SERIES
PULSE-RACING ADVENTURE

Book 1: The Decrypter: Secret of The Lost Manuscript

Book 2: The Decrypter and The Mind Hacker

Book 3: The Decrypter - Digital Eyes Only

Book 4: The Decrypter - The Storm's Eye

She's a museum curator, a doubter, and a skeptic. It all changed when the British government asked her to decrypt a code written in an unbreakable script on an ancient manuscript whose origin was as debatable as the origin of life. Then there was the issue of her long-lost parents.

Using her knack for history and technology, she bands with two faithful friends and is thrown into a dangerous journey of cyber espionage investigating the criminal, the unexplained, the scientific and the downright unthinkable.

More here: https://rosesandy.com/the-decrypter-series/

What Readers Are Saying About The Decrypter Series

"Takes you on a ride and refuses to let you off until you reach the very end."

"A brilliant read! I recommend this to anyone who enjoys mystery, suspense, thrillers, or action novels. The detail is astounding! The historic references, location descriptions, references to technology, cryptography....this author really knows her stuff."

"An action-packed adventure, technothriller across several continents like a Jason Bourne or James Bond movie, but with an actual storyline!"

"Brilliantly written. I loved the very descriptive side, which was a good

way of visualizing and getting to terms with each new place, as the action takes place in several different countries."

"The description is so rich, so immensely detailed that it just draws you in completely to its world."

"There is great tension and chemistry between the two main characters, Calla and Nash, that has you begging for more."

IN THE SHADOW FILES THRILLERS
A CROSSFIRE BETWEEN TECHNOLOGY, SCIENCE, AND INTERNATIONAL ESPIONAGE

Book 1 - The Code Beneath Her Skin

Book 2 - Blood Diamond in My Mother's House

A series about intelligent women caught in the crossfire between technology, science, politics, international espionage, and the men who drag them there.

Guaranteed action adventure in each book, you'll fill the need for thrills, savor satisfying cliffhangers as you follow a secret organization, **The Shadow Files,** and two of its former agents around the globe.

Sworn enemies, one is on a mission to safeguard the globe from economic corruption, and one swears he'll protect the victims.

Each book can be read as a stand-alone story.

More here: https://rosesandy.com/the-shadow-files-series-2/

ABOUT THE AUTHOR

Rose Sandy never set out to be a writer. She set out to be a communicator with whatever landed in her hands. But soon the keyboard became her best friend. Rose writes suspense and intelligence thrillers where technology and espionage meet history in pulse-racing action adventure. She dips into the mysteries of our world, the fascination of technology breakthroughs, the secrets of history and global intelligence to deliver thrillers that weave suspense, conspiracy and a dash of romantic thrill.

A globe trotter, her thrillers span cities and continents. Rose's writing approach is to hit hard with a good dose of tension and humor. Her characters zip in and out of intelligence and government agencies, dodge enemies in world heritage sites, navigate technology markets and always land in deep trouble.

When not tapping away on a smartphone writing app, Rose is usually found in the British Library scrutinizing the Magna Carta, trolling Churchill's War Rooms or sampling a new gadget. Most times she's in deep conversations with ex-military and secret service intelligence officers, Foreign Service staff or engrossed in a TED talk with a box of popcorn. Hm... she might just learn something that'll be useful.

For more books and updates, go to www.rosesandy.com

Printed in Great Britain
by Amazon

38070708R00281